Capital Consequences

Redemption, Revenge, Trust, Tranquility

Dawn Wright

This novel's story and characters are fictitious. While the businesses, locations, and some organizations are real, they are used in a way that's purely fictional. The opinions expressed are those of the characters and should not be confused with the author's.

ISBN: 978-0-9980787-2-4

Dedication

This book is dedicated to my late brother, Ryan. You would want my dreams to live on. May you continue your Wu-Shu kicks in Heaven among the bright blue skies. I love you to the moon and back!

table of contents

1: new beginnings
2: heated
3: picture this
4: one last time
5: missing you
6: surprise!
7: asshats
8: let's get pissy
9: the wedding planner
10: a new season

1: *new beginnings*

It was cold—frigid in fact. Looking off into the distance, my eyes settled on the little girl with wavy brunette hair, skipping in the scarcely-grassed ground, oblivious to the meaning of her surroundings. My tear-filled eyes turned back to the headstone to trace the top with my fingers. A sigh swept through my parted lips and eased into the crisp air. I dug a cold, frail hand deep into the comfort of my pea coat pocket, meeting a tissue and rubbing it. I pulled it out, looked at the little girl again, and began to sob.

Against better judgment, I lowered myself in front of the headstone, knowing that the hem of my coat licked the ground. My heels sunk quickly with the back of my thighs meeting my heels. It was difficult balancing myself with all this extra weight. Failing to support my weight above ground, the pointy heels of my black pumps eased into the soft mud, so I lifted my feet to reposition my stance. The wind tossed brown and orange leaves around my feet and whipped my hair around, as if it didn't already look wild enough. I didn't care.

What mattered was the fact that a person I once knew rested six feet beneath me. Massaging my temples, I cried like the burial took place yesterday, instead of two-and-a-half years ago. The sudden touch of small, soft fingers on my hand that rested on top of the headstone caused me to jump.

"Why do you cry every time we come here?" I looked into her wide, honey-colored eyes. She tilted her head at me. "Don't cry, Mommy. You said God gives wings to people who go to heaven." She skipped a few feet away from me.

"I'm not sure that all people get wings," I mumbled. Of course, she didn't hear me, and I didn't intend her to. Regardless of my misgivings, my heart was shattered. I didn't see the death coming. No one could have.

"Let's go, Autumn." She returned to me, and I took her tiny, trusting hands into mine, as my other hand rested on my baby bump, and we walked away from the graveyard and back to the parking lot with the sound of leaves, crunching under our feet.

Summer

Three-and-a-half months ago, my life overturned like an eighteen-wheeler on ice. I'd been fired, Brooke dumped Jackson, Emily dumped Eric, and Amber decided to make money the right way. During my months of creeping around with Ruben, the idea of losing my career plagued my thoughts. I'd convince myself that life would end if Fran were to let me go, but in fact, it'd just begun.

I sat on the window ledge of the spare room, absently taking in the scenery while contemplating life after waking up from a nap cut short by a disturbing dream. The room overlooked a city in motion of people strolling with a cup of Starbucks in one hand and a dog leash in another. Some walked with cell phones and briefcases, others with sling bags. Everyone appeared to have somewhere to go. Everyone except me.

After the New Year, Oliver suggested that I recruit from home by starting my own business, and Brooke jumped with excitement when she found out. Even though finding clients was supposed to be the hardest part of starting a business, Brooke's help alleviated the difficulty. Because she found some clients who jumped at the suggestion of hiring a recruiter to find talent for their companies, she drew up an agreement stating that she'd receive ten percent of my earnings per placement from her referred clients. Since my fee brought in a generous amount per placement, it worked out okay. And with two placements so far, my bank account recovered enough to make me feel somewhat independent again.

Still, it didn't mean that my role in the destruction of Fran's marriage—if it did end—didn't eat away at me from time to time. Even though my career didn't seem to suffer since approaching it on my own, my opinion of myself wouldn't let me forget my part in Fran's broken marriage every time Oliver and I kissed or snuggled at night. The suspicion remained with me that Fran lost love when I'd gained it because of my careless actions. And for this, the idea that I got off scot-free was a mere illusion.

Oliver and I were very happy together. As promised, we salvaged all the meaningful items from my apartment, like pictures and other sentimental valuables, and had fun shopping for new clothes and other knickknacks. My boyfriend wouldn't let me pay for anything. Since it was pointless to buy furniture going into an already-furnished arrangement, I was able to indulge in what really mattered—clothes and accessories.

My beyond awesome man encouraged me to let him take care of my financial and emotional needs. He flew in our moms during both holidays so that we could all get to know one another and catch up on lost time. The opportune time offered us a chance to take my mom house hunting as discussed last year. She swore that once she tied up loose ends with the sale of the house, she would be down here as a new resident. After our moms returned home, Oliver encouraged me to relax for the remainder of the year. Every day that passed deepened my feelings for him.

We worked well together. The adjustment was easy, and we were solid. Oliver made me realize that with the right person, relationships were possible as well as good. Speaking of relationships, Amber and Emily were on the first step to repairing their broken friendship. According to Emily, being totally free of Eric allowed her to have an open mind and to try to make room for Amber, though she still acted reserved around her. Speaking of healing, Amber learned to work on her confidence and managed to land performances for musicals in theatres, while Brooke decided that the best way to heal from a broken heart was to indulge herself in her work—even more than normal.

Brooke hadn't heard from Jackson, and she refused to chase him. As much as she wanted him back, she'd decided to focus hard on planning the wedding for Jacqueline Laurent's daughter. Unfortunately, Jacqueline almost fired Brooke because her performance suffered from a broken heart, but after she spoke with Jacqueline in confidence, she offered her advice that stuck with Brooke. Brooke told us that Jacqueline had told her that sometimes men can steal your dreams, but they shouldn't steal your money. Brooke slept on it and realized that she would always be a wedding planner, and no one should be able to take that away from her. She wasn't going to let Jackson's choice indirectly hurt her reputation or her business. It was bad enough that he'd pulled the rug from beneath her. Besides, Brooke didn't want to be anyone's victim, so she strapped on her stiletto boots and jumped back into the game.

Since Brooke had to spend Thanksgiving without Jackson, she traded in carving turkey for work. She kindly rejected my offer to carve the bird with my family, including Amber and Mara, and for Christmas, she declined Emily's offer to accompany her up north. Unfortunately, Brooke didn't make Christmas any more festive than Thanksgiving. However, she did manage to briefly stop by to exchange gifts with Oliver and me. Since Mara and Amber were with us at the time of her visit, she wished the two of them Merry Christmas, but still aimed most of her interaction at Oliver and me. Her thirty-minute visit consisted of forced smiles with eyes trying to hide nightly bouts of tears and long days of hard labor. By New Year's, she decided to wipe the love slate clean and commit to moving on without Jackson.

Emily welcomed the chance to surround herself by real love and decided to visit her family for both holidays. None of us could truly tell how Emily was getting by, especially since Brooke and Emily were healing from heartbreak and seemed somewhat distant in the presence of others. So many things had changed for all of us. It was hard accepting that the new reality that stood before us actually belonged to the three women I'd come to know and love.

I hopped down from the ledge and made my way to the living room. Waiting for ten o'clock to arrive before calling my client to make sure that the candidate showed up for her first day was one of those make-it-or-break-it kind of moments. That drove the office nuts when I was working for Fran; you never wanted to receive that phone call from a client in a rage blaming the recruiter for a failed candidate. Now, as an independent recruiter, listening to the *ka-ching* of five digits entering my bank account in ninety days if the candidate worked out was the only noise I'd want to hear. What a wonderful idea, becoming an independent recruiter, thanks to my lovely boyfriend.

After using the bathroom, one quick glance at the clock confirmed that it'd been past ten o'clock, but only by five minutes. I decided to call my client. As usual, when nervous, my mouth inhaled and collected air until exhaling with relief was an option. After receiving confirmation that she'd arrived, not only did the air fly out, but my limbs flung into a victory dance. *Ka-ching*!

Hours had passed. It'd been a long day.

Oliver stepped out of the elevator and before he could place the second foot on the wooden floor, I threw both arms over his shoulders like a whore in heat. No greetings, no inquiries regarding how the day went. Who cared? I wanted dick and needed it now.

In a hot whisper, I told him, "Oliver, I want you inside of me."

He stared back at me as if he had to adjust his vision. "Oh, you're ready to go." His eyes dropped and slowly coasted up my body, taking in a sexy image he hadn't seen in a while. His stare alone made my pussy tingle.

Wearing my new pink lingerie set with the sole goal of sexing Oliver before dinner, I'd taken a trip earlier to an independent lingerie store down the street. I told the sales representative to find me something that would get me laid tonight. She pulled a pink lace bodysuit from the rack and once she held it up, I knew it'd be coming home with me. And here it was, on my body paired with pink pumps. Every time he tried to pull back to talk or examine me, I'd jerked him close to keep his lips against mine. We'd already lost a ton of time from his hectic schedule over the past two weeks. I'd never felt so lonely.

He grabbed my face with one strong hand. "I'm not sure you really want it. How can I tell?"

Oh, so he wanted to play games. I could do that. "Please, Oliver." My hands caressed his chest in an up and down motion. They traced his shoulders and the back of his neck, too. "Please put it in me," I begged with a whisper.

Oliver didn't budge, but his eyes were weakening with heavy eyelids. He talked a good game though. He moved his hand to my neck, cupping it against the side. His thumb stroked my jaw. He whispered, "Were you thinking about me today?"

I arched my body into his, bending my neck to the side to cave into his hand, crushing it between my shoulder and jaw. His thumb moved to my mouth, strumming each lip slowly. "All day, baby, all day."

Oliver moved his dangling hand to cradle the other side of my neck. That other thumb stroked my cheek. Nothing but sweet torture between us. My nipples tightened under the pressure.

"Tell me what you were thinking of."

"Your dick sliding in and out of me . . . wet, slippery . . . messy. Come all over the place."

He squeezed his eyes and bit his lower lip before bringing his mouth to my neck, placing a sensual kiss against my skin. "Where did my come go?"

I loved when his voice dropped like that. He was barely surviving. "On my chest."

When he kissed my earlobe, my pussy danced. "Mmmmm. And then where?"

"My stomach." My hands wouldn't behave; and why would I want them to? They . . . they caressed his ears and neck while he wore me down with his breath against my skin and hands touching me in all the weakening places. My ears, my neck, my lips.

"What did you do with all my come?"

"Used it as lotion, rubbing that sticky stuff in until it became . . . dry . . ."

"I'll drown you in that Oliver lotion."

"Don't make me wait, baby. Oliver, please give it to me. I want it. Give me that dick, baby, please."

"Gimme that tight little pussy of yours."

He smashed his lips into mine, passionately, hungrily. The much-needed ache below intensified with each second our lips remained locked. I coasted my leg up against his denim-clad leg while balancing myself against his body on one pointy heel. Moans sang from my throat as his hands traveled ravishingly along my skin. I didn't know if he came home tired, but his aggressive hands told me how much energy he possessed. With one strong push of my pump, I lifted myself onto his body and squeezed my legs into the sides of his body. He transported us to the bedroom with one hand plastered into one ass cheek with a grip so needy, it fell into the valley of my cheeks.

I threw my head back, arching my spine to offer my pushed-up breasts into his face, drowning him. He licked the skin and bit the abundance above the material. I snapped my head forward, causing my hair to fall with ease like a parachute hitting the ground. He threw me against the wall, positioning his hands under my thighs to hold me up where he wanted me before unbuckling his pants. The rapid noise of his belt and zipper fed into my need to be devoured by this man.

I didn't make it easy for him. I held his tongue and lips hostage, leaving him to figure out a way to blindly prepare himself to unleash his sexual wrath upon me. I licked his mouth in circles, nibbled at his jawline, grabbed the back of his head like a predator ready for lunch. The heavy panting of his quick breathing tattled like a siren, his anxious heart beat against my chest like a magician trapped in a box looking for an out.

I lowered myself and detached from him to lower myself to my knees, wanting to taste him and all his labor. His flavor would tell me all about his day. He knew it was coming, so he threw his hands forward and steadied his palms against the wall. Facing his shaft, I licked its length before taking it into my mouth. His flavor tasted like a man who brought home all the bacon. I devoured his million-dollar manhood, sucking him hard and rotating my tongue on the tip, just to let him know how much I appreciated him. And when he started to pulse, I didn't break away like all the other times. I reached into the innermost Amber part of me and swallowed as he came.

Before I had too much time to think about my action, Oliver stepped out of his jeans, bent over, and lifted me up by the armpits over his head. My wavy hair flowed downward and onto his shoulders. Tasting his goodness spoke volumes to him. I could see it in his eyes. He lowered me onto the bed, gently, like his little angel in his care. In the middle of our bed with sprawled limbs, I flirted with the man I loved by slowly alternating my feet up and down the sheet as my hands played in my hair. Without taking his eyes off me, Oliver stood at the foot of the bed and pulled his shirt over his head, then tossed it to the side. Like a lion in the safari, he zoned in on me, making his appetite for me a priority and lending me the impression that I had nowhere to run. And I wouldn't. Beholden to his craving, I wanted to be eaten.

He eased toward me in the dark . . . slowly, with a crawl that accentuated the muscles on his arms. Oliver anchored one knee into the bed between my legs to search for the zipper trailing my spine. I arched my back just enough to give him room to unzip me, and when my bodysuit loosened, he eased it down over my golden skin. The pink material faded away from me as it cleared my ankles.

"Oh, mama, I could eat you for breakfast," he placed a kiss on each nipple, "lunch," then on my stomach, "and dinner," and then on top of my bare vagina.

Oliver opened my legs as far as they could split. Licking his lips, I could still see the sparkle of delight in his eyes despite the darkness. A smirk of a ravenous spirit eased across his face. He went all in and the minute his tongue slid against my walls and hit the clitoris, my foot arched like a skilled ballerina and an arm shot above my head, reaching for anything but grabbing nothing at all. In pleasure, I cried out the sound of random vowels as the wave of pulsating releases tortured my body. Oliver's tongue danced in my rain insatiably, cleaning up every . . . single . . . drop.

Emily

Emily closed the trunk of her new white Jeep Cherokee. After closing her chapter with Eric in it, she'd decided to get rid of all things that reminded her of him. With the house on the market, she'd begun her search for a new place to call home. Just when she'd fallen in love with calling that place home again with Eric, Amber had come along and revealed information that gave her bad feelings toward it.

As Emily approached her house with flat boxes in her arms, she heard a man call her name.

"Emily! Emily! Hey, wait up!"

Taken aback, Emily turned around to see a familiar man running toward her. *Zach?*

Catching up with her, he gasped to catch his breath.

"Zach. This is a surprise." Emily's eye's shifted about as she struggled to deal with his presence. Evident in her clenched jaws and less-than-enthused hazel eyes, she was hardly in the mood to socialize or deal with men.

His large hand covered her folded boxes. "Here, let me get that."

Emily didn't have a chance to reject him—he put the boxes in his arms as soon as he'd grabbed them, carrying them effortlessly. She shrugged and mustered a perfunctory, "Thanks."

Starting toward her house with Zach following alongside, she asked, "What brings you by, Zach?" The unfriendly tone wasn't lost on him.

"Emily, so sorry to impose like this, but I haven't seen you in a while, and I heard that that man moved out— again."

With an annoyed sigh, she stopped in her tracks to face him. "Oh, come on. Who—who told you that? Wait, let me guess." Pretending to think, she pointed a finger in the air. "Miss Mauzy?"

"Ding, ding, ding," he replied dryly.

Shaking her head in disbelief, Emily continued to amble toward her porch with Zach swallowing the gaps with quick strides. "Well, to be clear," Emily started, "I kicked him out. He did not leave me."

"Look, it doesn't make two hoots to me. I was just coming to check up on you."

Climbing the stairs, Emily couldn't escape the cold fast enough. A fidgety hand slid into her jacket pocket to retrieve the house key. Rehashing the aftermath of the fallout wasn't on the To-Do List, so she quickly inserted the key into the keyhole.

Emily's eyes burned into Zach's. "Well, I am fine. You see?" She stretched out her arms and did a mock curtsey without a smile. "Thank you, Zach, but if you'll excuse me."

Once the door opened, Zach let the boxes slip from his grip as she took them from his hands. He stared at her with his hands in his pockets accepting defeat. Reading the hurt in his eyes, Emily added, "Okay, now," as she gently closed the door, shutting out a man who was just trying to be a friend.

Amber

Amber stood in her pink denims on an escalator, waiting to reach the second floor of the Pentagon City Mall. Mindlessly toying with the drawstring of her white angora, hooded sweater, she watched the people below her eat in the food court. She'd just cashed Jacqueline Laurent's check for performing at her daughter's reception last week after the piano player's sudden hospitalization for food poisoning.

She thought it was hilarious how Brooke appeared to be the hero in Ms. Laurent's eyes, because she could fix something so unforeseeable with grace. Brooke surprised Amber by giving credit to her in the presence of Ms. Laurent. Nonetheless, she was so impressed with Brooke's resolve and grateful for Amber's talent, that she paid Amber an extra thousand dollars in addition to the original generous fee. Of course, Ms. Laurent showed the same appreciation to Brooke on top of her original fee as well. Either way, Amber smiled herself to sleep that same night knowing that that moment helped her and Brooke move along in the right direction.

Amber stepped onto the second floor and took a moment to read all the stores around her before choosing Express. Something about the spring skirt in the window called her name. As she marched into the store, she saw a

familiar face walking out with a very young lady on his
arm.

Oh, hell to the nah!

She couldn't believe this was happening. Just as she
started to put the past behind her, it moved up close and
personal and into her present.

Brooke

Brooke wanted to believe that she was drawn to a
specific Northwest Greek restaurant for its comforting
chicken soup *avgolemono*. Truth was, someone in the
restaurant had caught her eye. One incident revealed that
her man of interest turned out to be the owner. It happened
when she'd been given the wrong meal and had to drive
back to the restaurant in her Christmas present just to
politely fuss out the cashier. When he'd told her that she'd
have to speak with the person in charge, a very handsome
man emerged from the back. His gorgeous presence had
immediately extinguished Brooke's flame of anger. She
hadn't felt that kind of torture since Jackson. He'd proudly
declared himself the owner before listening to Brooke's
gentle complaint.

Brooke had found it hard to find her words as her focus
shifted from her wrong order to his appearance. Dark, wavy
hair and complementary brows sat over matching, deep-set
eyes. His full beard and height didn't make him look any
less like a sexy model in a perfume commercial, however,
his average physique would probably fall victim to
airbrushed abs. He typically wasn't her type, but his very
manly and exotic features made him hard to forget. And
when he apologized, she wanted to hear it a thousand times
over if it meant hearing that accent. But instead, she settled
for the refund and free corrected meal. Since then, they'd
share a smile while communicating with their eyes as she
frequented the place a few times a month. She just didn't
know his name.

Always dining alone at Pappas, Brooke strolled into the restaurant in her heels wearing an asymmetrical leather jacket over tight black jeans and headed toward the counter with a hungry stomach to order the same dish. It'd been two weeks since she'd last eaten at Pappas. Deciding to eat inside as usual, her eyes scanned the empty restaurant with anxious hands that gripped her purse. With no one in sight, the owner finally emerged from the closed doors behind the counter. Her bright eyes widened, pleased that her visit wasn't in vain. *Oh, my word.* Manicured fingers placed escaped strands back behind her ear. With a loose bun on top of her head, Brooke struggled to manage her longer tresses with one clip. She questioned if she should just take it down and let the strands wildly frame her face. Besides, she'd do anything to appear sexier to the Greek business owner.

Nothing could prepare her for his accent. The accent that made her vagina ripple whenever he spoke. He wiped his hands on a rag and threw it over his shoulder. It didn't surprise her that he wore his humorless expression, but when he asked, "Chicken soup *avgolemono?*" his thin lips curved into a smirk that played with her mind. She couldn't tell if he was thinking, *"I'm on to you, lady. It's not just my soup,"* or *"What else would you be ordering?"*

Brooke stumbled over her words. Maybe he found her predictability pathetic. "Y-yeah, uh, yes." Brooke reprimanded herself by calling herself stupid. She sharply reminded herself to get it together while remembering how well she handled her nerves with Jackson and figured that she could do it with this guy. "Thanks."

Still smiling, he asked, "For here, ma'am?"

She nodded once. "For here."

"Okay, then sit where you want." He gestured toward the almost empty dining room.

"Okay."

As usual, Brooke walked to the booth closest to the exit. She pulled her phone out to surf the Internet. With her eyes lowered and thinking of something to Google, she scolded herself again. *This is lame, Brooke. You ain't got nothing to Google.* Sucking her lower lip, Brooke decided to look at the pictures on her phone. Still a bad habit, she did it when she had downtime. Even though she advised herself to let go of Jackson because obviously, he wasn't going to call, looking at old pictures felt comforting in some strange way.

Pictures of them leaning into one another with parts of DC behind them filled her digital album. Jackson always took the pictures because of his longer arms. They appeared so happy, so full of promise.

"Ma'am?"

Brooke slammed the phone against her chest in a panic, and the handsome restaurant owner picked up on her awkward reaction. He quietly chuckled to himself, causing Brooke to feel foolish. "Yes?"

"I'm sorry to, uh, bother you." His eyes shot downward at her phone and back to her eyes. "But we are out of the chicken soup *avgolemono*. Can I offer you something else, on the house?"

Maybe he lied to her to force her to try something new. Brooke squinted her eyes at him and smiled from one corner of her mouth. "In good conscious, I don't know if I can keep allowing you to serve me free food every time something goes wrong, Mr. . . ."

"Damani."

He extended a hand. Normally, Brooke hated touching hands before eating, but Damani, the oh-so-sexy Damani, was an exception. She loved his exotic name. She loved his exotic look.

"Pappas."

Damani Pappas. What a hot name. He even got his surname plastered on the awning of his restaurant. Even better.

Placing her hand into his, she smiled and said, "Brooke Brazile, DC's premier wedding planner."

Touching him felt like a forbidden dare. Damani closed his large hand around her delicate fingers. His hands had seen many days of labor, and still, she wanted them all over her body.

Trying to play it cool, his eyes narrowed into smiles, his lips pressed to one side of his mouth. "I don't know what I find most intriguing, your handshake or your title."

Withdrawing her hand, a timid laugh tickled the air. Brooke's hair fell over one eye, so she replaced it behind her ear. "Yeah." Giddy, she didn't know exactly what she'd responded to. However, she was sure this older man had a clamp on her, and she didn't mind being anchored to the pull he possessed.

"You eat here a lot, I suppose. May I sit?" His hand gestured at the bench across from her.

Caught off-guard, she nodded. "Of course." With a streak of celibacy underway after her breakup with Jackson, Brooke resisted her inner bad girl that told her to go home with him tonight. Looking at Damani for longer than seconds at a time allowed Brooke to study his good looks. Damani had to be in his early forties. *An older man? This is new.* Something about it seemed hot. Brooke reminded herself to calm down since nothing indicated where they'd even go from there. Besides, who said he didn't have a wife waiting at home? His bare ring finger exposed his marital status, but that didn't mean he wasn't seeing someone special. That concern needed to be addressed immediately.

"I don't know what I should get. What do you recommend? Tell me something that your girlfriend or sister would order that's friendly on the waistline."

He quickly threw up a hand. "Wouldn't know, I have neither. But it doesn't hurt to sample."

Speaking of samples, maybe you can sample this vagina. And you can hurt it, too. Girrrrl. Do you remember who you are? You need to behave.

She felt victorious discovering his free-agent status and knowing that he didn't have a sister who left him traumatized. Because Brooke owned her bitterness toward Jackson and his sister, she questioned if she'd really moved on?

"Try the *horta vrasta*. Everyone loves it."

She raised an eyebrow. "The hor- who?"

Damani chuckled. "*Horta vrasta*. It's a dish of boiled greens. Very leafy. Try them." He stood up. "Let me go place your order."

"'Kay." It looked like she didn't have a choice. He'd already decided.

Amber

Amber couldn't believe her eyes when she saw Daniel Crosby coming out of Express with a cute, skinny blonde. Stopping abruptly in his tracks to take a phone call, he reached into his pocket to pull out his cell phone while handing his young bunny some money with the other hand. She hopped with a glow and scurried into Frederick's of Hollywood with her long hair swinging behind her.

Feeling as though the coast was clear, Amber tiptoed as she watched for sudden movements made by Daniel. She tried to run in the direction his back faced. He was so involved with his phone call, that he had a finger plugged into one ear with lowered eyes, listening carefully to the person on the other end. Oblivious to his surroundings, Amber crossed her heart as she took the final steps into Express.

Phew. Amber made it undetected. Her eyes darted around the store, desperately trying to locate the skirt from the window that'd caught her eye. Finding it, Amber hurried to the rack and sifted through the sizes and colors of the ankle-length spring skirt. As she placed skirts against her lower half without a mirror to reflect what it would look like, she bent her neck to assess if she liked it or not. She jumped when she felt three quick taps on her shoulder.

Amber spun around and was surprised when she saw Daniel looking at her with a grin. Her mouth formed an "O."

"So, it is you."

Amber didn't understand how Daniel managed to find her. She would give anything to get away. The last time this man saw her, he didn't even want to look her in the eyes. Now that his cubicle friends weren't there, he wanted to acknowledge her. When Amber accepted that she lost the hide-and-seek game, she blurted, "Um, when did she graduate from high school?"

It upset her that he thought he could just follow her into the store without regard to how he treated her last year at his job. He didn't even call to explain himself or to apologize.

Does he really think he has a chance?

"Nothing wrong with a college girl."

He placed a hand on her shoulder. Amber snapped it away from his grip. "Don't touch me." Her eyes glared into his eyes without blinking.

Daniel wiped his mouth with a hand. "Okay, sweetheart, I get it. You're still mad. But, baby, you can't come to a man's job like that unannounced. Do you think I would want her," he pointed backward with his head, "to come to my job? No." With a softened tone, he added, "Men can't be having random women coming to their jobs. Only solid girlfriends or wives. You know *that.*"

With the skirt still in her hands, Amber folded her arms with her tongue poking the inside of her cheek. "What do you want, Daniel?"

He flashed his palms at her. "Look, you two women are beautiful, but y'all ain't coming to my job. There ain't no way in hell. I was mad. You embarrassed me. You slipped past security and almost cost them their jobs."

"I didn't mean for them to get in trouble."

"They got written up for that, Amber. Look." His eyes softened. "I miss you, toots." He peeked over his shoulder as he slid his hands into his pants pockets. "What do you say you and I give each other what we like? I got money to burn that's going to that bimbo." Daniel leaned forward with his face close to hers. Amber remembered his halitosis and subtly held her breath. "Her tricks are in the little leagues, but, honey, you are in the pros. You can make a quick two grand this weekend. I miss your tongue. What do you say?"

Amber's ears perked up at two grand. She could pay one month's rent with money to spare and spend her piano earnings on everything else. Perhaps she could get a car out of him. All her friends had cars now, making her the only Metro-dependent one. Her teeth clamped down on her lip as she considered all the precious options if she were to accept his offer. *What will next week bring? More money, too?* The offer sounded so tempting.

Then she thought about Emily and Eric and how she played a key role in their breakup. It took months for Emily to face her again. The baby elephant in the room still existed when she and Emily came together. Even Brooke had seemed slightly cold toward Amber. On the other hand, Daniel was a free bird. Who could get hurt? What? The college bimbo? Lucky for the young bunny, Amber didn't want to collect anymore debt on bad karma.

Proud of herself, she smiled and replied, "Nah. I just don't think so, Daniel." She placed the skirt back on the rack with one arm behind her as she kept her eyes on him.

Daniel's jawbone tightened in disappointment. "Okay. But nothing is more important than money. Nothing. And everyone needs it."

The look of rejection on his face? Priceless.

Amber slowly placed more distance between them. "No." Walking backward, a smile stretched across her face. "All you got is money. I'll keep my pride, bruh."

Nodding, Daniel pursed his lips with pinched brows. He stood there stupefied, perhaps by the fact that he couldn't arrest her with the idea of money.

Realizing she forgot something, Amber headed toward Daniel and stopped in front of his face. Perhaps under the assumption that she'd changed her mind, a smile brushed over his face. Instead, Amber whacked his face with her hand. Using all her might, he received the message loud and clear. She pointed a finger in front of his alarmed face. In shock, Daniel's jaw dropped, but when he realized that he'd been assaulted, he gritted his teeth and his forehead wrinkled in anger. A chunky hand rubbed the red, sore spot.

"That's for playin' me like a fool at your job." When she turned to leave, she could hear Daniel fuss.

"Get out of here you gutter rat before I have you arrested for assault."

Amber didn't care. She smiled. It felt wonderful to keep her cash *and* her dignity.

Emily

Emily wasn't really paying attention to her television as she sat on her bed flipping through a house magazine. Deciding to come back to that, she picked up the *Apartment Locator* instead and sifted through the listings in the DC area. An idea popped into her head that maybe she should just rent an apartment in Northwest. Her cellphone on the nightstand rang, so she closed the magazine and tossed it beside her and stretched for the phone.

"Hello?"

"My little girl. How are you?" On the other end, her enthusiastic daddy sounded delighted to hear her voice.

"*Papi*? How have you been?" Emily needed to hear from someone who'd always been on her side. She situated her body on the bed and eased her back against her pillow.

"Your mama and I have been talking about you. And your sisters keep asking about you, too."

"One day I will give Lourdes and Valentina a call. I've just been so busy with this move and everything." She placed a hand on her head.

"Move? *Que*? *Por qué no—*"

Realizing that he was going to start his tirade, she stopped him in his tracks. "*Papi, espera. Espera, espera, espera. No era así. No iba a ser un secreto.*"

His tone softened. "Well why didn't you *tell* me if you weren't going to keep this a secret? Your mother and I are here to help you girls, but you all always try to manage without us. Why? *Somos tus padres. Sabes*?"

"*Papi*, I know, you and *mamá* are there for us, but we are grown. We cannot run everything through you guys."

"Look. There's no need to spend money on nothing. We have those two houses there. They're just sitting. I'll overnight you two keys, and you can take a friend to help you decide on which house to move into. Those houses are paid for, so you just deal with utilities. How does that sound?"

While it didn't take Emily by surprise, it moved her to know that her daddy would do that. She didn't know if it would make her feel helpless, but she also knew that apartment hunting sounded about as exciting as handing her money over to a stranger for nothing in return. On the other hand, buying a house or condo felt too permanent for now, especially since she wanted to be someone's wife again. The thought of not picking out a house with her future husband or selling her next home after selling her current one upset her in ways that she didn't care to acknowledge.

"*Papiiiii*, you would do that for me?"

"Ems, come on."

Ems made her think of Eric. She had to subdue the anger that simmered within. The thought of him used to make her want to cry. Now it made her want to hit someone.

"I acquired those properties so many years ago and kept them for our family. Now, tomorrow, you will have keys for each address. *Ta bien?*"

Grinning, she replied, "*Ta bien. Gracias por todo, papi.*"

They said their goodbyes. Once Emily hung up, she hugged herself, feeling loved again.

Brooke

Damani Pappas returned to Brooke's table with a plate of *horta vrasta* with a lemon on the side. He placed it carefully in front of her and said, "Give it a try. I will be back to find out what you think." He winked and walked away before she could reply; her stomach flipped.

"Thanks," she mumbled.

Brooke placed a hand over her midsection and exhaled. While she felt grateful that she didn't have to eat greens in front of him, his departure disappointed her. Deciding to be careful not to place too much on her fork, she took a bite and savored the taste. Pleased, she admitted to herself that Damani made the right choice.

Still, Brooke preferred not to eat greens in his restaurant. One smile with leaves in her teeth could really turn him away and humiliate her terribly. Brooke pretended to text whenever she checked her teeth using her cellphone's dark screen as a mirror.

She also kept an eye on Damani to make sure that he wouldn't pop up unexpectedly. It took her about fifteen minutes to eat, and when she finished, it was like he'd returned on cue to pick up her plate.

He smiled. "Good?"

Brooke nodded. She liked it when he smiled because otherwise she felt like everything between them only meant business.

"Told you that you would like it."

Brooke really wanted a date with him and needed another notch on her belt if she were going to ever rid memories of Jackson anytime soon. Remembering that he was the last person that she had sex with didn't help.

"It was very good, Damani. You'll have to make that for me some time again." Brooke smiled at him as their eyes connected without blinking.

"I can do that. What are you doing tomorrow? It'll be Friday, you know."

"Right. That's the only day that really counts," Brooke quipped. "Friday is fine. What time?"

"You'll have to excuse me but being a restaurant owner means long hours. But I guess I can trust one of these knuckleheads with the reins at times."

"Well, how are you going to enjoy the fruit of your labor if you don't even have time to peel it?"

A smirk and raised brow crossed his face. One to talk, she felt like a hypocrite.

"Hmm," he replied. He shook his index finger at her. "That's a good one. Well put. Never heard that one before."

Brooke smiled at him. "So then what time works for you since your schedule is so tight? I thought *I* was the workaholic?"

"How's eight o'clock?" Damani's eyes sizzled into hers as he waited for her response.

Brooke flattened her hands on the table as she prepared to stand. "Eight is great."

He moved to the side to accommodate her.

"You should at least let me tip you."

"You should."

Brooke didn't expect his candor. "O-okay." She began to reach into her clutch when he grabbed her hand and pulled it close to him. Brooke's knees secretly bucked. She felt a quick stab of pleasure in her secret region, but she didn't mind at all. It was awake! She needed a reminder that Jackson wasn't the only man in the world who could capture her sexual thoughts.

His eyes toyed with her soul. "Good day . . . Brooke."

Damani took her hand and stroked the top with his thumb.

Lord have mercy.

His brazenness flipped her stomach with anxiety. She had the feeling that this man wouldn't hold back on their first date, and at this point, she'd welcome a full bull charge of sexual energy. Damani struck her as a take-charge soul who wore sex on his sleeves.

Damani eased her hand toward her as his slipped away. "Staring into those beautiful eyes . . . that's my tip."

Brooke lowered her head, too shy to look up. She wanted his tip all right. Just not the kind collected in restaurants. Feeling bashful and out of her league, she twisted her lips timidly, trying to reconnect her eyes to his. All she came in for was soup, and instead, she would be leaving with a burn in her rosebud.

"Where do you want to meet?"

Damani cleared his throat. "How about I pick you up? Or, you can drive to my house if that makes you feel more comfortable."

"Hmm." She placed a finger on her lips. "Where do you live?"

"Arlington."

"In Ballston?"

"No. Just, Arlington, Arlington."

"I see. Finally, someone from Arlington without Ballston. Where exactly?"

Damani held up a finger. "Come with me." He led them to the counter with the cash register, stole a business card from the tray and scribbled his address on the back.

"There." He handed it to her. "Eight o'clock." He smiled. "Wait." He waved a hand to signal that he needed the card back, so she placed it on the counter. "My phone number— you may get lost."

Damani added the digits and handed the card back. He left the pen top protruding from his mouth as he winked and gave her a quick nod with his chin.

Brooke playfully eyed him suspiciously. "With GPS? I don't think so. See you tomorrow and thank you for the free *horta*."

When his finger shot up to his lips, he said, "Shhh."

Puzzled, Brooke tilted her head. When her head straightened, Damani leaned down and got close to her ear and whispered, "*Horta vrasta*," he corrected. "And we wouldn't want others to get jealous because you get special treatment, do we?"

The heat from his lips hit her ears, and from her ears, that heat had somehow burned her internally. Determined to play it smooth, she simply told him, "Thank you for the *horta vrasta*," hoping that she pronounced it correctly.

He grinned as she turned to leave. Brooke realized that she'd become a doer in the dating world. She'd bounced off the sidelines to take a step in the right direction, hoping to leave lonely days and horny nights behind her, even if for just a little while. And so, she walked away, wondering what tomorrow night would hold for them.

2: heated

Summer

"Here's your orange juice." I held out the glass for Oliver as he took it with his toast. "Baby, you should really sit and eat breakfast with me."

Eating eggs on the bar stool at the countertop—happily twisting from left to right like a kid in an ice cream shop—Oliver stood next to me trying to gulp down his juice before heading out.

"Ahhhh." He wiped his mouth. "Baby, I can't. You know I gotta go check up on some of my Wash 'n' Folds." He kissed my forehead since my mouth was full. "I thought you were going to straighten up around here. You're the one who told me to stop paying for that service now that I have you here."

"I've just been so tired, baby. I'm sorry. I'll take care of it today."

Oliver shrugged. "Let me know, Summer. Do we need the professionals back? My floors are looking bad. If you change your mind, use the credit card I gave you months ago for services and handle it, please. I can't do dirty."

Was this man implying that I was the dirty one? His comment made my heartbeat jog. When he started to walk away, my nerves suddenly exploded. My hands shook in the air.

"Okay, chill, Oliver." Flustered hands raked through my hair. "I said I will take care of it, whether it's by me or the professionals, okay?"

Oliver stopped in his tracks, and I spun around on my stool to meet his glower. "Look, there's one thing I won't feel bad about, and that's not living in a filthy ass home."

"Are you kidding me, Oliver?" I hopped off the stool. Full of incredulity, I narrowed my eyes at him. "Do you really think I would even accept that as my lifestyle? You saw my apartment, you know how I lived."

Oliver grew impatient and in a mood that I'd never seen. He gestured with a hand. "You exploded at me, Summer. *You* lost it—not me. And I don't even know what that was about. I offered you my card if you don't wanna clean up. I really don't care. But I *do not* want to come home to filth when you told me to trust you with that domestic duty. Either way, you gotta fix it. Because I ain't tryna do this with you again, Summer. It's silly and it's stupid. Goodbye."

Oliver gave me a lazy salute, snatched his keys off the countertop, and hurried out the door.

Not having a chance to say anything else, and not really wanting to, he left me feeling confounded. I couldn't figure out what my problem was or what made me treat him that way. He only wanted to maintain his way of living, and I was disrupting it. We'd never argued before, and it upset me to the core. The minute my phone rang, I sent a mental prayer to God to let it be Oliver.

Instead Brooke's name displayed. Too soon. My brows collapsed in disappointment.

"Hello." My hip shifted to one side with a fist resting against it.

Brooke paused briefly before speaking. "Gee. Are you okay?"

"What's going on?" Sometimes a girl couldn't fake a pleasant demeanor. Besides, that was the beauty of having close friends—you could be yourself.

"Uhhhh, okaaaay. Are you free right now? This is my first Friday off in a year and the girls and I are meeting up in Chinatown at noon. Can you come?"

Why not? Good friends and food were in order. "Sure. Text me the info. Bye." I wished I could've given her more to work with, but she had to take me the way I currently felt.

Brooke sounded doubtful. "Oooookaaaaaay. I guess we will see you then. Bye."

Hanging up with a sigh, I had to decide. Should I do the cleaning, or call the professionals?

Amber

Amber arrived at the Chinese restaurant first. She stood out front with her arms crossed staring at the traffic from behind her sunglasses. Dressed in her black mini skirt and matching sweater, she struggled to stand comfortably in her new heels. She sighed.

"Maybe I should go get our table," she said under her breath. "Too brick out here to be waitin' on these girls."

Once Amber placed her hand on the handle, an attached bell dinged at the motion of the door. The smell of rice surfed the air, liberating her nostrils from the pollution-filled atmosphere on the other side of the door.

Wearing a smile, a tall Chinese hostess greeted Amber with her hands behind her back as Amber approached. "Hello, may I help you?"

"Table for four, please."

"Table for four? Follow me, please." Her petite frame turned on one ballet flat, exposing a long, black ponytail at the base of her neck. The pleasant woman led Amber to a booth in the barely-filled restaurant. She stared at the old green diamond-patterned carpet that needed replacing. It was about as drab as the green curtains clinging over the dirty windows.

The lady gestured toward the booth lined with worn-out vinyl. "Is this fine for you?"

Amber nodded. "Yes, fine. Thank you." She sat down and removed her sunglasses before folding and pushing them to the side. The hole-in-the-wall experience reminded her of the Chinatown in New York with food so delicious you'd want to tip twice.

As soon as she picked up the menu, she heard a voice say, "Hey, lady. Don't eat without us."

Alone, Brooke approached Amber in fitted gym attire with her hair pushed away from her sweaty hairline into a ponytail. A white windbreaker over a matching spandex top and black leggings covered her fit frame. The workout added a natural glow to her beautiful face.

"Uhhh . . ." Amber appeared perplexed as she stood to hug Brooke. "You ain't drive?"

Brooke patted her lightly on the back before sitting down. "Girl, I'm so hot, and I don't wanna put my sweat all over you."

Sitting, Amber grinned. "I appreciate that."

Shorter than the host, their waitress appeared wearing a mid-length bob and a pleasant expression. "Something to drink?"

Brooke looked up. "Four waters, please." She placed a hand over her chest as she worked to steady her breathing while fanning herself with the other hand.

Amber held up a finger. "And an iced tea, please— sweet."

"Okay. Be right back." The waitress turned and left.

Brooke finally replied, "No, I jogged."

"I'm impressed."

Brooke fanned herself and stuck her tongue out in exhaustion. "You sure you want sugar in your tea?"

Amber flipped her hand out and shrugged with a grin. Innocently, she replied, "I know. That's how I like it."

Picking up the menu, Brooke shook her head as she opened it. "Your body."

"That it is." She really didn't need Brooke checking her for her life choices again.

Amber patted her hair down self-consciously, worried that she lost some strands from the last-minute ponytail that she barely managed to create. She decided to forego wearing a wig just for the sake of keeping it simple and made the same decision to keep it light with her makeup. One coat of mascara and an application of nude lipstick and she was out the door. Now that she had alone time with Brooke, she wanted to take advantage and clear some things up.

"Hey, I wanted to ask you something before the others got here."

"Okay." Brooke nodded seriously and shut the menu. Placing her elbow on the table, she slid a hand under her chin.

"I know you never liked me too much, and you annoy the piss out of me at times. I also know that what happened between Emily and me put a strain between you and me."

"Mmmm." Brooke's brows dropped downward.

"But do you think you can forgive me for breaking her heart?"

Brooke didn't say anything. The server returned with their drinks. They thanked the waitress, and Brooke requested a few more minutes before ordering. When she walked away, Brooke sipped her water and Amber her iced tea.

Finally, she replied, "I'm glad you were woman enough to bring it up, especially since you know your behavior offended me."

Amber fought her need to become defensive, because she knew she should be grateful that Brooke and Emily still wanted to have anything to do with her. Instead, she replied, "No one is really talkin' about it, but I don't want that funny air, you know, to exist among us. I'd rather get it all out and move on, because we can't pretend like we the same four girls from last year."

"No, we can't because we're not. But let's face the facts. You just didn't know it was Emily's Eric. But hopefully, at the same time, you've learned to keep your body sacred and away from married men."

"I have." Amber didn't ask for a lecture, nor did she want to be told what to do with her body as if she were a little child. However, it would be wiser to accept what

Brooke had to say so she could be done with it. Sometimes people just had to feel like they were winning just for the sake of moving on.

"Good. Then I think we should try our best to move on. Well, I can only speak for myself." She placed her palm on her chest. "Eric didn't belong to me."

Amber nodded.

"But we should kind of learn from everything we all went through last year. It was rough for all four of us. Really rough." Brooke picked up her glass again.

"Cheers." Smiling, Amber held up her glass for Brooke to clink.

Summer

I happened to run into Emily at the front entrance. All my stress about Oliver melted upon seeing her face. Hugging and entering the restaurant together, we spotted their booth and approached Brooke and Amber just in time to see them share a giggle and a quick toast.

We greeted each other with hugs and cheek kisses before sitting. It'd been weeks since we'd last seen each other. And for a pack of close friends like us, that felt like forever. But despite Emily tolerating Amber, their relationship balanced on a tight rope. Not wanting to push it, I sat beside Amber.

Brooke pointed a finger at me. "Lady, what was wrong with you earlier?"

The time for dishing had come. "Oliver and I had our real first fight."

They looked up from their menus.

"No way," Emily said. "What about?"

"Cleaning. I know, so stupid." I brought them up to speed. "Being a jerk, I flipped on him."

Slumped in the booth, Emily blankly played with the straw in her glass as she suggested, "Yeah, you'll want to preserve that one. He's a good one and we all know how hard it is to find a good man."

The sheet of discomfort snuck up on us like a ghost and silenced us. I peeked at Amber with a sideways look and she shifted.

The waitress came back with her pad and a smile. We all ordered an entrée except for Brooke. "Hot n' spicy soup, please."

"And?" I studied her, waiting for her to erase my confusion.

"And that's all. I have a date tonight." She handed the menu back to the server upon closing it as we all gasped.

The waitress left to put our orders in with the chef.

Astounded, we all asked in unison, "What?"

She nodded fervently.

"With whom?" asked Emily.

She pointed at each of our faces with her eyes. "A Greek restaurant owner."

"Shut up." Amber smacked the table. "They date black women?"

"What?" Emily asked. "Why wouldn't they?" Emily appeared almost irritated. Then again, it didn't take much for Emily to feel irritated toward her.

Amber shrugged with a defensive expression. "Umm, because most Greeks marry within their own race. That's all."

"Who said anything about getting married?" Brooke asked.

"Well if he dates you it could happen," Amber replied.

"Tell us more about this guy," I urged.

"Oh. Well, his name is Damani Pappas—"

"Damani Pappas?" Emily and I sniggered.

"Isn't it hot?" Brooke asked with a scrunched-up nose.

"It is . . . different," Amber responded.

"He owns that Pappas restaurant down the street."

"Can't say that I've heard of it before," I replied.

Emily sat up with interest. "Wait. That restaurant with the green awning, right?"

"Yup." Brooke's finger tapped the air once. "That one. He is soooooo freaking hot."

Amber raised a hand. "I hate to do it but, how do his looks compare to you-know-whose?"

Brooke nodded her head. "I know, we have to compare. It's only natural. Umm, he's not as tall or as built as Jackson. I think he's uncut. According to him, he works very hard, so I'm guessing he doesn't have a lot of gym time. So physically, Jackson wins hands down. The face . . . uhhhhh." She sucked her teeth as she tilted her head in thought. "Jackson had a gorgeous face, but they're in two different age groups. So, I can't compare faces."

Intrigued, I replied, "Older, really?"

"So, old and mushy?" Amber joked.

Brooke narrowed her eyes at her. Emily rolled her eyes. "Yeah but there's something rugged and masculine about him. Is there a such thing as an alpha metrosexual male? That'd be Jackson. Damani is ruggedly handsome—it's intriguing and new to me. Also, I think he's in his early forties."

"That is so hot," I replied.

"Check the balls," Amber added with a nod. "It's all in the balls. Been there, done that old thing."

I peered at her in good humor. "Yours were grandpa old and almost ready to see the light." I pointed a finger at Brooke. "Her old is "big daddy" old. There is a difference."

Emily and Brooke fell over laughing and Amber pretended to cover my mouth to ban me from talking. But when our food arrived, we all straightened to prepare ourselves for our meals.

Amber almost choked on her water. "Speaking of old, guess who I saw?"

"Eric?" Emily asked, creating an awkward silence. She raised one eyebrow and shrugged as her hazel eyes beamed into Amber's. Brooke and I looked at each other, and then at our two friends, and then back at each other again.

"I don't think Eric was quite that old, Emily," Amber responded with a look of disbelief that she would bring up his name. She placed the napkin in her lap. "And, no, it was Daniel."

I almost choked on my water. "Seriously?" My eyes shifted to Amber.

"Give me a break." Brooke leaned forward. "After he tossed you out on your ass, you ran into him?"

Amber nodded. "He had a young, blonde feline cat with him. When he gave her money to shop with, he followed me into Express to offer me cash for services."

Invested in the story, Brooke leaned in. "What'd you do?"

"I turned him down," she replied matter-of-factly. "I'm a changed woman I told you."

I gently smacked her hand. "Good for youuuuuuu."

Emily sighed, and without looking up from her entrée, she added, "Doesn't help me now." She tossed her napkin on the table.

We all raised our eyebrows and pretended not to hear that as Amber and I plucked the food on our plates with our forks. Brooke just over stirred her soup.

"Excuse me, I need the restroom." Emily stood up and walked toward the hostess to ask where the restroom was located.

Amber leaned forward and whispered, "Okay, when is she gonna stop throwin' that night in my face? I already apologized, and besides, I simply didn't know the man was Eric." She shook her head.

Brooke volunteered the first response. "She's a hopeless romantic, Amber. Eric was her first love. She has to take as much time as she needs. All we can do is be patient."

Amber pursed her lips. "And I'm supposed to keep taking a beating since Eric isn't around to help take some of the wrath? She can barely stand the sight of me."

"Shhhh," I warned with a finger against my lips. "Keep your voice down. She may hear."

She continued in a loud whisper, "Maybe she should hear. I'm getting sick of this. I thought we were making progress, but I ain't feelin' being her whippin' girl at random for one night of pleasure with a single man who happened to be her ex. Come on—*we were in West Virginia*, not DC.

Brooke nodded. "I understand, Amber. Maybe you should just talk to her *now.*" She sipped her soup from the spoon.

Emily stepped out of the restroom and made her way back to our booth. Once she sat, I gave Amber a nod to let her know that she should speak up.

"Hey, Em?"

"Yeah?" she asked with friendlier eyes.

"Can we talk now?"

"I thought that's what we were doing here the whole time." She tightened her ponytail by tugging the tail in two different directions.

"No, I mean a little more in-depth, me and you."

Tilting her head with a solemn expression, she said, "Sure. What about?"

"I'm asking a lot. I know I'm the reason you and Eric aren't together today, but—"

"Huh," she replied bitterly. "Now don't go giving yourself too much credit. He was in the wrong, too."

"I know, I know, but you and I are far from where we used to be in terms of our friendship."

Emily waved a hand at Amber before twirling lo mein around her fork. "Nah, nah, we weren't *that close.*

"Well, we were kind of close."

"No." She shook her head. "No, we weren't all that close. I mean sure, we went to parties and all, and I sold you my piano. But no, we weren't that close. So, we didn't lose too much blood."

"Okay." Amber rested her back against the booth cushion and placed her napkin and fork on the table.

Brooke's expression matched mine. We both tucked our lips inside our mouths and looked away with raised eyebrows.

Emily looked up at Brooke as she chewed. "So, what are you going to wear for Damani tonight?"

Brooke did a mock sulk. "I'm not sure," she whined.

I placed a reassuring hand on Amber's knee. She patted it to let me know she appreciated the nonverbal support. "Are you nervous?" I asked.

Brooke didn't hesitate. "Absolutely."

We shared a laugh, even though Amber's sounded strained. Obviously, she felt uncomfortable, and I couldn't help but realize that she must've changed. The old Amber wouldn't have let anyone subdue her, but this one was really upset by Emily's attitude toward her.

Suddenly, Emily interjected. "I'm moving." There was panic in our silence. We looked up as we finished chewing to enable speech.

"Where?" Amber asked first.

"To my dad's property. Well, one of them. But they're local properties, so no worries. I'm moving but not relocating."

Even Amber released a shared sigh of relief. Brooke placed a hand on Emily's.

"To Southeast." Emily's head bobbed, almost to encourage a sense of confidence in her choice.

"Say what now?" Brooke slowly slid her spoon from her mouth.

"South. East. You guys heard me."

"To the hood?" Amber tilted her head and frowned. "Sweetheart, I left New York for that reason. Why would you—"

Emily replied, "Actually, Southeast has come up, and it's been in the making for quite some time now. Being from New York, you wouldn't know." She pointed her head at Brooke. "And she wouldn't know because she refuses to even go that way."

"Damn straight," Brooke confirmed.

The fork in my hand pointed and shook at Emily. "She's right though. Oliver likes looking at real estate, because he was considering moving his mom out here, and he was blown by the costs of the upscale apartments. So yeah, it's changing."

Brooke shrugged. "Anyway, I stand by Northwest and I'm glad I won't be losing you. I would hate you for life."

Emily pretended to be taken aback. "Gee."

We snickered.

Brooke pulled a ten-dollar bill from her windbreaker pocket. "Well, ladies, I have to go. I need a nap, then I have to go shopping in my closet for tonight."

Amber looked confused. "Shopping in your closet?"

Emily smiled and told Amber, "Yeah, because she has so many new clothes with tags in her closet that it's like a department store for her."

"Ohhhh," Amber replied. "Must be nice."

She glanced up with a grin and batted her lashes. "Yeah. It is." Her attention shot at Emily. "Excuse me babe, gotta run, and this time literally." We all jumped up to say our goodbyes. "I don't stay sexy like this from sitting too long," she informed us as she waited for her hugs.

I waited for her to hug Amber. "Let us know how it all turns out."

She pointed at me. "You know I will."

When I hugged her, my nostrils caught a whiff of her pleasant sweet scent. "You smell good for a jogger."

Brooke laughed it off. "Do I? That's a Brooke Brazile for you. See you guys. Pray that my night goes well."

"We will," we assured her in unison.

The waitress returned to our table. "Ready for check?"

We nodded as we took our seats.

"And boxes to go, too, please," Emily added.

When the server left, Amber said, "Gee, Brooke's ten could almost cover the whole tip."

"Right?" I replied.

Seeing my friends—who slowly started to feel like sisters—boosted my mood as expected. Of course, I wasn't expecting us to be like we were when we'd first met back in September. That would've been naïve of me. But, I'd secretly reserved a piece of hope in the corner of my heart that Emily and Amber would've gone back to being chummy. Apparently, no cigar. In fact, Brooke was the only one who had something amazing to look forward to. And if her date was any indication of what she'd eaten, hopefully she could move on from her heartbreak and enjoy something hot n' spicy again.

Emily

Emily parked her Jeep and headed to her house. Her phone alarm went off, reading, 'Show home.'

"Ohhhhhhh, shoot," Emily complained as she stomped her foot. She'd completely forgotten that her longtime friend, Tim Sharpe, a real estate agent, knew someone looking to buy immediately. Sure that his client would find the home a winner, Tim made an appointment with Emily to bring him by. A cab stopped beside her Jeep, causing her to look back and stop in her tracks. Amber crawled out of the cab.

"Shoot, shoot, shoot," Emily whispered. "What is she doing here? I don't have time for this."

"Emily! Wait, girl!" Amber called, waving an arm as she ran toward her.

Emily wasn't in the mood to pretend that the visit wasn't at an inopportune time. She waited for her to catch up before she continued her way to her house.

"Amber, what are you doing here?" Emily didn't take her eyes off the ground as she marched toward her porch.

"I had to talk to you. It couldn't wait. Can I come in?" she asked through puffed breaths.

Emily sighed. "Well, I can't exactly send you back home now, can I?"

Emily saw the package at her doorstep and picked it up. She knew it was the keys from her father. The upper left corner read, "Quito Rosado."

"Look. I'm sorry." Amber watched Emily fumble for the house key. "But there is some funny air between us that I can't stand to inhale anymore."

"So plug your nose." Finding and inserting her key into the keyhole, Emily stormed into the house.

Amber followed her through the door without waiting for an invite. "Do you have to be so rude?" She tilted her head and narrowed her eyes at Emily.

Emily slammed her keys on the end table next to the front door and dropped the package on the floor. She crossed her arms, turned to face Amber, and said, "Look, I can't say that I enjoy your incursion when I'm expecting a very important visitor. Like now."

"If you hear me out, then it'll be quick."

"One minute." Her eyes widened. "Go."

Amber almost lost her words now that she had the spotlight. She lifted her chin. "Well." She crossed her arms and slid her slipping purse strap back onto her shoulder. "For starters, I think that you should stop giving me so much damn attitude when you know I would *never* do anything to intentionally hurt you. You gotta know that."

Emily's nose crinkled, and her eyebrows creased. "Really? Do I?"

"Yeah," Amber shot back.

"You see I think you could be more laconic about all this and save us the BS."

"*What are you talking about?*" Amber asked impatiently with outstretched arms. "Speak English."

Huffing with an eye roll, Emily shook her finger at her. "If I let you talk, you go on and on and on and never say anything relevant. Just be succinct about all this and say, 'Hey, Emily, I'm a whore who screwed up. My inability to work legitimately caused you to lose everything.'" Emily pinched the air. "That! That would make me happy."

Amber's mouth formed an "O." With arms reaching heavenward, she asked, "Why am I here? Why am I here?" She placed her face in the palms of her hands. When she lowered her hands and looked at Emily, she saw a face glaring with no regrets. "I'ma let that slide."

"Well, *thank you*, Amber. You are so kind, after all. I mean, you *are* in my house."

"Did it ever occur to you that I did you a favor?" Amber's foot tapped the floor.

Emily placed a hand over her chest as her voice squealed, "*Me*? Me? You did *me* a favor?"

Amber nodded once. "Yeah. I saved you from another divorce. Obviously, he was still a snake. I mean, Emily, come on. I had to speak up. He wasn't gonna say shit."

Emily scorched Amber with her stare. Known for being ridiculously calm as a child, Emily's sisters would go bananas when they thought she missed an opportunity to stand up for herself. And the more Emily listened to Amber as she tried to justify her actions, the more she realized people failed to take her seriously, because she was always known as the peace angel to her siblings. More and more, it was getting harder to wear those wings.

"What if you slipped on your bedroom duties? You don't think Eric woulda been the type to go fishing?" Amber clapped between each word. "He's a rich man who is used to getting everything his way—and fast!"

Emily mocked her clapping when she asked, "Why are you clapping?" Afterwards, she folded her arms. "So, you're going to tell me about my ex? You only knew him for one night."

"Well, look what he did." Amber's hands fell and slapped against her thigh.

"He was single."

Amber pointed a finger at her. "But he was capable, Emily." She poked her neck out at Emily and scoffed. "He. Was. Capable. What else was he hiding from you?"

With no need to indulge Amber anymore, Emily became hysterical with tears in her eyes. "Get out! Get out, Amber!" They would never see eye to eye on the matter and frankly, Emily was over it. She swung the door open. "Out!"

Amber turned to her and said, "My mistake was a favor. I did you a favor!" Her eyes glistened as she carefully stepped outside.

Emily stood in the doorway and yelled, "If you wanna do favors, keep your legs closed in the future." She slammed the door behind Amber and pressed her back against the door. She sniffed and found her way to the powder room to make her face look more presentable before her friend and potential buyer arrived.

Dabbing her eyes and nose with a tissue, Emily studied her reflection in the mirror. She decided to pull her ponytail down and flip her head over to shake her brunette hair loose. Standing upright, her hair gathered around her face. She rubbed her pouty lips together that complemented the small splash of freckles around her button nose. The knock at her door signaled her to turn the light off and head back to the foyer.

Emily swung the door open to two men, one of them familiar and tall, the stranger, slightly shorter. As she widened her door to accommodate the lean realtor and wide-shouldered client, she saw Amber outside standing at the curb. Emily figured she was trying to hail a cab or flash a leg for a new client. Either way, she couldn't care less. It wasn't her business and she'd rather it stayed that way.

Closing the door behind the two men, she greeted her friend, Tim, with two air kisses. "Tim, so good to see you."

Always meticulous and quite energetic, the brunette with pointy features glowed with a hand on his cheek. "Likewise, sweetheart. How have you been?" he asked in his borderline high and nasal voice.

They held onto each other by the elbows. "It's been rough but I'm getting through. Not gonna lie." Emily exhaled with a laugh.

"I'm sure, sweetheart. I know, I know how that feels."

They had a happenstance meeting at Starbucks one day and caught up. Tim told her about his breakup with his longtime partner, Chad, and how he thought he'd never breathe anytime soon. That was until a client called him to sell her DC mansion and the paycheck gave him oxygen again.

Emily gestured toward his client. "I'm so glad to show you my house."

"Forgive me. Emily," he told her with a business card grin, "This is Pharr Spradlin, Pharr Spradlin, Emily Rosado."

She shook hands with the young man who appeared to be in his low thirties. Emily liked her men older and something about him seemed kid-like. Maybe it was the curly brown hair that covered his ears and brushed his collar. Could be his super friendly eyes. Although, unless his parents were helping him to buy the house, he must've been doing something right to be able to afford it.

"Pleasure to meet you, Emily."

Emily raised an eyebrow. "Pharr? As in the opposite of close?"

He sniggered. "Yes, but spelled, P-h-a-r-r." He held up a palm and briefly closed his eyes. "I'm used to it. I can walk up to a lady and say, 'I'm Pharr.' Imagine how that sounds. I sound crazy." He laughed with Emily.

She nodded. "I like it."

"Thank you."

Emily plucked a quick finger outward. "Well, I'm going out back to give you guys some privacy, maybe even take a walk."

Tim nodded with a smile. "Excellent." He turned to Pharr and asked, "Well, should we get started?"

Amber

Amber spoke with Mara on her cell as she waited for an unoccupied cab. It'd been almost an hour since she'd spoken to Emily. For a street in DC, she was surprised at the low volume of cabs on Emily's block. "Yeah, I don't know when Emily and I will ever be able to patch things up. I think I made it worse by coming over here."

"You're an impulsive soul and sometimes that will get you into trouble. Just give her time before you apologize."

"I feel like a rotten egg." Amber sighed. "But you right, I guess. I just gotta wait it out before I come near her again with an apology."

"If you control yourself and gotta see her, just create a video and talk to yourself or go to your mirror and pretend to tell her there."

"That sounds cool, you know, if I ever decide to do that." Feeling tired, she placed a hand over her forehead. "Every cab that drives by got someone in it. Talking on the phone with you is making me forget that I gotta catch a cab. I gotta go. I'll call you later."

"Love you, Sis."

"Love you, too, Mara, and thanks for having my back."

"Anytime."

As soon as Amber hung up her phone, she spun around when she heard a voice.

"No luck with a cab?"

Amber saw a man who appeared to be a few inches shy of standing six feet, walking toward her. As he became closer, she could see his one-of-a-kind shade of blue eyes under straight eyebrows. His full lips attracted her attention after she found her way out of his magnetic irises. His hair was a little messy, but she supposed the contradiction of his sexy features could make up for that.

"No, unfortunately, each one seems to have someone in it. Kind of strange today. Don't you think?" Amber wanted to smile but she was a little too irritated by the fact that she was stranded in Emily's neighborhood and sad that she may have lost a friend permanently.

He revealed a beautiful smile. "Yes, especially in DC. You want a lift?"

Suspicious, she replied, "You don't even know me."

"I'm a gentleman." His hand touched his heart. "What can I say?"

"I don't even know your name. And what made you stop whatever it was you were doing to come talk to a chick like me flagging cabs?" Amber felt flattered, and she supposed his car had to beat sitting in the back of a musky taxi. She could use a break from the smell of worn-out leather that'd held too many funky asses anyway. Besides, it didn't hurt that the man was hot.

He looked askance at her. "A girl like you, huh? What do you mean by that?"

Amber couldn't go there with him. "Nothing, I just meant that, ummm . . . we don't know one another."

He pointed behind him at Emily's house. "You didn't see me go into that house right there?"

"I was on the phone so . . ." She held onto her purse strap with both hands.

"I'm going to buy that house. But I asked the lady in there—Emily—if she happened to know you. She told me I was on my own with getting to know you since you two were no longer friends."

Amber felt a stab in her heart, but she didn't let it show, or she'd hoped.

"So, I took a break to come get your name and number. I couldn't let you get away."

True, she felt flattered, but Amber didn't want to take this man down with her. In fact, she had to stop herself from suggesting that he run from her. "You're keeping them waiting?"

"She said she needed to speak with my realtor in private, and I already know I want this house. So, I chose to come and talk to you right quick."

Amber couldn't help but look at his clothes and then Emily's house. Appearances were deceiving at times, so beyond his slightly rugged exterior, she wondered who exactly the man was dressed in the distressed leather jacket and faded blue jeans. After she spotted the Timberland boots, she mentally ordered a lesson or two in the fashion department.

She couldn't suppress her curiosity any longer. "What do you do for a living?"

"I have my own construction business."

Wow! *Well that explains the rugged look.* "That's king right there, that's king." Amber wiped windblown strands of hair from her lips.

"You?"

"I offer piano lessons for a living. I know that pales in comparison to being a business owner."

"Hey, whatever makes you happy. My dad passed away last year so I inherited the company."

Ouch. Unfortunately, she knew how that felt. "I'm sorry to hear that . . . Well, I wish I had a name to go with my condolences."

"Ohhhhh, right." He smirked. "I forgot we were born with those things."

He made her laugh.

"Let's get this handshake out the way. Ladies first."

Amber placed hers into his. The lasting effects of holding hammers and carrying heavy supplies told a story on their own through his hands, and she liked it enough to want to get to know him.

Confused, she asked, "Huh?" as she accepted his hand.
"Your name?"
"Oh. Amber Hamilton."
"Pharr Spradlin."
"What?"
They stopped shaking their hands but didn't let go.
"Pharr. Here." He took his hands back to pull out a business card from the pocket of his jacket. When Amber read the business card and saw the spelling, she looked up at him and said, "I like that."
"Thanks. I get that a lot. Amber, huh? I like that name, always have. Never met an unattractive Amber yet."
She couldn't help but chuckle. "Wow."
A voice in the distance interrupted their chat.
"Pharr! We're ready!" They both turned to see a man in a business suit standing on Emily's porch calling for him.
"Right there." Pharr held up a finger and turned his attention back to Amber. "Where do you live?"
"Southwest."
"Oh, near the Waterfront. Okay, well give me a second. Here." He reached into his denim pocket and disarmed his vehicle with the keys. Amber's brows crinkled in perplexity. "A pretty woman like you doesn't need to wait out here. The midnight blue F-250 down this side. Let yourself in the passenger side."
"Pharr—" she began to protest.
He held up a hand in good humor. "Hey, I know where to find you. It's just a truck, not the card to my bank account. Besides," he tilted his chin up at her and looked at her from the sides of his eyes, "I have the key, remember?"
Reluctantly, Amber smiled, hoping Emily wasn't watching. She could just see her now, looking out the window and calling her a gold digger under her breath. "'Kay. Thank you." Amber nodded and hesitantly walked away from Pharr, almost wanting to walk far, far away instead.

Summer

I stood with my hands covered in rubber gloves, ready to scrub the toilet in our master bedroom when my cell phone rang.

"Oh, come on, man."

Peeling the gloves off, I quickly washed my hands with soap before grabbing the phone from the sink counter. Amber.

"Yes ma'am."

"Umm, I just had to tell you how odd this moment is right now."

"Why?" I stood in front of the mirror with my hand on my hip with hair that made me hot. Suddenly it occurred to me why hiring professional cleaners was a great idea. If I wanted a workout, I could go to the gym.

"I came to apologize to Emily. I know, I know, bad idea, won't happen again."

Luckily, she didn't see me shake my head in disapproval. She explained to me how things went between her and Emily, and how she was currently in a strange man's vehicle. This woman and her encounters with strangers.

"He's giving me a lift."

Amber surprised me with all her latest information. "Go for it, girl. That's a great ending to your crappy day. Consider it your Uber."

"Well get this. He owns his own construction company."

Leaning against the bathroom sink, I fanned myself with my hand. "Sounds like you're on your way to having your own Oliver. But, hey, do yourself a solid and hire professional cleaners when you move in together."

"Hey, if it gets me into one of these upscale Southwest apartments, I'd be happy to scrub. How sad is this? You were the only Southwest buddy I had, and now you in the same echelon of those two Northeast/Northwest heifers. I'm the only broke bitch left."

"Amber, if it weren't for Oliver, you know I'd be the other broke bitch, too."

"Well, you makin' money again, nowhere as much as Oliver, but with your new job, things can definitely put you on top."

One could only dream. "Amber, I wouldn't take it that far, but I could be a one-trick pony. There's no promise that I can eat tomorrow unless I get contracted by one of these bammas. And besides, if it weren't for Fran firing me, I'd still be making an average living. I mean, things are drying up on my end already. I wish I still had that job with Fran, but not with all that other crap though."

"Well, ain't that somethin'? You double-cross your boss and make out like a fat rat, and I double-cross a friend by accident, and I'm stuck teachin' perfect fifths for a livin' while findin' performance gigs. Grrrr. Why'd I stop sleepin' with men for money again?"

I felt uncomfortable talking about Fran and my wrongdoings. I felt uncomfortable for refusing to apologize for my initial success as an independent recruiter. I felt even more uncomfortable being caught in the crossfire of Emily and Amber's war. This sour conversation had to end.

"Giiiirl, you stay pressed about coming up. Look, don't forget to be grateful for all you've gotten on your own. But lady, right now, I have to scrub this toilet or else I just might find myself back in Southwest in no time."

"All right, well I just thought I'd catch you up."

"That's cool. Hey, if I move back, at least we can walk to the new shops there."

"I'm good with Southwest now. But I wanna come up and be in a better hood. My apartment sucks, yo."

"Bye, Amber."

"Yeah, yeah, yeah."

We hung up. Whew.

Relief swept over me. I loved Amber dearly, but her need to be rich was going to be the death of her if she didn't watch it. After a struggle with the rubber, my hands slid back into the gloves to clean the bathrooms, kitchen, and the floors in less than an hour and a half. My body was covered in sweat and felt extremely tired by the time I'd finished. If that wasn't enough, a sudden pesky throb attacked my head. Perhaps my headache came because my lunch had worn off, but it hadn't been that long since my meal in Chinatown. Besides, I wasn't too hungry at the moment.

Thirty minutes later, I emerged from the cold shower smelling like peaches and cream. My long, wet hair laid flat against my head, and a towel wrapped around my tiny figure. The knot gave me trouble, but that wasn't anything new. Trying again, I caught a glimpse of my body in the fogless mirror while readjusting the towel. To my dismay, my normally flat stomach had grown a slight bulge. *Really, Summer?* Oliver's fine cooking had gotten me in trouble!

The sight troubled me. Frowning, I shook my head and shut off the light. Looking for something to wear over my dark blue underwear set, an eyelet red shirt and jeggings made the cut. Heading for the kitchen, I intended to have dinner ready for Oliver before his return. Since he'd turned his phone off since my earlier attempts and hadn't tried calling me, it was safe to assume that he still didn't want to be bothered.

Before selecting something from the freezer, the sound of the deadbolts unlocking stole my attention. Closing the freezer door, I saw Oliver securing the locks.

He wore an unreadable expression once he turned around. "Hey."

Without thinking twice, I ran and jumped on him, feeling nothing but deep gratuity and showing it by wrapping my legs around his body while placing kisses all over his neck. My baby came home, and all was well.

Chanting, "I'm so sorry, sorry, sorry, sorry," and coming up for air, we stared at each other for a few seconds. I placed a kiss on his lips and whispered, "Sorry."

"I couldn't call you. My battery died and there was so much shit going on today. Work was a mess. I wanted to call you, but I had to let the phone charge."

"Nah." I lowered my legs to stand. "It's okay, sweetie, I'm just glad that you're home. I feel terrible for snapping at you, baby. Can we forget about it?" We grabbed hands and let them swing.

"Baby, it's okay I forgive ya'. But, please, lemme hire a professional to help you out now that you're working. Don't feel bad about paying for services."

Throwing my palms up, I acquiesced. "Oh, honey, I surrender."

He laughed. "Too much?"

I held up my thumb and index finger and almost made them touch. "Yeaaaaah. Just a lil bit."

Oliver smirked at me before his eyes darted around the apartment. "Hey, what's up here? Do I see shiny floors? You cleaned after all?"

"I did, baby, I did. I had lunch with the girls, came home, and cleaned. You were right. It was filthy. The longer you wait, the longer it takes to clean."

He tapped a finger on my nose. "Tried to tell you."

"Next time, I'm calling your old services."

He walked into the kitchen. "Good. Now, what's for dinner? Or should we call the professionals for that, too?"

Amber

The driver's door of the F-250 opened as Pharr Spradlin hopped in. He closed it and asked, "Take too long?"

Amber rolled her eyes playfully. "Originally, I was waiting for a cab that never came. Remember? So, thank you, Pharr."

He started the engine to take them out of the parallel parking space.

"Nah, it's my pleasure, really. So where is the first date going to be, your house?"

If Amber were drinking, she would've choked. "Umm, there?" She didn't want him to see her small apartment, especially when he probably lived in a mansion.

He chuckled. "Am I moving too fast? I'm tired, so I could really use a chill night in with a beautiful woman like you."

Again, Amber felt flattered. "Um, okay. Sure. I don't know if I got any food." She thought about seafood, but something about kissing him afterwards didn't sound too appealing.

"Dinner." Pharr rubbed his chin as he stopped at a red light. "Hmmm. How about the Waterfront? They got oysters there."

If he was game, then so was she. "Aren't they aphrodisiacs?"

The light turned green. "Isn't that the point?" Pharr glimpsed at her with a grin as he drove. "Actually, I read there isn't much scientific evidence to back that up anymore."

"Well, we can pretend." Amber returned the mischievous grin. "So how did you get that name?"

"Ever heard of Pharr, Texas?"

"Nope."

"Well, right before my parents moved from Texas, I was born. They named me after the city in which we lived. Kind of like a tribute because they loved it there. My dad did construction in Texas. We moved to Bethesda because my dad had to take over our construction company after his dad passed away."

"Why did your grandpa do construction in Maryland instead of Texas?"

"Ha. According to my parents, my dad and grandpa didn't get along."

"I see." Amber looked out of the window. She studied the diverse group of people walking the streets of DC. She realized that young people loved jogging and walking in crowds with their friends in the nation's capital. Amber grew nervous as they inched closer to the Waterfront. Soon it would be time to show him her place. Luckily, she always kept her home clean.

"So, what did you think of Emily's home?"

"Love it. Can you believe I'm renting an apartment right now in Rosslyn?"

"It's beside Georgetown, right? I'm still learning my areas."

"Right. I hate Georgetown. I don't even bother crossing the bridge into snooty world."

Amber laughed. "Don't let my friends hear you say that. We eat breakfast there a lot. Well, we did last year." The good old days. Back when things were simple, and her mistake wasn't looming over her head.

"Hey. If it works for you guys. The street crowd is just too much for me. I can't wait to get this house. I'm tired of renting—I feel like I lack a sense of permanency."

"Where does your mom live?"

"Still in Bethesda, in the same house where I grew up. She's a very self-sufficient lady. Exercises every day."

Amber laughed. "That's more than what I can say for myself." Pausing, she added, "Emily does yoga on Saturday mornings." Instinctively, she tucked her lips inward as she instantly regretted that unnecessary spill. She didn't know why she threw that in.

"Emily?" He looked confused for a second. "Oh, yeah her. Why aren't you two friends?"

"She feels I wronged her and she can't get over it, regardless of my apologies."

"That's too bad."

"Sure is."

They arrived at the Waterfront, picking up oysters, muscles, and fried fish. She directed him to her apartment as she nervously clutched the big paper bag to transfer the nerves of hosting to an apartment with no eye-popping features. Taking the bag of seafood in his arms, he followed her to her door after stepping off the elevator.

"So, how do you like it here?"

Perhaps he was trying to check if she really liked it there, as if she wouldn't move elsewhere if she had another option.

"When I moved from New York—that's where I'm from—I actually started out in Southeast. I got a sister who stayed up there for college. With me helping her out, you know, money can be tight."

"I see," he replied with a gaping mouth and raised eyebrows.

"But one day, I'm gonna get out of here."

At her door, Amber unlocked it with her key. Looking at him, she warned, "This is no Emily's home, okay? But I keep it very tidy and clean since it's mine."

"No worries, Amber, no worries. I'm not after your money, you know."

Grinning, she replied, "Good, because you'd come up real short." Holding her breath, she opened the door and gestured a hand toward her small kitchen on their left. "Welcome to my humble abode."

"I like it," he announced as he peered around with a smile. "It's got that cozy feel, ya' know?"

"Well, thanks." Amber suspected that Pharr was just being polite. Telling someone that their home felt cozy became a familiar compliment she offered the men from the streets with whom she used to sleep when they revealed less-than-stellar apartments. Locking the door, she instructed, "You can set it there, inside the kitchen."

"Okay." Pharr walked into the kitchen as Amber flicked on the light. They both reacted with wide eyes when they saw a cockroach on the counter. Amber gawked. In all the months that she'd been there, she'd never seen any pests in her apartment. She wanted to die from the embarrassment! The one time that she decided to allow a man to come back to her place for a normal experience, she had to put up with humiliation. Lesson learned.

"Oh, no! Oh!" Her hands flew up to her face.

Pharr acted nonchalant but moved in haste as he came to the rescue. He placed the big paper bag on the opposite counter and reached for a paper towel from the holder. The bug tried to escape, but Pharr managed to cover and crunch it in time.

"Hate those things," he said. "Where's your bathroom?"

Amber still had her palms against her cheeks. Still in shock and in disgust, she twisted at the waist and pointed down the hallway. "Down there to the right." He walked past her on a mission with the paper towel in one hand and eyes glued straight. She heard him flush the bug and wash his hands. Collecting her nerves, she walked into the kitchen to wash her hands and grab the big bag of seafood. Amber decided to place it on the coffee table in the living room.

Pharr emerged from the hallway and spotted her to the right in the living room. They flung their jackets over the sofa arms and situated themselves into the cushions. Still deeply mortified, she didn't know how many apologies it would take to erase any negative thoughts he may've garnered toward her. He reached for the bag to set up their food.

"I'm so, so sorry, Pharr. That was too nasty for words. I haven't had one yet, I swear."

"Amber, I'm in construction. Bugs are a part of my life in this business. But for your sake, please call the exterminator first thing Monday morning."

"I can call the office tomorrow. They can at least take my request on a Saturday. I'm just glad that you were here to help, but sorry for our appetites."

"Forget about it. What should we try first?"

He was ready to eat, and Amber knew that she would have to keep any additional thoughts about it to herself. She didn't want to ruin the night, so she decided to pretend to be over it as well. Besides, the idea was to forget about it, she reminded herself.

She suggested, "I guess we can get to the fried fish?"

"Cool. Television?" He adjusted their Styrofoam trays of fried fish and lined the sauces up on the coffee table.

"Sure." Amber reached for the controller and turned on the flat screen's sixty-inch picture. A Christmas gift she gave to herself.

"Glad you're not afraid of a big screen."

She grinned. "I ain't afraid of much of anything— except for bugs!"

They both reacted to her stab at humor as Pharr nodded in agreement while teasing her with imitations of her horrified expression.

It used to be true that she didn't fear much, but with her self-esteem shattered by recent events, it felt more like a lie and a far cry from whom she thought she was.

Calming down, he asked, "Something to drink?"

"Sure."

Amber needed this. A good man who didn't expect sex and who did little pleasant things for her. Amber just felt . . . normal. Normal. Her heart warmed at the idea of a man moving slowly with her and at the realization that she didn't have to part her legs after dinner. They were together, simply enjoying the company of one another. No skin, no lust, no bed sheets, no orgasms. Just a man and a woman delighting in hot food and television. And though this date cost next to nothing, it was the most extravagant one she'd been on, so far.

Summer

After dinner, Oliver and I cuddled on the couch to watch *Goodfellas*. My elbow rested in his lap and my feet nestled between a blanket and the crack of a cushion. I turned my face to look up at him. "That was a great dinner you cooked—and by the way, mister," I poked his chest, "your food is making me fat."

He glanced down and back at the television. "Oh, yeah? Well I don't see it."

"On my belly."

"Well let me see."

"No way, man." I turned my eyes back to the movie.

"Well, then be quiet. Pay attention, Summer."

Oliver rested a hand on my bottom. His hand went underneath the hem of my nightgown to stroke the skin of my thigh. As good as his touch felt, I couldn't resist the silent but aggressive pull of sleep. The next few hours were a blur as sleep won me over. A harsh nudge in my arm woke me up.

"What?" I demanded more than asked in a panic.

Oliver gave me an agitated look. "Summer, just go to bed."

"Well, just wake me up with more decency next time. Geez. You almost gave me a heart attack, Oliver." Pulling all my hair over one shoulder and wiping my hand across the back of my neck, the sweat glistening on my hand told me just how hot I'd become. I stood up.

"I'm sorry, baby. It looks like you're down for the count, so go ahead and go to bed."

"Fine, no problem, I'll go." Leaving, I complained, "Man, it's hot in here."

"Naw, it's just you, baby."

Sleepy, hot, and feeling out of sorts, I didn't know what to make of it all. It did convince me that the gym needed to become a part of my frequent routine. Maybe that would help. Women my age really couldn't dodge the benefits of exercising. Exercising had to become a priority. Otherwise, Oliver would classify me as "once hot," just like he did with his ex-girlfriends. Sliding into bed, I still felt hot, but it surely wasn't because of any sex appeal.

Emily

Emily started packing the items in her bedroom. She began with the bottom drawer of her dresser, since it held the garments she barely wore. Pulling out a stack of old underwear and socks, she realized it all belonged to Eric. She balanced the folded garments between both hands, but the hand on the bottom rested against something sleek.

"What in the world . . .?" She made her way to the bed and placed the stacked garments down gingerly, not wanting them to topple over. Carefully reaching for the slick material, a picture of Eric slid out in her hand. Surprised, Emily's mouth opened as she took in the lascivious photo.

Emily remembered taking that photo. They were on their honeymoon in that picture. Eric lay on the bed with tangled sheets between a bent and straight leg with his arms crossed behind his head. In fact, they'd just finished making love. The sheets between his legs revealed a delicious dick print that even her anger couldn't block her from enjoying.

In a daze, Emily pinched her lower lip with her fingers as she allowed herself to indulge in the moment. Happy and carefree in Aruba, they'd just finished swimming in the crystal blue ocean. He'd taken her to a beach party beside the ocean that night. Hosted by the resort, they danced with a crowd of vacationers. As she swayed her hips with the direction of Eric's large hands placed on her sides, in that moment, she knew they'd have countless vacations to book until death did them part. But death didn't do them part. His father did, and then Amber.

When the cell phone rang, Emily came back to reality. Picking up the phone, the name displayed across her screen surprised her. Staring at it with twisted lips, Emily debated whether to answer it. Tired of hearing the ringing because it reminded her of begging, she answered it with one angry tap.

"What?"

"Hello, Emily."

"Eric."

"Hi."

"What? Why are you *calling* me?"

"Because I heard that you're selling the house that I gave you. And if I knew that you wouldn't keep it, then—"

"Then what, Eric?" The blood rushed to her head. She'd grown tired of feeling like someone else's puppet. "What would you have done? Kept it? Do you remember why you gave me the house, Eric? Hmm? Because you felt guilty about divorcing me."

"Well, sell it back to me, how about that?"

"No. No, Eric." Emily clutched her temples.

"Why not, Emily?"

"Uh, well, for starters, someone else is buying it. The process on that has begun today. Second, I don't want to have *anything* to do with you. I don't want to have any ties to you, and, boy, does that sound great."

"I paid for it in full, and you turn around and let it go? You wouldn't be making one red cent if it weren't for me."

"Oh, but I will be making plenty of red cents from the sale. Thank you, Eriiiiiic," she teased. "Does it bother you that I will be one self-sufficient lady, thanks to you? And after all you put me through, you're going to cry about this house? Why do you want it back so badly anyway?"

"It's none of your concern. You know what? Do what you want. You're such a bitter bitch at this point that you will die alone. And you know what, Amber was so good, I'd pay for her again. Good luck, you ingrate."

Beep, beep, beep. He'd hung up on her.

"No that bastard didn't!" Stunned, Emily absently lowered the phone to her chest. She couldn't believe that he would say that. "*I'm bitter?*" she called out. "*I'm bitter?*" Even with open eyes, she couldn't make out a single object with clarity while standing in the middle of the bedroom. In a deep rage, Emily picked up Eric's old garments and hurled them at the wall. It wasn't enough. The green dresser lamp that she hated so much was next. "Errr!" It shattered everywhere when she hurled it against the same wall. Her enraged heart angrily thudded against her chest. The sudden pain in her head told her that she'd become upset way too fast.

"Bitter? Bitter? I will show you bitter!" She kicked at the dresser until she ran out of energy. *At least I won't have to clean that up.*

Plopping on the bed, she reached for a pillow at the headboard and cried into it with the pleasure of just letting go, with revenge scratching at the back of her mind.

Brooke

Well-rested and freshened up, Brooke settled on a sexy mini dress. The dress sent an intended message to Damani that if he played his cards right, then getting some would be an option. It wasn't her preference to sleep with a man on the first date, but she thought about Jackson, and how she bet that he'd gotten laid by now, even if it'd been meaningless. And if Jackson could do meaningless, then so could she—or could she?

There was no turning back now. Time passed with each moment she stood there fully clothed in a red, thin-strapped dress that hugged at the waist and flowed freely below with a sheer lining. Damani would be treated to a generous sight of her cleavage, and if he didn't get the picture, then he would be a better gentleman than Jackson. Brooke welcomed the day of not instinctively comparing men or sexual activity to Jackson. Sadly, she had a long way to go, because if it were possible to see, kiss, touch, or even talk to him at that exact moment, she would drop everything in a heartbeat to make that happen.

Brooke puckered her lips colored in a pale shade of red lipstick and gave her reflection one more look, approving of the black pumps and flirtatious loose bun on the top of her head. It was 7:15, and she didn't want to be late. Snatching her black trench coat from the rack beside the door, Brooke grabbed the red clutch on the end table. With a flip of the switch, she exited her condo in the dark and headed for the parking garage.

Once in her 5 Series, Brooke punched Damani's address into the GPS system and headed out. Typically, she didn't leave DC, so she needed help finding her way out of the city. Thanks to the GPS, she easily located 395 South and followed the signs. Instead of listening to music, Brooke chose to listen to her thoughts and the light pounding of the wind against her car.

"I think a car would be nice for you, Brooke. Why haven't you made that move before now?" He kissed her cheek, squeezed her tight and nibbled her neck.

Brooke placed her hands over his as they rocked from left to right. "I didn't want to spend more money than necessary. I wanted to leave my budget open for my mortgage and clothes and other necessities like health insurance and whatever else. It would just be easy to take one check and buy a car than to keep paying for it month after month."

"If you can afford to, do it." His hands went underneath her oversized angora sweater.

"The problem is, I don't know what kind to get. Maybe you should help me."

Jackson removed his hands and turned her around by her shoulders. He stroked her strands as they talked.

"What's your style: trucks, cars, sports car, vans, or motorcycles?"

"No!" Brooke's eyes widened. "No vans or motorcycles. One is for families with children and the other freaks me out."

"One day you may need that minivan, but for now, you need something that goes with your look. You need feminine and elegance."

She didn't want to cry, so she willed the tears away. Instead, she let her heart do the crying for her. He told her one day she may need a minivan after she clearly stated that they were for kids. So, if he didn't want kids, why did he hint that she may need one in the future? Certainly, he wasn't pinning her with another man, was he? Well, he didn't say "we." Either way, Brooke's anger intensified, so she pushed down on the pedal harder to see Mr. Damani Pappas sooner than later. It was just so hard to believe that now that she had a car, it wasn't headed toward the National Harbor, but Arlington. Nothing with another man felt right, but she had to make it feel right.

Thirty minutes later, and with minutes to spare before eight o'clock, Brooke pulled up to a white, four-level townhouse facing the traffic. Brooke sized up Damani's brick home. It didn't even appear to be ten years old in the dark. Before climbing out, she saw Damani standing on a high porch illuminated by the indoor light. Nervous, her stomach did flips. Struggling to control her nerves before entering the older man's home, Brooke wanted to tell the gymnast to calm down in there. Maybe it was more natural, but she was more confident and in control when she first dated Jackson. *Stop it! No more comparisons, Brooke, no more.*

Brooke approached his house with both hands tightened on her clutch. She climbed his generous sets of stairs to reach him in the foyer. Waiting at the top with raised arms, both elbows touched each side of the frame. In the dark, Damani looked suave in his black cotton t-shirt and black slacks. Standing in front of him, he grabbed both of Brooke's hands and kissed them slowly.

"Glad you could make it, Brooke. Come inside." With a big smile, he stepped to the side while helping her in with one hand.

Brooke smiled. "Thank you, Damani, for having me."

"You are one punctual lady. It's eight o'clock exactly."

Mmm. That accent. She could wake up to it.

Brooke looked around his home. Clearly on the second floor, they stood in his small but well-coordinated living room. Hazelnut colors dominated the sofa, rug, and coffee table trim. Brooke appreciated a busy man who could maintain his home. Maybe he didn't spend enough time at home to sully it.

"Lovely home, Damani."

"Thank you, sweet lady."

Kind of corny, but she ignored it. Stepping further into the house, something extremely delicious spoke to her olfactory sense.

Oh, no. Jackson cooked and so does Damani.

It proved too difficult not to compare the two men, especially after tonight. However, one thing became clear: Intaking Damani's cooking could only happen in moderation.

"Yum. What's that smell, Damani?"

"May I take your coat? Then I will tell you."

Brooke almost felt nervous about her dress. Correction—she felt completely nervous about revealing her dress. Perhaps it was too much? It really didn't matter since eating in a coat wasn't optional and neither was going home to change. Removing it off casually with her back already turned to him, her cheeks tingled with embarrassment, but thanks to her pigment, he'd never know. Brooke's knees didn't feel any stronger than the Thai noodles she ate the other night for dinner.

He chuckled. "Well, can I see the front?"

Brooke licked her lips before she turned at his request. She didn't say anything. When she turned, Damani's eyes locked in on her bosom.

"Well. You're more gorgeous than I realized." He nodded without looking at her face. "Nice. Very nice." Meeting her stare, he flashed her a quick grin. No doubt he scrambled to put his thoughts back together.

"Thank you. So, what are we going to eat?" she asked. *Before eating each other.*

"Follow me."

Brooke followed him to the contemporary kitchen, wondering if her dress sent him too strong of a signal. She figured time would tell. On the other hand, it would be cruel to reveal so much and let him go to bed empty handed, but as a woman, Brooke knew she had the right to change her mind about intercourse.

Damani bent over to retrieve the food from the oven with a gloved hand. "Okay, before you came, I made stuffed leg of lamb."

"Stuffed with what?" she asked.

"Peppers and cheese," he replied as he removed the glove from his hand. "I wanted to keep it light, so I cooked very little. A woman with such a nice figure has to preserve such a body of art, yeah?"

"That's for sure." She couldn't help but remember Jackson's feast on their first night. He surely didn't worry about her figure. Lost in her thoughts, she giggled.

"What?" His face jerked in her direction.

"Oh, no." Slightly embarrassed, Brooke didn't want Damani to think that she was laughing at him. "I was thinking of something, that's all."

"Okay, well, let's head to the table where you will find the rest of the food."

Grateful that he didn't dwell on her laughter, she didn't want to have to make up something or tell him about Jackson either. When they walked through the other open end of the kitchen, they walked straight into the dining room.

Hmm, she hadn't seen this before. A hazelnut-colored three-piece nook took the place of a traditional table and chair set. After a few seconds of consideration, Brooke decided that he had refreshing taste. As a restaurant owner, his choice made sense.

"This is so cute." They both chose the bench seating with backing.

"You like?" Damani grinned at her as he arranged the dishes and wine bottle to accommodate the entrée dish. He placed her portion of lamb on her plate before serving himself and then added a portion of rice to both of their plates.

"Thank you, Damani." She spread a cloth napkin across her lap.

Nodding, his fork pointed to the bottle on the table. "This wine, you know, is very special."

"Oh, really?" Before she took a bite of her food, she waited to hear his explanation about the wine bottle.

"I pulled this out for you. It is a bottle of 1961 Château Palmer, Margaux. It's a medium red wine. It goes for three grand."

Brooke's eyes widened. "Well I'm glad I wasn't eating. I would've choked."

"Yeah, well, good food, good wine. Right?" He placed a cloth napkin in his lap. "But it offers a great punch when going down. You'll see."

"Sounds like a warning."

"Hey, could be. But you will like it. So, let me pour us some." He removed the cork and poured them a glass before he replaced the cork.

"Don't forget the grilled grapes." His eyes flicked to a plate of grapes with grill marks on them.

"Oh." Brooke hadn't really noticed them. "Grilled?" She looked concerned.

"Yes," he replied, with a chuckle. "Grilled. You Americans just pick them from the stem and eat. We Greeks do some things a little bit different."

"I see." Brooke tasted her bite of lamb. *Delicious*! She closed her eyes to savor the taste. "Mmm, Damani. Mmm, mmm, mmm." She opened her eyes. "Do you want to make me fat? At least do it over time, not all in one night," she joked.

He smiled with delight. "Oh, come now. You seem very controlled."

She placed a quick hand on his. "You're right." Then she moved it to her chest as she laughed. When she realized that she was hypnotizing Damani, she collected herself. "You're a great cook, Damani."

"I hope so. My livelihood depends on it." He laughed.

Brooke laughed with him and more than she'd predicted. She worried that he would be stiff the whole night, but he wasn't, so her nerves went back to normal. They pushed through dinner with small talk as he described his most favorite parts of Greece to her, while she described parts of California to him. They intrigued each other over fantastic wine.

"So, Brooke, why wouldn't you move back there?"

"I couldn't. You know, it was good for college, but that was about it. I loved the state, but my heart is here in DC."

"Because of family?" He took his last bite of lamb.

Brooke hadn't covered family or lack thereof. She didn't want to bring up her mom, so she decided against elaborating. "Noooo, it's just because I grew up here in DC. I knew people here, plus, I came to conquer my hometown in the wedding planning industry."

He nodded and chewed. "I can understand."

Unlike her last relationship, Brooke decided not to hold anything back. She wanted to know what took her forever to ask Jackson. "Damani, do you want a family? You know, a wife and children?" If Damani Pappas was going to get mad at her, she'd rather know it now than later, especially before sharing her body.

He shrugged. "Of course. I mean what knucklehead wouldn't?"

Relieved, Brooke almost blurted out the name of a knucklehead whom she knew didn't want children, but she remained silent.

"I think that is the natural course of life. I'm just so busy with the restaurant, that I haven't—well, I did have a girlfriend, but we couldn't last. We clashed too much."

Brooke decided that he could share those details later. Talking about exes in detail too soon ruined appetites.

"How old are you?" She didn't quite mean to blurt it out so suddenly, but the suspense ate at her like a vulture on a carcass.

"Wow." He smiled. "Lucky for you, I'm not ashamed. I am forty-three."

Brooke's smile widened at the novel experience of dating an older—way older man.

"And you?" He took a swig of wine.

"Twenty-seven." She picked up the glass of wine as her eyes played with his above the rim.

"Well, you have a lot to learn still."

"Like what?" she asked before she drank.

"Like, uh, life." He removed the napkin from his lap and tossed it onto his plate. "There is nothing wrong with that. Be happy that time is on your side."

Brooke swallowed. Pulling the glass away from her lips, she happily stated, "Well, I am."

Damani grinned as he reached for a grape. "I told you to try these, but you didn't. Open your mouth."

Appearing a bit bossy, Brooke didn't mind. He wasn't dominating her, she reasoned. Besides, she'd grown tired of always being in control twenty-four/seven. It didn't get her anywhere with Jackson, she figured. And at work, she certainly exerted a lot of control and power. Letting

Damani hold some of the reins didn't bother her so much. So, she opened her mouth.

Damani placed the grape into her mouth. Instead of simply plopping it inside, he rested an index finger between her lips. Brooke closed her mouth, securing the grape and enclosing his finger. Using her tongue, she knocked the grape to the side and gripped it between her teeth, then she ran her tongue over and around Damani's finger. *What has gotten into me?* Guessing it could be the wine, she went with that and decided against looking for answers, as Jackson used to suggest.

Damani's dark eyes became heavier under the spell of Brooke's tongue. His face yearned for something more. Brooke removed his finger from her mouth, lowering it slowly down her chin, over her throat, easing it between the secret of her pillows. Clamping her bottom lip with her teeth, she pulled the thin material down to reveal one full breast, making Damani swallow harder than a hooker in the back of an alley. She slapped his hand over the bare breast, encouraging his fingers to massage her nipple. Aroused and unrecognizable to herself, Brooke tilted her head and dropped her eyes to his manhood. It killed her not to see any evidence of what she did to him.

"You like that?" she asked in a flirtatious tone.

He could barely process her question, as it took him a moment to respond. "Yeah."

A bulge appeared that wasn't there before. Leaving his hand to its own desire, she removed her hand from his to extend it downward to cup his reaction. She had to feel it. She'd never know what he had to offer if she didn't get to know what he was selling.

She turned a sensual tone into a whisper. "Mmmm, Daddy. What you got down here?" With the age difference between them, she couldn't resist.

Damani managed a grin that secretly begged for mercy. Barely able to contain himself, he shifted under her touch, at a loss for words. His head dropped back, succumbing to the sweet torture behind closed eyes. Brooke fondled his enjoyment package, secretly trying to stay in control as his fingers worked the sensitive network at the tip of her nipple.

She exhaled, hoping that the rush of air from her lips would offer her some sort of management for her lust. But it only intensified her need to act. To taste a Greek man on the tip of her tongue. Brooke fell to her knees like a woman under the desk of a business man, except she'd be under a table of a breakfast nook. She kissed his slack-clad groin. Ready, aggressive, hungry for sex. Sex with a good-looking man. Damani's head remained cocked back with outstretched arms while Brooke figured out how exactly she wanted to please this man.

Deciding that she could only give head to someone who owned her heart, Brooke stood and reached for her zipper. Damani's head straightened. Confused and probably disappointed, he watched her to witness her next move. Brooke lowered the material downward until it hit her ankles. She stepped out of the circle of material and walked away in her thong. Heading for the sheer drapes that dressed one of the windows, she pinned her thumbs inside the band of her thong and seductively moved her hips to both sides to ease it down her legs. Stepping out of the material, she moved behind the drapes, facing him as she gently covered her bare skin in the diaphanous material while wearing nothing but heels.

Damani leaned forward with his mouth agape. His hands washed his face, probably astonished that this was about to happen. Brooke's heart raced as she realized that he'd seen all of her and that there was no turning back. Another notch to pin under her belt, Brooke felt aroused at the mere thought of having Damani inside of her.

With her hands securing it behind her back, the drape sucked against her skin like a child to his mommy in need of protection. She wore it like a second skin, knowing that he could admire her body with only a thin layer of material separating them. Damani stood, approaching her with tension around his mouth, eyes glued to her places of power, hands knotted into fists of desire with determination to get to her with each step taken. Brooke didn't know what would happen next, but each breath caught in her chest with anticipation of the unknown and she loved every bit of it. The thought of his big hands grabbing her anywhere on her body became too much for her head to handle.

Come on. Touch me, Damani. Touch me until I pass out.

He stopped in front of her.

Her vagina pulsated. The rise and fall of her chest fell into a desperate rhythm. The craving to be devoured at the hands of this near stranger hit her nipples as they piqued at his attention, waiting for a sensual handshake. Brooke nibbled at her lower lip with eyes of worry that he would walk away for a reason unknown to her.

Then it all changed. He eased a slow hand upward, never breaking eye contact, until it touched her nipple. Stroking the peak with his thumb, the friction of the drape and his skin sent a wave of satisfaction through her stomach down to her womanhood. The flow continued as long as he stayed there and only intensified into an unbearable measure of gratification when his other hand slipped over her second set of lips with fingernails that gently scratched over the fabric, tickling her.

Closing her eyes with furrowed brows, Brooke swallowed hard, but when she opened her eyes to a set of unblinking pupils that stood certain of what they wanted next, Brooke had to place a request.

In a quivered whisper, she asked, "Take me?"

With full urgency, Damani ripped past the drape until it snapped. Before Brooke knew it, his manly hands took hold of her tiny waist and pulled her close against his clothed body. Their lips fastened as Damani rapaciously tasted her wine-laced lips and lust-driven tongue. Her back arched until she couldn't fold into him anymore. He lifted her against the window, pressing her butt against the cold glass as she squeezed both legs on either side of him. The drape fell behind him like a cape, cocooning them into a place of sexual privacy.

He kissed her neck. "I wanna go deep, baby."

Brooke helped him out of his dress shirt. Revealing a hairy chest and untoned midsection, Brooke could roll with it since he wasn't overweight. From the beginning, she knew he wasn't like Jackson, so her level of physical expectations had already been set. Besides, she currently wasn't too concerned with that. He had her vagina aching and for her, the fact that he'd already passed the first test already set him ahead of the game.

His hands worked double time to unfasten and rid his pants, and once they fell, he did the same to free his dick of his underwear. Brooke wanted to see what he had to offer, but she couldn't as long as she remained straddled onto him. Besides, she almost forgot to enforce his protection and wanted to slap herself for potentially making a costly mistake.

"Damani. Let me down. Where's your condom?" She'd only gone raw with Jackson, and no other man qualified for that yet.

"It's right here, baby." He stepped back slowly while supporting her legs to ease her down carefully. "I pulled it out my pocket before taking off my pants."

Brooke appreciated the fact that he came prepared, but she also felt a little irritated that he'd assumed that she'd be about sex on the first date. She decided to shrug it off since she proved him right.

"Okay. Good." Looking down, she saw his rock-hard cock, but it didn't have the length that she preferred. He fell a little short, but it wasn't exactly an embarrassment either.

It simply didn't compare to her ex. Brooke chose to move along with the night and to withhold judgment until after intimacy.

Donning the condom, Damani picked her back up into position and placed kisses over her bosom. He slid his mouth over her breast, taking the nipple, licking the areola. Brooke's vagina pinched at the sensation of new heights. She wrapped her arms around the back of his neck and snapped her head back to enjoy and savor the moment. His hands plunged into her butt as he lined himself up, easing his length into her paradise.

Brooke's toes curled when he thrust in and out. Slowly burning her walls, Brooke liked what he had to give. His hand pulled her hair down, creating strands of messiness behind her head. He gripped the fallen locks between his fingers, tilting Brooke's head to one side. With an open mouth and squeezed eyes, Brooke's thighs tightened with each thrust into her pussy. Her nails dug into his shoulder blades, fighting the pain of pleasure building up between her legs. He laid kisses over her shoulder and along the sides of her neck. Each pump into her knocked her viciously upward. She gripped the strands of his wavy hair and briefly imagined that Jackson had a hold of her. But since his hair and feel didn't add up, she had to destroy her fantasy and stick with reality. Besides, she didn't want to remain stuck in the past by pretending. So, she went all the way back in and let Damani have her full mental attention.

When he pulled out of her, Brooke was forced to get back into the moment. Besides, the moment wasn't too bad. She had a man with dark, smoky features staring back at her, reflecting nothing but desire. He turned her around and took her from behind. With her hands splashed against the glass, Brooke's face rubbed against the glass as he pushed against her ass. That moment, Brooke realized that she had a long way to go. Even though she'd physically started the process of being with someone else, her heart and mind stood far from graduating. Those two areas proved difficult to control. However, one step in the right direction had to be enough for now, and since it was happening, she had to go with it.

Brooke felt turned on by his need to have her. It made the urgency within grow more intense and at that point, she really had to have him. He pulled out again and lead her to the rug stretched out in front of the sofa against the wall. Sitting down on the rug, he lay down waiting for Brooke to sit on his dick. She eased it inside until all his length hid within and commenced riding with her hands behind her head. Damani placed his hands on her breasts and played with her pleasure points. With three sensations coming in at once, Brooke wanted to reach the finish line with thoughts of his age and bossy nature. Having fun with a man she barely knew, Brooke ended the race with a big trophy at the end and with Damani coming in at a close second.

Amber

After the seafood dinner, ESPN, wine, and a movie, Amber witnessed Pharr struggling to stay awake. She raised an eyebrow at him as she gave him a half smile. "Tired?"

Slouched on the couch with folded arms, Pharr's eyelids shot open. "Oh, Amber, I am so sorry. I need to get out of here and get home."

"It's up to you. I know I've kept you long enough, but you welcome to stay." Sitting up, she pointed her knees in his direction.

"Amber, I didn't get much sleep this week, with searching for a house and building and all." He straightened and stretched. "I don't want you to think I'm a bore."

Amber shook her hand at him. "Oh, hell no. Please don't feel bad. We can always do this again if you want. I still had fun with you."

"Really?" He gave her the playful side eye.

"Really. Look, if you gotta go, I got this mess here, and we can do this again. How's that sound?"

"Like a plan, for which I'm grateful." He chuckled and stood. Pharr stretched one more time. "I think that five-second nap revived me, or at least long enough for me to make it home."

"Come on, silly. Lemme walk you to the elevators."

Jokingly, he asked, "Why, is your neighborhood that bad?"

"Ohhhh, so you got jokes." Amber grinned at him.

Pharr smiled with closed lips. "Kidding."

"Trust me. After where I've been, you gotta come harder than that to get under my skin." Amber led him to her front door. She unlocked it and headed for the elevators then pressed the bottom button.

"Wait."

Amber turned around, curious as to what Pharr had to say. "Yes?"

"I had a great time." He peered dreamily into her eyes.

"Oh. Well, me, too." She punched him playfully on the chest. "Thank you for the ride and dinner." Amber couldn't remember the last time she went on a date as a lady and not as a client. It felt strange, but good, not having to take or give anything. It was just two genuinely nice people enjoying each other's company, and she wanted to keep it like that.

Pharr grinned. He bit his lower lip. Amber could see the wheels turning in his head, reading her. There was nothing a man could do that would throw her off. After being around so many men, it became obvious when they wanted more. And she was right.

As soon as the elevator chimed, Pharr leaned in to kiss her, and in her peripheral, she could see the doors to the elevator fly open, revealing a Black couple. An overweight woman and a tall, thin man stood there, looking at Amber and Pharr.

The woman complained, "Nuh-uh. She too busy kissing to pay attention. Miss, you comin' in?"

Without facing them, Amber faintly answered, "No."

"Ain't this something. She done wasted our doggone time."

"I don't mind watching," the man told her.

The woman puffed. She fussed, "Pfft. What? You ole nasty mutha fu—" as the doors slid to hide them.

Amber and Pharr shared a quick giggle as they resumed kissing, with her enjoying his full lips on top of hers—it'd been a while since she had a genuine kiss. The best part was that these lips belonged to the face of a young man. She liked how he lightly bit her lower lip and tickled it with his tongue. *Whoa. So much so soon.* He placed a hand on her shoulder and gently pushed her back until she stood against the wall next to the elevator. She placed two hesitant hands on his shoulders, then behind his head. His silky strands tickled her fingers like a feather. She closed her eyes, leaving the rest of her senses open. When she allowed herself to let go, she felt like her old self, but this time with more dignity.

Pharr's hands weren't so well-behaved. They started on her back and then lowered to the back of her legs. Amber didn't want him to think that he had easy access just because she wore a mini skirt. As their kiss intensified, Pharr's hands walked up her legs and under her mini skirt and rested on her butt. Amber wore a thong and could feel his bare hands on her flesh. He gripped her cheeks and massaged them with desire. Quiet moans escaped Amber's mouth as she wondered if a random neighbor would come flying out of a door to see her kissing a man in the hallway.

She decided that she could keep an extra ear out for the sound of locks or a creaking door.

He kissed her chin. "Amber, I wanna go back inside and make love to you." Pharr's tone became low and breathy. His blue eyes burned into her dark browns as he waited for her to contest or confirm with some sort of permission.

Unsure, Amber evaded his gaze with a turn of her head. He waited for a response with his hands on her hips. When she turned her attention back to Pharr, she replied, "As much as I would love to, I can't. Not today, not this way."

"We can go slow. You won't regret it," he suggested. His lips attached themselves to her earlobes. Kisses dropped on her ears.

An uncomfortable and brief smile hit her face as she placed her hands on his chest. "No, please, some other time. All right?"

Pharr seemed to have gotten the message, because he nodded with disappointment. "Okay, Amber. Yeah. Some other time."

"Are you mad?" Amber wiped across her upper lip as he stepped backward and toward the elevator.

"No." He pushed the button. "Just use my business card to call me. You promise?"

With a smile, Amber replied, "Of course, Pharr. I'll be in touch."

The elevator chimed. "Real soon?"

"Real soon," she assured. "And thanks for the lift and seafood, Pharr. I really appreciate every kind thing you did today, even if I didn't gratify you in the way you wanted."

Pharr closed his eyes and shook his head. "No, Amber. You don't owe me anything. I'll just take the verbal gratitude and wait for your call. Have a nice night." He stepped into the elevator.

Amber spun quickly on her feet. She managed to tell him, "Good night, Pharr," as the doors shut, officially separating them for the night.

3: picture this

Summer

  A few weeks later, I had an appointment with my doctor. Unable to recognize myself any longer had become unbearable. The last straw was when Oliver made a comment after briefly seeing me shirtless. I felt so embarrassed when he told me that maybe his cooking wasn't as healthy as he'd thought. Obviously, he knew that he'd spoken without thinking by the sudden look of compunction on his face. His words were like a smote to my ego. That's when I knew, it was time to see a doctor.

  Maybe the doctor could tell me why my metabolism was failing me. I felt fat and tired. It was amazing what a ten-to-fifteen-pound weight gain could do. No wonder I found myself subconsciously gravitating toward dresses. Even the girls started sizing me up during our lunch dates. Brooke suggested one morning for breakfast that I try the "low-cal" menu. Pretending not to hear Brooke, I saw Emily nudge her.

  After filling out paperwork and sitting in the waiting room, the nurse stepped out from behind a door to call my name. Gathering my purse and entering a bathroom as instructed, I urinated in the little cup and set it in the specimen window and headed toward the designated room. Sitting in a chair next to the examination table, I answered a series of questions as the nurse plugged my answers into the computer. She took my blood pressure and weighed me. Sitting back down in my seat, the nurse continued with her questions.

  "Are you pregnant?"

  I crinkled my mouth and fought back a slight chuckle. "Pshh. Me? No."

  "And when was your last period?"

  "It was mid-January, I believe." I nodded at her, my expression matter-of-fact.

Her look of concern had officially turned into a frown. "And yet today is February the twenty-seventh, Ms. Stevenson. Are you irregular?"

My eyebrows furrowed as I bit my upper lip. My eyes fixated on the wall. "Uhhhhh . . . no." Suddenly, my palms became sweaty and my heartbeat rapid. I looked back up at the nurse. "Why?" Great. I knew where she was going with this. This lady was trying to confirm my worst fear.

"Well, because you're late, Ms. Stevenson."

Late? What was she talking about? This lady didn't know my body. Besides, sometimes periods could do what they wanted to do. "N-n-no." Shaking my head rapidly, I became panic-stricken and the nurse could see it.

"The doctor will be in Ms. Stevenson."

"No. N-no. I'm just fat because my boyfriend cooks really well. See?" I jumped up and pulled my top up to reveal my slightly protruding stomach. "This is *not* a baby, just extra calories sitting around." My hands and voice shook.

"Ms. Stevenson," she said, trying to pacify me by caressing the air with her hands. "The doctor will be in shortly. Go ahead and change into the gown and then have a seat and wait here."

Reluctantly changing into the crappy gown, the wait felt like an eternity as the nurse left me there alone with my thoughts. Taking a seat on the examination table, my mind ran away with thoughts of Oliver. I didn't know how Oliver would feel about becoming a father even though we had the means to support a baby. *I* didn't even know how I would feel about it, because I never sat down and dreamt of marriage and family. My list of endeavors and goals centered around having a successful career. The time to call someone felt right, but regardless of the many names programmed in my phone, there was still no one to call.

Emily

Emily stared at the photograph of Eric. No amount of hatred could refute the fact that he looked irresistible in the photo. The picture reminded Emily of a hot cologne advertisement, daring a woman to get up and go home after a hot and steamy sexual encounter. No woman would be able to just get up and go home if she turned around to see a man like that posing and staring at her. Before she knew it, Emily found herself fanning her face with the picture. *Hatred, Emily, hatred.*

Emily jumped at the sound of a knock followed by the doorbell. She dropped the picture on the counter and scurried around the kitchen island to yank the door open. "Zach! Never thought I would be so happy to see you."

"Yeah, well . . . I can't believe I agreed to do this for you." He sighed as he stepped into her home.

"Remember, you were the one who traumatized me the first time we met. I think this will even the score." Emily closed the door behind her.

"Emily, I already apologized. Remember that?" He peered at her from underneath the peak of his baseball cap.

"Zach," Emily said impatiently. In a firm tone, she continued. "Look, I don't have time for this. You must do this before eight thirty. And I must get to work. Bad enough I had to call in late this morning. I don't need you making me later than what I promised, nor do I want my call to be in vain. Your son and his classmates are waiting for me."

"Okay, well, now that I kind of have you at my mercy, so to speak—"

Emily sighed.

"—I know I said I would do this to make up for what I did to you, but I do want something in return since I could get in trouble if I'm caught."

"What's that?" she asked with folded arms.

"A date. One date, Emily, or you can forget about this favor. I've been trying to get you to see me differently since that one incident, and now that Mr. Perfect is clearly out of the picture, or at least not literally . . ." he joked.

Emily's eyes narrowed.

"Well, I want at least one fair chance with you."

Emily shook her head in disbelief as she tapped her foot. "Fine." She dropped her folded arms and left Zach standing in the foyer alone. She returned with a stack of pink papers. Pushing them into his chest, Emily ordered, "Here, get to work, cowboy. And you better follow through. If I don't receive confirmation, then there won't be a date. Got it?"

With a smirk, Zach tipped his baseball cap at her. "Got it."

"Okay, the address is on the top page. Now, please, Zach, hop on it, because I got to get to work."

Zach reached for the door.

"And Zach?" He stopped and turned to her. She gave him a toothless smile. "Thank you. I really do appreciate this."

"Whatever this will do for you, I don't know. But I hope you get what you're looking for." He nodded and passed through the open door, leaving a crack for her to follow.

His last words rang in Emily's head. If Zach did what she asked, she knew that she would get exactly what she was looking for.

Brooke

The cigarette smoke smacked Brooke in the face. A slight grimace hinted that she couldn't take the smell of the smoke seeping into her nostrils.

"I'm sorry, Brooke. Is the cigarette too much for you?"

"I'm sorry. I just can't do cigarettes. I tried to bear it but it's too direct and as long as we're in here, I'm gonna feel suffocated. Please forgive me."

"No, no, it's no problem. Come on. Let's go outside and get some fresh air."

Brooke and Jacqueline Laurent stood up and pushed in their chairs. Jacqueline snatched her long fur jacket from the back of her chair. Brooke slid into her leather jacket and grabbed her clutch from the table.

Jacqueline called Brooke out of the blue to invite her for lunch. Brooke felt reluctant, but she also wanted to talk to someone else from another age range. Many times, Brooke wished to call her mother, but she knew that the mother-daughter ship had long since sailed before coming into port. Besides, she needed to find out how the marital bliss was going with Jacqueline's daughter, Veronique.

They stepped outside of the diner and onto the busy K Street sidewalk. The weekday crowd consisted of men in business suits topped off by wool coats and women in pencil skirt suits. Brooke cringed when women passed in tennis shoes and slacks. She'd much rather stomp the pavement in heels and deal with the consequences than to wear tennis shoes without workout clothes. Adding to her mental list of other fashion disasters, she wanted to rescue Jacqueline from her too-loose mid-length skirt and one-inch heel dress shoes. Next to Jacqueline, Brooke felt like a fashion icon in her black skinny jeans, high-heel platform pumps, and ivory ripped hoodie. Sometimes Brooke wondered if she should've been a fashion consultant instead of a wedding planner.

"Tell me. How are you getting along without Jackson?" Jacqueline asked as she re-lit another cigarette. She fastened her jacket in a quick attempt to block the knock of wind from her frail body.

"Good. I'm good." Brooke sensed that she sounded weak in conviction, so she decided to elaborate. "Umm, honestly, I'm making a little headway with a new man, but it's just not the same."

"You compare him to Jackson, huh?" She puffed her cigarette as she suspiciously eyed Brooke with a raised eyebrow. They ambled in no particular direction, just away from the diner but in the same direction as their parked cars.

"Hmm. It's kind of hard to refrain, but I try not to."

"Don't. They are two different men and you will never see what this new man has to offer if you don't see him for who *he* truly is."

They didn't say anything for a few seconds as Brooke pondered Jacqueline's words. "I understand. But I can't seem to get over the fact that Jackson felt like my soul mate."

"You believe in those?"

"What, soul mates? I think I do. I mean, they don't have to be everything that you want or have imagined, but I believe in strong connections." Brooke glanced at Jacqueline as they strolled.

Jacqueline exhaled a puff of smoke. "Brooke, let me remind you of something."

"Okay."

"People admire your beauty and your success. They praise everything they love about you. This, you are used to." Jacqueline inhaled and gestured in the air with her cigarette. Brooke didn't see her point and waited anxiously for her to continue. "Now darling, please. You told me a long time ago that you wanted children, right?"

"Yes."

"You're so used to having it all. You have a body, a gorgeous face, and a stellar career that only you can handle. But my dear, have you ever stopped to think where a man and children fit into the whole picture of your life?"

Brooke stopped walking. She felt a slight blow to her stomach. "I don't . . . I don't follow you." She shook her head as she fought back the inexplicable irritation.

"Brooke." Jacqueline stopped walking to face her. Strangers walked around them. Jacqueline took one of Brooke's hands into hers. She could feel the many years Jacqueline spent on this planet and number of puffed cigarettes held between puny fingers. "Did you ever stop to consider how you will learn to handle the stress and the weight of a man and even one child?"

"Jacqueline, many women do it every day."

"Sometimes, young women like yourself fail to ask questions. You guys have a monkey see, monkey do type approach. Sometimes, older women like myself fail to share information. My dear—" Jacqueline patted her hand and released it as she looked away. Brooke watched her old friend choose her words wisely.

"What? Say it. *Please.*" Brooke felt desperate, like she'd gone her whole life wanting the wrong things.

"What if you don't get it all? What then? Or, what if you do get it all? How will you handle it?"

Brooke didn't hesitate. "But I will have it all. I will," she declared.

"Having it all, Brooke, is everyone's choice. We all can have it all. The problem is that having it all for a moment in time comes with a price that no one likes to pay or talk about."

Brooke considered Jaqueline's point with a look of disappointment. "You sayin' it's a myth?"

"No, it's a reality."

Agitated, Brooke shook her head. "Okay, either you're talking in riddles, or I'm really slow."

"Come with me." Jacqueline placed a hand on Brooke's back and gently ushered her to a bench located away from the sidewalk. "Sit, please."

Concerned, Brooke took a seat next to Jacqueline on the bench. She felt grateful that Jacqueline put out her cigarette with a crush of a heel. They both looked out into the traffic.

"*Vouloir, c'est pouvoir.*"

Brooke shot a look at her. "What?" She moved her hair away from her face.

"To want is to be able." Jacqueline cleared her throat as she crossed her legs. She met Brooke's eyes. "It's a French saying, and in English it means, "Where there's a will, there's a way."

Brooke nodded slowly. "Okay. But why'd you say it?"

"If you want it all, you better be able to do it all."

"But I told you I know I can."

"You think you can." Jacqueline coughed and looked away, but turned back to face Brooke when she asked, "Do you have a problem with me trying?"

"People say many good things about you, and then you begin to see no reason why you cannot conquer more. I mean, look at you." Jacqueline waved a hand up and down at Brooke. "You are flawless with money at your disposal."

"What are you saying? I should turn fat or ugly or become unemployed to convince you that I'm capable?" Brooke couldn't hold back her attitude, but she didn't care. "I've known since I was a child that I would have everything I have ever wanted. And just because I'm grown, I'm not gonna stop now."

"I'm not telling you to." Jacqueline wasn't fazed by her attitude. She remained calm.

"Then what *are you* telling me to do?"

"I'm telling you to think. Why do you want children?" With her legs still crossed, Jacqueline placed intertwined fingers on top of her knee. She examined Brooke's reaction sideways with a grin.

"Because that's what some of us women want." Brooke's hands flailed. "I . . . I don't know what you want me to say." Brooke grew increasingly frustrated.

"The truth. How many do you want to have?"

"Like two. No more than three."

"Will you cut down on your hours to care for them? Will you put them in a daycare?"

"I will have to have them first in order to know." Brooke had somewhat calmed down as she realized she hadn't asked herself those questions before.

"Will you sacrifice your career, if need be?"

"Why would I have to? I can still plan weddings."

"Not at the same rate as you do now."

"I know."

"Do you? Let me ask you something. What if someone else in DC moves into your territory? What if you are no longer the prime of all wedding planners? How would you feel? You don't have a team, Brooke. You like being the only one in the spotlight. How would you even handle being dethroned for a family, let alone a man?"

"Okay." Brooke held up an index finger. "I can handle a man, at the least."

"Until he wants more of your time, sweetheart. You and Jackson didn't even make the one-year mark. Are you even aware of how much time it takes to make a relationship work?"

"I successfully made time for him," Brooke said undoubtedly.

"As a boyfriend, sure. But a husband will require more." She uncrossed her legs and pointed her knees in Brooke's direction.

"He was fine with it, Jacqueline. Really. We made it work." Brooke started to panic. *Did Jackson use the passing of his sister's daughter as a catalyst to deter me from thinking we were right together? Was he just protecting me?* The last thing she wanted was to show her vulnerability to Jacqueline, but the poker face became harder to wear.

"Look, honey, you are great at your job as a single woman. A *single* woman. Now, when was the last time you were in a relationship before Jackson?"

Brooke became fidgety. She twisted her fingers and lips. She bit down on her lip as she avoided Jacqueline's eyes. Eventually, Brooke stole a quick glance at her.

"My point exactly. As gorgeous as you are, you have no experience in relationships, because you didn't want any distractions."

Brooke felt a hammer drop on her head. In a panic, she stood up. "I gotta go."

Jacqueline stood up and grabbed her arms. "No. Listen."

Brooke's eyes became glassy. It scared her that she may have ruined her relationship with Jackson other than for the reason he'd told her.

"Brooke. It's not that men are always afraid of successful women. Yes, a small group of lousy men are, but for the most part, they just want to know that there is a real place for them when they come home after work. Listen to me."

She tugged Brooke's arm to win her full attention. Brooke reluctantly met her stare with a sense of vacancy behind her look.

"You have to be willing to get a wrinkle or pudgy stomach or lose a client to other people more frequently for the sake of children and a husband. You didn't realize this did you? You thought that you would be the same old powerhouse-wedding-planner Brooke with flawless skin and a tight body. No amount of expensive clothes will ever hide the insecurities that you will feel after losing steam."

"I can hire nannies!" she exclaimed with a sense of hope and defensiveness.

"Sure," Jacqueline replied sarcastically. "Just make sure that they leave as soon as you get home. Otherwise, you will be the mom who chose to pamper her career and not her babies."

Brooke wiped a tear.

"Let's walk." Jacqueline started to move.

"Wait."

She stopped and looked back. "Yes?"

"Do you think that's why Jackson really left me?"

"Brooke, I don't know. Call him and ask. But you can have it all, as long as you know that some areas will be in the red most of the times. You may already have it all right now by your own standards and not society's. The concept should be based on your terms. But if you find that you don't, and you want more, just remember what I said. *Vouloir, c'est pouvoir.*"

"Do you have it all?"

Jacqueline replied without hesitating. "Oh, honey, I stopped measuring a long time ago. Having it all for me came down to just simply having a spirit of gratuity. I'm happy, so in that sense, I suppose I do." She smiled with a take-it-or-leave-it type of shrug. Brooke followed her with the realization that Jackson was wrong. If she were the type of person who always needed to know the answers to the future, then she would've inquired about her own desires more thoroughly long time ago.

Summer

A lady with brunette hair brushing her shoulders entered the room. Anxious, I stood immediately. In the few seconds it took her to close the door behind her, I tried to read her demeanor to guess her answer regarding my possible pregnancy. *What would Oliver think? Would he walk away? Was this what he wanted?* It seemed inconceivable that Oliver's child could be inside me. Children and marriage weren't part of the plan, let alone a relationship!

When she turned to face me, her honey-colored eyes curved upward as she asked, "How are you doing, Ms. Stevenson? I'm Dr. Westin."

Exhaling a nervous sigh, my hands rubbed together rapidly. "Nice to meet you. I'm—am I pregnant?" Even a greeting felt like a waste of time. I just wanted the facts.

Getting straight to it, Dr. Westin smiled with sealed lips and answered, "Indeed you are. Congratulations, Ms. Stevenson."

An unrecognizable sound came from my throat with a sharp inhale. Staring at her eyes full of confusion, she realized that I failed to jump for joy. My eyebrows collapsed in despair, and even with open eyes I couldn't see. Suddenly, the Sahara set up shop in my mouth—it'd suddenly become parched. My stomach housed my heart. My shaky knees matched the rhythm of my breathing. The walls of the room turned into ocean waves. She could tell I was beyond nervous—frightened, in fact. Squeezing my fingertips with a crinkled forehead, my heartbeat raced faster than any horse in The Kentucky Derby.

"No, Dr. Westin. Please. You don't understand. M-m-my period just happened."

Remaining calm with one hand in her white coat, she nodded once and said, "Okay, I—"

"How long, Dr. Westin? If you're right, then how long has this baby been inside of me?"

"How about we do an ultrasound?"

"Oh, my God!" Tears washed over my eyes as I stared at the ceiling, the computer screen, the counter—anything but Dr. Westin. "Oh." I fanned myself. "I need water. Quick. I need water. *Please* get me some water." My hands wrapped behind my head as I saw Dr. Westin's legs head outside.

"Nooooo." Taking a seat on the examination table, my nails dug into the blue padding of the examination table. The vinyl felt good under my nails as I tried to transfer my agony into something tangible. Anything.

Returning, Dr. Westin stretched her arm out toward me. "Here you go, Ms. Stevenson. Here's your water."

Dr. Westin handed me a cup of water with eyes that failed to mask concern and pity. I grabbed and gulped it while Dr. Westin took a seat in the chair at the foot of the table. It wasn't that I felt calmer, just numb from the massive amount of fear. My eyes looked to the left of Dr. Westin as hers fixed on mine. Sniffling, tears fell while I held the partially-full cup in my lap.

"Summer?"

Glassy eyes slowly rolled to hers. My mouth wouldn't close. I felt like a zombie.

"Summer, how about we get started on that ultrasound and get those questions of yours answered?"

I held my head in my hands before pushing them through my hair. "Okay. Yeah."

She pulled out the machine and explained what the procedure would entail. The next thing I knew, the hem of my shirt sat underneath my breasts and I had one arm behind my head. I tensed once the cool gel hit my stomach.

"Relax, Summer," she instructed. I took a deep breath and exhaled, appreciating her reluctance to proceed until I became more at ease. She smiled. "You're doing great."

As Dr. Westin proceeded with the transmitter, it was hard to not think of anything, so I decided to look back on my life. Maybe it could tell me how I ended up on top of the examination table with my nerves on the floor.

I struggled not to think about my free spirit in 2016. I'd just received a significant promotion, rented my own apartment, and started a fling with a married man. Then once I'd chosen to kick Ruben out of my life, a terrific man replaced him—Oliver. My flooded apartment drowned my independence, and then I moved in with my wonderful man. To intensify the chain of life-changing events in 2016, my boss ended up finding out about my fling with her husband and then fired me. To put the cherry on top of my screwed-up sundae, two of my best friends turned into enemies. Now in 2017, in addition to my new life as an independent recruiter, I was about to find out how long I'd been carrying this new addition of my own. I sighed after mentally recounting the major events that seemed to have successively happened in my life.

Emily

Noon came, and it was time for Emily to take her lunch break as she walked away from the cafeteria. In fact, Emily couldn't wait to be rid of her class so that she could check her cell phone for messages. From her calm strut in the hallway, no one would be able to tell how excited and anxious she felt on the inside. With a smile on her face, Emily nodded to fellow teachers in passing. She closed the classroom door behind her and sat at her desk. With a tug of the drawer, Emily saw her purse and reached inside for her phone.

When she turned it on, a notification displayed for seven missed calls and one voicemail. Smiling, Emily bit her lower lip and chuckled. Just as she'd suspected and expected, the seven missed calls revealed that they'd come from Eric. She accessed her voicemail and heard a hostile message. Eric had demanded that Emily pick up her phone or at least call him back. So, she did. His phone rang once before he answered.

"How. Dare. You? How dare you!"

Sensing that he was foaming at the mouth, Emily nonchalantly crossed her legs and grinned over the phone, refusing to let him get the best of her.

"Eric, what is wrong with you? Is everything okay?" she teased.

"Emily, don't you play with me! Do you know what you just did? Huh? Answer me, you little—"

"*Eric*. What on earth are you talking about?" She placed a hand over her heart.

"I know it was you. I know! No one else had that picture but you. You took that picture!"

"Eric, please calm down." She secretly prayed that he would die from a heart attack.

"Placing copies of that picture all over the parking lot and on cars? You really want to go there? You really want to humiliate me? Do I need to remind you that you are a teacher? I have photos, too."

Emily knew that he was lying. He'd begged her to take nude photos, but she was always too shy to do it. "Umm, no you don't."

"You have really done some damage over here," he growled. "Why are you mad, hmm, Emily? Because I told you I would take your friend again, or because I called you a bitter bitch? Hmm?"

Hearing that again pissed her off, but she did her best to control herself. Uncrossing her legs, she leaned forward, placing both elbows on her desk.

In a firm tone, she replied, "Look, honey, I really don't know why you are calling me, let alone blaming me, but I couldn't care less about your opinion of me. You want to sleep around with my friend, then pound away, but don't call me with allegations that you can't even prove. I've moved on, and so should you."

Eric let out a choked laugh. "Moved on? Moved on? I highly doubt it. You will pine away for me for as long as you live. You will always be checking for me, crying for me, blaming me, because you loved me, and I broke your little heart. You are *so* fragile, you had to take revenge. But guess what? I can always get another job if it comes to that. But what about you, hmm? You will still be the single woman who will eventually need cats, because men won't stick around with a bore like you to even impregnate you accidentally. So, you enjoy your little victory for this round, but I've won the whole fight. I'll be married with kids long before you."

Emily could feel her organs move into her throat. A bore? No husband? No kids? Did he really think that about her? Was he really calling her a loser? No matter what, this man always seemed to hit the biggest nerve. She didn't know what to say except, "Eric! Heartbreaks are ephemeral, but—"

"Stay the hell away from me, or you'll regret it."

Beep. Beep. Beep. He'd hung up on her just like the last time.

No . . . No. No. No. No. No! Did Eric really come out swinging even though she thought she'd delivered him a knock-out punch? She lowered her phone and squeezed it in her hand.

Emily felt her mouth twinge. Felt the blood rush to her head. Felt her breathing grow more rapid with each second. Felt her palms grow moist. The rage within had reached a boiling point. With no other way to respond, Emily exploded.

"Errrrrr!" Emily hurled her cell phone across the room. It barely cleared her target, given her weak pitch, but it hit the wall opposite of her and shattered upon hitting the floor. Emily raked an anxious hand through her ponytail as she struggled to gain composure. She buried her face in her hands as she concluded that regardless of the outcome, revenge was still the best dessert on the menu.

Brooke

"Hello?"

"So, when can I see you again?"

Brooke rubbed the back of her neck. "D*amani.*"

"What? Too much? I don't even know where you live. You keep coming to my restaurant, and you even know where I live, but I cannot say the same about you."

Brooke was used to having her space. At the same time, she could hear Jacqueline warning her that men would want more time at some point of the relationship. Perhaps the time was now. If she were in love like she was with Jackson, then she wouldn't have cared. However, he wasn't Jackson, and her heart had a wall that blocked off new men from intruding on Jackson's territory, but she knew she had to try.

"Okay. When?"

"I want to come to your place tonight. Give me your address."

Brooke remembered that he was bossy, so she knew she wouldn't win. She told him her address.

"Okay, baby, I have to run. See you tonight, yeah?"

"Yeah." Brooke folded one arm over her waist. Ever since she had that talk with Jacqueline Laurent, she hadn't been the same. Brooke felt very unclear about what she should want from life. Every scenario that Jacqueline had thrown at her, she had to picture. She grew up knowing the answers and vision for her future before she'd formed her questions. Now she felt like a stranger in her own head.

Summer

Arriving home later than planned, Oliver had the day off. He'd told me last night that he had a special run to make today. When I tried to goad him to spill the beans, he'd resisted with the defense that it'd all be revealed in due time. After aimlessly driving his Corvette around all day, the moment of truth had come. The elevator opened, and I stepped out and into our home. He stood there, cooking.

"Get out of that elevator and come give me a kiss."

Feeling lifeless and dull, my heart felt punctured. Oliver pulled my motionless body close with me trying to hide my puffy eyes. He pulled me from his chest and kissed my forehead.

"How's my sexy lady?"

I didn't want him to stare at me. It would've been helpful if he hadn't even noticed me, but that wasn't Oliver. Oliver was an attentive one-woman man. I, on the other hand, was an irresponsible rat who didn't think to plan, living life ignoring the consequences. I was a finger-crosser, always hoping to have a favorable outcome. Not like Brooke, planning things out and working toward the plan. Not even like Emily, backing away from trouble and taking the straight and narrow path. Just me, a free bird who believed in having fun and living according to my own rules. But I'd learned that I lived in a real world, and what a rough lesson that was.

He stared at me through his beautiful eyes. "Something wrong?"

And there it was; he noticed. I offered a wan smile. "Just so, so tired." I smacked his shoulder with the back of my hand. "So, what did you do today?"

"I'm glad you asked." His arms extended with pride. Oliver pointed a finger at me and smiled. "You are going to love me."

"I already do," I replied blandly.

Reaching for a small, black box on the counter that I'd never noticed, Oliver handed it to me and said, "Open it, baby."

Reluctantly, a shaky hand accepted the box. *Please tell me that this man isn't about to propose.* I couldn't withstand another life-changing surprise. Not today. Not even tomorrow.

"What is it?" Holding the box in my hand, I eyed him with frowning brows and eyes of doubt. Frozen, unable to move. Didn't want to.

"Open it." This man stood with a posture of pride.

Nodding with my bottom lip prisoned between my teeth, I lifted the lid in hesitation, trying to ignore the flip in my stomach. Once the lid popped open, my jaw dropped. I picked up the key fob and asked, "Is this a key to a car?"

"Yes. Papa Oliver bought you your own car."

My mouth dropped. I felt like the worst creature in the world.

"How about a brand new, fully loaded, hot pink Corvette? Huh?"

Suddenly, I covered my face to hide behind an uncontrollable sob with the key ring looped around my index finger. His hands fell on my shoulders.

"Baby. What's wrong? You never had a good man, huh? Come here."

Unable to face him, Oliver tugged my body toward him. Tears ran into his shirt, because I couldn't handle how a man like him could be so sweet to a woman like me. He kissed my head. Oliver stepped back and pried my hands away from my face.

"Look at me, cupcake. Look at me," he requested gently.

My pathetic eyes fell into his. "Why?"

"You're not happy? I can take it back. I just thought that you would want your own car."

"I . . . I don't deserve it." My emotions bubbled to the surface. My voice became stronger and louder. My hands gestured around us. "I don't deserve *this*. I don't deserve this treatment and surely not your car." My voice faded, strangled by my own tears. "I don't deserve . . . you."

Confused, Oliver examined me. Taken aback, he sighed loudly.

"Summer." I could see the glassy glint in his eyes. The tone in his voice told me that I'd crushed his spirit. "Why are you acting like this? This is not the carefree Summer I took out to IHOP. Where is that girl? What's wrong with you?"

"I'm here." My hand pressed against my chest. "I'm *here*," I insisted without believing it. Somewhere inside I still existed, but where? I felt trapped.

"Where, exactly? Because I don't see her."

"I love you, Oliver, I do. But I question if I can be all that you need or want anymore." Hearing those words out loud ripped my heart. The man I loved shook his head. "I told you I was never any good at this." I cried, "I ruin lives. You should've run. You should've run!"

"Sweetheart. You are acting like one of my crazy exes. I told you how they changed, and now you're doing it. You're gaining weight, snapping at me, always tired, you cry for no reason, and now look at you. You come back home with swollen eyes, and still, you say nothing's wrong."

Sounding gross, I flinched at his words. Why would he want to be with a wreck like me? I placed a hand on the counter to steady myself. "Please, Oliver," I pleaded. "Just put on your fastest tennis shoes and run."

Oliver narrowed his eyes as he looked into mine. "With an attitude like that maybe I should." He grabbed his keys from the counter and walked around me.

Immediately, panic deluged my being. Who knew if I'd lose him for good. But at the same time, keeping him would be selfish and unfair. He deserved a woman who had her crap together, someone like Brooke, but just not her. Realizing that I had to let him go, there was nothing I could do but rest my head on the counter and weep.

Amber

After a few touches, Amber was ready for her date with Pharr Spradlin, who waited downstairs in his pick-up truck. Considering that her party mesh dress had only cost her twenty-five dollars, she felt happy and sexy in all black. Her shoulder-length wig that brushed past her shoulders was in place and complemented her black eyeliner penciled on both lids. The look was new to Amber. Though Pharr would delight in seeing a lot of skin, she felt toned down and classy. Despite the ticking clock indicating the time to depart, Amber couldn't seem to break the eye contact that she had with herself in the mirror.

Who is this new girl?

This Amber felt more confident in areas unlike the old Amber. She may've been known for being brash, but that was partially because she didn't care what people thought. This Amber started to care, because she believed she deserved a better reputation. Her only concern was that she didn't become someone unrecognizable. Though the old Amber used to be raw, she had fun. She didn't want her somewhat polished personality to make her boring, and she certainly didn't want to morph into an Emily. While she mildly admired parts of Emily's personality, she loyally embraced the girl from New York who lived by her own rules and not those of society.

Exhaling, she grabbed her matching purse from the bed and headed out the door. Amber heard a neighbor disarming a door. She turned her head to see a tall, thin man locking his door. Amber noted his handsome looks once she arrived at the elevators. He caught her staring as he turned to approach her. The bald, dark brown man wore a trimmed beard that surrounded thick, succulent lips. Amber could feel herself being pulled into his dark eyes, which made it hard for her to break her stare.

What a fine drop of chocolate. I could drop to my knees right now. Lord, give me strength to behave.

She heard the deep voice say, "Hello." He nodded with a smile that revealed perfectly white, straight teeth.

Amber couldn't talk, but managed a silently mouthed, "Hello," which made him chuckle. She cleared her throat and looked away. Her bashful response upset her. *Where has the old Amber gone?* She felt like a fool for crumbling so overtly in front of a man and blamed the slow elevators for allowing her to be in that situation in the first place. The sudden elevator chime relieved her. They stepped inside together, with him gesturing that she step in first, of course. She thanked him with a nod since she couldn't seem to talk.

As soon as the doors shut, he asked while looking straight ahead, "You live here?"

His very masculine voice robbed her composure, leaving her to feel nervous with a desire to get to know him better. A quick glance at him reinforced her shaken confidence. "Yes."

He turned his head to face her when the elevator landed on the main floor. "Good. Then maybe I'll see you around." Before she could reply, he stepped off first, leaving Amber unnerved by the fact that had he proposed the idea of going back to his place, she probably would've ditched Pharr for a chance with the man without a name. Realizing that a part of her old self still remained tucked inside somewhere, she stepped off the elevator smiling as she headed toward Pharr's truck.

Amber hopped in and asked, "Where we gonna eat?"

Pharr looked at her like she had two heads. "Um, you better give me a kiss when you come into my truck looking like that." When he grinned, Amber mirrored his expression and leaned over to give him what he wanted.

She ended their tongue-free sensual kiss and asked, "Well?"

Pharr's desire ruled his eyes as he pulled back. "Well what? We could forget it all and you can give me a tour of your bedroom."

"Stop." She giggled and added, "I'm starving. Please, tell me where a gal can get some good grub tonight."

"I booked a reservation last week to a restaurant in Northwest called The Prime Rib. Ever heard of it?"

"Well, that was quite presumptuous of you. How'd cha' know I wouldn't reject you?" she teased.

"Because I'm cute." They grinned at each other. "Do you like steak or seafood? Because that's what they specialize in."

"We ate seafood together. Come on Pharr, you know the answer." Amber noted how good he looked in his suit jacket and couldn't resist telling him.

He cranked the engine and headed toward the restaurant. They made small talk over country music on the way there. Amber did her best to pretend like the country tunes didn't bother her. It was a first, putting up with a genre so far from her preference. But she didn't want to step on his toes.

Once they arrived in Northwest, they entered the fancy restaurant. When Amber opened the menu, the prices amazed her. Her eyelids jumped.

"Whoa, Pharr."

His eyes rolled from above the rim of the menu to meet hers. "Whoa what?"

"Damn. Everything here is almost forty dollars," she replied as her eyes continued to scour the menu.

"Amber, it's no big deal, really. Whatever you want, I can provide, so go ahead and order at your leisure."

The skinny-framed waiter with blonde, collar-length hair popped up at their table to fill their glasses with water. "Good evening, my name is Mike, and I will be taking care of you tonight. Can I start you off with something to drink?"

"Amber?" Pharr offered.

Amber reluctantly removed her eyes from the menu. She couldn't believe the prices. Even Daniel Crosby didn't dine with her at fancy restaurants. The most she managed from him was inexpensive Chinese platters. The well-paying clients in New York always ordered in, so she never saw the prices. So, in a way, Amber considered this her first real date at a fancy restaurant. She felt out of place and somewhat like a poser, because this wasn't her style. Dressing up for dinner with a man sitting across from her in a jacket fell out of her comfort zone.

"Coke, please."

"*Amber*?" Pharr said through gritted teeth. Her eyes shot up at him. She shrugged with a look of confusion. He cleared his throat and told the waiter, "In addition to her Coke, please bring a bottle of red wine."

"Okay," Mike replied with a nod. "Which one?"

"Your 2003, please, uh, upon the arrival of dinner."

"St. Emilion?"

"Yes," Pharr replied with a nod.

"Very good," Mike said. "Would you like to look over the appetizers?"

"Amber?" Pharr offered.

"Tell me. Y'all got mine-strone soup?" Even though she didn't see it on the menu, she wondered if there was a chance they'd have it.

Mike's mouth twisted in confusion. He smiled. "I'm sorry, can you please repeat that?"

"Mine-strone?"

"Umm, I'm not sure I'm following you." He appeared uncomfortable at the possibility of letting down Amber and Pharr.

Amber looked at Pharr, who also had crinkled eyebrows. "Mine-strone, you know what I'm talking about?"

"Mine—wait. Minestrone?"

Amber realized that she'd been pronouncing it as a two-syllable word, "mine" and "strone." When Pharr pronounced it correctly, she felt like hiding under the table. The only response she could think of to casually blow her embarrassment off was to wave her hand and say, "Oh, well, yes. See, I knew I wasn't crazy. Minestrone."

Mike instantly felt relieved that his lack of understanding wasn't his fault. "Oh," he said with a smile. "Right. No, ma'am, we don't have that." He pointed at the soups listed in front of Amber on the menu. "See the listing here? These are the ones we have."

Well, damn. All that embarrassment for nothing. These clowns ain't even got the soup.

Amber decided to peer up at Pharr. He looked embarrassed, clearly realizing that he'd brought Amber to dine at a place that was out of her league. She felt exposed as an imposter and realized that even her best smile couldn't earn her one hundred points now. Looking back at the menu, she decided to choose the least expensive appetizer advertised for ten dollars.

"Roasted tomato soup then."

"Sure." Mike turned to Pharr. "And you, sir?"

"Petrossian cavier, please."

Amber's mouth dropped. She wondered if he was trying to save face with the waiter by ordering expensive dishes to counter her inexpensive selections.

"Very good," Mike said before leaving.

"Yeah. I'm sure it is very good," Amber said in disbelief to which Pharr replied, "Amber, I don't take dates to McDonald's. I hope you understand that."

"I hope you understand that the last time I accepted a date to McDonald's was in high school. But good Lord, you ain't gotta do this."

"Hmm. You're the first woman I've seen fight a good meal, that's for sure."

She felt ridiculous. "Okay, I'm not sayin' I shouldn't be eating like this, but I don't think we gotta be here. We coulda gone somewhere a little more modest."

The truth was, Amber wasn't used to proper dining and dates. Typically, she had to always give something in return. She had difficulty comprehending that a man would take her out to a fancy restaurant and treat her like an actual lady. While she was used to being in the homes of rich people, she was nothing more than a guest who blended in with the other attendees. However, tonight was different and one-on-one, more personal. A man gave her attention without expecting anything in return. She couldn't explain to Pharr without admitting to her being a former prostitute of a certain proportion. Instead, she figured it was best to let him believe that her discomfort stemmed solely from the belief that she'd seen herself as a common hood rat who'd never experienced anything finer in life.

"Just enjoy, please. You've done enough already." He took a sip of water.

"And what's that supposed to mean?"

"It means that you ordered a Coke, a side of minestrone that doesn't exist, and ten-dollar soup."

Amber flushed on the inside with embarrassment. She really didn't know how to respond to his viewpoint. Tonight proved that she belonged right there in her Southwest apartment until she worked on her own to build herself into a new lifestyle. Until then, Amber realized that she needed to stop trying to drive in other people's lanes.

A weak smile brushed across her face as she wondered if she should just excuse herself from her dinner date. She knew any of her friends would come take her home, except for Emily. On the other hand, she knew that the girl from New York wouldn't dare turn down a free, quality meal. Amber had concluded that she would eat now and decide what to do about Pharr later. This time, she appreciated the old Amber for sticking around.

"I sure did order that, cuz that's what I wanted," she shot back calmly. However, it appeared Pharr wanted the other Amber, so she'd be more than happy to give her to him. And since Amber had studied the menu earlier, she knew which entrée would make a statement. "And I already know what I want for dinner."

"Do you?"

"The roast prime rib." That was half a hundred dollars. Pharr's eyebrows shot up as he nodded. She was sure he probably thought she'd hustled him. A grin coated her face. "Can't wait to sip up a bottle of wine more expensive than my cable bill."

Summer

Unaware of how much time my head spent resting on the counter crying, I felt two strong arms grip me from behind. Jerking up and refusing to turn around, his body leaned into mine from behind as he barely rocked me.

"Baby. Baby, baby, baby. I have bad news. I can't find my fastest tennis shoes anywhere. So, I guess you're stuck with telling me what's wrong." His sexy whisper should've soothed me.

I spun around in his arms, losing it with smacks against his chest repeatedly and tearing up once more. "Why do you gotta be like this? Go on, Oliver! Go—just leave! I can't take all your goodness. Can't do this anymore."

Oliver struggled to get a hold of my wrists, but once he did, he yelled, "What's your problem? Huh, woman? What? Tell me." His face almost covered mine as he waited for an answer, refusing to let me go, so I let him have the truth since it ate me alive.

"I'm pregnant! Okay? There, stupid. Ya happy? I'm pregnant!" I jerked from his weakened grip once he heard the truth. "That's why I'm fat, sloppy, tired, emotional, and all that stuff that you hate. Okay? Now what are you gonna do with that?" He tried to process my outburst with a blank stare. My hand flung behind me toward the direction of our bedroom. "Do you wanna go back and look a little harder for those running shoes now?"

His large hand wiped over his face as if he had water dripping from his head. He blinked once. "We're . . . we're pregnant? And gonna have a baby, Summer?" Oliver stared at me. I barely nodded. "Wow." His shock turned into happiness. "I'm gonna be a daddy?" He laughed with joy shining in his eyes. "Oh, my God. That's what I'm talkin' about!" Oliver turned his back to me as he bent over. He straightened and turned to me, but his smile faded when he caught a glimpse of my face. "Why am I happier than you?"

I reached for my purse to pull out the picture of the sonogram. "Here."

Oliver took the tiny envelope and opened it with his eyes glued on mine. With lowered eyes, I ran my tongue over my lip. A shaky hand slid the picture from the envelope. Oliver studied it with glassy eyes. Looking at me, he said, "I'm gonna be a daddy."

4: one last time

Summer

$\mathscr{I}$t'd been weeks since finding out about the bun in my
oven. Nobody knew except for Oliver, not even my mother
or closest friends. Unfortunately, the other secret that
brewed inside of me left me feeling like a coward for
hiding it. While I wanted to tell my girls, it would be wrong
not to tell Oliver first, although telling them first would
give me the much-needed courage and support. What was I
supposed to do?

Thursday night, and the ladies were coming to my side
of town to eat at Rail One—a clean, well lit, and sizable
diner that stayed open past midnight. The other diners
consisted mainly of sets of friends and young people, but
for the most part, the diner was nearly empty. I arrived first,
which made sense considering my proximity, and took the
liberty of ordering four glasses of water with lemon on the
side, and a pot of coffee, under heavy fluorescent lights
with a nose seduced by the smell of pancake batter.

"So, do you want to wait for the rest of your party
before ordering anything else?" the young, red-headed
woman asked.

"Yes, please. Thank you." She nodded and walked
away.

Before my mind could drift away with a foray of
worried thoughts, Amber came barging through the diner
doors wearing a short, blonde wig. I chuckled. She slid into
the booth taking the seat across from me.

Shaking her head, she greeted me with a, "Girl," as she
fumbled with the zipper to remove her hooded quilted
jacket to expose a white cashmere sweater. Amused, my
eyebrow cocked. "Most people are sleeping at this time in
Virginia, but the people driving were so slow."

Confused, I asked, "You—you drove? You have a car
now?"

Amber flipped a hand at me. "Heffa, please. Brooke still kee-hee-heeing and shit on her cell. She scooped me up and drove us here." Grabbing the glass of water with a straw, the plastic flattened between her purple-painted lips as she sipped.

"Oh. Hey, that was nice of her. I wouldn't want you on the train at this hour."

With the straw still between her lips, she looked up at me as if she didn't hear me correctly. "Um, Summer, just months ago you were doin' this, too. And besides, I'm from New York," she reminded me in a tone that questioned my intelligence.

"True." Tapping the table, I decided to take advantage of Emily's missing presence. "Hey. How things going between you and Emily?"

Amber shrugged as she straightened. "Still mute. You know what, sis? That other Amber was *not* workin' for me. She was becomin' docile and just plain borin'. I'm gonna be me again, with no apologies."

I smiled and placed a hand over hers. Besides, who was I to judge with an unplanned life growing inside with a past that included sleeping with a married man? "And that's all you should be."

"No, Summer, I have apologized to her repeatedly for somethin' that I didn't even plan. I gave up sleepin' around with men. And if she can't get over all of that, then sorry for her. Besides, Eric wasn't even *with* her."

"I *know*, I *know*. But, please, just play nice tonight. You know Emily's a little fragile."

Amber nodded. "I'll play nice but that's about it. I ain't holdin' back nothin' no more. And the fragile thing? Not really buyin' all that."

Before I could respond, the doors to the diner flung open. Emily and Brooke entered together and pointed in our direction once they spotted us. Surprisingly, Emily slid in beside Amber and Brooke beside me. Maybe Emily preferred not to face Amber. Time would tell.

With lots of energy despite the time of day, Brooke said, *"Hey, guys."*

"Man, that was a long phone call," I teased.

Brooke batted her long lashes. "It was Damani. He was going to bed and wanted to tell me goodnight. He said he couldn't go to bed without hearing my voice."

"What's up, ladies?" Emily mustered as she removed her fluffy coat.

Amber and I replied, "Hey," to her in unison.

The server returned. "Are you guys ready to order?"

Brooke ordered first. "Yes. Sunny-side-up eggs and toast, please."

Emily raised a finger. "A garden salad with light dressing."

Amber closed her menu and handed it back to the server. "A well-done hamburger and onion rings."

My turn, I closed my menu and handed it back to the server. "The same but with fries. Thank you."

"Okay, I'll be back with your food, ladies." Looking more tired than the first time she approached our table, she walked away.

Brooke eyed Amber and then me. "How can you two eat like that at this time of night?"

Amber answered first. "What? You don't eat like that any time of the day, Brooke?"

"Well," she replied matter-of-factly, "once a month maybe. But I can't exercise as hard as I do just to replace it with dripping fat and carbs. Disgusting. And I'm thinking about becoming a vegetarian, but I can't seem to shake the love of chicken."

"You're black," I replied, and we giggled.

"Lord knows I'll eat animal with pride till the day I die," Amber proclaimed.

"Me, too," I agreed.

Emily smiled. "Yeah, I love pork. We Puerto Ricans love our pork."

Brooke sneered. "Ew. You three are gross. You have hog on one end and dripping beef on the other."

I shrugged nonchalantly. "Well if it ain't mooing, then I ain't chewing."

"Okay?" Amber high-fived me.

Emily chuckled and shook her head.

"So, what's up y'all?" I asked.

Emily looked up. "I have something to say, just wanna go ahead and get this out the way. Please?" She turned her attention to Amber. Emily took a moment to find the right words as she placed a hand on Amber's.

Amber jerked a little, clearly surprised by the sudden gesture of kindness.

"Look, the last time you were at my house, things got out of control. We said some things in anger. But having weeks away from you did me some good."

Amber nodded and smiled. "It did. Not botherin' you seemed like the right thing to do."

Emily nodded. "Yes. But I really came to realize that Eric was not the man that I thought he was. The more I thought about it, the more I realized that his words about the one-night stand made me angrier toward you than it should have."

"Why's that?" Amber asked.

She shrugged. "Well, he compared us, implied that he liked it and just slept with you because he was curious . . . I mean being curious enough to pay for it?" She shook her head. "That whole thing creeped me out." She waved a hand at Amber, her eyes wide eyes with horror. "I mean, you saw his penis!"

Amber hung her head low in shame.

"Shhh." Brooke shot a look of panic at Emily with furrowed brows. "Keep it down, please. Don't embarrass me."

I smacked her arm with my hand. "You? How about us?" She nodded.

Emily didn't pay us any attention. Instead, she proceeded. "Amber, I know you two were strangers, and I had to get past that. You did apologize to me. When I sat back and thought about it, I wasn't willing to lose a friend for a man who broke my heart at random. So," she sighed and stared into Amber's eyes, "will you take me back?"

Amber grinned. "Honey, it's more like will you take *me* back?"

I felt so happy to have my girls together. The tension had become more than what any of us could stand. Brooke and I watched them hug and rock side to side in the constraint of the booth as we released an, "Awww," in unison.

After the arrival of our food, we ate, eager to share any news in our lives. I suspected that no one could top mine.

Brooke inhaled sharply as she remembered something. "Amber, how are things with you and that guy Pharr?"

Amber waved a dismissive hand. "I don't know, honey, you tell me. He fell off the face of this planet."

"What?" we all asked, except for Emily. I noticed her subtle look of guilt as she begun to chew slowly.

"What happened?" Brooke asked.

"I just said I didn't know," Amber replied. "I mean, I didn't even get to at least suck the lollipop. We were talking about it one day, making plans to hook up, and we had a date. He told me that once he met with Emily and his realtor, we would go on a date that night. Never heard from him after that." She popped an onion ring into her mouth. Preoccupied with the crumbs on her fingers, she couldn't see the look on Emily's face.

I elbowed Brooke and nodded at a slouching Emily— the only quiet one. Brooke took to the clue and replied with a look of realization that Emily didn't seem comfortable.

Since she'd made up with Amber, the silence didn't make sense.

Brooke didn't waste any time. "Emily. Why are you so quiet?"

Without responding, Emily shifted and continued to poke around in her salad. She sat up. "I . . . I may know about that," she interjected reluctantly.

Amber looked almost desperate. "You do?"

Dropping her fork and looking at all of us, she bit her lip and nodded. "I needed to get some type of revenge for the whole Eric breakup thing."

Amber slapped her hand on the table. "What?"

Emily nodded. "Yes, okay, yes. After we wrapped up the closing process, Pharr told me how happy he was that he ran into you that day when you came over to my house. And then he was telling me how happy both of you were, and that you were rough around the edges, but that he could overlook that. I suggested that you may have an STD. I—"

"You what? You implied that I had somethin'?" Amber's mouth dropped.

"I figured that you shouldn't have a good man that you met on my watch. Basically, Pharr and Eric have connections to me. You wouldn't have met Pharr had you not been in *my* neighborhood." She inhaled with eyes on the table. "Childish? Perhaps. But I feel better."

Our mouths fell open. The newly mended fences were unraveling again right before our eyes.

Emily became slightly hysterical. "I was angry, okay? Angry. You slept around with so many men, didn't want a relationship, tore mine to shreds, just to move to happily ever after? How could you be so happy after doing a rotten dance on my parade? Karma failed me, so I wanted to make sure that you had something coming."

"Wow." Brooke shook her head.

"That's deep," I added, taking a bite of cow.

Amber exhaled and stared at her food. Emily grabbed her arm. "Look. And I am so sorry, Amber, but that was the only way I could move on, to know that I could rob you, too. I'm sorry."

"But I didn't know your man was '*your man*,' Emily." Amber folded her arms.

"Was Pharr even your type? Y'all looked crazy together anyway."

Amber shot her a sideways glance. "That's not the point, Emily. You did a stick up on me, girl. Not cool."

Brooke and I widened our eyes at one another.

Emily sighed. "I can call him. He would believe me if I told him it was a petty shot since he knew you and I were on the outs."

"I don't think I could face him now." She ran a hand over her blonde wig and jerked her chin in the air. "It's okay. We were too different anyway. To be honest, he tempted me to use him for money. I wasn't really head over heels, but them pockets were lined yo. But I need to find a normal man on my level, even if that means going back to black." Amber cracked up laughing at her own comment. She shifted in her space. "That sounds so wrong. I know there's good black men out there."

"Yeah," Brooke said, "you should really let that color thing go. Jackson was a black successful man with a great head on his shoulders. We just wanted two different things."

I added with a shrug, "And I got Oliver. Besides, you were around a rougher circle in New York, probably straight-up knuckleheads. Let it go."

"So, you forgive me?" Emily hugged Amber's arm with batting lashes. We all waited in silence for Amber to decide.

She peered down at her as the mock disappointment seeped from her expression. "Oh, fine you ole sneaky bitch." My squared shoulders collapsed with relief. The progress hadn't been lost.

Emily clapped like a happy seal. "Yay! I was so scared you would go New York on me."

Amber turned her shoulder at her with mock offense. "Girl, bye."

Emily laughed. "Well, I went . . . *something* on Eric."

My brows popped. "Whatcha do?"

Emily looked naughty as she grinned. "I, um, in exchange for a date, got Zach to do me a favor."

Brooke threw a hand over her chin. "The penis whipper?"

"Oh, come on. We've moved past that, remember? But, yes, him." Smiling, she continued, "Well, when we were on our honeymoon, I took a nude picture of Eric in the bed with the blanket wrapped around his legs, but with more than a tip slip hanging out."

Shocked, but too hungry to say anything, I continued to devour my burger. Even Amber noticed my ravishing behavior as I licked the ketchup from my fingers. "Damn, I don't think you supposed to lick the pole?"

Everyone stopped what they were doing to look at me. They all caught me with a finger in my mouth. My eyes shot at each of theirs, slowly pulling my index finger from between my lips. "Uh."

"Ew." Brooke wrinkled her nose with disgust.

My strained grin barely hid my slight embarrassment. They turned their attention back to Emily. They deserved to know why I ate like a hungry horse.

Brooke urged Emily to continue. "So, then what?"

"Well, I made pink copies and had Zach go to the lot where Eric works and distribute the papers under the windshield wipers of the cars. Hours later, he called me over and over. When I called him back, he was irate."

Amber shook a finger at Emily. "Fragile you are my ass. Gee, man. You had my and Eric's number and you used it. I got your number, now."

"Tell me about it," Brooke agreed. We all chuckled.

Emily tried to sound innocent when she asked, "What? I think I have reached a point of being tired of getting burned. I can no longer take crap lying down." With her hands on her hips and full of pride, she announced, "I'm a new woman."

Our expressions told her that we were impressed.

Amber added, "Well, you don't have to worry about me testing your declaration."

Brooke twirled an impatient hand. "Tell us what Eric's gonna do to you."

"I didn't admit to it. That really pissed him off."

"Does he plan on paying you back?" I asked, chewing a fry.

"Oh, he already did." We looked at her in amazement with curiosity. "The arrogant bastard crushed me like a little bug with an Armani shoe. He told me that I'd wind up with nothing and he'd have a wife and kids before me. Can you believe that jerk?"

We didn't know what to say.

Brooke pointed a thumb at me. "Well, the only one in a solid is this girl here. The one who didn't even want a man was Miss Wavy Locks."

Immediately, I felt guilty about having what the other girls wanted. "Do you want a man now?" I asked Amber.

She sighed and shrugged. "I mean, I wouldn't bite a man who wanted to come home to me. On the other hand, I ain't interested in dating any man way above my level, financially, anyway. Those men are too much in one fashion or the other." A naughty grin crossed her face. "But I sure would marry one."

"Well, you guys are going to hate me now." I inhaled and held my breath as I waited for a response or reaction, whichever came first. They stared at me.

"Well, what? Tell us," Emily demanded.

I could only shut my eyes to gather my confidence. Collecting myself to announce that I had something that I wasn't sure that I'd ever wanted and what appeared to be everything to Emily and Brooke, I announced, "I'm pregnant. Twenty weeks in fact." The silence covered us like a sheet of fog. Their wide eyes communicated their thoughts. It all made me feel awkward and regretful for saying anything. "I said I was expecting a baby, not placing a legit hit on Fran."

Amber squared her shoulders and tapped her fingers on the table. "Then? Is this good news?"

"I . . . I don't know."

"Shit. Isn't this something?" Brooke stated more so than posing a question. She slammed a balled-up napkin on her plate. "I want to say congratulations."

Irritation started to brew on the inside. "So then do it."

Brooke placed a hand on my shoulder. "You're getting everything that you've never wanted."

Something about what she said sounded ridiculous, because Amber started to chuckle, and Emily surrendered to her laughter. One by one, we'd all succumbed to the laughter.

Emily sniffed and wiped the tears of joy and laughter. "Sweetheart. Congratulations though, really."

"Yes, *thank* you. Finally. After making fun of me for getting myself into a pit hole of hell."

Once they composed themselves, they stared at me in consternation and confusion. Brooke cleared her throat. "Wait. You call life with Oliver hell?"

I hesitated. It wasn't really what I meant, but the right words failed me. "Well, no. It's just that—I love him. I really do. But everything is happening so quickly. Just before Thanksgiving, I was a woman who lived alone, happily, might I add, and I was jumping on the Metro to get everywhere. Now, do you want to know what happened?"

"Yes," they all replied.

"I came home to show him the sonogram, just for him to turn around and tell me first that he got me my own little pink Corvette."

Brooke dropped her fork and held up both hands. "Okay. I'm done. I'm done."

Amber leaned forward. "And I'm still flagging down cabs? Well, you lucky broad."

Emily concluded, "So I'll take the baby, Brooke will take the man and Amber the car. And you keep his condo since your home was flooded. You have it all."

Amber narrowed her eyes. "Yeah. All that *we* want." She crossed her arms and grinned. "Oh, hell. Congratulations, Summer. Someone has to be happy here."

Emily placed a hand over her chest. "Yeah, we're sorry for being so lackadaisical about your news. Again, congratulations, honey."

I smiled with a fake pout. "Thank you, Emily, and thank you, Amber." We turned to Brooke who had her nose in the air.

"What?" she asked as if she were unaware of what was expected of her.

Emily gritted her teeth. "Brooke."

She sighed and turned to face me. "You remember the first night you came to my condo?" I nodded with fondness in my eyes. "Well, I guess I can say that tonight, I feel the way you felt that night."

"What? Overwhelmed and jealous?" I admitted.

Brooke nodded. "If that's how you felt, yeah. But that night you really impressed me. You told me that you'd love to have what I had. Well, I have to be a big girl, too, right now." She placed a hand over her heart and stared deep into my eyes. "I'm . . . this is so hard to say, but I'm jealous. I'm not angry, I'm not mad, just simply . . . jealous."

No one said a word; Brooke had the floor. I nodded in disbelief that Brooke Brazile could ever be jealous of me, but it was harder to believe that she would admit it in front of the other girls or at all. And maybe a long time ago I would've reveled in her jealousy, but today, it didn't bring me any bit of pleasure. We'd all become like sisters. If I could pass on my pregnancy to Emily or Brooke, I probably would. Lord knows they would appreciate the process and all that it stood for. Sometimes I'd lain in bed, and no matter how many times I closed my eyes at night, it seemed near impossible to imagine myself being those after-daycare-soccer moms or even a nursery décor-hunting mother. Hearing Brooke spill her heart out made me wonder what it was about this whole thing called a blessing, that I was missing.

"You were such a wild bird. And now you're about to be caged in the comfort of the arms of the same man night after night, with his child, living in the lap of luxury. You really did hit the jackpot, Summer. You could stop working and he wouldn't even care. Hell, you're even making a good living on your own so far."

"My recruiting has hit a rough spot."

"Still. I mean, my God, Summer, look at how much you have compared to last year. But I get the feeling that you seem uneasy or oblivious to it all." Brooke stared at me as if all the answers would come spewing from my mouth.

I looked down at my plate, swallowing a lump with a secret that killed me on the inside. Whether or not I should tell Oliver first seemed so irrelevant. As my emotions started to stir from my stomach to my throat, I realized that no amount of swallowing was going to push away the sadness. The server showed up and we gave her permission to clear the table.

"Did I go too far?" Brooke asked. A tear fell out the corner of her eye and onto the table.

I shook my head without looking up. Emily sniffled and Amber sighed. The mood had shifted. No one laughed, no one pried with excitement, and certainly, no one made jokes. Reluctantly, I looked up.

"There's a problem," I blurted softly.

"What?" Amber asked anxiously.

"You guys cannot say a word." Succumbing to the tears, my voice cracked under a choked throat.

"We won't," they agreed quietly in unison.

"Oliver is so happy, but this baby can't be his."

"Oh, God." Brooke placed her forehead on the table. "This is one *wicked night*."

"Excuse us?" Amber blurted.

"Sum*mer*," Emily added.

The teacher tone in her voice raised my feelings to an emotional state. The tears hit the rims of my eyes in no time. Perhaps a seat in the naughty corner would fit the crime. The last two weeks have been nothing but constant berating for putting myself in this position and for not telling Oliver. Unfortunately, I'd become one of those women who shared everything with her friends first instead of with her man. Preferably, my mom should've been the first to know, but the idea of disappointing her seemed unbearable. She'd already met Oliver, for Pete's sake! She loved him, so this would make her so disappointed in me. I needed my mother to continue to believe that I could handle life in the nation's capital as an adult and on my own. But she probably questioned my ability after finding out that I didn't buy rental insurance.

Grimacing with narrow eyes, Emily stretched an arm toward me and tapped the table with her fingers to get my attention. "I'm so sorry," she apologized.

Brooke placed a hand against my back, calming me with circular motions.

Waving a hand, I assured her, "No, it's fine, it's fine," as I dabbed the corner of my eyes with a used napkin that I'd used during my meal. "Stupid hormones." A half chuckle sneezed from my throat.

"Well how do you know that?" asked Amber.

"The time of conception. Oliver and I *always* used a condom in the beginning."

Concerned, Amber asked, "So does he think the condom broke or something?"

I shrugged.

Brooke squinted at me. "So, *who* is the baby daddy?"

Amber interjected. "Wait. Let's call that talk show dude who does paternity tests."

After shooting her a look, she cleared her throat and pushed her straw between her lips. Then with a raised eyebrow, I beamed my laser glare at Brooke. "Who do you think?"

Emily's body jerked. "*Ruben*?"

My expression confirmed her guess.

"Oh, my God." Amber's hands covered her nose and mouth. "Oh, my God."

Brooke placed her head on the table again. Knowing that my life made her act in such a way drove me crazy. "Would you stop?"

Brooke straightened immediately. "I'm sorry but, Summer, your news takes the cake. What are you going to do?"

"She has to tell him," Emily said.

Amber shot an annoyed look of at Emily. "Like hell she does."

"What?" Brooke replied.

Emily snapped back. "Do you think lying will help? Oliver isn't the dad and he deserves to know that."

Amber fired, "Says the girl who lied on me about having an STD."

This was spiraling out of control. My life became the cause for an open debate and had created war among my friends.

Emily's jaw dropped. "I did not *say* that you had an STD, I simply said—"

"Ladies, ladies," Brooke snapped. She tried to whistle with her fingers to break up their ill-disposed exchange, but it ended up sounding like a dry blow between two fingers.

I turned to her with a frown. "What the hell was that?"

She shrugged. "Girl, I don't know." She stretched an arm out and tapped her hands against the table. They stopped and turned their attention to Brooke, the referee. "Stop it now, stop it."

I felt relieved, because I didn't have the energy. "Thank you, Brooke."

She placed a quick hand on my shoulder and said, "You're welcome. Look. Oliver may have had a broken condom—"

I shook my head. "No. He's not a possibility."

Brooke tilted her head. "Summer, what do you mean?"

"The timing." I played with the collar of my shirt. "Amber, remember the night when you and I went to eat dinner at Fran's?"

Her eyes lit up as she smiled. Her index finger flicked at me. "Oh, right. You mean the night you and Ruben—"

I couldn't let her tell my story, so I interrupted her. "Yeah, yup, that one."

"Okay. So, what about it?"

I gestured a hand toward Brooke and Emily. "Well, I have to tell them."

"Right."

"All right. Amber and I dined with Fran, and that night Ruben followed me to the bathroom and ravished me. He didn't have time to fish for a condom, and I didn't think of one. I was too preoccupied with the thought of Fran catching us, that protection totally went out of the window.

I met Oliver that same night and had sex with him to get over Ruben, but he used a condom."

"And Ruben didn't . . . withdraw?" Brooke asked with full attention.

"No."

"Why did that phrase 'luck of the draw' come to my mind?" Amber grinned.

"Shut up. Really, please," I told her.

Emily gave her a playful punch to the shoulder. "That's for Summer."

"Thank you."

Brooke appeared disturbed or confused. "Hold up. You didn't question or wonder if you were pregnant after knowing he ejaculated without withdrawing and you didn't feel symptoms?"

Hearing her say that aloud made me feel stupid. "I . . . I guess I was too preoccupied with so much and then I got what I thought was my period over and over. January was the last time I had any blood."

"Huh?" Emily said. "I'm confused. You still got your period?"

"I thought it was, but my doctor said I was spotting. It wasn't for too many days. I thought my periods were shortening."

Amber raised a hand. "Like mine. Mine last for a few days. They used to be longer when I was a teenager. But then again I heard that's the normal scenario for women."

Emily could only stare without blinking. "This is bizarre. You were pregnant and didn't even know it."

"Tell me about it," I replied.

"Well, at least we know why she was getting fat," Brooke added before sipping coffee.

My jaw dropped. Before she could take another sip, she gave me a glance from the side of her eye and placed the coffee back down to defend her point. "Well, honey, let's face it. Your heels were crying under all that weight. And when was the last time you wore any of your skinny-girl outfits? You might as well don a poncho at this point." She lifted her coffee cup again to sip. I shook my head at her bluntness. At least I'd grown accustomed to it.

The tired server reappeared. "Anything else, ladies?"

"No," we replied in unison.

Removing one hand from her apron pocket, she slid a ticket onto the table. With a weak smile, she said, "Have a great night." We wished her the same as she shuffled away on tired feet. I slid the bill my way.

Emily joked, "Damn. Remind me to move to another continent when I get pregnant to avoid Brooke's fashion critiques."

Amber added, "Right?"

"I had symptoms that mirrored my circumstance at each moment."

"Like?" Emily asked.

"I thought I was getting fat because of Oliver's cooking. I was crying a lot, tired, and getting headaches, because I'd lost my home and was dealing with the whole Fran and Ruben thing. But when I just didn't feel physically right anymore, I figured it was time to see the doctor. I hadn't even realized my period hadn't come in February even though the month had almost passed. I'm normally very much on top of it. I was falling apart."

When they realized I wasn't done, they all looked at me with horror-filled eyes.

"And I've been snippy with Oliver. I've been an emotional basket case. I was coming off as insecure and no fun to him. But now the baby thing has made him totally understanding."

Reluctantly, Amber asked, "Is that it?"

I thought for a moment. "That is it." I nodded to confirm my answer.

"Phew." Amber wiped her forehead with the back of her hand. "So, a surrogate sounds good to me."

We all managed to squeeze a grin from our tight lips. "Gee, I really do know how to lighten a party, huh?" No one responded, so I answered my own question. "Yup."

"How's Damani?" I asked Brooke.

Before she could respond, Emily interjected. "Wait. Are you going to tell Oliver or not?"

I shrugged. If I had a gun I would've probably shot her for killing my attempt to deflect. "I don't know. I mean I guess I would have to. But *when*, is the question."

"Try asap," Brooke answered.

"I could lose him."

"Summer." When Brooke grabbed my hand, I knew that what she was about to say would finalize my decision. "You have two choices. Tell him now and let him decide to stay or go. Or never tell him and lie to your baby and Oliver and walk around with a secret that will gnaw at you until you die. At least if you tell him, you may just lose a man. But if you take option two, you may lose him and your baby if the truth comes out in the future."

Amber offered, "Also, they may never know. So, she should be fine."

Brooke jerked her neck to face Amber. "Amber, what if the baby gets sick and needs something from Summer or Oliver, and then the blood comes back exposing her lie, then what? Families often find themselves getting tested for one another if one member falls ill. I wouldn't do it. You never know."

Amber backed off with both palms surrendering. "Okay, then. Tell the man."

"You are so right. How can I have it all and still make a mess out of it?"

Brooke replied, "Now that you know what you have to do, we need to talk about my life now."

"You are a mess!" Amber declared with a laugh.

I chuckled.

Emily sat forward again. "Okay, then. Tell us how many times you've slept with Damani. By the way, is he girthy?" She motioned around her stomach. "You know, there. Not . . ."

"No. Oh, God, no." Brooke grimaced. "But he's not ripped. He's soft." She jerked her chin in the air. We tittered. "But," her index finger flew up, "he always makes time for me, and I love that."

"Don't all daddies for their daughters?" Amber ribbed.

Brooke narrowed her eyes at her. "Ha. Ha. Well, Damani is only forty-three."

We hooted at her words.

Amber retorted, "Come on, get to the good stuff. What else?"

Brooke's dimples flashed as she smiled with quick bats of her lashes. "Well, we've had sex like five times. He's good." She started to count on her fingers. "We did it in his bed, in my bed, on my couch, on his couch . . ."

Amber yawned. "That don't even begin to hold a candle to where Jackson banged you." She held up a finger. "On the back of the club wall . . ."

Brooke scowled, "Hey, we'll get there. Relax. It hasn't been too long. And we don't talk about the 'J' man anymore. Okay?"

"Really?" I gave her a dull look. "Is he really off-limits?"

She nodded unconvincingly. "Yup."

"Do you feel for him yet?" Emily asked.

Brooke took a while to answer. She played with her fingers. "Well." Her shoulders slouched. "No. I mean I could, but I don't want feelings right now. Unfortunately, the 'J' man still has a stake in my heart. Besides, I should break things off with Damani, or scale it back some."

"You were just batting your lashes," I pointed out.

"Well you owe me now, sista'." Her eyes locked with mine with expectations of collecting a payback. "I gave you stellar advice, and now I need some. What to do?"

I almost choked. "You're asking me? I'm way past pre-heating the bun in my oven, and I have to tell the expectant diner that he can't eat it, because it's for another diner. Yeah. I have nothing to offer. You may wanna ask her." I pointed at Emily.

Caught off-guard, Emily shifted. "Well. I mean, yeah, I guess I can offer a thing or two. What do you need to know?"

"Should I break it off?"

"If you're looking for a long term, and he feels right so far, no. But if you're hoping to win Jackson back, then call him up and see if things have changed on his end."

Worried, Brooke replied, "I can't do that."

"Then move on, Brooke. If you have too much pride, move on, and stop looking back," Emily told her.

Brooke tapped the table with her fingernails. "Do you know what Jacqueline Laurent told me?" We shrugged and shook our heads. "She told me that I better be sure that I can handle it all if I want it all. Like women can't balance these days."

"Some of them can't," Emily replied. "Children take a lot of attention and so do husbands. Maintaining a household goes beyond chores and finances. Spouses and children are a lot to deal with. My dad was a real estate guru and my mom was a lawyer. She worked seventy hours before they dated, and she had to cut back to sixty when they married just to spend a shred of time with my father. Once she had my two sisters and me, she had to cut down to fifty and then to forty. Eventually, she just decided to stay home to give us all her attention since my dad could carry the financial load anyway. My mom pretty much saved enough throughout the years for our college education and was okay to let work go."

Processing the information with her chin resting on her palm, Brooke squinted. "Was it her passion?"

Emily nodded fervently. "Oh, she loved the law, and she thought she'd be doing it forever. But she fell in love with family and loved us more."

Brooke could only say, "I see," as she sat back against the booth.

"Maybe Jacqueline has a point," Emily continued. "You can be kind of selfish."

Astonishment flashed in Brooke's eyes.

"I mean, you can barely wait to talk about your life in conversations, like minutes ago."

Amber agreed. "Hello."

"So, she is right. Balance is key, and you better be sure that you can handle not being number one with children in the picture."

Brooke defended herself with a finger in the air. "Well, if you're going to insult me, do it right. I'm not kind of selfish, I am selfish," she admitted with a quick nod.

"Okay, but Brooke, give it some thought, but don't overdo it. You have no clue how you'll feel about much of anything in life until it happens. That's life. You're such a planner that you crumble at the idea of possible monkey wrenches. Monkey wrenches make us stronger. I should know." Emily smiled through her melancholy expression. Amber stretched an arm around Emily and pulled her close. Emily peered up at her and mumbled, "Thanks."

Full of thought, Brooke bit her lower lip. "Thanks, Emily. Thanks guys for listening. Look, normally I'm in bed by now. It'll be a while before I stay up this late again. Can't sacrifice beauty."

"Yeah, I'm sure Oliver will be calling me any moment now. But before we take off, I want to tell you ladies something." They appeared afraid to inquire, so I quickly added, "Thank you."

"For what?" Emily lifted and dropped her shoulders.

"For always listening to me in the past as I rambled away endlessly about Ruben and Fran. I never really made it a point to thank you guys with all that's been going on."

They smiled and took turns patting my hand.

I straightened. "On that note, ladies, I've got the bill and tip. Go."

Amber's eyebrows shot up. "Well, you know how much I love being treated to a free meal. Thank you, boo."

I waved my hand at her. "Nah, when you have great friends, it's nothing. Now go."

"We don't let pregnant women walk alone to their cars this late." Amber smiled and threw in a wink. One nod told her that her offer had been accepted.

I flipped the bill over and placed a fifty down to cover everything. They all thanked me as we stood up and walked to the parking lot. We all hugged and vowed to meet up again sooner than later.

Driving home in my new Corvette, my hand subconsciously rubbed my belly when I found myself stuck at red lights. Only minutes away from reaching home, another red light popped up. At one-thirty, the streets belonged to me. That was, until a car with music at a head-throbbing volume pulled up beside me. I turned to see the annoying person with whom I had to share the road. Staring back at me from the muscle car was a bald, ethnic-looking man who appeared to be around my age. With his tattooed arm hanging out of the window, he puffed on his cigarette, grinning at me between puffs. The sinew in his biceps popped with each lift of his forearm. Cute man.

Humored, I grinned at him and rolled my eyes to myself. Staring straight, my single days came to mind. Before I would've never hesitated to flirt back with a cute man showing me attention, but with a dedicated man at home and a baby on the way, it wouldn't be cool anymore. Obviously, he didn't like me ignoring him, because he gunned his engine at me to make me notice him again. The light changed and without looking back, my foot pushed the pedal to move forward. Thank God.

Unfortunately, another red light waited ahead. I thought about detouring to avoid him, but the layout of Ballston almost matched the same unfriendly set up as DC. So, we found ourselves together again at another red light. Stuck. This time, his engine roars weren't good enough, and neither was the volume of his music.

He turned the music down and yelled, "Hey, beautiful! What's up?"

I knew what would happen next, but something inside of me felt like ignoring him would be mean. On the other hand, indulging him wasn't cheating either, right? So, I rolled down my window to confirm my suspicions. I didn't say anything.

With a lowered voice, he said, "Nice whip. You look good in your Corvette."

"Thank you." I decided a smile couldn't hurt.

His hand lowered from the steering wheel to the exterior side of the door. A big palm rested against his green paint job. "Is there any way I can get your number right quick? I know the timing ain't great, but, uhh, can't let you slip away without asking."

One quick glance at the green light and in my rearview mirror verified that no one waited behind me. Turning back to the man who wore danger like next season's trend, my finger flew up to signal him to hold up a minute. Unsure of what compelled me to do it, my hand quickly dug for a pen and paper to scribble the necessary information to make a connection. My arm stretched across the passenger seat as far as possible, and he opened his door to hop out to meet me halfway. When he jumped back into his car and opened the small paper, he looked up at me and smiled.

"Nice name . . . unique even."

Nodding, my lips curled at him before punching it to make it through the green light. Once home, I removed my clothes as quickly as possible to join my already-sleeping man.

Brooke

Brooke responded to the knock at her door by peering through the peephole. Friday morning, and she hadn't recovered from her late-night dinner date with her friends. Her eyes felt puffy and her hair was disheveled. She hadn't even brushed her teeth, which was the top priority upon waking in her rule book. On her tippy toes, she could see a very familiar face staring down as he waited. Damani Pappas! *What is he doing here?* Didn't he know that a diva required notice?

Taking a quick last look in the mirror before opening the door, she yelled, "Be right there!" Brooke really wanted to strangle him for putting her in that position. With a few finger strokes through her hair, she decided that she already looked her best under the circumstances. At least she always wore nice lingerie to bed instead of patterned cotton pajamas.

Brooke opened the door. Before she could get a great look at Damani or have a kiss planted on her lips, she held up a finger. "Be right back." She allowed him to let himself in as she raced down the hallway to her bedroom. "Make yourself at home!" Rather than stick around and risk embarrassment due to her breath, she decided it was best for him to believe that she was in the middle of something and scat. She closed the door to her room and locked it.

Brooke chose to clean her teeth first. Worried at the prospect of him smelling breath that was anything but fresh, she snatched her electric toothbrush from the drawer and brushed. Brooke opened her mouth and raked her tongue across her top teeth. "Much better." After a quick rake of her comb through her hair, she ran into the closet and put on a pair of Adriano Goldschmied jeans with a white tank top to replace her lingerie gown. Braless, she stepped out of her closet and met Damani in the living room.

He sat on her sofa with an ankle resting on one knee and an arm stretched on top of the backing. When she entered, his attention shifted to Brooke from the flat screen that he'd turned on. Reveling in her appearance, his teeth bit down on his lower lip as his eyes reviewed her from top to bottom and up again.

"I see." He stood and met her in the middle of the living room floor.

"Really?" With fingers intertwined and eyes locked on one another, they stood toe-to-toe, flirty with one another. "What do you see?"

"A beautiful young woman." Damani freed one hand from her grip to caress her butt. "One who makes me feel good inside and makes me remember that work is not so much fun."

"Speaking of work, I do have to get dressed soon. I'm in the crucial stage of the wedding process."

He sighed, tracing her back and butt. "But I can't get enough of you, Brooke. I think about you a lot. I try to think of other things I can do to you."

Brooke tilted her head and eyed him with playful suspicion. "Is that all you want from me? Sex?"

Damani grinned. "Yes. And a lot of it."

She couldn't tell if she minded his honesty. While Brooke wanted to keep it light with Damani, she didn't want to give her body away over and over without some possibility of a real payoff. It contrasted her principles to sleep with a man with whom she wasn't committed. But then again, she figured she may've already breached her own rule.

Nothing else came to mind but, "Oh." She flashed him a disingenuous smile but could tell that Damani read it.

He grabbed her chin with a thumb. "But, you also intrigue me."

"Why?" Brooke's expression turned plain as she waited for his response.

"Because I like the way you carry yourself. You do everything on your own, but you make room for me."

Brooke appreciated his observation as well as the credit he gave her. Her raised shoulders eased upon hearing his words. "Thank you."

Damani placed his hands on both sides of her face. He kissed her lips and pulled back. "You're so feminine. You're a lady, delicate but strong. I like your balance. It drives me nuts. But you're an animal in bed."

They laughed at his words and connected with another kiss. As he grumbled in pleasure, she became more aroused. With her eyes closed and caught up in the moment, her mind started to drift to Jackson, but she couldn't figure out why. Her heartbeat jolted with a quick ache as she recalled how Jackson used to compliment her about the same thing. And she'd gotten so good at brushing thoughts of him to the side, especially during inopportune times, but the idea of him easing from her heart scared her. What would life be like if it didn't include missing Jackson? He *was* her first love. It only felt right to pretend that she was in his clutches once again, even if the thought made her want to cry.

Even though both men's lips felt so different, she couldn't resist the role play that intruded her thoughts. She wanted to pretend that Jackson's lips touched hers. As Brooke's mind chanted Jackson's name over and over, she began to feel her brain slip away from her body. Her mind felt detached from reason, but if it meant indulging in her fantasy, she didn't really care.

The only thing that mattered was pleasing her achy heart with thoughts of Jackson. Brooke didn't understand where the sudden desire to allow Jackson to high jack her mind came from, but as wrong as it was, it truly felt right. Her mind fought between thoughts of Jackson and Damani's words: *"Yes. And a lot of it."* Damani's statement of wanting constant sex with her and her yearning for Jackson made Brooke realize that she and Damani had a long way to go before becoming a real couple. And if she was right, then Brooke felt like a little fun in the meantime didn't hurt nobody. Damani never said that he'd wanted more with her, so she gave herself permission to have fun, especially since he didn't have to know.

Not wanting to see the real man in front of her, Brooke kept her eyes shut as she lifted the shirt above his head. In her mind, the shirt belonged to Jackson. Soon, it had become Jackson's belt. As the seconds passed, everything had become Jackson. For those brief moments, Brooke felt the fantasy-filled Band-Aid cover her heart. For a moment in time, the chronic pain had subsided. And for the first time in months, she felt whole again.

Brooke took that feeling and ran with it. When would she really feel that peace again? Before she knew it, she'd been swept into his arms. Refusing to open her eyes as their lips continued to kiss as he walked, Brooke whispered, "Oh, Jackson." When Brooke realized what she'd done, she instantly broke free from the kiss as her eyes stared into his with consternation.

"Jackson? Who is Jackson?"

Amber

Amber smashed the cigarette into the tray and stood up from the dining room table. Her only Friday appointment cancelled on her via email this morning. Unfortunately, her wide-open day translated into a loss in revenue. A loss in revenue posed a threat in Amber's ability to pay the bills, which reminded her that she needed to see what she owed. After days of ignoring the mailbox, Amber anticipated a junky box and didn't want the mailman to struggle to fit any more mail into her space if she didn't remove the contents now. Sighing, she slipped her bare feet into her animal slippers and snatched the key from the kitchen counter before making her way to the elevators in a tank top and pajama shorts.

When she arrived at the mailboxes and opened hers, just as she'd thought, it'd become crammed with mail.

Amber huffed. "Great." She carefully pulled the mail from the box. After gingerly tucking the mail under her right arm, she headed back to the elevators. As soon as Amber pressed the button, the same elevator that took her down, waited to take her back up.

"Hold the elevator, please."

She turned to see a familiar face approaching her. *The man I met when I went to dinner with Pharr*! She didn't want the handsome man to see her in her sleep attire. Her feelings didn't matter, because he couldn't hear her, and he'd already stepped into the elevator with her.

When he recognized Amber's face, the handsome man grinned. "Oh, it's you. I think you know which floor I need." He had his hands locked together, resting against his crotch. Amber willed herself not to look for a dick print.

"I do." She pressed the button to their floor.

Still grinning, the tall man glazed down at her from the other corner of the elevator. "What's your name, luv?"

Ooooh, that deep voice.

"Amber." She wanted to ask him if she could see his bed but didn't know how to be forward with men from whom she hadn't planned on collecting cash. Returning eye contact proved to be harder when she didn't have to worry about exercising power to get what she wanted. While Amber appreciated being a retiree from the prowl, the trade-off became adjusting to coming on to men like other women would. In fact, no longer being on the prowl meant being the prey for once. Regardless of the discomfort, Amber enjoyed being the hunted.

"Don't cha wanna know my name?"

Maybe he liked teasing her just to watch her squirm.

"Okay." Amber felt like a teenage girl trying to keep her crush on an older guy under control.

"It's Cane."

Amber nodded as she folded her lips inward. "Okay." That's a good name, she figured. There weren't many Canes walking around. First Pharr, then Cane. The name was very hot on him. When the doors opened, they both stepped off. Amber didn't know what else he wanted her to say. "Do you wanna come in?" Oh no, she realized. Did she really just say that? Her hand almost flew up to her mouth in embarrassment.

Cane didn't hesitate. "Would love to."

"Great." Amber remembered that she didn't have a chance to pick up, so she crossed her fingers in hopes that nothing dirty laid around. On the other hand, she relaxed as she reminded herself that she lived neatly. After she unlocked the door, Amber held it open, so Cane could pass through.

"Nice." Cane nodded as he observed her apartment with his hands in his slacks. "Looks a lot like mine."

"Thanks. Coffee? A smoke? Coke?"

"If you talkin' four twenty, yeah I'll smoke."

"Man, I haven't hit that four twenty since New York. But, nah, I mean cigarettes."

"You smoke?" His face appeared slightly concerned.

Amber nodded shamelessly. She locked her hands behind her back.

"Not such a good habit for such a beautiful woman."

"So I've been told."

"Well, nah I'm good. I just wanted to learn more about my neighbor."

Reading Cane didn't come too easily to Amber the way it did with other people. He appeared mysterious, possibly serious, and extremely sexy.

Amber shrugged. "I'm a smoker who teaches piano lessons and lives alone." She'd learned her lesson from her time with Pharr. No more making apologies. She didn't wear that outfit so well. "You?" Her finger skirted the end table that sat next to the door. She wasn't used to small chat and felt awkward trying to host a hot stranger.

"Love working out and making that bread at The World Bank."

Wow. Another man with easy cash flow. Amber felt a jab of discomfort but tried to act unfazed. "That's what's up. You live alone?'

"Nah. I wish. My younger brother stays with me until he gets back on his feet. Little knucklehead." He pointed a long index finger toward her door as if they could see his apartment. "And I live across the hall from you."

Amber didn't know how well she liked that when she heard him say it. It worried her that he would expect too much of her time, or that he would randomly intrude on her space. Shrugging on the inside, Amber decided to cross that bridge if she came to it.

"Tell me Cane, how old are you?"

"I'm twenty-seven. What about you?"

"At the beginning of April, I'll be thirty. So, when do you turn twenty-eight?" Realizing their age difference, though it wasn't significant, Amber felt the need to know just how long it would be before his next birthday. Twenty-eight sounded a whole lot better than twenty-seven since she'd be thirty soon. She also felt an awkward air between them but suspected more from her end since it probably stemmed from her recent male encounters.

"I just turned." Sensing disappointment, Cane shrugged as an apology.

"Would you like to sit down?" She gestured toward her sofa.

"Actually, I gotta head out to work, but are you down for hooking up later on tonight?"

There it was. Amber wasn't sure if he wanted a date, or if he wanted to swing by her place. "Now is this a legit date?" A forced smile attempted to mask concern.

"Yes, it is."

"Okay, then. Make sure you dress like it is. Just because you live right there . . ." she teased as she waved her finger pointing at her door to hint at the location of his apartment.

Cane laughed. "I got you, I got you. I won't show up in my pajamas. Who knows, I may take you clubbing."

"That actually sounds great. Would it be so bad if I were to bring a friend with her man?"

"Not at all." A large hand flew up. "But first, I want to spend some time with you tonight before we head to the club."

Grinning, Amber said, "I got cha. See you tonight then, Cane."

He nodded and flashed her one last perfect grin before heading out of her door.

Summer

The bed shook at the sound of the alarm. I forced my eyes to open as they resisted the hint of sunlight that barged through the blinds. Oliver stood after slamming the alarm button to quiet the chime.

"Arghhh!"

"What, Oliver?" Sleep still clogged my voice.

He spun around to face me with a grin. "Nothing. Just that waking up some mornings can be so hard."

"Well do you have to report today?" Sitting up with a yawn, my wavy hair fell carelessly around my face.

"You're so beautiful, Summer. Today, I just want to spend the day with you."

Those words pinched my heart. This man genuinely loved me, and I felt like a rotten soul who would lose him for being truthful. I didn't know what to say except, "So what'd you have in mind for today?"

I wrestled with not knowing if we should have one last beautiful moment together before the inevitable and unfortunate breakup, or if I should just grab my big-girl panties and tell him now before we went any further. Another unfortunate issue to consider was finding a place to live. Luckily, Oliver insisted that I save my earnings from recruiting independently, or my financial situation would be minimized to paycheck-to-paycheck living again. He would need his credit card and Corvette back, too. But if it meant having him by my side, there would be no hesitation in giving up every fine piece of luxury living. I chose to make one last memory with him before the breakup.

Oliver sat down beside me. "How about . . ." He placed a large hand over my little baby bulge. "How about we go to New York for the weekend?"

I'd never been to New York! Unfortunately, as tempting as that sounded, it wouldn't look too considerate from Oliver's point of view. He would think that he'd been used for the trip before announcing my news, and if the truth came out in the Big Apple, I'd be the Big Bitch for ruining our trip. New York would have to be after he knew the truth, although, the idea of taking Amber to surprise Mara excited me as well. No, now I had to do what was best for Oliver, not Amber, nor myself.

With my hand resting on his, I removed it from my baby bump and placed it on the comforter followed by a pat on his hand. "Sweetie, can we just keep it simple for this weekend? I do appreciate the offer, Oliver. I do."

"But I saw your face." He smiled and so did his eyes. I loved that, and it'd be sorely missed. My heart sizzled with an ache. "You were excited, so why not?" Cutting me off before responding, he asked, "And, uh, isn't Amber from New York? Maybe we could take her."

I wanted to cry but held back the tears. Any man who would think of his girlfriend's friends won the prize as a keeper. "Yes. You are one-of-a-kind, baby. But I don't know, I guess I don't feel like packing or something."

"Baby, don't be obtuse. You know we can buy you some clothes when we get there. Just bring your essentials. My treat."

I fell over laughing. "Isn't it always your treat?"

He barely poked my belly. "Yes, it is, but since I love you, I can't seem to stop spoiling you. You stole my heart at IHOP." He shrugged, rising to his feet. "What can I say?"

I laughed. "Aww, well I love you, too, Oliver."

"If you do love me, then choose. Where to spend the weekend, or at least the day?"

"Hmmmmm, how abouuuuuuuuuuut . . . National Harbor?"

His nose wrinkled. "Why?"

"Why not?" I raised my shoulders and smiled.

"If it's what you want, but I wanted to give you more. Hey, by the way, what time did you get home last night?"

"Late. Almost two, I suppose." The comforter and sheet swept over my body with one quick tug. My tiny feet supported my tired body and additional weight all the way to my closet—the closet I would miss so much when Oliver kicks me out on my tail.

"Did you have fun?" He headed toward his dresser.

"I did indeed."

"That's good. I wish I had more time to hang out with my boys. But you know, work hard now, play later."

I poked my head out of my walk-in closet to see his face. "Well, don't you have time for a quick game of pool to play with the guys?"

Never looking up from a pair of wrinkled jeans before giving them one harsh shake, he answered, "If I did, then I wouldn't have told you that I didn't."

"Gotcha." I went back inside my closet, or the one that Oliver moved out of to accommodate all my crap, to find my outfit for the day.

Brooke

Lowering his arms to set her back onto her feet, he straightened slowly as he smoothed the front of his shirt with a flat hand. "What did you call me? Jackson?" Squinting at Brooke, Damani panted with a tilted head. His hand gripped her wrist with slight pressure to ensure their distance.

Brooke couldn't justify her actions, nor did she want to. The fact remained, Jackson still had a huge part of her heart, and Damani didn't stand a chance of taking over it. Alarmed, she placed her fingers over her bottom lip as her eyes swelled with disbelief. "I'm sorry," she said quickly.

Damani released her wrist and stepped back. "Did you just call me by another man's name?"

Her voice began to crack as she cried. "Damani . . ." Now would be the time to tell the truth. "I . . ." She tried to speak but ended up raking her hands through her hair. "My last boyfriend was my very first love. We broke up before Thanksgiving, when I found out that he didn't want children."

Irritation tunneled his being and robbed his handsome face. "Yes, well, clearly that is not me." His eyes darted to the floor to locate his shirt. Finding it beside the leg of her table, he snatched it up and donned it hastily as Brooke begged.

"I am asking you to forgive me, Damani." Brooke took steps to meet him face to face. "I'm trying to get him out of my heart. I really am." Her palms crossed her chest, tears raced down her face.

Unbothered, he fastened his belt. "What? Was I Jackson the first night we made love, too?"

Brooke knew that he wouldn't believe her even if she denied it, but she had to be honest. She pointed her finger at him. "No. No you were not."

Completely dressed, with a harsh glare, he informed her that, "I will never be a second fiddle. I did that growing up in my family, and I'm not a child anymore." He took long strides to walk around and away from Brooke.

She didn't follow him to the door as she cried, "No, wait. Damani! Damani! *Please . . . wait.*"

But Damani didn't wait, nor did he look back. Even though Brooke was the one who walked away from Jackson that night, seeing Damani do it to her offered insight as to how Jackson must've felt when she did it to him.

Emily

Emily lay in her bed staring at a book. She found herself reading each sentence twice, struggling with her waning concentration. When her cell phone rang, she left the book open in its current position and flattened it over her chest to keep her place. Her other hand reached for the phone on the nightstand.

"Hello?"

"So, how about that date you owe me."

"Oh, my gosh, Zach." Her hazel eyes rolled in her head. "Are you really going to hold me to that promise?"

"Well, if I don't, it won't get done. A deal's a deal."

Emily found him handsome, but dating felt like a complication that she just couldn't handle along with the move and the surrounding issues with Eric. However, he did humiliate Eric, and he earned some redemption points. Emily sighed, "Well, when and where?"

"I think we should go out."

"You would. Okay, anywhere but your house. You seem to recall what happened the last time I came there, right?"

"It's in the past. Get dressed."

"Wait, now? What should I wear?"

"How about if we go to a restaurant? Some place nice and simple."

"Fine."

"And be ready in a half-hour?"

"Zach." Emily released a sarcastic laugh. "Goodness, you do know you're talking to a woman and not one of your buddies, right? That won't do for a woman. And you're lucky I just showered. I still need an hour."

"Well, I would think that the shower already taken would knock off a few tics, but what the hell. A lady says she needs an hour, then that's exactly what the lady gets. See you soon."

"Bye." Emily jumped out of the bed with a good-natured smile on her face. Some change just may do her some good.

Summer

After seeing a movie and hanging out at the mall for some new maternity wear at Oliver's insistence, we finally made it out for a night at the National Harbor. Oliver parked his Corvette and hopped out to assist me. As he skirted around his car to open my door, the nervous gas inside my stomach developed. Enjoying the day's outing felt impossible, because the devil's voice on my shoulder overpowered my positive thoughts with taunts about how this would be my last great date with the man I loved.

When my door flew open, I stepped out with my right wedge-clad foot first. Oliver made me retire my pointy heels until the baby was born. Only good guys think that way. I couldn't help but lament over the fact that I could lose everything, just when I'd started to believe.

Oliver gripped my hand to help ease me out. "Thank you, boo."

"Anytime." He smiled the way I liked; it made my heart flutter. "What did you want to do here?" His hand looped into mine. "What was so great here that you just had to pass up on New York?"

"Simplicity."

What a lie. Unfortunately, having people fooled became a mastery of mine. The thought stopped me in my tracks. Without looking up, I could see him staring at me to find an obvious wrong. Despite my awareness of his stare, my face twisted with realization. Fran pinned me as sweet, my mom still thought of me as the same girl who left for college, and Oliver thought I was worth a shot even though I campaigned against monogamy and children. Gee, I seemed to have fooled everyone, including myself.

"Hey." He tugged my hand to get my attention. His eyebrows furrowed. "You okay, baby?"

I collected myself quickly when it occurred to me that he could be worried about the baby . . . Ruben's baby. "Oh, yes. I'm sorry, I was just worried that, umm, oh, nothing. Let's go eat or something."

Partially convinced, he nodded. I took the initiative and began to walk. If my goal was to form one last good memory, I should at least get it right.

Amber

Amber jumped at the knock at the door. "Oh." She replaced the mascara wand back into the tube and closed the medicine cabinet. Walking from the bathroom to her foyer to open the door for Cane, she tugged on her tight, red mini skirt and adjusted the plunging, crème-colored V-neck blouse one last time. Without a bra, Amber hoped that Cane would receive the right message. It'd been way too long at this point.

An open door revealed Cane standing with flowers. Delighted and touched, Amber couldn't help but feel shy by a man's genuine play for affection. "For *moi*?" It would take more than flowers to impress Amber, but she decided to play his game anyway.

He extended them until they touched her chest. "Well, I don't want them," he joked. Stepping through her threshold, he eyed her blatantly up and down with his hands in the pockets of his black slacks. "Wowwww."

Amber chuckled as she stood there with the flowers in her hands. "You like?"

"I do, I do, I do." He bit his lower lip as he stared at her legs. "Girl."

Amber went inside her kitchen to find a vase. Of course, she didn't own one. After looking into two cabinets, she decided to stop pretending to herself like she was that type of woman. She spun on her toes to face Cane as she shrugged. "You know I don't have a vase," she admitted.

"You don't own a vase, huh?"

Amber shook her head with a naughty grin. It felt great to be her normal self without the shame of where she came from and what she had. Between the paying clients and men like Pharr, Amber couldn't care less if she never encountered a man from the other side of the tracks again. But she did feel like a Martian on Earth as a woman without one vase. That just proved how starved of romance she'd become. It also told her that she'd placed too little emphasis on her domestic life over the years.

"Ah, well." He waved a hand at her. "Put those suckas on the counter and let's get going."

"Wait." Amber placed them on the counter carefully before she turned to face him. "What about us talking before we go?"

Cane didn't seem too interested in talking. "Amber, this is me. I'm straightforward and a little rough around the edges. I know I brought you flowers and all, but really, I'm starved and ready to party. Maybe we can do this tidbit some other time. Ya' know?"

Amber felt like she was in New York again. And, of course, she wouldn't have the opportunity to find that out because he didn't want to talk. These were the men she'd surrounded herself with before coming to DC: direct, emotionally unavailable, and not romantic. Amber had fantasized that Cane would be the balance between rich men like Eric and Daniel who paid for sex, and rich men like Pharr who were used to the finer things in life despite having dirty nails. Apparently, Cane would probably turn out to be a reminder of her roots. She met him in Southwest DC, in the same apartment building as hers. Although many successful men come from low-end neighborhoods, it didn't mean that he couldn't turn out to be like Oliver or Jackson. She tabled her judgment in favor of going with it.

But all she could say was, "Well, let me not pretend that I don't know how this story will end, even though I've read the book." Somewhat bummed, she grabbed her purse from the dining room chair and said, "Let's go."

Cane shrugged and followed Amber out of the door.

Five minutes later, they arrived at a seafood restaurant after walking down the street. Settled in, they didn't say much to one another once the server took their orders. Staring at the dessert menu, Amber decided against out-eating her date on their first outing, so she put the menu away.

Amber pointed at the doors. "I live right next to this restaurant and never managed to eat here."

"Well, when you live close to something, you think you'll take advantage, when in reality, you take it for granted because it is so close."

Amber nodded. "True." She felt much more confident in a place like this with Cane, versus her first night out with Pharr when she tried to be more refined than sugar. "So, as we wait and sip our water, tell me more about the man sitting across from me."

Cane ran a hand over his black sweater. "All right, since you keep pressing a bruh to talk."

Amber threw up a cautioning hand. "Hey, wait. Is this somethin' that you don't wanna do? You keep actin' strange when I ask about us talkin'. Am I missing somethin'?"

He raised his eyebrows as he sighed. "Well, Amber, we don't know where this is gonna take us, so I think we should stay on cruise control. Don't nobody need to be all personal and all."

"I ain't." Amber felt bothered by his insinuation that she tried to interview him like some nosy woman. "I just think that this part is normal. I should know who's treatin' me to a dinner. I'm just talkin' basic shit."

"Girl, you may have to kick in a little bit on this bill. I bought you flowers and this place ain't all that cheap. It ain't a drive-through. I can tell you that right now."

Amber was taken aback. Her back slammed against the chair. "Umm, hel*lo*, I know where we are. But this is a date, and you need to act like it." Just as she'd considered walking out on him, the server arrived with two plates.

"Crab cakes for the lady." The plate rested in front of her. Once the aroma hit her nostrils, she knew she wasn't going anywhere. "And fried flounder for you, sir." He placed the plate in front of Cane and asked with a smile, "Will there be anything else?"

Cane replied, "Is it gonna be on the house?"

The server's brows frowned. He released an uneasy snicker. "I-I'm sorry, I don't follow . . ."

"You asked if we needed anything else." A hint of irritation seeped into Cane like food through an intravenous cord. "Will it be free?"

Amber placed a hand on her forehead, averting her eyes to the table, wanting to flee.

This negro.

The server released a forced laugh. "Oh. Got it. No, sir. I wish I could."

"Then nah, son. We good."

"No thank you, sir," Amber replied politely.

With a clasp of the hands, the server just replied, "Enjoy."

Amber didn't know if Cane was just too rough around the edges or if she'd been more refined over the years than she'd realized. She decided to forego confronting him over what just happened, and to heed the modern advice of choosing one's battles. Rather than carry on about who was going to pay what, Amber decided to let it go for the moment. She realized that she could let him be a jerk and pay for her own meal and never see him again or refuse to pay and let the chips fall where they may. A lot of things scared her throughout her life and losing him for good wasn't one of them. So, she concluded: Why sweat the small stuff?

After a few minutes of silence, Cane decided to break it. "So, Amber, why so quiet?"

Amber swallowed a piece of crab cake. "Well, everything seems to be off-limits."

He squinted his eyes at her and replied, "Stop trippin'. I just don't want an interview, especially on an empty stomach. That's all."

"Oh, so you're saying when you're full, I can ask away?"

"Well, as long as you don't get carried away."

"Hmm." She nodded. "Then we will have to see about that."

Cane grinned and slid a piece of flounder into his mouth. About twenty minutes later, the server had already cleared the table and Amber and Cane sat as they awaited the check.

"So, do you really prefer that I pay half?" Feeling chilly, Amber caressed her arms until they warmed up.

"That shirt looks really nice on you, Amber. Back to your place?"

Naturally, she almost told him that they could as long as he paid. The problem with that, was that she would be selling herself for a meal and that made her feel like she would be relapsing. Instead, she just said, "Cane, I ain't paying for this meal tonight."

Nonchalantly, Cane shrugged. "It's all good. It is *all* good, Amber."

"Then why'd you bring it up at the beginning of the meal?" she persisted.

"Cuz it's true, girl. I got bills, and this ain't one that I'm tryna pay tonight. And since you don't wanna help a brotha out, guess I'ma have to do it."

"Brotha works at The World Bank." Amber frowned with a shrug.

"*Brotha*, just got hired."

Stunned, she leaned forward so he could hear her whisper. "Cane, you are on a date, the first one with me, might I add, and you not even tryna impress me or anything. What's up with that?"

Cane snickered. "Why should I front? Would you rather me pretend to be something I ain't just to please you and then change later? I ain't no bitch. That's trash, man."

Amber didn't know what to say. On one hand, he made sense. She could see where he came from because a lot of people try to impress their dates only to become another person down the line. In fact, as she considered her experiences—including her decision to be herself thanks to the horrendous date with Pharr—she decided that she should be grateful that Cane chose to be himself. True, just like the other men, Cane would probably be a disappointment, however, she had to appreciate the fact that he didn't pose as someone on another level.

"Then how much should I pay, Cane?"

"Thought I already told you I would, especially since you agreed, and you didn't throw a fit, and believe me, women these days can throw them. I'll pay it all. Good?"

"Women wouldn't throw fits if men would step up. But whatever, it's good. Go 'head and pay."

After all the debating, Amber wanted to ring his neck. When the server came back with the bill, Amber watched as Cane opened the check presenter. He grimaced when his eyes dropped down to the total.

"Man." He reached for his wallet and pulled out a fifty and three singles. "Let's go." On his feet, Amber felt the pressure to rise with him. She couldn't believe he stressed over paying fifty raggedy dollars.

"Wait, Cane. I don't have any cash on me. Where's his tip? I know that those singles only cover the tax." Amber pushed in her chair as she waited for him to explain.

He didn't look her in the eyes as he said, "I ain't here to pay him. He'll be aight. Let's go."

What a cheap bastard!

She'd hate to see what he'd give a girlfriend on her birthday. Embarrassed, she marched in her high heels toward the door faster than Cane. Once they reached the concrete, she turned to him. "Cane, we live right here. How am I gonna show my face here again anytime soon?"

"Then dine somewhere else." He spoke as if it were nothing as they walked back to their building and approached his Scion in the lot. Cane disarmed it and Amber stood beside the door as she waited for him to open her door. He was about to open the driver door when he noticed Amber standing there. "Girl, God gave you those hands for a reason. You betta use them."

"This is the least you can do." Amber crossed her arms and stared at him with a raised brow.

"Girl, I fed you. Now you being spoiled. Come on, get in." He hopped in before Amber could reply. "You women cry for equal rights but don't wanna lift a finger."

She sucked her teeth and murmured, "Unbelievable," before hopping in. Closing the door behind her, she replied,

"You men want pussy pie but don't wanna be enough of a gentleman to earn a slice."

"I paid for dinner. Amber you more high maintenance than I thought." He shook his head, starting the engine.

Astounded, Amber looked at him as she buckled her seatbelt. "Me? High maintenance? Maybe you should meet my other friend."

"Is she pretty?" Cane looked at her, waiting for an answer.

"Motha' . . ."

"Maybe we should head back to your unit for that alone time."

Like he'd get this pussy? Not a chance. Not even a sniff. Fifty dollars and he think he's done something.

"No, the club."

"It's all you. Between the flowers and the dinner, I'm done for the night."

How could a man with such a manly voice behave like such a child?

"Honey, my meal was only twenty dollars. You didn't spend the whole amount on me. Besides, is this even your car? I'm having a hard time believing that you even paid for it."

"That's none of your business. It's mine."

"Whatever. Take me to the club."

"Well, it is before midnight and women get in free, so you'll only have to pay for me."

Amber rolled her eyes until they landed on the scenery outside of the window. From having men pay for her to her having to pay for a man, it all felt like bull to her.

"And you gonna bring that friend?"

Amber didn't want to bring a friend to meet him tonight after all. She was too afraid that he would embarrass her, and she knew that any one of them would need more notice than this, so she replied, "None of them could make it."

"Oh, well. Their loss."

"Which club we going to?"

"The one on F Street in Northwest."

"Fine."

The demanding line outside hinted that the club would be a blast. She already mentally deducted one hundred dollars from her bank account when she factored in paying for him as well as the drinks. She just wanted to have fun tonight. It'd been a long time since she'd gone clubbing, and she planned on dumping him after tonight anyway.

Summer

After our meal, we headed outside and decided to walk off the food by cruising the sidewalk. People huddled in crowds laughing and talking, while couples and families strolled casually along the strip. Different scents filled the air. Car fumes battled the aroma of grilled food while the smell of perfume snaked through the air in a race to hit my nostrils before the cologne from different men. It occurred to me that my bought time neared its end, thus spelling the demise of Oliver and me.

I stopped walking to fight the bout of nausea with cupped hands over my mouth.

"Is this walking okay for you, baby? I know the meal was probably heavy and all, plus you're carrying our baby in there." Oliver's happy grin flipped my stomach.

What would make me throw up first? The idea of hurting him or the smell of mixed scents?

I was about to break his heart before the end of the night. I needed a trash can or a bag. My feet scuffled as quickly as possible to a trash can to purge my emotional anguish through my vomit. Oliver rubbed my back, comforting me like Fran did, undeservingly.

Embarrassed, I reached into my purse for a napkin, avoiding the curious stares of surrounding strangers. I dabbed my mouth at the corners.

"You okay, baby?"

"Ugh, this pregnancy." More lies. Well, partial truth. "I'm fine."

"You don't need me to hold your purse, do you?"

Slightly irritated and failing to hide it, I told him, "Baby, please, I'm good." The nicer he behaved, the worse I felt.

"Okay, baby, relax. Didn't mean to push."

"No, you've done nothing wrong." Horrible didn't suffice to describe the turmoil inside. It seemed more appropriate to be annoyed at my tired feet than Oliver's concern. "Baby, it's me. My emotions are all over the place. Sorry."

"You're entitled. Let's just enjoy a silent walk. It's already noisy."

After a quick glance at him, a smile graced my face. Thinking of a way to break the news to him every time our eyes met, my creativity failed me. It felt better to look away and ahead. I reached for his hand to avoid being a distant jerk and to show that he was still needed. Instead, I decided to study the crowd as a distraction and enjoy the slightly chilled temperature.

"Are you cold, Summer?"

I couldn't be mad at a man who thought of everything. "I'm fine, baby. You?"

"Nah. I'm a man, we can handle anything."

Under the circumstances, a smile would seem like a mockery, so instead, I decided to say nothing. Keeping my eyes ahead, I fixated on a baby in the stroller, whose feet nearly kicked the wheels. "Don't you hate that?"

"What?" he asked.

"Parents who let children sit in strollers at that age. That child needs to walk."

"Well, don't worry, Summer. We'll be great parents. We won't raise brats or overly dependent children." Oliver grinned at me. I bit my lip.

"I'm just saying . . ." But I shouldn't have said anything at all, at least until this man knew the truth.

"Right."

As we continued our walk down the street, I noticed the gang of college-aged people standing in a circle, laughing and simply being loud. Oliver gave my hand a gentle pull to walk us around them. Before we reached them, half of the gang pulled apart from the other half in a rowdy bout of laughter. As they pulled apart, a familiar, tall, handsome man speaking with an attractive woman stood out. I couldn't see her face too well, but she had a nice figure and beautiful skin. It had to be Brooke, because I knew the man was . . . Jackson? Was it him? Instead of going through the group, I stopped in my tracks, causing Oliver to stop, too.

Confused, he asked, "What's wrong? You okay?"

My hand absently patted his as my stare froze on the man I knew as Jackson. I just needed him to turn around to prove it instead of showing me his profile. "No, no. I'm fantastic, baby." Unfortunately, the woman turned out to be someone else.

"Then why do you look like a zombie?" Oliver stared at me with furrowed eyebrows. "Summer." He sounded irritated by my silence.

Words seemed impossible to form. Finally, my lips cooperated. "Look. Look. Oh no, that's him. He has another woman."

"What?" Oliver snapped his neck to see the person in question. "Who?"

"Jackson. Brooke's ex. He is there and with another woman. She's going to die."

Oliver snaked his neck to locate Jackson faster. "Wh—wh—oh. Jackson. That's that guy from Emily's dinner. Ohhhhh, yeah. I remember him."

"Brooke is gonna die," I repeated in a trance.

Oliver snapped his neck back to face me. His face hardened into a serious mask as he looked at me. "Then don't tell her," he ordered, as if it were an obvious option.

My eyes met his. "*But I have to.*"

"No, you don't, Summer. You have enough to worry about, like this baby, without trying to stick your nose where it doesn't belong."

Even though his words stung because he hadn't a clue as to how right he was, I couldn't help but stare and obsess about what Jackson was doing. He stood with his hands in his pockets as he chatted and listened to the other woman. He nodded and appeared to hang on her every word. She stood with her arms crossed, then reached out and squeezed his shoulder with a small palm. I fought the urge to go up to him to make my presence known, but clearly it would piss Oliver off. This newfound knowledge of mine had to be in violation of Girl Code. But what could I do? Oliver would challenge me every step of the way. Instead, I decided to take one last look at Brooke's handsome ex and walk away.

I crossed my arms over my chest. "Let's just get out of here."

My eyes remained locked on Jackson and the attractive woman. He reached out to pinch her cheek. She grabbed his hand with both of hers and rested her cheek against it as they smiled with eyes lost in one another's. Maybe my man was right. If this would kill Brooke, then she would be better off alive and ignorant. Maybe I should change my name to Summer 'Secret' Stevenson, because every time I thought secrets were behind me, something else would put me in the line of fire again.

Emily

With a satisfied stomach, Emily had her eyes glued to the big screen. She and Zach agreed on a romantic comedy that turned out not to be so funny at all. They sat at the top of the auditorium with a small audience below. She couldn't deny the way the dark made her feel next to a man whom she'd actually found handsome. Yes, Zach did turn Emily off the first day they met, and she did feel odd that Enzo was oblivious to the connection she had with his father, but he'd actually grown on her in the past months. It became easier for her to embrace their fondness.

Emily thought about Eric from time to time; she couldn't deny it. Deep down, she also knew that it wasn't healthy to hang on to a man who'd constantly disappointed her. It'd become rather tiresome and painful to look back. The time to embrace the future without Eric had long pass.

Now, Emily could look forward to adventures as a single woman. Although she'd overdosed on the consumption of nervousness, it didn't rob her ability to be wild and carefree. Maybe that would explain the sexual energy that desperately needed to be release.

The movie might as well have been on mute, because Emily started to focus on the thoughts in her head. She thought of reasons why she should touch him or at least give him a try. Zach was handsome but different from her usual business type. He'd grown out a three-inch beard to match the length on top of his head combed to one side in one big wave with a side part. He had gentle blue eyes and kissable lips under a moustache. How would she ever know if he could please her if she didn't try? What she *did* know, was the amount of meat he had stored in his package.

Now fidgety, Emily found herself pinching her bottom lip with her thumb and index finger as she contemplated making a move. Remembering that she only lived once, Emily stopped analyzing and placed her other hand on his knee. Besides, why should she be nervous? She wasn't nervous the day she called him over to do her dirty work to hurt Eric. It didn't make sense to second-guess herself now that she had her hand on his knee. Emily secretly wished that she had an inch of Amber's temerity sometimes.

Zach responded by placing his hand on hers. Swallowing a lump of doubt, Emily turned to meet the stare she sensed in her direction. In the dark, Emily could see the wheels turning in his head. She couldn't make out his indifferent expression. She gathered that he wanted to see where she intended to go with her bold gesture. In that case, to make herself clear, Emily decided to proceed with her second move.

The subtle masculine scent of Zach's cologne drifted into her nostrils. Emily thought that she should express to him what it did to her. She pointed her crossed legs toward Zach and turned her shoulders to match the same direction. Placing a hand on the shoulder farthest from her, Emily brushed her nostrils against his neck and inhaled.

She lifted her glossy lips to his ear and whispered, "Mmmmmmm. Zach. You smell so good."

They made eye contact in the dark.

"Emily? What are you trying to do?" he whispered.

Emily didn't doubt that Zach wanted more, but she knew that he wanted her to vocalize a form of permission or confirmation. Obviously, he didn't want to cross any lines like he had done before.

"What do you want me to do?" Something about the dark made her come alive in a way that felt impossible in the light. The sexy tone woke up through a whisper.

Why couldn't I always be in the dark?

"Hmm." He half-heartedly laughed. Emily didn't want to lose the momentum. Her hand moved away from his knee and closer to his manhood to massage his upper thigh. With a cracked voice, he warned, "Emily. Don't start something you're not willing to finish." The stern expression on his face still managed to come across as gentle.

"Ohhh, I think I can finish," Emily flirted. She served a naughty chuckle to him like a game of ping-pong, waiting for him to toss one back.

"I mean it," he added with a tilt of the head. "You know how I feel about you."

"Shhhh." Emily placed a kiss on his neck and then his earlobe. "Don't disturb the viewers."

Zach placed his hand on her bare knee and eased it between her thighs. Now she knew the truth behind the invention of miniskirts. Emily helped him as she parted her legs slightly to accommodate his large hand. His other hand contacted the back of her neck and into the back of her button-up blouse. Zach moved his hand on her right shoulder to pull her closer to him. He placed his lips on hers, and for the first time in months, Emily tasted the flavor of another man's lips. It made her forget about Eric, but she questioned if she should've tried this remedy sooner, or if she felt positive because she was now truly ready to move on. In any event, it didn't matter since her body appreciated the contact with another human.

The kiss wrapped Emily up in pleasure; dormant moans came to life. She pulled back in fear that the other audience members would hear.

"Should we get out of here, Emily?" Zach asked out of breath.

Emily tasted her top lip. "No. We shouldn't. That won't be necessary."

"I told you, Emily, not to start something—"

"I'm not." Unsure of what came over her, Emily located his belt in the dark as her hands hastily worked to unlock his treasure. She could feel the rapid tap on her shoulder.

"Emily? Emily? What are you doing?" he whispered with concern.

"Shut up, Zach. Please." Before she knew it, Emily had easy access to his open package. Emily's fingers tugged his waistline as she signaled that she wanted Zach to lower them.

"What? Here?" The quick flash of light from the screen revealed the disbelief on his face.

Emily just tilted her head at him and bugged her eyes. Zach lifted his hips and eased his jeans down just enough to expose his excitement. Emily grinned at him and whispered, "I knew you could do it."

She lowered her thongs to her ankles and took a seat on his lap. From the corner of her eye, she watched him fumble for a condom in the dark before he donned it. Her move silenced Zach as she aligned herself with his shaft. Large hands wrapped her tiny waist as she slowly raised her body up and down. To balance her weight, she gripped her hands on the arms of Zach's chair as her heels scribbled the floor like a crayon in a happy kid's hand. Before a loud sound of satisfaction could escape, one of Zach's hands covered her mouth to muffle her. Emily's head angled as her chin tilted upward. All her cares in the world ebbed as the pleasure that Zach brought overtook the thoughts in her head.

Emily jettisoned her fear of getting caught, but as she had once heard, that only heightened the excitement. Despite the sensation that took over her mind, she had a quick realization that she would have a great tale to finally share with the girls. Maybe she would be caught. She would be the teacher who had a trashed reputation because of a lewd act. Maybe she would make the radio and the deejays would share her story to commuters in the morning rush hour. The horrible thoughts that rushed through her mind only pushed her to the edge faster. If she could sing to the top of her lungs, she would have. However, a suppressed feeling in the depths of her chest and throat would have to do. Once she realized that it was over, she jumped off his lap and left him to fend on his own. Giving him privacy, she turned her head. After hearing the release of pleasure in Zach's throat and recovering from her own peak, she shifted her glance sideways and clamped her lower lip in satisfaction.

"We gotta get outta here," he suggested while fastening his clothes.

"Sure." The movie was corny anyway, and Emily accomplished her mission. It was a good quickie.

They headed toward the exit. Emily saw a few heads turn in the dark as they left the auditorium and headed down the long hallway that lead to the exit to the main foyer.

Emily followed Zach to his Expedition in the parking lot. He eased her up and into the passenger side before he made his way to the driver side. Before he cranked the engine, he turned to her and asked, "Do we need to talk about what happened in there?"

"I got you off; you got me off. There, we talked." She faced forward.

"Emily, if you don't want me to make a big deal about it, then tell me so. But whatever you do, please don't pretend like we saw the credits scroll with an empty bag of popcorn."

Rolling her eyes with batting lashes, she turned to face him with a perfunctory smile. "Don't make a big deal about tonight."

"If that's what you want." He fumbled with his keys before inserting the right one into the ignition. Emily noted the disappointment in his voice.

"Zach, let it all sink in first, okay?"

Hastily, his eyes shot at her profile, and with an irritated tone, he asked, "Would Eric have to let it all sink in?"

Emily snapped her face in his direction and peered at him with instant anger. "That's not right and you know it. Don't you dare bring my ex-husband into this."

Zach flicked his palms up, regretting his choice of words. "Sorry, I'm sorry, Emily. I went too far. I know that now."

"You damn right." She folded her arms and averted his eyes. *How dare he?* Emily wondered why men thought they had a right to pry whenever they gave a woman an orgasm. She would be sure to keep the lines in the sand drawn and visible.

"But, Emily, I've been watching you for a while now. For months. You've been reserved, proper, and private." He pointed to the theatre. "Now you do that. When are you just going to let it go?"

"Let what go?"

"Him—the past. You've been acting out of character and I'm willing to bet it has something to do with Eric."

"I don't know what you think you're talking about. I don't care about Eric no more than you care about Heather."

"I have to care about that wench. She birthed my child. But you need to remember what you had me do to him just recently. You mean to tell me you've let him go? Because if that's letting go then what does it look like when you're holding tight?"

"Take me home now. I've had it."

Zach obeyed and eased out of the parking lot. Emily couldn't take another minute of his inanity. Which was all it was, right?

S*ummer*

The moment of confession lingered between us like a ghost that only I could see . . . sense . . . reach out to touch. It was my illusion, and mine alone—something that Oliver didn't even know existed. Except, this ghost existed in the pit of my stomach. I could feel it. It would take telling Oliver what he didn't know or seemingly suspect, to cleanse myself of the misery festering inside of me. If humans could shake courage into their systems with a shoulder jiggle and a neck roll, then at this moment, I should feel the difference.

The elevator opened, allowing us to step into our home. *Our* home. How much longer would there be luxury in saying that?

"Whew," Oliver sigh. "Nice day with you was all I needed. Still, I wish we were in New York though." He rubbed his stomach as he turned to watch me remove my shoes.

"It was a lovely day, Oliver." My grin was sincere but strained. "The best."

Oliver smiled and removed his shoes and baseball cap. "Would it be wrong to admit that I just want to take you in our bed and have Summer pussy for dessert?"

Grinning, I blushed on the inside, saying nothing. Oliver eased toward me with arms outstretched. "My pregnant princess." He placed a quiet kiss on my forehead as he squeezed my shoulders. "When this baby is out, I want us to explore our sexual wild side even more with some home props. There are some things I never got to do to you."

"What makes me so special?" I chuckled. Hopefully he would stop with the intimate comments, because chances were, I wouldn't be around to fulfill his fantasies.

"You're perfect." He kissed my cheek as a hand cupped my neck. "So sexy. I want you. I secretly watched you the entire day. You were oblivious."

I couldn't talk. Our eyes met and locked. Something was wrong, and I didn't want to hide it anymore, especially with all his enthusiasm. My hand fell on his shoulder and slid down his chest. Not knowing where I would find the strength, I abruptly blurted out, "We need to talk."

Oliver nodded once. "Okay." He stood with his hands in his pockets with his weight shifted to one side. Waiting.

My fingers rested on my hairline before sliding through the hair on top of my head. Deciding on the right words, I bunched some hair at the top with a fist, but then concluded that there were none. "Oliver." I exhaled and averted his stare of calm anticipation. Turning my focus back to his handsome face, I proceeded. "Did you ever wonder how you got me pregnant?"

Oliver chuckled. "Are-are you serious, Summer? I put it in, that's how." His expression read, "duh."

I sighed. "Honey."

This was going to be a long night. My cell phone rang from inside my purse. I snatched it from the kitchen counter. Brooke. My finger flew up to excuse myself. It was either annoying or fortunate that an interruption would occur just as my courage did.

"Hello?"

Brooke sounded upset. "I'm in Rosslyn already, and I need to see you. You're home, right?"

"But, Brooke, I'm a little busy." The sudden flashback of seeing Jackson with that woman made me dread the idea of seeing her.

"Summer, please." I heard her sniff. "It'll just be a moment."

Reluctantly, I agreed." Okay."

"Great." She hung up and I texted my address immediately. Oliver stood there patiently with a locked jaw and crossed arms.

"Is everything okay?"

"Y-yeah." I placed my phone on the counter. My thumb pointed at the elevator behind me. "Can we just talk after I see Brooke? She sounded upset and needs to talk."

"Absolutely. Hopefully she can find parking though." Oliver kissed my face. "I'm gonna go shower right quick, sweetie. It'll give you guys some privacy." He walked away.

"Oliver?" He turned around. "Thank you, baby, for everything. I do love you."

His face twisted into a confounded expression. "You say that as if I doubt it. But I do love you, too, Summer." Oliver disappeared behind our bedroom door.

How was I going to do this? I exhaled the breath that I didn't know I was holding. As Oliver showered, I decided to change into my comfy pajama set and wait for Brooke while watching television. About ten minutes later, we met at the elevator that lifted her to *our* home.

"I'm so appreciative of the time you're giving me, Summer," she admitted as she forged into the living room.

"It's no problem, Brooke. Really."

She gestured with her clutch as she spoke. "Okay, well, let me get right to the point." Her red eyes snitched that she'd been crying. Knowing Brooke, she touched herself up before coming over. "Emily's phone went straight to voicemail, so I had to intrude on you and Oliver. Otherwise—"

"Brooke, please." My hands flagged her down. "You are fine. Just tell me what I can do for you." The last thing I needed was for her to think for one moment that Oliver and I should be discussed, especially since she didn't know whether he knew my secret by now. The focus had to stay on her, so she could leave as soon as possible. It was bad enough I had to downplay my anxiety while in her presence.

She sighed, obviously a wreck. "Right. Damani and I were kissing this morning, and I called Jackson's name. He stormed off, and now I'm worried."

"What? That'll you lose him?" I wanted to warn her that she was barking up the wrong tree for help if that were the case. About to lose my man myself, I wished someone could tell me how to hang on to him.

"No. Well, yes—maybe. I'm really worried that my past with Jackson is going to haunt me and prohibit me from moving on for good." Seeing Brooke so frazzled felt odd, especially compared to the Brooke I remembered meeting the first night we'd hung out. Nothing short of grace, she projected a calm and confident lady in control. To see Brooke Brazile in a state like this really made me nervous as to what I might encounter after spilling the beans to Oliver. Speaking of Oliver, he'd just cut the shower off.

"Brooke, maybe you should have given yourself more time to heal. You were in love with him."

"But don't you think that dating someone else would speed up the process?" She looked at me as if I held a book of answers, when I was the one who played the other woman in my boss' marriage. Where was my permission to give advice?

I couldn't help but think of Jackson and the mysterious attractive woman. Then Oliver's words rang through my head. I didn't want to kill her. On the other hand, maybe Brooke needed a push in the right direction. My hands slapped my outer thighs in defeat. "I don't know, sis."

Brooke tilted her head heavenward and stretched out her arms in despair. "Argh! I would do anything to get that man out of my heart if he ain't coming back." She lowered her chin and asked me, "How long does it take to mend a broken heart? There should be a biological time limit that pumps out the last piece of love you have in your blood for another person. Look at Emily!" she suggested with wide expressive eyes. "No matter how many times that man beats her up, she can't get Eric out of her system. To this day, this man still gets the best of her."

Great. How long would Oliver be in my system then? I stood there in silence, letting her vent. Besides, there weren't any answers that I could offer. Emily really would've been the better choice here.

"That's another reason," she said, pointing her clutch at me, "that I had to choose you tonight. You and Oliver are nice and stable. Emily is not in a position to discuss love. Um-um." Brooke shook her head.

I saw Oliver hesitate before coming out of the bedroom. He looked at me and nodded, silently cuing me to tell Brooke about Jackson and the other woman.

My voice barely carried above a whisper, as I said, "Umm, Brooke?"

Pacing with a lowered head, she stopped and looked up at me upon hearing her name.

"You-you should really forget about Jackson."

"Don't you think I'm trying? What have I been saying, Summer?"

"No—really. It's for the best, because I think he's forgotten about you."

"What? Because he doesn't call, right? See, that's what I was thinking—"

"No, Brooke." My voice livened, audible and steady. I pressed my palms against my hairline. If somebody wanted to clunk me over the head right now, I'd be fine with that. The night kept getting darker and darker, and not literally either. With her full attention, it was time to take advantage. "He's got someone else." The words couldn't come out any faster.

Her back straightened when the news hit her. Trying to process my information, she turned her ear to me with squinted eyes. Pointing her hand at me, she asked, "And how do you know this, Summer?" She crinkled her forehead waiting for me to elaborate.

"Oliver and I spent the day at the National Harbor. I spotted him there with a woman. It looked intimate. He didn't see us." Closing my eyes only amplified the silence. Opening them revealed an ugly reality. Brooke tried to hide the wind that'd been knocked from within. Her hand flew over her heart as she stared away and gasped for subtle breaths. Her mouth twisted, her eyes never blinked.

"I'm sorry."

I couldn't offer her anything else. I had my own pool to swim out of and unfortunately, my burden had already left me weak with no strength to spare. I felt awful. Although my words had just devastated my friend, I couldn't help but feel positive that I'd made the right decision in telling her the truth. Here Brooke stood, pining away for a man who'd moved on. Logic would allow one to believe that since they didn't have too much history together, she should've moved on by now, that she was being ridiculous, because she didn't even have one year under her belt with the man. The same failed logic could apply to Oliver and me. We barely had six months but something about us clicked, and for that, I could totally see why time didn't always measure the feelings of the heart.

"No." A quick tear fell from her eye as she continued to stare in a glassy-eyed trance. Her eyes shifted uncomfortably about, her hand absently looked for something to balance her. It located a bar stool. Out of breath, she managed to blurt out, "I need to goooo," in a quivery voice.

Brooke was desperate for fresh air. Normally, I didn't do the touchy thing, but when any of my friends become this upset, all my isms go out the door.

"Brooke, come here." Never looking at me, with a mind disconnected from her surroundings, Brooke staggered over to me as she bled from the heart. She had just about collapsed in my arms, but I was there to catch her. With her cheek resting on my shoulder, I gripped her tightly as she recovered her strength.

"If he never comes back Brooke, don't ever feel bad for sticking to your guns. Brooke Brazile is not a settler." I peeled her from against me and gripped her by the shoulders as I looked into her devastated eyes. "But if he's meant to be, then he'll be back."

Brooke nodded in silence. Our eyes connected and, for a moment, I could see a hint of strength. I kissed her on the cheek and directed her to the elevator with my hand in hers. "If you need more time to collect yourself, stay here for as long as it takes. Please."

"No." She shook her head and squeezed my hand. "Thank you, Summer. I'll remember how you took care of me at this moment, because I would love to call a mom, but mine is no use. So, thank you and tell Oliver I said, 'hi.'"

A nod assured her that I would. My heart ached at the thought of having a deadbeat mom. I was grateful to God for mine. Everyone needed to experience having at least one good parent. But Brooke didn't have that.

I watched the independent woman who yearned to have it all crumble in despair when she realized that she couldn't conquer men like she had her career. And then I turned to face my man in the doorway as he stared at me with compassion for Brooke. I couldn't wrap my head around the fact that I was a grown woman who'd behaved like a selfish kid over the past months. My negligence may have ruined a marriage, but it was certainly about to ruin a man's love and respect for me while breaking his heart in the process. *Go, Summer!*

Amber

Finally inside the club, Amber sat on Cane's lap and bopped her head to the hip hop music with a margarita in her hand as she felt the alcohol kicking into her system. Cane wrapped his arms loosely around her as he checked out the dancing women. She leaned back against Cane to face him and yelled, "How do you like it?"

He yelled back, "The women here are hot!"

Amber rolled her eyes. *Did he really bring up the women in front of me? Who does he think he is?* "Oh! Well, did you see the men? Some of them are really packing down there!"

Not fazed at the least, he asked, "Is that what you think?"

"Well you're not the only one who can check out other people, you know!" Amber struggled to speak over the music. She gulped the rest of her margarita.

"Would you be mad if I found a hot girl to join us in bed tonight?"

Amber wasn't sure if she heard him right. "What?"

Once Cane repeated himself, Amber stared at him as if he had three arms. "Excuse me?"

He shrugged.

"Honey. You won't be thinkin' of any other pussy when you up in mine. And I don't need another woman's help to bust your nut. I got so many tricks a magician would be jealous." Amber jumped to her feet and peered down at Cane and his cocky grin.

"You're no fun," he yelled as he adjusted his collar.

Amber crossed her arms and casually replied, "What can I say? A girl can bring the steak *and* potatoes to the table. What I need your peas for?"

Cane stood up with a smirk. He leaned closely into her ear to tell her, "I think you need to find another ride home."

Appalled, Amber's mouth dropped open as her hands dropped to her hips. "You blowin' me right now. You gonna make me hail a cab?"

"It shouldn't be that hard . . . magician."

Amber's eyes frowned at him.

"Amaze yourself and find a ride. 'Xcu' me." Cane moved her with a hand and walked away.

Amber followed him and placed an angry hand on his shoulder. He spun around. "I paid for your tired ass and you mean you just gonna bounce like that? Oh, that's trash, man." She wiggled her fingers with a backward wave. "Give me back my money then."

Cane looked her up and down before he replied, "Pshhhhhh. You wish!" and walked away.

Amber really wanted to follow him and jump on his back in anger. The street girl from New York threatened to boil over and show off, risk a trip to jail tonight, but the refined woman reminded her to never try to fight a man—an ignorant man at that. Realizing that her twenty and a date were gone like a bill sucked into a cold slot machine, she decided to step outside for fresh air. Hearing her phone ring, she pulled it out of her purse.

"Hello?" she answered impatiently. The temperature had dropped, and she regretted not bringing a party coat.

"Hi, beautiful. Remember me?"

"Umm, no, you don't have it like that just yet. Drop me a name or I'm hanging up." She desperately searched her purse for a cigarette.

"We met in traffic, Amber."

"What? Traffic? I think you have the wrong person." *Damn.* No luck. All her cigarettes were gone.

"No, this is the number you gave me. You have the long wavy hair."

Confused, Amber pulled the phone away from her ear to stare at her screen. "I never met no man in traffic, and I certainly don't have long, wavy hair unless one of my wigs count."

"So, lemme guess. You weren't driving a pink Corvette that night?" He remained calm regardless of the rejection.

"What? Huh? What number were you trying to dial?" She placed her back against the brick wall of the club.

When he read off Amber's number, she realized that a dear friend must've given her number to a stranger. She sighed and shook her head. "I'm gonna kill my friend. I'm going to kill her . . ."

"Then it ain't you?"

What the hell? "Are you hot?" Amber realized that unless this man was a criminal, he certainly couldn't be any worse than a cheap, no-good-excuse of a man named Cane.

"I got muscles, a fast car, and tattoos. You?"

"I ain't never have no trouble picking up a man." The only problem seemed to be keeping them, Amber realized.

"That's what's up. What you doing tonight?"

Amber liked his voice and figured that no friend of hers would ever send an ugly man her way, so she decided to play. "I'm standing outside of a club that is over."

"It ain't even past midnight. What are you talking about?"

"It's over for me. Can you come to Northwest on F Street?"

"Yeah, I can do that but, you gotta give me about twenty minutes."

Giving time didn't drain her wallet. "Doable. Call me when you get in front of the club. Kinda car you got?"

"A green Pontiac GTO. It's an antique. Be there soon."

"All right." Amber hung up the phone and turned to the boy next to her chatting with another guy. They barely looked over twenty-one. "Hey. You got a smoke and a light?"

The two guys turned to her and grinned. They looked like skater boys with their ear-length, dirty blonde hair and super baggy pants. "Yeahhhhhhhhhh," the one against the wall replied. He reached into his pocket and handed her two cigarettes. "Since you're cute and all, have two." His eyes stared into Amber's without a flick of an eyelid. Amber reached out to take them.

"Oh, bless you, boy."

"No problem. And that light?"

Amber popped the stick into her mouth and balanced it between both lips as she nodded once with her chin.

The guy replied, "Trey, give her a light, man."

"Sure." Trey pulled out his lighter and lit Amber's cigarette.

Amber inhaled and puffed. "Awesome. Thanks guys. You are the heroes of the night."

They chuckled, and both replied, "Anytime."

They re-engaged in their conversation as Amber puffed while she studied the scenery. Many cars passed by with thumping music. The intersections and sidewalks were populated by college-aged club goers. Amber studied the way everyone dressed. No one seemed to have any fashion imagination. Coming from New York, she knew what true fashion risks looked like and she felt a lot of people everywhere else missed the mark. Most people slapped two plain garments together and called it an outfit. When they called themselves being dressed up, they tended to overdo it and, instead of making a statement, they just looked like they were ready for a business meeting. She shook her head in disapproval. Unfortunately, she found herself nearly losing her New York sense of style the longer she lived outside the Big Apple.

Finished with the cigarette, Amber decided to save the other one for a later time in the night. If the mystery man didn't smoke, she knew she'd be out of luck and wouldn't be able to bum another one. Stores? Forget about it. Finding a gas station or 7-Eleven at the drop of a hat was like looking for a needle in a haystack sometimes in DC. The nation's capital had sporadic placings of those, but the neighboring states, Maryland and Virginia, were filled with them. And gas stations and 7-Elevens were lifesavers in a tristate area that seemed to fall asleep by nine unless it was the weekend. New York never slept, but, on the contrary, the DC-Maryland-Virginia area, or the DMV as the locals called it, slept too much.

Minutes later, Amber saw a dark green antique pull up next to the curb in front of her. A bald man blasting reggaeton searched for her. Finding parking in DC was always nearly impossible, so she knew he'd parked illegally. Amber hurried over to his passenger side. He noticed her and grinned.

Not bad at all, Summer. He seemed to be somewhat tough-looking in his basic black t-shirt. She immediately noticed and adored his tattoo-clad sinewy arms.

"I'm Amber," she told him.

He grinned and replied, "Hop in."

"Heeeey, that's my jam." She stuck her tuck out, wormed her body from her hips to her shoulders and snapped her fingers to the music as it ended.

He smirked with a side eye. "Just to let you know, *mami*, I don't do handshakes off the clock." His wide mouth curled up at the ends, each lip made perfectly the same in size.

She shrugged. "Well, shiiiii, bruh. Neither do I."

Now this was more like it. So far, she liked the guy. A man with a different culture to offer sparked instant chemistry with her unlike Pharr and Cane. She'd become too comfortable with dating the same kind of men which limited her dating range. So, she appreciated Summer that much more for bringing a much-needed experience into her life. Amber mentally thanked her dear friend for the hook-up and decided to embrace the night.

He laughed. "I see you got good taste in music."

Offering the same expression back, she replied, "I see you got good taste in women."

Locking stares, they burst into laughter simultaneously. Once they gave into a high-five, he said, "Let's roll."

The man she'd never met cut the tires with a few rotations of the steering wheel and eased into traffic. Amber subtly tasted her lips with a tongue slide the minute his muscle flinched like an eye wink, made to taunt her like dessert to a dieter.

"Where do you live?"

Grateful for the question, it interrupted her lust down Fantasy Lane. "Maryland. Takoma Park. But I'm about to move to my aunt's house in Arlington."

"You playin'. Does everyone I know live in Arlington? Maybe I should move there, too."

He grinned. "Nah, my aunt is getting back with my uncle, but her lease won't be up. She can't afford to break it. She has a whole year left. I live with my big family and need my own place. So I'ma move in her home and work it out at the end of the year. I'ma live in Arlington where the *Español* be poppin'."

"Not in Ballston?"

"Nah, I can't do Ballston. Too uppity for my taste."

Amber noticed that he drove toward the Maryland border. She didn't care. Starved for adventure, Amber welcomed the mystery, especially in the dark. She didn't even know the man's name! This was who she was—a woman who lived with reckless moments of unplanned adventure. Trying to be a straight arrow led her to dead-end zones of boredom. The thought alone of being a little bad with a hot man of a different culture struck a horny chord within her vagina.

"It's not that bad. My friend lives there. It's really nice and she loves it."

"I like a little roughness going on. Makes me remember where I came from."

Amber laughed. "I know what you mean. I try to fit in, but I hate it. I like being who I am."

"Represent then. Represent."

At times, the wind would pick up and push into them like New Yorkers on Fifth Avenue.

"You cold, *mami*?" His brown eyes effortlessly upheld sexiness even while being soft.

"*Mami,* again?" Amber laughed. "I like that. I'm good."

Those sultry eyes brushed her up and down from behind a high arm that steered them left. "That, you are."

Amber did her best to ignore her giggling vagina. *Behave, girlie. Stop pulsating.* "So, where you from?"

"From Mexico to Maryland . . . Yo, we goin' to Maryland. *¿Ta bien?*"

Amber's brows pinched in confusion. "Huh?"

Chuckling, he clarified. "My bad. Is that all right with you?"

Sexy, sexy. She nodded with a grin. "Sure. Drive me back though?" In fact, he could drive her anywhere. With looks that sent silent messages down below, who cared?

"When?" He took quick glances at her as he drove.

"We'll see what the night holds. You still live in the house of family members though, right? And we going there tonight?"

"Yup and yup. Only if you good with that."

Amber smiled. "I'm a New Yorker. I can handle it."

He looked intrigued. "Oh, *si*? I figured with that accent of yours."

"*Si*. I'm starting to miss it though. The more I try to do the right thing down here, the more I realize how much I miss it."

"Where you livin' now?"

"Southwest."

"Close to the hood, huh?" he teased.

Amber laughed. "I'm down the street from a rough section. But it's all right. I'm used to the rough life. I just feel like I ain't makin' progress in life being a piano teacher and performer, you know? But what about you? What do you do?"

"I temporarily work in an auto body shop part time."

"No college? I hate college, too."

"Huh?" he looked at her with a slightly furrowed brow. "No, I went. I got my bachelor's. Don't let the tattoos fool you now," he joked with a chuckle. "I graduated top of my class at the University of Maryland. I also work part time at a law firm. You don't have a degree?"

"What?" Amber was surprised. She felt like she just couldn't escape overachievers if she wanted to. Did everyone think she was a loser or something? "No, I hated school. High school was it for me."

"Why would you hate college? You need an education, *nena*."

"I . . . no, I . . . I find studying boring. What'd you study?"

"Political Science."

"*Shit*. What can you do with that?"

"Be a lawyer. I live with family because instead of paying rent, I've been saving for law school. I don't wanna have a lot of student loans, plus the law firm will pay for half my tuition. So why wouldn't I go? But I gotta take what I got and go. I start school this fall if I'm accepted."

"How'd you end up working with your hands?"

"Hmm. I love using my hands, I'm good at it. My cousin—God rest his soul—started teaching me at the age of five how to work on cars. But when I got into school, the law intrigued me."

Silent, Amber thought for a moment. *Is everyone doing better than me?* Sure, she'd left the money-for-sex lifestyle alone, but where was the payoff aside from her newfound dignity? Amber couldn't believe that she'd hopped into the car of another man who wasn't what he appeared to be. It occurred to her that these Washingtonian jokers were slick. No matter what, a successful career seemed paramount. Most women would be happy to keep finding men with advanced goals, but she felt silly for almost wanting an underachiever.

What does this mean? Am I an underachiever? And if she was, why did she have qualms about leaving that status?

Almost scared to talk, Amber asked, "Where you gonna go?"

"Georgetown. I've made that my aim for years. I aced the LSAT. It was tough, but I did my thing. Now I gotta see what the university says."

Amber wanted to choke. This man unloaded many surprises. "What the hell is the LSAT?"

"Law School Admissions Test. It's one of the deciding factors for admitting applicants."

"How old are you?"

"Twenty-six."

"I thought you said you hated the uppity stuff?"

"I love the law, and I gotta make a living. Firms can be full of stuffy people, and some are cool and friendly, but that's money on the line. It is what it is. I don't wanna come home to it though."

Amber nodded without saying anything. Instead, she observed the sights on the other side of the window as they turned into a neighborhood of old houses—split level and two stories. Even the dark couldn't hide the age of the vinyl-sided homes. Street lights illuminated the overgrown lawns and driveways crammed with multiple cars. On the same street of his house, they'd already passed a residence with a group of men drinking from a paper bag, talking while heads bobbed to music from the car on which they sat. Car hoods became stools and bumpers footstools. They always had to know who came through so when her date's car coasted by, the men's eyes held contact with Amber's until they were faced with taillights of the green muscle car. But between her old neighborhood in New York and her prior residence in Southeast, this was familiar to Amber and frankly quite comforting. At least she felt unjudged and within her element. Hell, she could hop out his car and walk right up to those men and just kick it. But with one turn of the wheel, that possibility flew out the window once he eased into a pothole-ridden, concrete driveway that led to a hunter green home.

Amber squinted and pointed ahead of her. "Your house is green, right?"

"Yup." He smirked.

"Okay, what's with you and green?"

"Right?" They unbuckled their seat belts.

Amber had a thought. "Hey, ummm, will I be the only sista up in there? I mean, no one else has a chocolate lover or something in there?"

He snickered. "Just you. No lovers, no chocolate. Don't worry, you'll be fine. *Mujer*, I got you."

Amber's expression turned naughty. "With those muscles, I'm sure you do. Where your room at?"

"In the basement. I know, grown man living with the fam but in the basement. Typical. Right?"

Amber didn't say anything. She really didn't care if he slept on the roof. It wasn't like she was trying to marry him. Didn't even know his name nor did she care. She just wanted to get laid. Besides, she knew she was in no position to be judgmental. So, she just told him, "Doesn't matter to me. I'm done with being brand new."

When they climbed out, he grabbed her by the hand. They made their way to the front of his house. She prayed that they could bypass the upper level, go around to the back, and enter that way. Certainly, he had an alternate access that was more convenient for her. But at the end of the day, she didn't scare that easily. In fact, it felt like old times. Boy, did she miss her native home.

Her mysterious man opened the front door with a set of keys. Though before the house appeared dark in the front, the party of relatives hollered in the back. Of course, she thought, as she rolled her eyes. She wouldn't have been that lucky to go unseen. As they eased down a dimly lit hallway, Amber could smell food . . . something like tortilla and lime. Though she had eaten earlier with that loser of a neighbor, she could almost eat again. Her olfactory nerve woke up and she thanked the Lord for being in the home of people who actually cooked. The tasty smell teased her appetite.

Voices rose and fell as music in Spanish played in the background. Amber hadn't any idea of the genre. He whispered to her, "Country Mexican music. I know a certain someone is up."

Amber smiled and bobbed her head. "It's okay. Life ain't all about hip hop either. It's good to hear different music."

Amber chuckled and stopped as they bent the corner and entered the kitchen. A man in a ribbed white tank top sat at the table with two young females. She couldn't help but notice his very protruding stomach and heavy mustache. He held a Corona in his hand with a lime wedged on the rim as he exclaimed, "Heeeeeeeeyyyyy!" once he saw Amber's friend. The two other women just looked up and grinned at Amber's new friend, before shifting their gazes at her. They both leaned on the table with folded arms as they chatted with the man.

The skinny girl with straight brunette hair that swept over her breasts appeared to be in her low twenties. "Hey, stupid. *Tío* is talking bad about you. He says you shouldn't go to college."

The girl smiled at the man she called "stupid," but didn't bother to acknowledge Amber. Maybe she was used to him bringing home random chicks, or maybe they didn't want to see a black woman there, Amber considered. The slightly overweight girl just glanced up now and then as she played with her iPhone. Amber doubted that they were sisters. The overweight girl had black, wavy hair that was around the same length as the skinny girl, but she was cute at the least.

Amber's friend just told the girl, "Whatever, Jalissa. Hey, this is my friend, Amber."

Jalissa barely waved when she said a lazy, "Hiiiiiii." Her eyes darted from Amber to *tío*. "You should just go to bed, *tío*," she nearly demanded. Pretty, but likely immature, Amber noted.

"*Tío* and Pilar, this is Amber."

Pilar, the chubby one, glanced up for a second to say, "Hey, Amber. Nice to meet you."

"Thank you, Pilar. Nice to meet you, too."

Tío looked at Amber from head to toe with a smile. "Ah! *Beuno! Ella es muy bonita!*" He offered his hand to Amber, to which she shook, and told him, "Nice to meet you, *tío*."

Jalissa snickered. Amber's friend whispered, "*Tío* means 'uncle' in Spanish. You can call him that, but his name is Raul."

Amber whispered back, "Ohhh, I see," as Jalissa took furtive glances at them with a smirk. Amber watched Raul take another long sip of his Corona.

"Also, he says that you're very pretty."

She knew about five words in Spanish. *"Gracias."*

Raul turned his head to look at her to smile with a nod.

"All right then. I'ma catch you guys later," her friend told them as he placed a hand on the small of Amber's back.

"Nice to meet you guys," Amber said before she left the kitchen with him.

Jalissa said something to Pilar in Spanish. They chuckled.

Amber didn't worry about it. Either it was about her or not, but she didn't care. If Jalissa couldn't say it in English, then Amber wouldn't reward Jalissa's lack of bravery with any further attention. Passing through a living room lit by a lamp, a man emerged from the hallway. Amber wasn't used to fine living herself, but with wood panel walls and brown carpet, she knew that the room needed a makeover. The room existed in simplicity with just a few pieces of furniture. A pattern of flowers covered the yellow sofas. Yikes! Amber cringed. She wondered if she'd entered a time machine via the living room and just wasn't aware of it. Even with the smell of tortilla wafting through the air, she could still smell a slight scent of something worn and dated. Maybe the carpet? Whatever it was, Amber couldn't wait to pass through the room. She could only hope that his room in the basement didn't smell like that as well.

The man who emerged called out, "Crisanto! Man, where have you been today? We were trying to go fishing."

So, his name was Crisanto, Amber realized. That sounded beautiful to her as she eyed him sideways with a raised eyebrow with hands clasped behind her back.

"Nah, man, I had things to do." The two men locked hands and gave each other a tap on the back. "I couldn't leave the shop before six anyway."

"Man, that shop be working you." The guy's eyes shifted to Amber.

Crisanto picked up on it and said, "Oh, this is Amber, my new friend. Amber, this is Luz, my cousin."

Luz appeared to be friendly as he held out a hand for Amber to shake. Like Crisanto, she noticed that he didn't have an accent at all. That disappointed her. "How you doin', Amber? Nice to meet you. Cris is a good guy here. Hard worker, too."

Amber giggled. "Nice to meet you, too, Luz. So far, he seems good. But hey," she shot Crisanto a wicked look, "anything can happen."

"Wow." Luz ran a hand through his buzzed-cut head. "On that note, I'ma leave you two alone then."

"All right, Luz, check you later." They locked hands once more before heading in opposite directions.

"Hey, Amber." Amber turned to look at Cristanto. "Call me, Cris, please. Crisanto is just too much. He does it to be funny, but he knows I hate it."

"Cool. No problem." Amber nodded.

Cris grinned and placed his hand on the small of her back and led her to the door on the other side of the living room. The smell of tortilla transitioned into a neutral smell, and the sounds of Jalissa and Raul slowly disappeared, along with the Mexican country music. Amber eased down the old wooden stairs first, as Cris followed from behind. Once she reached the landing at the bottom of the stairs, she turned to wait for Cris. She noticed an open space with couches and a generous-sized flat screen. Two hallways offered to take them away from the living room, but Cris pointed to the one right across from them.

"There."

Amber followed his finger as she felt his hand on the small of her back again. He guided her body to the last door on the left. "Right here."

Cris turned his doorknob that led to a dark and well-scented room. As he reached for the light, Amber told him, "Don't."

Turning to face her, Cris hesitated. "What's up?"

"I don't want you to do that. I wanna just lay in bed beside you."

"Lie."

"Excuse me?" Amber was confused.

"Lie. You said you wanna lay in bed beside me, but, uh, you should say lie in bed." Sensing that Amber wasn't amused, Cris added, "I-I'm sorry. Sometimes I feel that people can't take me for a hidden nerd with muscles and tattoos who works on cars with a love for the law."

Amber grinned with a stressed forehead. "Well, I prefer that you let me believe that you're dumb as a rock with sexy muscles."

Cris chuckled to himself. "We can lie together."

"About what?" she asked.

"Huh?" Cris grinned. "No, I mean on the bed."

Amber sighed to herself. Was she in over her head again? She was with the walking dictionary. Before that she was with a self-centered, broke jerk in a suit and before him she was with a young man with dirty nails who turned out to have deep pockets. Getting to know a man instead of hiding behind the exchange of sex for money proved to be harder than it appeared. Men were full of contradictions these days, and frankly, it convinced Amber that her old method of male interaction wasn't as bad as going through this trouble to connect with men on a genuine level. At least her superficial interactions with men never left her feeling down on herself. She felt empowered and in control. The difficulty with dating came when it forced her to hold a mirror up to herself. Then she believed, she didn't measure up. But why?

"Right."

Amber slid her feet out of her shoes and chose one side of his bed. Cris slid next to her, shoulder to shoulder. In the dark, they lay as they stared at the ceiling.

"So, you thought my friend in the Corvette was cute?"

"She was hot. Her car made her stand out. I like cars but when I saw a hot girl driving it, that was even better. But I think you're hotter. Don't tell her."

Amber giggled. "Scout's honor—I won't."

"Why'd she do that? Why didn't she give me her number?"

"Relax. Don't bother puttin' a Band-Aid on that bruised ego of yours. She got a man."

"Oh. Well, this little hook-up she did paid off."

"You think? I think so."

"Yeah . . . I do. So, you live alone, right?"

"I do. My sister is a freshman at Columbia University and lives there."

"Wow. Smart girl. You sure you not as bright as her?"

Amber fell silent. She hated talking about the past. It hurt too much. "I didn't do too bad on my SATs," she confessed.

Cris turned his neck to face her. "You playin'?"

Amber chuckled. "I know, lie and lay, don't nobody really know that shit. The fact is, I did better in math than literature and all, but I was aight. I lost a few marks with the language part. I mean, I'm a girl from Harlem who stayed in the streets. But for real I did good enough to choose a geeky school. Now I'm like, dumb as a doorknob. Spent too much time worrying about money."

Intrigued, his eyebrows pinched when he asked, "Then why'd you skip college, Amber?" His eyes studied her face, hers the ceiling. She couldn't face him. Mara didn't even know that Amber's SAT score reflected a promising entry to college.

"This stays between us." She saw him nod. "I'm just lazy. But now I can see that laziness don't pay off. I never wanted to do the work in school. I enjoy short cuts since I'm a fast learner, but that made me cocky and lazy." She crossed her hands on top of her chest.

"Why you think that is?"

She shrugged. "I get bored easily. I know in middle school, I was ready to grow up and pay bills. My parents never saw my full potential. I didn't apply myself. They knew they had two brilliant children. Teachers warned my parents about my potential and pretty much told them that I held myself back. I did just enough in school to keep from gettin' ass whoopins and banned from hanging out. My triflin' ass stayed doin' my math homework on the bus." She sighed and flung a dismissive hand. "I didn't worry or care about college, and my dad didn't have the time to push us though. Bills were the topic and priority. Money got all the attention in my family, ever since I was a tiny tot. In my little head, I thought I could adult better than my mom and dad. Like they were doing it all wrong. In my little eyes, they made it harder than it looked. Mara, my sister, she was different though. She loved to study."

"I'm sure your parents are proud of you now. Maybe you should tell them about your SATs."

"I wish I had told my dad and coulda told my mom. My sister is all I have left. In middle school, my mom was a crime victim, and my father had a heart attack not too long ago."

"Damn. I'm sorry, Amber. For real." Cris turned on his side and placed a palm on her stomach.

"Thank you." She tapped a finger on top of her other hand. "She died in the late spring of eighth grade. Yeah, in high school, it was hard to focus without her, but I managed. I almost dropped out in ninth grade, but I couldn't let Mara see me do that. My dad woulda kicked me out, too." Amber paused before turning on her side to face him.

Cris shook his head and grimaced. "I call him *tío,* but Raul is my father." He shrugged.

Surprised, her eyebrows raised. "Why you call him that?"

"I'm not too proud of my dad. But, a lot of people call him *tío*, and at times I find myself doing it, too. You'd never know that I got my brains from him. But he pissed his intelligence away with alcohol."

"Really?" Now it was Amber's turn to be intrigued. "What was he like before the alcohol?"

"Ummm, I never really remembered a time when he didn't drink, but it got worse over the years. He used to be a financial advisor. My dad let work get in the way. Then when my mom and dad started having problems, she turned to another man. It ruined him. The more he drank, the worse he performed and now, he just drinks. He's a broke ass who killed his potential. He was on top of the world."

"Ain't that how we all start?"

"My mom couldn't stand being in this house. She moved to be alone in an apartment in Silver Spring."

"That's deep, Cris. I'm sorry to hear about that."

"Nah, nah. I'm used to this crap."

"Parents . . . They're either dead or divorced."

"Dead while alive," he added with a bitter snicker.

Amber agreed with a, "Tuh."

There was silence for a moment before Cris asked, "How old are you?"

"What do you think?" She grinned. Amber shifted her stare to his face.

"High twenties."

"Bingo. I'll be thirty in April. Too old for ya'?"

"No. I could use a woman with a few more years on her than me," he teased.

"Good. I got some things I can teach you." Amber placed a hand on his jaw line then down to his neck.

"*Quiero aprender.*" He lowered his full lips to hers. She didn't know what he said, but it sounded good to her.

When their lips touched, Amber felt the quiver rattle from her stomach to her vagina. Amber loved the way Cris' hand felt as it caressed her from her midsection down to her upper thigh and under the hem of her mini skirt. Both hands cradled his jaw and neck as his hand explored her butt. The power of a thong, Amber thought. His hand moved from under her skirt to under the plunging V-neckline of her blouse. Without a bra to fight with, Cris' hand squeezed each sensitive nipple, sending a tingle downward that her pussy could feel. Amber moaned as the younger man climbed on top of her. She didn't want him to stop torturing her tightened nipples as she realized that she could kiss him forever. His lips were like no other man's. Maybe because he knew what to do with them set him apart from the others.

A jarring sound at the door made her jump. "Cris! Cris! Open the door! I need help getting your father upstairs!" Amber knew it was Jalissa. *What a jerk.*

Straddling her body, Cris peeled his t-shirt from his muscular body. Amber managed to see a six-pack abdomen in the dark with some writing on it. He hastily tossed his shirt to the side before his face approached hers once more to kiss. Jalissa relentlessly pounded on his door.

She really hated to break off their passionate lip and tongue engagement, but Jalissa threatened their moment. Out of breath, Amber asked, "You need to get that?"

"Ignore her. My dad does this crap all the time. They can work it out while I work you out."

Cris continued what they'd started by tasting her full lips, brushing each lip with a lick, tasting each one with a naughty, gentle clamp. He removed her top and yanked off her mini skirt, leaving Amber on top of his comforter wearing nothing but a thong.

Sitting up and taking in the sight of Amber's nearly nude body, Cris mumbled, "My pin-up girl just came to life," right as he removed his jeans.

"Cris! Cris!" Jalissa banged on the door. "Open up you jerk."

"Let's give her something to hear if she wants to stick around for the performance," he said.

"Oh, I can perform." And in a sexy tone she added, "But let's make sure it's real." Cris covered her lips with his and soon, Jalissa was no longer a factor. Cris retrieved his protection from the nightstand beside Amber before ripping her thongs away from her hips. Bending over her again, he parted her legs and dived in with his tongue.

Cris' tongue explored her lips and then painted her walls before rolling up to Amber's pleasure point. Her midsection wiggled under his taste, her fists gripped the sheets as her eyes rolled up in her head. She wanted to speak Spanish but didn't know any. The few words she did know would be too silly to mumble. He couldn't do anything with '*hola*' or '*dinero*.' She decided to stick to her English and sounds of excitement as he slowly lapped his tongue against her pussy.

Amber swung a leg over the back of his neck, securing him into her nest of love. He gripped her by the outside of her thighs and continued to submerge himself into her sea of treasures. Cris didn't stop until she came. When she did, her leg dropped from his neck, her hips shot up, her back arched with her feet, and she cried out under the intensity of his work. Biting down on her lower lip, Amber's hand shot out and repeatedly whacked his bed before calming down. Cris raised his head and wiped his tongue across her stomach with his shiny lips. Sitting up, he donned the condom before pushing himself into her; Amber cried out.

He wanted her badly, that much she knew. He'd become aggressive, torrid, in fact, driven with need, a desire to conquer. And Amber wanted to be conquered, ravished, thrown all over the bed. Amber wanted him to bang her out so hard for all the weeks of missed action, that she'd struggle to walk. She loved how he threw her calves over his shoulders before lowering himself closely to her. Hovering above her, Cris worked it out as the top of her thighs kissed her stomach and her knees her breasts. After a few minutes of Cris sliding in and out of her, he straightened to remove her legs and slapped her on the side of her thigh.

"Get on your knees."

Amber nodded, and when she moved, her pussy farted. She knew he made her body proud. It'd been a while since anyone had awakened her vagina. Though she felt confident that he heard it, she didn't care. Men knew a good sound when they heard it.

Happy that she had a man who took charge, he waited for her to settle into position before plunging into her from behind. Cris steadied her with his palms pressed into her hips before ramming into her from behind.

"Yeah, Daddy. Go, *papi*, go! Work it!" She moaned and begged. "*Papi*, please! Ohhh! Do it! Oh, *papi*! Tear this shit up!"

"You wanna go to Mexico, huh?" He smacked her butt with a hard whack. It sent a harsh bolt of a stinging sensation through her butt to her vagina.

"Take me to Mexico, baby!"

"I'ma take you to Mexico with this big dick. Gimme some of that Big Apple, *mami*."

Moaning loudly, Amber said, "Yeahhhhh, you give me some of that auto shop dick."

Thrusting into her repeatedly, he replied, "Don't let me tune you up, girl." He placed his hand along her jawline and down to her throat and squeezed around it. Amber knew this was her man. Maybe not commitment-wise, but just to be her go-to, if nothing else.

"Mmmm." He'd strained her voice at this point. "You like to rotate tires. How about you rotate this pussy?" Regardless, she made sure he heard her.

"I'ma tour your city, all right."

He squeezed her neck tighter and grabbed her by the arm with the other. Once Cris anchored his body into her, he pushed harder into her backside. He was a rough one for sure, and she knew this dick would be trouble. It may be the one to have her biting her nails at one in the morning. She hadn't felt this threatened since Harlem. Rich men in Virginia and DC had the pockets, but if crossing the border meant getting that good stuff, that good loving, then she'd go to Maryland anytime.

Why didn't any of those hoes tell me Maryland had the good meat? I'm done with District dick.

Feeling her breathing run short and her internal supply next to nothing, she knew she'd hit a danger zone. Without saying a word as she began to feel lightheaded, Cris went in harder during his last two pumps and released his hand when he came with a few grunts.

Immediately, Amber fell flat and rolled over, coughing. Cris ripped her legs apart and placed his fingers into her to finish her off for a second orgasm. Somewhere between pain and pleasure, she enjoyed the sensation as she swallowed and rubbed her throat. With the orgasm just right there, her eyes shut down as the last thing she read across his stomach said, 'Pain for Pleasure.'

Damn right. She rolled her eyes in her head with fluttering eyelids as she grabbed the sheets once more.

She'd wanted to do this with Cane tonight. Even her "come hither" outfit didn't make a jerk like Cane behave. Perhaps Cane didn't take her seriously because of it. In any event, it just didn't matter, because she was happy that one friend's move allowed Cris to come into her life. Amber didn't know how long it would last, but she sure did enjoy it for the night. And if this was what going to Mexico felt like, then *adiós* America!

Summer

Brooke was gone, and I was here, standing in the middle of our living room, wanting to cry out for help. "I don't want to talk about Brooke, Oliver. Not right now." He eased his way toward me.

"Okay, baby, I want to know what she interrupted between us."

I'd reached the point of no return, so I had to blurt it out. "This baby."

"What about this baby?" Oliver didn't seem concerned. He seemed suspicious, and almost prepared to be let down. I couldn't chalk it up to paranoia.

"Have you ever wondered how you got me pregnant? I asked earlier."

"Again, I put it in you."

"Oliver, stop it!" I snapped. Oliver jerked his head back at my explosion. How could he be so dense? Was it a joke? "We never went without a condom. And you always checked it afterwards. Did you ever see a leak and never tell me?"

Through gritted teeth he replied, "No, Summer. I didn't." He'd grown angry now. "Did you cheat on me and never tell me?"

"Cheat? No, Oliver. Why would I want to do that?" A flash of me confiding in him about sleeping with a married man made me realize that I didn't want to go there, so I waved a hand at him and replied, "Never mind, don't answer that." He shrugged. I decided to calm down because, after all, I was in the wrong, not Oliver. And it would've been careless of me to endanger my baby with heated emotions. "Oliver." My hands rested on my belly.

"What, Summer?" He glared at me with pain in his eyes. "If you have something to tell me, just say it."

"I don't know how to do this," I cried. Tears welled up and my voice quivered. My eyes rolled upward as a silent prayer to God to assist me with my confession to the man I loved. "Oliver, I had one night of unprotected sex with Ruben. He and I had sex . . ."

"What? What, Summer?" His demand to know more sounded far from a question. I noticed his balled fists at his side. I had pushed this man too far so many times. Tonight, might've been the last straw.

That dreadful nugget developed in my throat. My chest turned hot and strained. "Oliver, remember the night you rescued me from Fran's house?"

"Yeah, what about it, Summer?" There was a flicker of fire in his eyes. A vein of stress attacked his temple.

My finger directed his eyes to his fireplace. "We sat there and drank hot chocolate, and I confessed something to you. But I left something out because I thought it would be something irrelevant, and I saw no reason to rub it in your face."

"Spit it out." His lips turned downward, the frown lines started to form on his face. I didn't know who or what I was getting. Scared, I'd never seen this kind of look on Oliver before. I could only believe that I'd always be safe, no matter what.

"The same night I met you, was the last night I had sex with Ruben. It was the only time that he didn't put on a condom. You and I stopped using condoms weeks later after meeting. But that night, he made it hard for me to get away and—"

"Did that bastard rape you?" Oliver's lips twisted in fury. His shoulders bulged at the idea that he may have to rearrange someone's face.

"*What?*" My chest heaved. "No, Oliver, no he didn't. He came on to me and I tried to resist, but—"

Bitterly, Oliver tried to guess. "It was a *another forbidden* moment." He threw his hands up. "Am I right? Is there something forbidden about us?" He eyed me suspiciously. "If-if we're not forbidden enough, you gonna walk?"

"Oliver, please stop." No amount of imploring eased my anxiety. I patted my chest with cheap conviction. "I have grown and matured since then."

"Oh, give me a break, Summer! You haven't *grown*," he declared with eyes full of disgust. "Are you saying something about this baby not being mine? Do I have to put it bluntly for *you*?"

I didn't have the heart to confirm it with a nod or with words, but only through silence and a dead stare into his eyes. "The timing matches the night he and I last had sex."

Oliver stood with fists resting on his sides, without averting my eyes. The mouth that would never hesitate to smile at me now turned downward in disgust. Gone were the smiling eyes, nothing but disdain. At a loss for words, I just stood there, feeling as though an apology at this point would mock the situation.

After the stillness between us, he finally murmured, "Look at you. You don't know how to fix your own mess, because we know at this point words can't even suffice."

I literally felt embarrassed. The carefree girl had gone too far. I was a child having a child, and that hurt to admit. Clearing my throat, my eyes dropped to the floor.

"Summer Stevenson, look at me." I couldn't until he yelled, "Look at me!" I jumped. "You knew the day you came home with the news that this baby wasn't mine, right?"

Though it was hard, I didn't want to be yelled at again, so I nodded vehemently with a weak, "Yes."

"So, why didn't you tell me that?"

"Because when I'd finally mustered the courage to tell you that I was pregnant, you went off on the deep end with excitement about being a dad. Had you seen the sparkle in your eyes, you would've seen how cruel it woulda been to take that joy away from you."

"Summer." He exhaled. "That is one weak excuse, you know that? I woulda rather you stole one moment of happiness from me than a build-up of joy." When he put it that way, it made more sense than trying to work it all out in my head. I watched him shake his head at me in disbelief. His attitude toward me stabbed me in the heart.

"Is all you want to do is play with other people's lives? You're good at shittin' where you sleep. Do you want to ruin people? Are you that much of a loner that you live to keep it that way?" He became relentless, like an animal had taken over him. "I mean, you are selfish. Look at what you just did to your friend. You told her about her ex knowing she couldn't take it." Was he really blaming me after signaling me to tell her? "You just had to get that off your chest even if it meant hurting someone else, even when I warned you to let it be."

I was either astonished or confused. "What?" I could barely talk. "You told me to tell her with a nod. I saw it!"

"I nodded to let you know that I could tell that you needed more time with her. I don't think you should have told her that kind of information with a heart that fragile."

"You're being a hypocrite! You just told me not to spare your joy, and now you tell me that I shouldn't have been honest with my own friend?"

"A-ha!" He laughed bitterly but with amusement. "How rich is this? You couldn't wait to be honest with her, but you shoved what was best for me to the side for weeks. Amazing, Summer! Just amazing."

"She needed to know that she should move on, Oliver. That's the only reason why I told her so fast. I didn't want to smash her with that knowledge tonight."

Oliver tsked a rapid finger at me. "Summer, you need to realize that you are not God. People like you are nothing more than puppet masters, trying to make people dance to your rhythm."

Feeling the emotions rushing to my face, I exploded into tears with my face in my hands without expecting nor deserving a touch of comfort. Though it seemed useless, I had to stand up for myself with one last plea. My hands flew outward as I cried, "I'm sorry!" The tears splashed onto my bosom. "I'm sorry, Oliver! I'm sorry! Please, don't hate me!"

Tapping his foot, he clenched his jaw as he looked away and back at me. He fought back tears. I certainly didn't want to see him cry, but at least I knew that hatred didn't consume all his emotions.

"You know . . ." Thinking, Oliver wiped his chin before speaking. "You used to warn me that you weren't the relationship type." Staring at me, his eyes hardened. "And it shows."

I shook my head, a quick cry shot from my lips, mucus eased onto my upper lip. "No, Oliver. No, I love you." My chest became too heavy to support. It caved under pressure like a criminal under interrogation. My spine wore thin, brittle like hair in the battle of a windy autumn day. The weight in my head no longer dense, became as light as nonexistence. By the grace of God, I stood . . . weary, worthy of nothingness. In a moment of despair, I found all my love for Oliver, a little too late, but deep nonetheless.

"Summer, I need to get away. I'm going for a ride on my motorcycle."

What? He had a motorcycle? I wiped profusely at my tears and tried to clear my voice. "What motorcycle? You never told me you owned a motorcycle."

He snarled at me. "Well, I guess you're not the only one who has secrets, huh?" He reached into the closet near the front door and yanked a motorcycle jacket and helmet from the top shelf. Without looking back, he headed toward the front door.

"Be careful," I warned through tears and a broken voice.

Turning to me with a frown, he said, "Ohhhh, I think we passed careful a long time ago."

The untamable panic within nearly destroyed my knees. "When will you be back?" Instead, he shut the door and left me there all alone.

I wanted my dad. For the first time, I understood what it was like to yearn for and need a father. It took seeing the man I love walk out that door, to understand that something about me, never allowed a man to stick around.

I had no one to blame but myself.

5: missing you

Brooke

Two weeks had passed since Brooke decided against contacting Damani after he'd stormed out of her house. Nothing in Brooke's life felt right. Her career had lost some of the ability to fulfill her like it once had. Now she was beginning to see that independence wasn't everything. Sitting on her window ledge, Brooke jumped down when she heard the doorbell ring.

She knew who it was because she'd invited her friends over. An open door revealed two of her close friends, Amber and Emily. They barged in and hugged in a huddle as the door shut behind them. Brooke never knew just how much she loved her friends, until a thread of their fabric had begun to unravel.

"Come in, guys," she told them somberly. They all headed to her living room. "Sit."

Distraught, Emily and Amber sat on the sofa while Brooke sat in her new chair and a half. She sighed. "I don't know where to begin."

"This is terrible," Emily stated.

Amber shook her head as tears fell down her eyes. "I miss Summer so much. When I needed someone to talk to, she was always there. And now that I finally found a man to brag about, she's not even here to hear about it."

Emily held her temples. "I don't even know what Oliver is thinking. I call his phone, and he won't pick up. Did he even get to find out that she was *not* carrying his child?"

Brooke sighed. "I remember the last night I saw her. She sounded so stressed, but she put her troubles to the side just to help me out. Every time I go back to Oliver's, he never answers the door."

Emily sniffed. "Poor guy. He must be worse off than us."

Amber shouted, "They were in love. They were so lucky to have one another."

Brooke stood up. "Okay. Let's go kill some mystery. Get up. Who wants to drive?"

Emily responded, "Well, I have my jeep."

Amber said dryly, "Are you kiddin' me? You know it's you or Emily."

Brooke raised her hand. "Well I can. Let's go. This is just absurd, and we need to find out what's going on with Oliver. Summer would've never done something like this to us. I'm going to either hug or kill him."

Brooke pounded her fist on Oliver's door. Emily whispered in her slight raspy tone, "See, I don't think he will answer."

Brooke jerked her head back to tell Emily, "Don't be so negative. We will stay here all night if we have to. Just because Summer is gone, I don't think he would move out."

Amber offered her opinion. "Some people don't like staying behind with memories. When my father died—"

Emily and Brooke shot a look at Amber and just as they were about to speak, the door flew open. Oliver squinted as he stood there. The once-handsome man looked a mess. The new presence of a beard proved that he hadn't shaved in some time. Brooke knew he was distraught, so she acted on impulse and gave him a hug. Oliver accepted the hug with his palms up before he allowed himself to hug Brooke back. Following Amber and Brooke inside, Emily moved to keep the door from hitting her as it closed.

"Oh, Oliver. I'm so happy to see you again. I was wondering how you were doing," Brooke cried. When she pulled away, she stared at him with her hands placed on his shoulders. "Why haven't you answered your phone? Why haven't you answered your door?"

He shrugged. "Working hard under stress. Can I get you guys anything?"

"Yes," Brooke replied firmly. "The truth."

Oliver rubbed his head and dropped his hand. "You guys don't know what happened to Summer?"

They shook their heads in unison. Oliver replied, "Just sit." He pointed at his sofa set. "Right there." He followed them and took the sofa chair. He leaned forward with wide legs and rested his elbows on each one. Before he could talk, he looked at them and explained, "Brooke, the night you came over to see her was the last night I saw her." His eyes were glassy. A tear fell. "If I could take back all of the terrible things I said to her, maybe I could sleep just one wink. One." He measured an inch with a thumb and index finger.

Amber's face contorted with anger. "Are you more worried about your sleep than Summer?"

"Amber, stop," Emily pleaded. "The man is distraught."

With a voice above a whisper, Brooke asked, "So why did you say mean things to her?" With eyes wide open and glued on him, Brooke waited for an answer as a tear fell down her face. Her finger tapped the arm of the sofa.

"Summer had me believing that that baby of hers was mine."

When they didn't seem shocked, Oliver squinted suspiciously and said, "But wait. I guess you guys already knew before she told me, huh?"

"Yes," Brooke admitted. Brooke felt the need to defend her friend since she wasn't there to do it for herself. "The night we met at the diner—that night she came home late— she confided in us. Oliver, I'm not saying it made it right, but Summer was scared. She loved you, man. She told us that she had to do it. Summer wasn't proud to have another man's baby in her stomach."

With devastated eyes, Oliver met her stare. "And what if she's with that man now? Hmm? What if she decided to run off with that loser Ruben? She always told me how she found it hard to resist the man's charm. I bet you she ran off the same night to tell Ruben when she thought I gave up on her. You know, sometimes, I wonder if my feelings for that girl were one-sided."

"No," Emily replied. "Absolutely not. Summer is madly in love with you."

Amber added, "What we need to know is what happened to her. Where is my best friend?"

Brooke asked, "Oliver, why didn't you answer my calls. Did you have something to do with her disappearance?"

"Yes! Had I not yelled at her like I did that night, she would be here. I have one phone in the house and the cord was unplugged. I didn't realize it until today. Other than that, I use my cell. Summer would call my cell. I didn't know where any of you lived, except for you, Emily. When I finally went to your home, you weren't there."

"No?" She shook her head. "I'm sorry. I hadn't a clue. You coulda left a note."

He shrugged. "I was too anxious to think of that. Well, I don't have your phone numbers or last names. Summer mentioned it once or twice I suppose, but I don't remember. She ain't on social media. I didn't know where to find your jobs. Summer took everything from here that belonged to her. I thought she was cutting ties with me. I even drove to Delaware; her mom wasn't there either. That's why I'm shocked to see you ladies here, and now I'm all worried up."

Brooke was frustrated. "You coulda' Googled me."

Oliver plucked his head. "It didn't occur to Google someone using one name. Besides, I focused more on her than contacting you guys."

Brooke rolled her eyes. "She doesn't answer her phone. I thought that maybe you guys went on a vacation or something. But I knew she would tell or call us, so I didn't get comfortable with that thought. But you didn't call the cops?"

"I thought she left me. All of her things were gone. It made sense. When people break up, they stop communicating. I left her that Friday night and didn't return until Monday night. Let me put it this way: I coulda brought another woman over, and she wouldn't have seen a trace of an ex. Now, you tellin' me that doesn't sound intentional?" he challenged.

Amber must've become pissed, because she stood up instantly and asked, "Okay, but what does that have to do with us? I'm worried that she doesn't think she can or should deal with us anymore. Did you make her feel like a low person or something? Because she would *never* cut us out like that. Never."

Brooke appreciated Amber more at that moment than at any other time. She stood up, too. "Yeah. What did you tell her that night? This is odd."

Amber and Brooke both folded their arms. Oliver sighed and wiped his tired face as he sat back in his chair. "I, umm, I accused her of wanting to ruin lives."

"What?" Brooke cried. "Why would you say that, even though—"

Oliver interrupted her. "Please, sit down." When his eyes dropped up and down Brooke's body, she sat. "I heard her tell you about Jackson."

Amber sat.

"I was there when we spotted him."

It would've been so easy to make this all about Jackson, but with a best friend missing, her lost relationship paled in comparison to Summer's absence. Brooke knew where to find Jackson if need be, but she didn't know where to find her best friend. Brooke could only say, "I'm worried about my friend, not Jackson."

Oliver ignored her. "I warned her not to tell you. But she had to be honest with you right away and make you feel worse rather than comfort you and just pretend as if she knew nothing."

Brooke shot back, "No, what she did was give me the dose of reality I needed. I was becoming pathetic. Summer rescued me."

Amber interjected. "And besides, I need to thank her for sending me a chance at love."

Puzzled, Oliver asked, "What?"

"Oh, well, your girlfriend gave my number to a man and he called me. It was like a blind phone thing. But, hey," she raised both palms in the air, "as odd as it sounds, so far, I'm happy. And I have no one to thank but my dear friend, Summer."

Clenching her teeth and holding her head, it was obvious that Emily didn't feel so confident that Amber should've revealed that information at the moment, especially since Oliver questioned his trust in her.

Oliver shook his head and looked away. "Wow. Funny how she had so much time to fix and meddle in other people's lives, but not her own. Just . . . wow." When no one said a word, he shrugged. "Hey, whatever. All this talk about her doing good, but she messed with Fran and Ruben's marriage, and had she not done that, she wouldn't be carrying his child."

"We don't know that," Brooke shot back.

Oliver stood up. "Look, all I care about is finding out what happened to the woman I love. We can work out all this other stuff later. It feels real trivial right about now." With gritted teeth, he smacked his chest as he confessed, "I feel like I'm about to explode."

A symphony of sniffles filled the room. Emily wiped her nose and said, "He's right, guys. Doesn't matter who we want to kill. We need to get up off our asses and find our girl—right now." Shaky and weary, she stood and the other two followed suit.

With a raised eyebrow and clasped hands, Brooke asked, "Okay, then. Where do we start?"

"Okay, for starters, we need to check all home phones and missed calls and any voicemails," Amber suggested. "Our cell phones should be glued to our hips."

Brooke shook a finger. "Also, her mother is key. We know she's a nurse. If we can locate her mother's hospital, then we can find out where Summer is. Maybe the mom won't disclose Summer's location to Oliver, but to her girlfriends, I'm sure she will."

"Unless Summer warned her mom not to, out of fear that you guys would spill to me," Oliver said.

"In any event, let's get moving on this," Brooke directed. "We have to call around to all local hospitals in her home city until we find her mom."

"What's her mom's name?" asked Amber.

"Rebecca Stevenson," Oliver answered.

"Awesome," said Amber. "But, Oliver, you can still help us find the right hospital, and if you find it first, then tell us so we can call the mom."

"Of course." He sighed and rubbed his forehead. "Let's get started. Remember, just ask if you can speak to nurse Rebecca Stevenson. Let's not ask if she works each place we call, let's assume."

They all nodded and got down to business.

About thirty minutes later, Emily rejoiced with a proud, "Yes!" Everyone looked up to see Emily's elbow poke the air behind her in celebration, as she claimed, "I found her mom."

"Great." Brooke approached her to hear Rebecca's location.

"She works at Bay Hospital in Delaware City," Emily announced. "They said that the mom was on vacation. So, that may explain why Summer and her mom both appear to be missing."

Oliver had his hands on his hips. "Maybe," he mumbled with a sigh. "Let's hope that they're together. I hope Summer's not looking for her own place to live, because there's no way Rebecca could vacation in peace knowing her daughter was missing."

"That's true," agreed Emily.

Brooke didn't know if she should feel relieved or bear the fact that their unconfirmed doubts of their friend's whereabouts didn't bring any sense of peace. Her heart was still heavy considering the amount of loss that kept on mounting. No mom, no Jackson, no Damani, and now, no Summer. No one realized Brooke's sudden mental withdrawal even when she nervously raked her hands through her hair. She'd grown accustomed to living without her mom, but it didn't mean that she preferred it that way. Being that her mom didn't turn out to be mom material, it made her realize that fantasizing about having the perfect mother was a moot desire. She had what she had which amounted to nothing. Brooke was dealt the no-parent card, but being used to it didn't necessarily make it any easier, especially at a time like this.

Men were another story. Either you had one of your own or you didn't. There wasn't a gray area regarding commitment. And right now, Brooke didn't have one. There was the man who got away, just because she wanted something that he didn't. But he did have her heart, however, she really wanted that back. Damani was something else. He wanted her heart, and they probably wanted the same things in life. Though he seemed obtainable, she couldn't reach for him when her hands were tied to Jackson. But did it make sense to let Damani slip away even though Jackson had clearly moved on?

And what about her friend Summer? Brooke really appreciated their four-woman crew. Being reduced to three didn't feel right, especially when the headcount already included herself. Having a close network of best friends was the second substitute for family for which one could ask. It didn't matter how annoying each one could be or even if they weren't annoying at all. They each came with flaws like anyone else and just like family, you'd want them around. Brooke admitted to herself that none of them could throw stones. They could only unite and find their friend.

Emily

Sad and alone, Emily closed her briefcase full of graded papers while she mentally crossed off another day left in her home. Moving day would be here in a matter of days. Although Emily had been looking forward to moving, the last thing she'd expected was to feel the way she did. It meant that Eric would have to work hard to find her. All her memories of him cooking in the kitchen would be gone. The memory of the moment he walked away from her a few months after their wedding stuck like glue. Kicking him out on Thanksgiving replayed in her mind repeatedly at random times.

The bottom line had already been clear. It was time to move on and let it all go and start over somewhere else.

Turning off her lamp and lying on her side, Emily placed both hands together flat against the pillow, resting her cheek against it. The outdoor breeze felt perfect. Emily knew that the right conditions existed for her to have a good night's sleep. Despite drifting off for perhaps ten minutes, she awoke to the strum of a guitar outside of her window, accompanied by a vocal.

"What the—?" Emily jumped out of her bed to see the ass disturbing the neighborhood and in particular—her. Without raising the window, she peeked outside to see a familiar face looking up toward her window in hopes of grabbing her attention.

The ass was Zach!

Zach stood in her tiny front lawn strumming a guitar singing a love song.

"Zach!" Emily yelled in a loud whisper. She lifted the window, so he could hear her better.

"Shut up out there!" Emily heard from a distance. She didn't want anyone blaming her for the disturbance in the little time she had left.

"Pssst! Come up. Wait there." Luckily, Zach stopped strumming as Emily raced down the stairs in her sheer black lingerie. Forgetting to grab a robe, she snatched a wool coat from the coat rack next to her front door and slid into her black pumps that had been tossed to the side after work before opening the door. There Zach stood, in a cowboy hat with a guitar in tow.

"Howdy."

Emily pulled him in by the sleeve of his leather jacket. "Get in here, and quick." Briefly, she stuck her neck out of the door to check to her left and right to see if any neighbors were watching. She slammed her door shut and spun to face a smiling Zach. "Are you nuts?" Emily folded her arms as she waited for him to answer.

"What? You've been looking sad lately and you surely haven't been picking up your phone either. I'm scared to cross the lawn to come over and knock even."

Emily laughed. She thought she was mad at him, but any man willing to sing to her in the middle of the night at the cost of being affronted by a neighbor was truly all right in her book. Sadly, she admitted with a shrug, "I guess I am sad right now. But as for the serenade, no, I, uh, I actually liked it. I was just caught off-guard and scared of the attention, that's all."

In fact, Emily couldn't deny just how much she'd been turned on by his attention. All the components came together, seducing what little restraint remained within the threads of her grasp. The dark mass that covered the sky. The kiss of light that emanated from the promise of the moon's nightly visit. The sheer material from which her skin played peek-a-boo. The dress clothes that framed Zach's every inch, almost as if tailored specifically for his perfection.

Everything.

With a smirk rolled over her face, Emily peeled the coat from her shoulders and arms in one graceful motion as she eased toward Zach, with one foot in front of the other. Zach studied her with a frozen gaze.

"So, you think the answer is to strum your guitar on my lawn at ten o'clock at night singing a 2003 pop hit?"

"Well, don't you like that song?"

"I love it, Zach, but come on, that's beside the point."

He shrugged nonchalantly. "Well what's the harm?"

"The harm *is* Zach, is that the neighbors—"

"Aw." He waved an irritated hand at her words. "Neighbors shneighbors."

Watching him watching her, Zach's eyes devoured her barely-covered frame with a stare that licked her up and down that left her wet in the right place. Her manicured hand kissed his shoulder with a touch strong enough to kick him against the window.

"Sit," she ordered with a snarl that even had her questioning who she thought she was. Maybe she couldn't answer that, but she knew who she wasn't: the scaredy-cat that everyone remembered her as.

Bewildered, Zack struggled to expel words from his gaped mouth while taking refuge in the crevasse of the wall and the floor.

Removing his hat and placing it on her head, Emily firmly stabbed her stiletto above Zach's groin. He watched helplessly with arms parted wide, resting them against the window ledge. She captured him with her stare, and without a word, he knew what to do next.

"That hat looks so sexy on you." Zach licked his lips.

Two large, hungry hands slid up the length of her shin and calf. Wearing a smirk, she steadied her body on the one foot placed behind her, hanging both hands loosely at her sides. Like a ruler over a peasant, she stared down at him with expectations of him to please.

Zach craved her like a man deprived of many meals, which also made her pussy match the knocking rhythm of that in her chest. His desire proved that he relished in the moments she chose to share her body with him. Like a grateful man determined to make the best out of each moment, he placed kisses against her smooth, peach-toned flesh.

Each kiss involved lips that sucked in her goodness, touches involved hands that owned each moment like it'd never come around again with fingers that raked her skin as if mere contact fell short on sufficient.

Emily owned this man, and she wasn't even trying to buy.

However, she wouldn't reject a man whose lips eased up the meat of her thigh and near the heart of her pleasure. No way. And if he ravaged her with touches on just her legs, there was no telling what he could do to her delicious orchid. Like a young man stolen by the lust of an older woman, Zach looked up at her with an expression that told her he was going deep. She grabbed him by the peak of his gelled hair wave and pushed him into her womanhood.

"Mmmm." She took a softer tone. "This is a teachable moment, sir."

His eyes closed with a smirking mouth. "Just like a smell that I wanna taste."

Zach's hands eased downward, over the front and sides of her thighs and back up again. The band of her panties came down with the clench of his teeth as his hands worked the back, until she stood in her bra and stilettos. Zach chuckled. "Oh, yeah, baby. Lemme show you why men really grow beards."

Confused, Emily watched as he eased forward for space before reclining until his head met her wooden floors.

"Limbo this way, baby."

"What?"

He twirled his finger at her. "Limbo . . . this . . . way."

Looking doubtful, a confused Emily tried to match her actions with his words. As she did, she ended up collapsing on top of his neck.

"I'm sorry!"

"I'm not."

Immediately, she felt the tingle from his hairs against her bare lips as she rocked to regain balance.

"Oooh. That's feels . . . good."

"That's the point. Sit on my face."

"Excuse me?"

"You heard me. It's what I want."

Shy and perhaps embarrassed, she giggled. "Oh, Zach. Think I'm gonna crush your face."

"The best way for a man to die."

Emily chuckled.

"Well why else would I ask you to move over here with me on my back? For a teacher, you're surely coming up short on the wild side."

Fueled by another character jab of always playing it safe, she decided to throw caution to the side faster than a pair of dirty underwear. "Oh, you have asked for it."

"Come on, Miss Proper. Give me a lesson in eating with etiquette."

Emily situated herself until her second set of lips covered his mouth. His tongue coated her with licks, and as Emily rocked her hips back and forth, the intensity collected, hardening her nipples into two tight bundles of nerves. Emily tweaked her nipples, arching her back and her feet. She moved one hand to her head and through her long, brown strands.

"Yessssss!"

She rocked continuously in a sweet rhythm that Zach had no problem matching. Zach's tongue stroked her pussy like a plate left with a one-of-a-kind family sauce; he didn't leave anything behind. Clearly, he came on a starved stomach.

Tasting her fingers, she moaned and cried his name until her strands of hair intertwined with her fingers and slid into her mouth. Her body quivered, her eyelids fluttered, she hollered, gripped his pants for support and then exhaled before she collapsed.

He tapped her thighs, because her abdomen covered his face. "Um, sweetheart. I can't breathe."

Sitting up, Emily laughed at his muffled voice. "I'm sorry, babe." She wiggled back until her legs parted over his chest. She noticed the glaze from her pleasure all over his mouth. "Wow," she said while panting softly. "That was so good. Really needed that."

"Glad I got a good rating." He sighed with a smile. "My turn?"

Aside from Eric's, Emily never had a penis in her mouth before. She had a feeling he would want that, whether or not he vocalized it. In a pensive state of mind, she rolled her tongue around her cheek.

"Is that a no?"

He played it chill, but Emily wouldn't dare let him down. "Umm, no. It's not a no."

He reached up to play with the ends of her hair. "What is it then? Never done it before?"

Her mouth twisted. "No, no. Of course I have."

"So, is it what I think it is?"

"What do you think it is?"

"Emily, you don't have to hide from me. Talk to me."

She bit her bottom lip. "Eric. Who or what else would it be?"

He moved his fingers from her hair to her chin. "Look at me."

She did.

"Baby, that man is gone. He ain't thinking about you. But you got a nice, long, hard penis waiting right—I would say in front of you—" They laughed. "Behind you. Right here, baby. It's tasty, clean, and all yours, ready to be sucked."

She playfully squinted her eyes at him and raised her hips to ease toward his face. In a flirty tone, she asked, "Mr. Lerner, are you trying to turn me on?"

"Ooh, baby. You keep it up. I'm gonna bust in no time."

Emily still felt reserved and even though she wanted to be an adult about it, she just couldn't commit the way Zach wanted her to. She removed his hat and shook her hair. "Do you have a condom?"

He grimaced with regret. "'Fraid not." Zach took the hat from her hand and placed it beside him on the floor.

She returned the expression. "Okay, then. Can I ask you something?"

"Can you hurry? I'm kind of horny here."

Good. Then maybe he'll do things my way.

"I was wondering. Can we try this my way?"

He couldn't disguise his doubt. "Umm, what way is that?"

"Hang on." Emily stood and hurried to the kitchen and opened the door to the pantry. When she grabbed what she needed, she winced at the possibility that he would embarrass her. Grabbing the box and hiding it behind her back, she tiptoed in a hurry to the horny neighbor starved and stretched out on her floor.

"What cha got there?"

Emily quickly gathered her nerves. She swung the product in front of her. "This."

"Plastic wrap? Huh. What, umm," he cleared his throat and twirled a hand, "what are you trying to do with that?"

Emily exhaled. "Hear me out. Look. Giving head isn't quite my thing. I'm scared of that going in my mouth. So, I want protection." Feeling shamed, she offered, "I'm sorry?"

Zach chuckled bitterly. "Wow, Emily. Umm, what? You think I'm gonna give you something?"

Great, now she felt like a jerk. Maybe she should've just been straight with him. "No, Zach. This is all me. But I have the right to protect myself. Before you judge, here, let me try."

He rolled his eyes. "Knock yourself out."

Emily felt stupid as she sat beside him to expose the infamous penis that freaked her out last year. She could almost laugh at the situation for finding herself right where she never thought she'd be. This would be the last man she'd ever thought she'd get down and dirty with.

"Watch." His goods had been freed from the button and zipper by her reluctant hands. With her back turned to Zach, Emily grabbed his stiffy with huge eyes, worried by the thought of putting his bare penis into her mouth, especially given the size. She wanted to call Brooke for advice, because she knew that Brooke could be quite conservative as well.

Am I doing the right thing?

Or, she could call Amber and listen to her encouragement about finding her inner animal. Emily preferred to think of it as her expanding and owning her sensuality. She didn't think that the deed was dirty, just intimidating. It felt more important to love the man she wrapped her lips around. Presently, that wasn't the case and unfortunately, she couldn't keep his dick sitting out while it became cold and soft.

Emily took a deep breath, struggling not to stare at his business. She slowly unwrapped the plastic from the roll and severed it against the teeth on the bottom of the box. Wondering how she was going to pull it off, she bit her lower lip as she grabbed his dick by a plastic-coated hand and wrapped it up as carefully as possible.

Zach sighed. "Emily? Damn, baby."

Refusing to look at him, she held up a finger. "Hold up, Zach. Hold up. I got this."

Fueled by determination not to let him be right, she eased her face toward the pinkish penis suffocated in plastic. Admittedly, she felt childish and wrong, but she couldn't bring herself to go for it. Channeling Amber, with her index finger and thumb circled around his width, she opened her mouth and dived into action. Zach moaned a little, but the plastic made things rigid. She couldn't stroke his shaft without upsetting the placement of the plastic.

When she sucked his tip, the material would retract into her mouth. Realizing that the effort was a headache as her saliva and tongue inadvertently loosened the plastic wrap, the wheels in her head turned desperately as she scrambled for another solution.

"Innovation at its finest, huh?"

Emily raised her head to look back at a non-thrilled man with one arm behind his head. He wiggled his brows at her.

Defeated, she frowned with slumped shoulders. He took his free hand and stroked her head. "Baby, come on. Put those nice lips over my penis and give it a little taste. But first, unwrap the piece of candy before you put it in your mouth."

She wanted to laugh—hell, she'd settle for a giggle. However, nothing was funny when the desire to perform oral sex on him escaped her. Unfortunately, she'd have to let this nice man down. She uncoiled the plastic from around his penis and balled it up with one hand.

"Zach . . ."

"You can't." He sat up. "I know."

"I'm sorry. I really am."

"I know you are. It's not for everyone."

"I have to love a man first. It's me."

"It's admirable. It's okay. You shouldn't go throwing those precious lips around any ole man anyway." He fastened up and sat beside her with one arm resting over a bent knee.

She snickered. "I don't know what's wrong with me." Her hand stretched over her heart. "Sometimes I feel like I am uninhibited. I mean, you saw me. Right? In the movie theatre, we had fun. Right now, we had fun. But when it came time for me to do something that a lot of women do with no problem, I couldn't."

"Did you survey real women? Where do you get your facts from? TV?"

Confused, she wrinkled her brows at him. "Huh?"

"Who told you that plenty of women like to or even perform oral sex?"

"I mean, pshhhh, don't they?"

"Yes. There's some who do, and some who never will, and then you have women like you. They simply want to do something that special with special people. I'm more upset that I'm not too special to you right now."

Emily smiled and placed a hand over his shoulder. "You're such a great guy. I mean, really. What can I do to please you like you've pleased me?"

Zach smirked. "You know, Emily?" He flicked his wrist at her. "Don't worry about it. I'm happy. I got to be intimate with you in a way I dreamed of since the day I met you." Raising both hands, he claimed, "I'm good."

"And, so no orgasm for you?"

"Men can manage. Believe me."

"I can ride it. Is that fair?"

Zach wore a prideful grin with his eyes closed. Opening them, he placed a hand on her shoulder. "Sweetheart. You're a good woman who deserves all the good things in life. Baby. This one is on me. Go on upstairs and get some sleep." He passed her the panties she had on before things got heated.

"Thanks." Sliding them up her legs, he turned to the side to offer her some sort of privacy. "Done."

He turned his face in her direction.

She sighed. "I can't sleep." While grateful for the physical release, it still didn't erase her emotional struggle. After the orgasm, reality still sat around like a lousy visitor, and she just wanted it to go.

With the sudden misery painted across her face, Zach sensed something was wrong. Concerned, he rubbed her shoulder.

"Emily? Everything okay?"

"No, no, no, Zach. It's just that one of my best friends is missing and the rest of us, including her boyfriend—or maybe ex—are all upset. She moved out and no one has heard from her. Before you ask, we've called her mom and everything. Nothing."

Zach grimaced. "I'm sorry, Emily. I really am. What can I do?"

She shrugged. "Nothing. She's out there somewhere. We just have to wait and see what happens. We all miss her. You being here and just asking is enough. Thanks."

"Well my pleasure, Emily. You know I'll always be there for you."

Her strained smile did its best to reflect her warmed heart. "I just feel like she moved on or something."

Zach poked his tongue against his cheek. Clearly, something was on his mind. "Speaking of moving on, did you—from Eric?"

Two excited hands flew up after she rolled her big hazel eyes. "Yes."

"Okay now, just making sure. You're too beautiful to wait for one man. I say toss him and move on."

Emily blinked slowly one time as she allowed a doubtful smile to cover her face. "Thanks."

"Look, Emily. You can have some other man, who will pay you attention, a man who will work hard to make you smile. You think I would let that wretched Heather steal my life and happiness with her antics? Noooo. I let her go; she was a poison. Toxic. And-and-and Eric, he had his chance and took advantage of your love. Now that he knows what it's like to hurt, he may treat the next woman better." His gentle blue eyes seared into hers and almost into her soul. "But, babe, I know what it feels like to hurt. Some other woman did it to me, so I won't do it to another . . . if I know what's good for me."

Emily giggled as she wiped her runny nose with a finger. She hadn't noticed how his kind words and attention made her emotional on the inside.

"I just don't think he respects you, that's all. He did enough to distract you. But now that you have a clear head, think straight, Emily. I hate to see you move, but, sweetheart, if it will do you good, then I say *adiós*." He motioned a goodbye in one wave.

She smiled and stifled a laugh. "Won't you miss me?"

"Of course, sweetheart, of course. But you know what? I risked getting caught by the cops for you, because I wanted to protect you. I wanted to nail that bastard for you. I only made you agree to a date, because I knew that was the only way to get you to go out with me after what I showed you."

Emily placed a hand on his knee. "Ohhh," she pouted playfully. "About that. Please, Zach, I have long since let that go. You should, too."

He held out a hand. "Well let's shake on it. You let go of Eric, and I let go of me accidentally showing you me shaking my penis."

That sounded so strange to Emily, but what sounded even stranger was deciding to let go of Eric once and for all and having a witness there to ensure it. Hesitating, Emily sighed as she decided. His hand waited there for her to grab, to take control of her life and future. And while the handshake didn't mean that the hurt or love would immediately disappear, it did mean that she would be deciding to take back some sense of control. It meant that if by the off-chance Eric were to come back asking for another try, and she knew that was about as likely as the Democrats and Republicans working together, then she would have to reject him because of the handshake. So, she shook it.

"Oh, hell. When was the last time I took control like this?" With her hand in his hand, they shook hands for more than five seconds. He grinned from ear to ear.

"Great job, Emily." They retracted hands. "Now you *have* to move on."

Proudly, with a tilt of her chin, she grinned and affirmed with both hands locked on top of her knees, "Yes, I do."

"I've been meaning to tell you something."

"Oh."

"What we did at the movies was wrong. I shoulda' been the strong one and denied you."

Emily couldn't listen any longer. Gently, she interrupted with, "Zach. I'm a grown woman. I knew what I was doing and frankly, I don't regret it."

"Because we didn't get caught. But darling, come on. That wasn't you." He squinted at her. "You don't have to take on another personality to prove a point."

"I wasn't trying to prove a point, Zach. I was just horny, like you said earlier. I needed a release and you were there. I wish people would stop putting me in a box."

"You're right. I'm sorry. But are you saying you have no attraction to me otherwise? Had I been a monkey, then what? That would do, too?" He placed the hat on his head.

Emily realized her poor choice of words and attempted to soothe him with a hand on the leg. "Zach, you know that came out all wrong. No. I am attracted to you. I mean—

hello. Clearly, I am. I just buried my vagina into your face. I am a very selective creature, trust me. It's just that, with you I feel safe, and I do find you rather cute, especially when that hat isn't hiding you and all," she teased.

Zach grinned faintly. "Okay, I'll take that, but I'm gonna show you how a real man should treat someone like you. It'll also let you see what I'm capable of. Had we not shaken hands earlier, I would bring up that unspeakable incident, but—"

Emily tsked a finger at him. "Unh, unh, unhhhhh. No going back. Remember?"

Zach fingered the rim of his hat. "Well, hell, if you can enforce the rules, then I surely need to follow them."

"I need to give you my new address . . ."

"Can you text it to me?"

"Sure."

"I'm glad I stopped by, but you and I both know, we need our sleep now. I just had to see your face. Seeing you puts me in the best mood."

Feeling touched by his kindness and words, Emily nodded with a faint smile. "Thank you—Zach."

They stood simultaneously. After he found his guitar, she escorted him as he headed toward the door. When he leaned in for a kiss, a quick flashback of her sitting on his face made her dip back and tap her cheek.

He chuckled. "Of course."

A peck of affection landed on the side of her face. She opened the door and told him, "Good night now."

He nodded once. "Night, Emily."

She closed the door behind her. Holding her head with a grin, she felt amazing after accepting his gift, but horrible for not giving him one in return.

Amber

Sunday morning, Amber found herself outside with Cris, pretending that the cold breeze didn't bother her so much in a thin, lime, V-neck t-shirt and blue jeans. Amber flashed Cris a naughty grin as she watched him watch her scrub his muscle car with a soapy towel. He gave her the job of washing the car while he scrubbed his rims.

"This is heavy duty, you know." She made sure to push her butt out with every stretch.

Squatting, Cris warned, "Keep that up and you're gonna find yourself in a position in front of these neighbors."

Amber watched the sinew in his bicep pop as he scrubbed. "Oh, I won't be the only one in trouble. You're a few seconds away from being in danger yourself."

"I may have to take advantage of you while we have an empty home. That doesn't happen often here." He stood and wiped his hands on his loose-fitting jeans.

"So, absolutely no one got left behind in the whatever residence?"

"You got all the spots, baby. Time to hose it down. And no, for once, no one is in the Perez household at the moment."

Amber had spent the night after they crashed from late movie-watching. When they woke up, she'd expected to take a walk of shame into the kitchen, but much to their surprise, everyone had left. Relieved, Cris decided to wash his car with Amber's help.

"Where do you think they went, Mr. Perez?" Amber dropped the heavy towel in the bucket of water.

"Well, some of the elders went to church. I'm sure of that. But it's the youngins I'm not so sure about."

Amber pursed her lips as she shifted her weight onto one hip. "Do you go to church?"

Cris looked up as he picked at a nail. "Sometimes. You?"

"No. I never felt good enough."

He snickered. "Amber, that's not what church is about. You come as you are and let God work it out. You don't judge yourself. Did your parents go?"

"All the time." A sigh escaped as a passing memory flashed of her mom wearing a large hat with a Bible in her hand standing next to Amber's dad. "My parents were so happy to go. I remember my Sunday's best attire and my patent leather Mary Janes. Loved those shoes." Amber got lost in her own thoughts. She remembered Mara every Sunday, difficult and tired. Despite the fight of resistance going to church as a kid, Mara was always the first one to stand in the congregation to sing a hymn. Amber didn't know it then, but she knew it now: Those were the good ole family days. Now, her family consisted of one sister until she could make one of her own.

"Sounds like fond memories." Cris studied her as he indulged in anything she was willing to share. "Maybe I can take you with me one day. You never know what a sermon may do for your soul."

Reluctant to inquire, Amber squinted and tilted her head. "Are you Catholic?"

Cris laughed. "Because I'm Mexican, right?"

Amber waved her hands and giggled. "No, no, no. I'm just sayin' . . . Oh," she stomped a heel. "Come on. You know most Mexicans are."

Cris pointed a finger at her. "Well, hey. You must be Baptist, and lemme guess—fried chicken after service?"

Amber laughed so hard her stomach almost ached. "You know some of those heavy Baptist women can put their feet in some fried chicken." Once she regained her composure, she answered, "Yes. We were Baptist."

Cris shook his head. "Knew it. Black people are usually Baptist or Methodist," he teased.

She snickered. "Why all the denominations, do you think?"

"It goes back to the history of religion. Each of them did some things differently. Maybe if I can get your butt back to school, you can study that for yourself." He folded his dirty rag and threw it down next to the bucket of water, so he could slide his hands into his pockets.

"Ohhhh, noooo." Amber smacked a hand on her forehead as she cocked her head back. "Are you gonna be like a campus recruiter or somethin'?" She lowered her head and removed her hand to see his expression.

"Nope. I ain't gettin' paid." He pointed an index finger at Amber. "But I'll personally recruit you."

She shook her head with pursed lips. "Mister, I don't think so. I'm too old. It's too late." Tired of standing, she decided to use his car as support as she rested her curvy bottom against the driver door with folded arms.

"Amber, you told me that you play and teach the piano, right?" When she nodded, he continued with, "Well, why not go and get your bachelor's in business and learn how to expand your business selling your services? You can even partner with someone. Try to study *something*," he implored her.

"Cris. Four years?" She held up four fingers. "*Four years*?"

"The market is full of older people wanting a change. College ain't just about teeny boppers anymore. The face of college has changed and so should you." Approaching her with a smile, he picked up her hands. "You are young, brilliant, and you got some work experience behind you. Plus, you got a gift. You should be the most focused freshman on campus. Besides, you don't even look a day past twenty-five. You wanna wait till people can accurately guess your age? Hell, do it online."

Amber chuckled. "Errr."

"Yeah, keep it up, Amber. Don't challenge yourself. You'll regret it." He poked her midsection. "Now bring your Baptist buns here." She released a tiny startled screech when he yanked her close and tied his arms behind her back. "Beauty and brains are never a miss."

"I'm too old," she groaned.

"If the colleges don't put an age restriction on learning, why should you?"

She shrugged.

His voice grew with excitement. "Besides. You said your SAT scores were good, right?"

"And?"

"So, you're smart."

"Oh, please. I took those in high school."

"Yeah, so your brain may have some dust on it."

Amber punched him in the stomach.

He grinned. "Good hit." Cris' expression straightened. "For real, Amber. You got work experience and they may ask for a resume, which might work in your favor. I'm sure in all of these post-high school years, you were productive."

Amber could only muster a perfunctory smile as she decided to embrace him to hide her face. Experience. Resume. Those two words in the same sentence made her cringe as she considered what she'd been doing all of these years. She'd been sleeping with men for money, something that Cris had no business knowing about her. In fact, Amber had determined that no serious man in her future should ever learn about that.

Brooke

"*Woo-hoo. Woo-hoo.* Over here, Brooke!"

Brooke turned when she heard her name as she walked into the crowded La Madeleine. She saw a smiling Jacqueline Laurent waving her frail hand in hopes of catching her attention. Brooke returned a brief smile before heading toward the table with her new friend.

Brooke took a seat across from her friend and unfastened her leather jacket. "Thanks for meeting me, Jacqueline." She set her Burberry clutch on the table.

"No, it's a pleasure. I took the liberty of choosing a salad and tomato soup for you." She pushed the extra tray in front of Brooke. "And a glass of water."

Dying of thirst, Brooke felt happy that she did. The hunger pangs in her stomach started to tear at her insides. "Good call. I appreciate that." She took a long sip of lemon water and a few bites of her salad.

"So, tell me. Are things better?" Jacqueline stared at Brooke over the rim of her glass as she swallowed her mango iced tea.

"Before we get into my life, how's yours? And what about Veronique? Is everything still great with her and married life?" Contrary to always wanting to discuss her own life with friends, even Brooke knew that sometimes it was just great to hear about other people.

"Very well. Thank you for asking. She is house hunting with her husband. Me, on the other hand, I'm happy fundraising. But I'm also worried about you."

Brooke twisted her mouth to one side. "Well, I blew things with the new man. I let my past ruin my present. But I'm debating whether I should try to work things out with him, since it was my fault. I do think he's right though. I'm not over Jackson."

Jacqueline waved one hand as the other cupped the glass of iced tea. "The best way to get over someone else is to date someone else. Otherwise, you sit around obsessing over the last man who didn't work out. I mean, if Jackson hasn't called you then perhaps it's time to seize the day." Jaqueline grinned, no doubt proud of her own advice.

Brooke anxiously rubbed her hands up and down her thighs as she chewed and nodded. "I see. And, according to my friend, who by the way is missing—" A wave of melancholy blurred her vision. In a broken voice, she managed an, "I'm sorry." Pointing a finger in the air, Brooke took a moment to push the lump back down her throat as Jacqueline studied her face with a concerned stare.

"What, darling? What? Oh, my goodness, are you okay?" She pulled a tissue from her purse and offered it to Brooke. Jacqueline searched Brooke's face for an answer.

Brooke fanned her face. The last thing she wanted to do was draw any attention to herself in an eatery. Luckily, it wasn't too full. "My pregnant friend is missing. We are all doing all we can to find her. This is the third week and we haven't seen or heard anything."

"So sorry, my dear." Her tiny arm reached across the table to stroke Brooke's arm in comfort. "So sorry, my dear. She will come back. You'll see."

Brooke nodded. "Well, anyway, that same friend saw Jackson with another woman. So, he's moved on." Brooke sighed and poured out her thoughts in frustration. "You know, I just called you because I needed to talk with someone who's not in my face all the time. You're like a breath of fresh air."

Brooke really wanted to tell Jacqueline that she was the closest person she had to a mother, considering age and wisdom, but she decided against that to avoid freaking Jacqueline out.

Jacqueline smiled. "Anytime, Brooke. Anytime. Let's not be strangers. If you need something, you call. I was sold on you the day you put together the best wedding my daughter could have ever had. I would like to say that I feel indebted to you, but that would subtract from the fact that I genuinely like being around you."

The sentiments warmed Brooke's heart, especially at a time like this. "You're sweet. But I feel strange now. I mean, for the first time, I don't have the answers to anything in my life."

Without hesitation, Jacqueline replied, "This is life, Brooke. One day we know everything and the next, we know nothing. Embrace moments like these."

Brooke frowned, and so did her eyebrows. "Why would I wanna do that?"

Jacqueline leaned forward. "And what does despair teach us, hmm? From despair, we grow strong. It makes us think. For if we always knew the answers, we'd become self-centered and opposed to others' opinions."

Brooke slumped as she took in the wise words. Even with the fork resting in her hand, she couldn't eat.

"You tell me something. When you thought you knew everything, did you seek advice as much? Did you care what others thought?"

Brooke allowed that information to marinate into her brain as she absently shoved salad into her mouth. She decided that Mother Laurent was right. When she had the world in the palm of her hand, she was a child in a fantasy world, but nonetheless it was hers. And as an adult, she had the real world in her hands. Reflecting on happier times, she didn't welcome others' opinions, because she had everything visualized and mapped out. Therefore, listening to Jacqueline's direct but wise words immediately told her something: She was going to be all right. Just because she didn't have the answers, didn't mean that there weren't any solutions.

With that, she grabbed Jacqueline's hand with a wan smile and told her, "Thank you. Now you tell me. How'd you get to be so smart?"

Smiling, Jacqueline shifted in her seat. Leaning forward she replied, "Oh, honey. Not only have I been around the block," she leaned back in her chair, "I built it," and winked.

Nodding her head to Jacqueline's comment, she high-fived her with a grin of admiration. Intrigued, Brooke vowed to be a woman who would build her own block.

6: surprise!

Summer

She touch of my mother's hand on my knee comforted me as we drove in silence toward Oliver's condo in Arlington. Mentally strained from rethinking where I went wrong, I needed my mother more than ever. Without her strength, I felt positive that a mental asylum would've done me some good. She eased the rental car behind a parked car on the street in front of Oliver's building. All of the memories, good and bad, flooded my mind. The inundation of mental visuals made my stomach flip with nervousness.

"Are you all right?"

My gaze shifted from outside of my window to my mother. The sun highlighted her golden wavy locks that rested carelessly around her shoulders. Her crow's feet appeared as she studied me through narrowed eyes. Nodding without saying a word, both of my hands gripped the safety belt.

Finally, whispering a, "Yeah," in distress, I felt numb and tired.

My mother reached over to hug me. "Remember, pumpkin, just as we discussed, if he gives you a hard time and you feel uncomfortable, or if he ain't home, call me and I'll turn around. Otherwise, I'll be heading toward Delaware."

"I will, Mom. Thank you so much. I am so sorry you spent the whole time comforting me. I'm sure you didn't imagine caring for your grown daughter like she was four."

"Stop." And when my mother used that tone accompanied with a hand in the air, I obeyed. "You handled things the best way you knew how. He'll get over it. Now go on. You've wasted enough time with me and spent enough away from your man and friends. Time to get back to normal. Go on. Mama will be fine." My mother knew me better. Instead of giving me a chance to hem and haw over what happened, she took the initiative to free me from the car when she reached over to unbuckle my seatbelt. It slapped the door. "Out," she commanded with a thumb pointing behind her, in the opposite direction of where I really needed to go.

Reluctantly willing my hand to the door latch, one leg followed the other. When both of my sandals hit the ground, I resisted my tears, but all my emotions seemed stronger than the willpower in my little body combined with the little bit borrowed from my mom. Without closing the door, I hid my face in both my palms as I cried hysterically. It was all too much: seeing my mom trying to hide her concern, seeing her sitting in the car that would take her away, and seeing the building in front of me that once housed a happy relationship. Despite the sunny day that Mother Nature had offered Virginia this early April, my emotional state was cloudy with a chance of storms.

Behind me, I could hear the driver door slam. Facing the crowd of pedestrians that happily strolled the sidewalk on this blessed sunny day felt impossible, so I left my face hidden in my palms. The firm grip at each wrist lowered them, exposing my puffy eyes and distraught face. My mother lowered my hands as she took them into hers.

"Sweetie." Her lashes batted as she tried to keep herself together. "Don't make your mommy cry. What on earth is the matter, huh, baby?" Her voice sounded tender . . . heavenly. She tilted her head at me as her pity-filled green eyes pierced into mine.

"Everything. I don't want you to go. I need you, Mom." My barely audible voice cracked. I could see a few curious faces taking quick, furtive glances as they walked past.

She grabbed my chin. "Don't be foolish, honey. You are strong—stronger than you think. Yes, you slept with a married man and got pregnant. You did do your fair share of dirt, but our actions have consequences, and we don't like them because that's what a consequence is. But you've been dealt the road of twigs and now you have to walk it, uneven terrain and all. But if Oliver is the man that you think he is, then he will pick you up on the rockiest places, so you won't have to endure all of the discomfort." Her thumbs wiped at my tears as she cupped my jaw.

I wanted to smile, but my stress wouldn't let me. "And what if he chooses to stay away?"

My mom smiled and straightened her head. "Then you get a bike. I can be that bike. I'll put you in the seat behind me and pedal, because you'll always be my little girl. Remember, when one solution fails, there's always another." My mother gave my face one last shake between the palms of her hands.

I nodded and dove in for a desperate, tight hug. It was time to pull back and be a big girl. Letting the leftover tears fall from my face, I gripped her hands and told her, "I'll go now. I'll call you if I need you."

"Let me help you take—"

"No, Mom, but thank you. I have a carryall and a purse. I think I can manage."

She nodded in agreement, knowing that if she helped me with the bags, then she would have to help me with my real baggage. "Now you go," I assured her with the same renewed strength I'd have to use to face Oliver. "I love you, Mom. Thank you."

"I love you, too, sweetheart. And you are most welcome. Wait here." My mother grabbed my purse from inside the car and retrieved my carryall from the trunk. I thanked her and closed my eyes as she inched forward to kiss my forehead. Either I'd see her again while in labor or in a matter of minutes. As much as I loved my mother, the former appealed to me the most. I opened my eyes to see the back of my mother's head as she approached the street to hop into the driver's seat.

"Drive safely," I called with a slight turn of my neck barely looking over my shoulder.

"I always do," she called back.

I listened for the sound of her driver's door to shut before gripping my tiny hand on the handle of the carryall. Staring at the fairly new brown building staring back at me, I encouraged myself.

Big girl, big girl.

Entering the main entrance, I took the elevator to Oliver's front door. Still in possession of his key, it didn't seem appropriate to use it, but that day I couldn't leave it behind since I had to secure his home upon moving out.

Stepping off the elevator, the door to my past stood there like a taunting monster. Suddenly, I felt somewhat embarrassed and even presumptuous showing up with a carryall as if he'd been expecting me today. With my pride on the line but thrown to the side, I stared at his big, wooden door. My brain took note of the trim, partly as a stalling tactic, but also because I was used to taking the elevator straight to his kitchen and hadn't really noticed it before.

Nervous as hell, I bit my lower lip and squinted my eyes, knowing that it was show time. He'd either want me or he wouldn't. I knocked: one, two, three. And I waited for him to answer the door to my future.

Brooke

Brooke whispered a confession to Emily as they headed toward Amber's apartment door with gifts. "I've never been here. What a shame. We've been friends for how long, and this is the first time we've come to her home?"

Emily shook her head in shame. "Yeah, I know. Crazy, right?"

Brooke knocked on Amber's door with the hand free of her purse and party bag filled with a bottle of champagne.

"I bet she thinks we forgot that her birthday is today," Emily whispered.

"On a Tuesday, no less." Brooke gritted her teeth. "Yikes."

"Who is it?" Amber called from the other side of the door.

"Open the door, hoe," Brooke called. She snickered quietly as she turned to Emily. "She'll know now."

When the door flew open, Brooke and Emily called, "Surpriiiiiiiiiise."

Amber—wearing a scarf, pink stretch pants and a white cable sweater—covered her mouth with both hands as she widened the door with a foot. She cried a muffled, "Ohhhh."

"Happy birthday, Amber!" they announced simultaneously. Brooke felt accomplished knowing that they surprised her.

Amber stepped to the side and held onto the knob to let them pass. "Get in here, you two. Come on inside." After she closed the door, she followed them into her living room.

Brooke looked around her friend's home. Obviously, Amber had been all alone watching television. On the coffee table was a plate with traces of fried rice and grease. Brooke couldn't imagine a birthday like this. To worsen matters, Amber seemed to be clicking through channels or chose to settle on the evening news. Brooke managed not to crinkle her forehead in disapproval. She hated the news from local channels. She didn't want to hear about a kid who'd been shot in his neighborhood, nor did she want to see strangers who hadn't seen a mirror being interviewed. They always seemed so dire. No, if Brooke had to be in the know about the world or the nation, then it'd have to come from the dedicated news channels with more focused topics. Brooke loved watching intellects duke it out using their viewpoints. Looking away from the flat screen, she realized that Amber's tiny, dim living room could stand some light.

Vertical venetian blinds covered the patio door and prevented natural sunlight from shining through. Her sofa seemed to have needed reupholstering, evident by the cushion dip of too many asses. Brooke cringed on the inside as she couldn't help but compare her home to Amber's. It wasn't out of spite, but in fact, it was to assess what exactly Amber must've been missing from living in such a cramped, low-budget apartment. Brooke had to admit that sometimes, one's home truly reflected that person's finances.

Brooke hooked two fingers under the strings of the champagne bag to hold it up. "Where do you want me to set this?"

Amber placed a finger on her chin. "Ummmm, set iiiiiit," she waved a finger from left to right before choosing her coffee table, "there."

"Okay." Brooke placed it on the coffee table and readjusted her falling purse strap. She favored a sunset-colored Salvatore Ferragamo shoulder bag today instead of her typical preference for a clutch.

Emily sat her gift down on the piano bench.

Amber enthusiastically invited them to sit down on her sofa. Brooke didn't want to let her reluctance show, so she flashed a brief awkward smile and slowly bent at the knees to sit. She could only pray that Amber bought it new. It wasn't the worst couch by far, nor did it appear dirty, but Brooke wished that she'd purchased her a new couch instead of what she had with her for Amber's birthday gift. Emily happily took a seat next to Brooke.

Amber stood in front of them with the coffee table between them. "You know, I just wish that Summer was here."

"I know. It sucks without her. But let's focus on your day, Amber," Emily suggested. "I know we've all been stressed and freaked out by this whole situation with Summer, but I gotta be honest. If I can just forget about her for an hour, that would be great. I am *so* worried."

"I agree, Emily. I agree." Brooke stared down at the floor in thought. When she looked back up at her somber friend, she decided to switch gears. "Girl. Open Emily's gift. Come on."

"No, wait!" Emily stood suddenly, startling Amber and Brooke. When she noticed, she said, "I'm so sorry, but first there is something she—well *we*—need to all do."

Puzzled, Amber asked, "What's that?"

Emily froze, and with her hazel eyes locked into Amber's deep brown eyes, she said, "We need to have a couple of drinks."

Amber pushed a slow fist into the air. "Ye-esssssssssssss!"

Emily walked away to the kitchen to retrieve glasses. "Where's the corkscrew?" she yelled.

"In the drawer next to the fridge!"

Brooke giggled. "You guys are on your own once I get one down.

Amber's arms collapsed at her side. "What? Noooo. I'm the birthday girl, and what I say goes. Two. Then I won't beg anymore."

"You know, I'm light and I ain't a big drinker. You have to know what one glass will do to me." Brooke smiled as she rested her face against both balled hands.

Emily emerged from the kitchen with three glasses and a corkscrew. She smiled from ear to ear and handed a glass to Amber. "One for you."

"Thank you, ma'am."

She made her way to Brooke and handed her a glass. "And one for you."

Brooke nodded once in return and sighed. "I will try, guys. But drinking makes me slightly nervous, you know."

Emily sat her glass down on the coffee table and walked over to the bags that she'd placed on the piano bench. She shuffled through some of the bags before she said, "Aha. Here it is. *Voilà.*" With her hand craned around the neck of a wine bottle, Emily showed off her gift to Amber. "Amber, this is your first gift from me. If you don't mind me being frank, this bottle is one from the collection that Eric left behind in our home. The selection is expensive."

Amber's face glowed. "I don't mind at all."

"I mean, I don't drink heavily, but while I cherish what he left behind, it'd be nice to give at least one away."

"Thank you, Emily."

About half an hour later, the three ladies cackled in the tiny living room with shared stories from their lives before meeting each other, along with stories that included all of them.

Brooke, the least drunk, called out, "Ladies, it's time to open more gifts."

Summer

Two shaky feet somehow grounded me as I waited for Oliver to open the door. The knocks from my tiny fist didn't hold a candle to the ones coming from my heart that pounded against my chest. I just wanted to get the show on the road at this point. Seconds later, sounds of footsteps came from the other side of the door. I braced myself. The same demanding heart that beat down my chest seconds ago, passed out and dropped to my feet like a TKO upon the sound of the disarming locks.

Was I really about to come face to face again with the man who had my heart?

Seconds later, the door flew open to reveal a familiar but weary face. Oliver! The air held captive in my mouth escaped in one big pant. Those exotic eyes widened with surprise. That full mouth that used to kiss me passionately slightly parted as his brain tried to process my presence. His arm lingered at his side while the other dropped slowly from the door, keeping it ajar with his broad shoulders.

He gasped. "Summer."

Nodding vehemently, my hand cupped my mouth and tears started to fill. "I'm here, Oliver."

"For good?" He tilted his head in confusion, reluctant to allow happiness to take over without gaining all the facts.

I could only nod and sniff.

"Come here, you." He leapt at the chance to grab me. "Come here." Grabbing me close, he looped his muscular arms under mine and lifted me up. My little arms clutched his neck and held on for dear life. "Get in here." Oliver spun and settled me down inside his condo—or maybe it was *our* condo.

I watched him hastily pull my carryall and purse inside before closing the door. He settled the carryall next to me with my purse on top. Without reservation or restraint, I blurted, "Am I still yours?"

Oliver pulled me close and kissed the top of my head. Without hesitation, he replied, "Of course, Summer. Of course." Before I knew it, he'd snuck a long, hungry kiss against my lips. The moment stabilized my raggedy heartbeat, proving just how much I wanted him.

My stressed lips relaxed into a smile full of teeth. "Oliver," I began with a quivery voice. "You have no idea how—"

"Where did you go?" he asked impatiently. "Do you know how worried I was about you? And your friends?"

"I do, sweetie. I do." I inhaled sharply. "My friends. Now that I have you, I can call my friends."

"No." He put a hand up to stop me. "You deal with me first." Alarmed, before I could say anything, he explained, "Summer, you haven't put me first the way I do you. You didn't let me help you first when your apartment flooded, you chose Fran. You got pregnant and let me think I was the dad, but your friends knew first. You thought it was more important to share vital information with Brooke before confessing yours with me, and then you managed to have time to find a man for Amber, when your first order of priority shoulda' been to tell me that I was *not* the father of your baby." Looking away, he collected his thoughts before continuing. "You didn't even tell me that you slept with that slime ball the same night as me until your back was up against the wall."

Yeah, my back was certainly up against a wall that night. Consternation swept through me from head to toe. I decided not to defend any possible points against him because the truth was, I couldn't. Even if possible, I didn't want to. He was right. I hadn't done a good job at all with putting his feelings and our relationship first.

"You're right." He responded with a quick raise of his eyebrows. But something he said did make me curious. "H-how did you know that I found a man for Amber?"

"Because they all came over here recently to demand an explanation regarding your whereabouts. They miss you and are worried sick. So was I, and I wanna know what happened to you. The only reason why I haven't badgered you about your disappearance is because you look fine."

"Okay." Rubbing my belly, I bounced on my toes. "First things first. I want to say how much I missed you. My heart was being ripped to shreds every day that I was away from you. But I want to tell you that I am sorry."

The waterworks were on again. What was it about today? I just couldn't seem to catch a break. I attempted to steady my voice as the words spewed. "I am so sorry for being a girlfriend who only thinks of herself. Obviously, I have a lot to learn since this relationship stuff is new to me. It's hard to learn to think about putting someone above me when for so long, I just had to worry about myself." I placed my hand over my heart. "I promise to do better, Oliver. I will, because I don't want to lose you."

He simply nodded. "I appreciate that, but this wall between us can't be torn down unless you tell me where you went. Why couldn't we get a hold of you?"

I couldn't help but say, "See. Even without trying, I managed to ruin your and my friends' lives."

He shrugged in confusion. With wrinkled eyebrows, he asked, "What the hell is that supposed to mean?"

I bunched my wild hair with one hand and pulled it to the side, holding onto it for support. My preference was to avoid speaking about this, but it wasn't optional. Choosing to remain strong, I proceeded. "I didn't leave you, Oliver." I stomped my sandal lightly in frustration. "Well, I did and, I didn't. When you left on your motorcycle and didn't return the next day or call, I decided that your actions spoke volumes. I thought the classy thing to do would be to remove myself from the situation."

Between my belly, sandals, and the weight of the story, I needed to sit. I walked over to the sofa and took a seat. Oliver followed suit and sat on the other side of the sofa after he took the initiative to bring me a glass of water. I thanked him as he passed it to me. After taking a long sip, I placed it on the coffee table.

Rubbing my printed maxi dress-clad belly, I continued. "I called my friend, Max, and he brought his wife. She helped me pack and he moved my crap like no one's business. They insisted I stay in their guest bedroom for a few days. Couldn't face my girls. They knew too much, and I knew they'd be in my ear with too many opinions. My mom happened to have called me and I broke down over the phone."

Nodding, he told me, "I'll go to Max's house tonight or tomorrow to get your things. That's where they are, right?"

I nodded. "I appreciate it."

"Not a problem."

Oliver's knees faced forward with his feet placed flat on the floor. With crossed arms, he turned his neck just enough to make eye contact. Serious, he appeared to be listening with tight lips and strained brows. I would've done anything to see those familiar smiling eyes.

"I told her that you and I were in a bad spot. She insisted that being stressed would be no good for the baby, so she came Tuesday morning. My mom was on vacation and arrived with two tickets to California. I thought some time away would do us some good, you and I. Besides, I really needed my mom. I'd intended to call everyone as soon as I'd arrived. It seemed like a good idea to get away first before speaking to anyone. It felt so good to be with my mom. She offered me clarity and tranquility."

"I think that's fair." He cleared his throat as he waited for me to continue.

"Well, we arrived at Newport Beach to visit my aunt. This aunt . . . is my dad's sister. This visit was something that needed to take place years ago, and so, we got to know her. I heard an earful of stories about my dad. It was good for me, Oliver."

"And I am very happy for you." His face didn't reflect those sentiments at all. "But what about a phone call Summer to at least tell us that you were okay? I came home to a missing girlfriend, wiped out traces of you, no note."

"I just needed to breathe." Closing my eyes, I reiterated, "I just—needed. To. Breathe." I opened them and continued. "And when my phone died, I found relief in letting it remain dead. Didn't bother buying a new charger since I left mine here in the nightstand. It was a relief to rely on my own brain again and to see if I could hear my heart. I couldn't hear my heart anymore here. There was too much noise, too many opinions. Everything started to make me feel like a failure. I had to get well."

"And did you?"

"I believe so. Yes. And I'm sorry, I am so sorry that it had to be—" I closed my eyes and sighed. No. "I *chose* to do it this way."

"Thank you."

"I had to reevaluate who I was, who I'd become. So, yes, I let you guys down by disappearing. However, in the end, it was for the best."

"And who are you?" he challenged.

Boy, he wasn't going to make this easy for me. "A woman who is stronger than she thinks and knows what she wants." Wasn't quite sure how much stronger I'd become, but to admit that nothing had been resolved after leaving so dramatically would only piss him off even more. On the flip side, at least he was receiving some truth for once.

Oliver looked at me without blinking. "And what do you want, Summer?"

"You. I want *you*." My hand drew a circle. "And this life."

Still looking resistant, he nodded. "Good."

"Again. I'm sorry."

"Don't."

"Don't what?" I couldn't win, and that broke my heart.

"Don't apologize." He stood and walked in front of me. I looked up at him. "You're pregnant, and I want you to soul search and do what's right for you before your baby comes."

"*Our* baby."

With a turned head, he didn't say anything.

"Right, Oliver? This is *our* baby, no matter what."

"You did what you had to do as a mother. You put that little one first. I can appreciate that. That's growth, Summer."

The slow smile forming across my face almost made me cry. Almost. Problem was, I didn't think it was possible to produce any more tears.

"Problem is, you dipped, when the most courteous thing to do woulda been to shoot a text to at least Amber, who appears to be your favorite, to inform *someone* that you needed time away. Not to let us go bat-shit crazy over your whereabouts." He walked away and headed toward the bar counter with his back facing me. Without turning around, he added, "Summer, I fear your judgment calls sometimes. You need to learn to think things through."

"I know, okay? I know that now. What the hell? You just complimented me." I could feel my breathing becoming shallow as the anger threatened to simmer to the top.

He turned around. "Listen, I hope you know that your absence has taken a big toll on my life. No gym, barely a wink of sleep, I couldn't focus at work. If it weren't for the cleaning ladies that I had to hire back, my laundry and crap around the house wouldn't have gotten done. So, excuse me for sounding insensitive to your bad choices."

Bursting into tears with my face in my hands, I didn't think that being pregnant would wreak such havoc on my emotions. But how could I not feel bad? Oliver felt disappointed in me like my mother did when she discovered that I'd slept with a married man. Did I not make anyone proud?

I felt the cushion next to me sink. Hands pried mine away from my face. Before our eyes could meet, I buried my face into his shoulder.

"I'm sorry, baby. I'm so, so sorry. I need to stop exploding at you." He kissed my forehead. His muscular arms gripped me with love. "Had I not exploded at you the first time, then maybe you woulda never left. Just don't tell your buddy Brooke. She scares me and she's quite protective of you."

I pulled back and in a quivering voice asked, "What do you mean?"

"When they came here, I admitted to being rough on you. She wanted to know what I said to you. They were pissed at me."

I nodded; he wiped my tears away. "Sounds like her."

"Yeah." Both of his palms stroked my hair from the top down to the ends. "On my motorcycle ride, I had time to think."

"Where did you go anyway?"

"To a bar and then to a hotel. Trashy sounding, huh?" I could only respond with a half-grin. "I almost got into a bar fight with this jerk, too."

My eyes bulged in surprise. How much damage could I do to this man? I was indebted to him for years to come. The only way to make this all up to him was to prove my love by giving him whatever his heart desired. "Why?"

"Oh, you know he was mad drunk and got angry when I didn't want to get all chatty with him. They had to separate us, and we both got thrown out."

"Oh my gosh, Oliver." I sniffed and tried to stop my crying. He waved a hand at me.

"No, no, no. Don't even stress about it. I'm fine, he was drunk. No one got hurt. Case closed." When he put it like that, I agreed.

"But why didn't you ever tell me that you owned a motorcycle?"

"I didn't intend on using it anymore. Before I met you, I almost had an accident. Swore I'd never ride it again, but when I left you that night, I needed to take the edge off and hopped back on it. But it's gone. I gave it as a gift to someone at the bar and hitched a ride back with a friend."

"That's a lot to take in, Oliver. And that was mighty generous of you."

"Yeah, I didn't have the energy to sell it. What I wanted to say was that on my ride down I-66, I thought about how we could rectify this."

"Yeah?" My lips twisted nervously.

"Forget that this is Ruben's baby. Let's pretend like he doesn't exist. You and I will raise the baby together."

I bit my lower lip from the inside. My heart sank. I didn't care about Ruben, but this was his child, and despite the way Oliver or I felt about that, Ruben had the right to know. My child would have the right to know where the other fifty percent of his or her genetic makeup came from. This is not what I wanted, not at all. Oblivious to my objection, Oliver rambled on.

"I can step up and be the dad. Ruben is bad news and should stay on his side of town. Besides, he could be in Cuba by now, long gone." He spoke so matter-of-factly, like his plan was foolproof.

"And why would you think that? We weren't so special that he would lose his mind and uproot himself from all that he has and knows because of me."

Oliver shrugged like it was a game, or at least I took it that way. "You may have imprinted him."

"Oliver. You wanna strip away her Cuban roots?" My tears seemed to have dried up as panic took over.

"Baby. We can pass your baby off as mine and yours. *Don't make it so difficult.*"

I hid my irritation. This man thought long and hard about my baby's future without considering my concerns. "I . . . I don't know. We'd have to wait and see. We don't know what our baby will look like."

"Hmm. You said, 'our baby.' Did you mean mine and yours, or yours and his?"

I really didn't know except that it meant me and a father. Oliver posed a good question. I answered him the best I could, in all honesty. "I see this baby as having two fathers."

Oliver shifted and grunted, "That ain't what I wanted to hear." He stood and walked toward the bar stools.

I did the same. With his back to me, I replied, "Well, Oliver, whether you like it or not, Ruben is the dad. Ultimately, I see it as mine and yours."

Oliver turned to face me. "Biologically, yeah. But that's where we have to draw the line. That's all he gets."

My ears started to warm. I couldn't believe this man! Placing a hand on my chest became a useless effort to suppress the emotions that rose to the surface. *"Oliver, that is my choice.* I am the mom, and I think that Ruben has the right to know that he has a daughter or son coming into this world." Tears of anger made their way to my eyes. Here we go again. I couldn't control them if I wanted to.

Oliver pointed a fierce finger at me. "No. No, Summer." He became hostile. Those friendly eyes took a back seat to squinty ones of anger and a voice housed with a need to be heard. "You've made all kinds of decisions without me. Consider me this time."

My arms flew outward. My tone of voice went up. "Oliver are you kidding me? Seriously? Listen to yourself. I'm the mother. What's good for this baby has nothing to do with you, me, or anyone else—just the baby. *He* or she is gonna wanna know where his or her eyes came from, the nose, the mouth, whatever it is, the baby's gonna wanna know who he or she is. Everyone loves to know about their parents' background. I don't want this baby to rely on false information. How is that right, man?"

Hands on his hips, Oliver shook his head in disbelief. "Summer. You can forget about Ruben, all right? This over-cologned guy is gonna have his hands all over my girlfriend. I know he's gonna try something, especially knowing that he has a baby with you."

I was out of my head. Was this the same man that I met at the party that night? *"Oliver.* Don't you think I have a brain? Like I'm just going to let this man put his hands all over me?"

"Summer, he's already had his hands all over you." Oliver may have been furious, but not as much as me.

"Why are you talking to me like some sort of jerk?" His head snapped back in surprise. I hated yelling, but it felt like he wasn't listening otherwise. "I am a grown woman, and if I don't want a man touching me, then he won't be touching me." I threw my hands in the air. "You are acting so impossible." Anger suppressed my breathing. He smirked at me like I had a problem, but I knew he was being the childish one. "Look. This baby is mine and I would truly like to think of this baby as yours, too. I wish this baby was yours and not his. I wish to God that it had worked out that way, but it didn't. So now I have to digest what I've done and handle it. Ruben needs to know, and he will."

"Why? Why, Summer? What will he appreciate about all this as long as he's with Fran?"

"Oliver. Fran doesn't matter. I never want to talk about her again."

He raised his eyebrows. "Soooooo Fran won't ever be around this baby?" He wasn't asking me, he was challenging me.

"Oliver, I won't have to let Ruben see my child without supervision. I'm the mom."

"That's not my point. The point is, have you ever considered the fact that she may be around that baby for some unforeseen reason, even if Ruben is in another room, briefly?"

Impatient, I asked, "*What is your* point?"

"She-she-she . . . she could pinch the baby or something. You don't know, Summer."

His desperate thought was so funny that it almost made me laugh. "Fran wouldn't do that."

"You had sex with her husband multiple times and now you're gonna have his baby. Oh, okay, Summer. The lady would burn your hair in your sleep if she could." We shook our heads in unison. "My rule stands. Ruben ain't gonna know this baby."

"Stop it! Stop it, Oliver, right now!"

"Don't yell at me in my condo, Summer!"

"Oh." My tongue poked my cheek as I rolled my neck at him. "So, it's just your condo?"

"Don't be foolish, Summer. Of course not. You know what I'm saying."

"Whatever."

Everything seemed to have been spiraling out of control as I had images of me dialing my mom's cell quickly with a nervous finger, all the way to the girls hugging me upon seeing that I was okay. Anything else I could see—except for what was standing in front of me—felt better than this. Since it hurt my head to yell, I decided to make a rational decision and lower my voice, while keeping it firm.

"Well, quit trying to rearrange my life. You are not my husband." I started to pace with my hands on the sides of my head. "In fact, Oliver, I don't need this. I can't do these relationship things. I told you that, but you didn't believe me. Now I'm sitting here with another man's baby in my stomach with a man who is trying to keep them apart. No. No, no, no, no, no." I stopped pacing long enough to tell him, "I can't do this to you, and I can't do this to Ruben, I can't do this to the baby. I can't do this to anyone."

With that, I spun around and located my carryall with my eyes and found it near the front door where Oliver had left it and hurried toward it.

"Wait, wait, wait, Summer. Where do you think you're going?"

He had either desperation or deep concern in his voice. Couldn't tell. But without a chance to spin around, a hand grabbed my arm and did it for me. I saw the stress in my boyfriend's eyes.

"Where are you going, Summer?"

"I'm going to call my mom. I'm going to move back to Delaware." Did I mean it? I didn't know. I wanted to believe that it was the truth, but there was no time to think. I just needed to get out of here.

He sighed. "No, you're not. I'm not gonna let you get away so fast." At least he stopped yelling, because I really didn't know that I had a screamer on my hands.

"All you do is yell."

Oliver choked out a stifled laugh of disbelief. With a thumb pointed at his chest, he asked, "I yell? Me? Are you serious, Summer? I've been putting up with your moody butt for so long now, and you think I'm just supposed to sit here in my home and curl up? No."

"I did not say—"

"Look, I know you're pregnant. I get that. But you have been snipping at my head, and I've been dealing with a lot from you. Your lies, you putting me last, your big ole social circle." Suddenly, I felt like a failure in the role I played in his life. "I, on the other hand, have a business to run and a home to maintain. I opened my heart to you, and I feel like you do things to mock my gestures." He stopped talking. We said nothing. We stared at each other. Finally, he held up one finger and requested, "Give me one good reason why I should agree that Ruben have a role in this baby's life—aside from him being the biological father."

Crossing my arms over my chest, I started with, "Well, Oliver, being the daddy should be reason enough. But if I must delve deeper into the issue with you, then it's because," my face softened as my heart ripped just a little to reopen an old wound, "you know what happened to my father. No amount of wishing at night will ever allow me to know my father."

Oliver's hard facial expression crumbled like a soft cookie.

I ambled away a few feet as the thoughts in my mind connected to my heart. My palm rested over it. I met his pensive gaze and continued. "Oliver, many days, even as an adult, I catch myself doing what I used to do often as a teenager."

"What's that?" He shoved his hands into his pockets.

"Looking into a mirror to find a piece of my father in my features. My dad and mom had an airtight marriage. She didn't want to marry anyone, but he managed to steal her heart. So, I guess you can say I got my mom's free-bird spirit. I don't know." I shrugged, picking at my thumbnails.

"Suppose so. So, what did your dad do to win over your mom?" Obviously, he hinted that he needed help taming me.

"There was just something about him, according to my mom. But when you ask me to deny the baby to know Ruben, I imagine my mom doing something so foolish like that to me and me ending up hating her." I scurried to Oliver. My tiny hands squeezed his arms. In a gentle tone, I told him, "I would give anything to have my dad. Anything."

Without saying a word, he nodded, looking down. "I see."

"Do you, baby? You got to understand that this does not make Ruben the man that I want to be with or the man more fit for my child. He is just the right thing to do." I took two fingers and placed them under Oliver's chin to show him that I needed to see his eyes. "You are the one who I want to serve as a great role model for our child. And this time I mean yours and mine."

Oliver's mouth tightened to one side of his face. I could see the wheels turning in his mind. Did he doubt me?

"Let's make a deal."

Should I be scared? Reluctantly, I replied, "Okay. Depends on what it is." Becoming fidgety, I folded my arms to hide my nerves.

"Get a paternity test. Prove that he's the daddy, and I'll support his visitation rights. And, Summer, that's the only way I can move forward with this idea of yours to include him."

I reached in deep and pulled out the firmest card in my pocket. "Well, I have a stipulation of my own."

"What's that?" He crossed his arms.

"You cannot talk to me again in that tone. I will not accept that treatment in my life." I pointed at him. "*You* are starting to stress me more than this situation."

"Summer—"

My hand flew up. "I'm not done. I love you, but I am the mother. I will be the one who will be in hours of agony pushing the baby out after months of growing inside of me. *Me*. Not you. I will decide what's best for this baby. I wanted to include you, but you're trying to run power over me, and I don't like it."

Maybe he would throw me out, maybe this would end us. Both possibilities broke my heart, but living this way another day was not an option. I swore my heart stopped beating after laying down the law.

Oliver stood there for a moment, nodding in silence. "I'm sorry. I guess I've been stressed about all of this and conducted myself poorly. I'm very sorry, Summer."

"However, you made good points. I'll change my actions, and you change your behavior. Otherwise, we go our separate ways."

Oliver couldn't hide his dismay. "Please, don't say that."

"Oliver, we won't—*I* won't go on like this. My well-being comes first."

He pulled me close and nibbled affectionately at my ear. "Baby, I'm sorry. I'm sorry, I'm sorry, I'm sorry. I'm an ass."

We rocked together in an embrace, and for the first time today, I didn't feel like crying. I felt too empowered.

In a low tone, I said, "I'll get that test done."

It seemed reasonable and something that needed to be done anyway. Condoms or no condoms, it wouldn't be smart to rely on my theory alone. Science was the answer this time. I smiled at him, hoping to catch his smiling eyes, but I didn't. I just nodded and pulled him close. His lips kissed the top of my head as my hands rubbed his back. Warm, soft, calm, and supportive. This Oliver, I knew.

Emily

Watching her two friends interact, Emily sat with her legs crossed with an elbow resting on a knee and a fist supporting her chin. She smiled to herself, grateful for a positive moment to remember among friends.

Amber turned the gift card over and back to the front side. "I can't believe that you bought me a *five-hundred-dollar gift card from Macy's.*"

"Well," Brooke replied, "I'm more of a Saks girl myself, but one garment there on that gift card and it's over. And since you're trying to be taken seriously as a professional here in DC, then you really need to bring your A-game, and let me tell you, good business attire will separate you from the rest of the competition. I mean, you're from New York City. Shouldn't you always represent?"

"Uh, right?" Amber cackled. "Seriously, I can't thank you enough." Amber's palms pressed against her cheeks. "Was starting to look too Washingtonian."

Confused, Emily asked, "What? What do you two mean? DC people cannot dress?"

Amber shrugged with a grin. "Let's just say that a sense of style don't really stand out here like it did up there. Come on, New York is one of the top four fashion capitals."

"And my college was in a city that neighbored another fashion capital of the world. Therefore, I know a good look when I see one, too." Brooke winked at her.

"Wait a minute." Emily held up a finger. She would stand but the alcohol wouldn't let her. "You're implying that you two have style and I don't? Is that what you're saying?"

Amber and Brooke looked at one another with smirks. Brooke shrugged and nodded. "You do okay. Maybe we can all take a trip to New York or even L.A."

Amber defended her point of view. "Well, wait. In New York, it's more about imagination, takin' risks and lettin' your personality shine through. To me, everyone looks the same here. I mean, Brooke always brings it."

"I guess . . ." Emily decided to observe the scene the next time she stepped out in public. Until then, she decided to take their word for it and move on.

Delighted, Brooke smiled and ushered a proud hand toward Amber. "Well, thank you. Nice to see that we can agree."

"Today we get along. Tomorrow, we'll see," Amber teased.

Brooke held up a finger. "But there is one more gift."

"Whuuuuuuh?" Amber gasped.

"Yeah." Brooke stood up and handed her a rectangular box from her purse. "Look under the tissue."

Emily wiped a tear from her eye as she witnessed the whole gift-opening event, realizing just how much she loved her friends and missed Summer. In their own world, Amber and Brooke didn't notice Emily drowning in her own sentiments. It was thoughtful of Brooke to spend so much on a friend that she'd taken a while to appreciate.

"I love this purse." Amber gawked at it as she held it up by the short strap.

Brooke waved a quick finger at her. "No, no, no, no, no darling. This is a wristlet, you gotta learn your stuff.

Upon closer examination of the gold-plated tag on the front, Amber placed a hand over her heart. "Burberry. Woooooooooow." She grabbed Brooke and rocked her in a drunken hug. "You hate me. Why'd you do this?"

Brooke pulled her off by a grip of the shoulders. "What? I mean, I was not your biggest fan, but hate? I didn't hate you, but what I do want is for you to be successful with the gift that God has given you. That's all."

Amber fell over laughing, shaking a finger at Brooke. "Sneaky, sneaky. But this gift card and pur—wristlet, Brooke, come on." Between the emotions and the alcohol, Amber's face became sappy. "I mean, why are you givin' me so much?"

"Well, not gonna lie. I re-gifted the wristlet. I bought it a while back and just never got around to it. I went shopping at the mall, passed Macy's on my way to Saks and realized that you should diversify your preference. You like Express, I know, but sometimes you gotta try new things. Plus, Macy's got clothes for your career. I know you're trying. I see ya'. You'll be surprised at how much great clothes can make you succeed faster. *This* is where you shoulda' spent your money—on more sophisticated clothes back when you were turning tricks for cash."

Amber nodded. "Thank you, sweetie." She'd begun to cry. Not dramatic tears, just plain tears of appreciation.

"Now open mine." Emily jumped and clapped like a seal.

"Oh, let us see." Amber salivated with a grin.

Emily held out a hand of caution as she passed Amber the bag with the other. "Now let me give you the disclaimer. Warning: Brooke has outdone me by a mile, and I wasn't looking to compete." Amber and Brooke laughed. "Now go."

"It's all good, honey. I don't care if it was a box of tea. A gift is a gift."

Brooke playfully eyed Amber up and down with a mock attitude. "Um, now you tell me. If I knew that then I woulda just stopped by the grocery store and did just that."

Everything sounded funny to a drunk Amber. She struggled to steady herself. "Now come on, let's see what Emily got me." Amber reached into a bag and pulled out an envelope. Confused, her eyebrows crinkled. "An envelope?"

"Open it." Emily took a sip of wine knowing Amber would love it.

Amber snorted with laughter. "Okay." Curious, Brooke stood over Amber's shoulder on her toes to catch a better look at the contents of the envelope. Amber struggled to pull out the piece of paper from within, but when she did, she tilted her head in confusion. "Tickets?"

"Umm hm." Emily felt proud, regardless of the lackluster reaction.

Amber's jaw dropped. "From New York City to DC?" She took a few staggered steps to Emily and held out the tickets to give to Emily. "Washington DC to New York City?"

Shrugging, Emily replied, "Sometimes you just need your family."

Choked up, Amber's eyelids became heavy and her eyes glassy. "I can't believe this." She threw a hand over her chest. "Seriously. This—this means a lot. Like, more than you could ever know."

"Well, you getting her here and you there can be costly. I figured I'd help out with that. You get a trip and she gets a trip."

Amber squinted. "What? Ain't this too much? You're a teacher, Em. I don't wanna take all your ends."

Emily may not have been flashy like Brooke, but she knew how to manage her money. "Oh, honey, thank you for your concern, but I'm a single woman with a brain. I think I'm all right."

Amber snapped her fingers. "All right now." She sniffled and chuckled. "Why are you two doing this? Either I'm a charity case or you two are two terrific girlfriends."

Brooke wore a naughty grin, and with one raised eyebrow, she said, "How about both?" With a laugh, Amber knocked her on the shoulder. Brooke bit her lower lip and added, "No, seriously, we encouraged you to change and wanted you to know that we got your back in the process. We know this isn't easy, being without family, wanting things, competing with others for jobs, trying to make it in this area. Besides, we know how much you need a break."

Amber nodded slowly. "You right. You are absolutely right," she sang. "It's been hard and it's my fault though. I shoulda been well-off from collecting money from men all these years. I worked hard for that money. I've put up with smelly balls, wrinkly balls, short penises, bad breath, fat mother—"

"Okay." Brooke flung a hand of submission into the air. "We get the point. Just remember that the next time you're tempted to do something silly with your money, that's all. Besides, the past is the past. Gotta move on, right?"

Emily twisted her lips. "Looks like we all do. We're new women now. Or, at least we're trying to be."

Folding her arms with a distant stare, Brooke nodded and shrugged.

"I know that's right." Amber shrugged in disappointment. "You guys, these gifts are so thoughtful and handy. All my earnings from teaching goes to my rent and utilities. I'm barely makin' it. But on the real, I'm grateful to have that much."

"What happened to the gigs and stuff?" Emily asked.

"Uhhh, I do get some phone calls sometimes, but that's been slow, too. Sometimes I think I'm gonna get called for a performance, but the prospects warn me that all other things gotta come together first."

"Amber, I'll try to promote you to my clients. You know, for those who don't have a piano player and want one, I'll recommend you. Who knows, I have two weddings this month. I think I can make something happen. You'll be fine if you stick with me."

Amber didn't show any restraint when she blurted. "Man. How much you gonna get paid this month from that?"

"I don't always like to share my finances with anyone, but I guess this month I will. You guys are my inner circle, even though we are *missing* someone." Amber and Emily nodded and sighed. Brooke continued. "Combined, I'll make around thirty grand."

"Sheesh," Amber replied.

"I know, she's a machine. My dad would love her." Emily remembered her dad working around the clock to make sure that the family never went without.

"But don't go repeating that," Brooke warned with a finger pointing up. "Which brings me to my next point: I have to go to bed. Tomorrow, I need to update my social media page, plus my client is a jerk. I will be so glad when I'm done with Ms. Victoria Williams. Her dad is spending a ton of money on this wedding. Meanwhile, all she does is obsess and cry. I worry that her fiancé will wake up and realize that he can do better and call it all off. I tell you, if it weren't for my love of this, I woulda quit a long time ago, because people like Victoria can really wear you down."

Emily suggested to Brooke, "I don't think he will break anything off. It sounds like daddy is loaded." Amber fell over laughing. "Well they may not last long, like Eric and me, but best believe, boyfriend is marching down that aisle."

Brooke smiled. "True. But first, Amber needs your new address. We gotta get moving."

Emily wished that she was leaving her address for Summer as well when she scribbled it down on a piece of paper Amber gave her. "Here. Come by whenever you like."

Amber thanked them profusely as she led them to the door. After all of the hugs and kisses on the cheeks, Amber snatched the door open to see a familiar face standing there, ready to knock.

Summer

I stood there in consternation looking at my friends studying me like a foreign organism in a petri dish.

"Summer?" Obviously Amber couldn't believe her eyes, as mine darted to Brooke's awe-struck face and Emily's expression of concern.

I wagged my head vehemently.

"Come here." Amber ushered me in with a fast wave as they pulled me into a huddle of tears and hugs. The door slammed behind me.

This felt like home, and not the structure housing us. These arms, the scent of their perfumes, their voices. It was indescribable to see Oliver, but it was a big relief to be reunited with my girls, especially since they'd become my rock.

"I've missed you guys so much." The tears came back. Good tears. I had a gift for Amber in my carryall, which was why I'd decided to stop by her place first. The bag I carried held two souvenirs with the gift.

We released each other to find that there wasn't a dry eye in the foyer. Emily waved her hands into the air. "What happened?"

If I didn't feel so overwhelmed, the running mascara under her eyes would've subjected me to laughter. She looked like a clown.

"Guys, it was so crazy. I just got back today."

"Well, you better start talking, because I lost sleep over you and had to try a ton of tricks to make sure that my beauty didn't suffer irrevocably." Brooke placed her hands on her hips. "Guess who the last person was to put me through something like this?"

"Jackson," we all guessed.

"That's right," she confirmed. "And let me tell you, my face almost didn't recover from that."

Brooke's level of vanity humored me. Sincere, she wasn't playing and made no apologies for how she preferred to look or carry herself. I missed that so much.

"Come in, come in." Amber pulled me by the hand and we all plopped on the sofa—except Amber, who chose to sit on the coffee table. They stared at me intently, as I eased the story out, worried that they would hate me. I felt a hand rub my knee, my shoulder, and even saw some pouty lips. I even told them about my reunion with Oliver.

"How was meeting your aunt?" Brooke asked.

"It-it was nice. Really nice. My mom doesn't come from a big family. She lost touch with a lot of the ones still living. But meeting my dad's sister was what I needed to help heal."

Amber shook her head. "Good for you, really, Summer."

"You coulda called though, just once." Brooke didn't look too happy with me.

"Guys, I did a crappy thing, and I can only hope you can forgive me."

Emily's pretty, compassion-filled eyes solemnly stared at me. "But you let us think the worse until we located your mom's place of employment. Then we feared you left us for good. That hurt. *You* hurt us, Summer."

"Big time," Brooke added.

Perhaps Amber realized that I was drowning, so she offered me a hand above water that I desperately needed. "Yes, she dipped suddenly, but she had to get well. Sometimes, we all need space to be better for the ones around us. Hell! But first of all, for ourselves. You got a lil bigger." Amber's hand flew up when she saw my green eyes widen. "But relax. I mean it in a good way." Amber rubbed my leg and asked, "Well, how do you feel?"

"Physically, I feel fine. Emotionally, not so much."

Emily shrugged. "But you're home now, and we should all just let this go."

Brooke agreed. "She's right. You need to think about your baby and forget Oliver if he's acting up. He can get the boot if he's gonna be a jerk about this."

Amber fell over laughing. "Now, Brooke, that is wrong. You know she can't do that."

Brooke shrugged casually. "Why not? Jackson and I kicked each other to the curb, and we're just fine."

"Says who?" I asked with a smile. "You mention his name every chance you get."

She crossed her legs with mock dignity. "Well, it's natural. He was my first love."

"Mmm-hmm," I teased. "Don't worry, Oliver won't be a problem anymore if he wants to hang on to me. We had the talk that should've gone down weeks ago."

Brooke wagged a finger at me. "That's how you do it."

Thinking, I sighed. "I have to tell Ruben the truth, like now. Guess I just fear Ruben's reaction. What if he brushes off the baby?"

"Well, if he doesn't want the baby then that's good news, especially for you and Oliver. You can raise the baby without his interference," Amber answered, as if she had the whole thing figured out.

"Amber, how is that a good thing? I don't think anyone understands. I don't want this baby to not know who his or her daddy is. By name is not enough. I want the relationship to be there. It's not about what Oliver and I want, only what's good for the baby. Brooke knows what I'm talking about. We didn't have fathers. I mean, don't you know what I mean? Wouldn't you want that for your baby?"

Brooke thought about my question with her eyes focused on the floor. "I'm a selfish person. Summer. If the relationship between the baby's daddy and I was rocky, and I was involved with another man who I loved . . ." She appeared befuddled. "Maybe I would have to be in your shoes to know. But I do know that it is big of you, and you should do what's right. Do what you can live with."

Emily nodded in agreement. "That's what I say. It's your baby, your ex-fling, and your man."

"Now I need you guys," Brooke admitted. As usual, I welcomed a break from discussing my life for too long. We stared at her as a sign to continue. "Should I call Damani?"

Without hesitation, Amber replied, "You have major pride issues. A man is a man. Listen to your gut. If it gnaws at you, feed it and call the man. I think you should call Jackson, too."

Brooke snapped her neck to face Amber. "Oh, I did not ask you about Jackson. Remember, he moved on. Stick to the script."

Amber held up two palms as Emily and I giggled. She pointed a finger at Brooke and with a grin she said, "Take it easy. Don't think you own me now because of those gifts. But that's my final opinion."

Brooke reached for the pillow behind her back and used it to playfully hit Amber against her arms. "Take that!"

Amber guarded herself with her arms as she laughed with her head turned away from Brooke. "Quit playin' Psycho Barbie!"

Brooke laughed as she moved back into her seat placing the pillow back in its place. "Talkin' all that trash to me."

"You ole rough broad," Amber joked.

Grinning, I said, "You guys are nuts, and this is why I need you all in my life." That couldn't be more truthful given the amount of stress Oliver and I were under.

"You better keep your lil golden ass on the east coast next time." Amber stuck her tongue out at me.

Holding up both hands, I said, "Lesson learned. At least for now."

Brooke asked, "Who can blame you for trying to get away? Hell, I need a vacation."

"I think you should," Emily said, looking at Brooke. "Look at how it ended—with you mentioning another man's name. It was your bad. I would have left, too."

"Summer?" Brooke waited with her eyes expectantly beaming into mine.

I waited a moment to ponder her dilemma. If I had to face my ex-fling, then she should be brave enough to call an ex-lover. "I have to call Ruben, so grab your tits and do the same."

Amber rejoiced by shaking her hands in the air. "Looks like you're out-numbered," she taunted.

"Shut up." Brooke looked for something to throw at Amber until she located a balled-up piece of tissue paper next to Amber. She picked it up from the coffee table and threw it at Amber, who blocked it off with her hands.

"Ha-ha." Amber stuck her tongue out at Brooke.

Brooke shot her the middle finger and Amber mirrored her action with two of them.

"Easy, ladies," I said, playing the referee.

"Oh, I don't pay the ole snot any attention." Amber squinted her eyes and nose at Brooke and wiggled her head at her.

"I'll take those gifts back, woman. I have the gift card receipt," Brooke threatened her with a wave of her index finger.

"Nooooo," Amber pretended to look concerned. "I'll be good now."

"You better." Brooke crossed her legs and settled back into the sofa.

Emily folded her arms and chuckled. "No more drinks for you women."

Brooke frowned. "See, I'm out of control and this is why I'm in need of my bed. Thank you, guys, for the advice." We all assured her that it wasn't a problem. She leaned forward to catch a glimpse of my face. "And, Summer, I really do hope this all works out for you. Just call me and keep me posted. I am so sorry if we made you feel like you had to take off. I'm sorry. Come here." She stood and helped me up by the hand. We hugged, caressing each other's backs.

I pulled back to tell her, "Thank you guys for always being supportive. I really do love you guys." I caught a glimpse of Emily and Amber's faces.

We wrapped up the party after I distributed my gifts to my friends. Brooke and Emily gushed over their Newport Beach t-shirts and cellphone covers. Amber couldn't be more thrilled when she received the box of business cards and pens that I had made for her. Many weeks ago, we'd all decided that Amber needed things that would propel her toward a better future. Now, she just had to keep making the strides to get herself there. And with all of us behind one another, how could any of us fail?

7: asshats

Brooke

Brooke puckered her electric red lips at herself as she modeled her cobalt blue peplum top with a pair of roll-cuff skinny jeans. The outfit matched her mood: bold! Stepping outside with a loose, high bun, Brooke enjoyed the early spring breezes that frequently skated across the back of her neck as she walked the streets in search of a cab. Today felt better outside on the sidewalk amid the DC lunch crowd than in the confines of a car.

Reaching Seventh Street, Brooke flagged an approaching cab. Once she told the cabbie her destination, she grasped her trifold clutch for dear life while she prayed she wouldn't regret swallowing her pride. Minutes later, the cab neared his restaurant.

Damani better appreciate me going out on a limb.

Brooke didn't know whether to ask the cabbie to wait, or just let it go and hail another after pouring her heart out to Damani. Deciding on the latter, she slipped the driver cash and slid out of the cab. "Keep the change," she told him before closing the door.

He grunted and said, "Thank you," as he pulled out into traffic.

With two hands on her clutch, she held it close to her chest before walking into the restaurant. She hadn't been back for a great Greek meal since she'd let Damani down.

The more she'd thought about it, the more she felt like a jerk for sending him home disgusted. My God, she realized. Maybe she did send her future husband home. He seemed open to children and marriage from the times they'd talked. It was just a matter of him finding the right woman as well as the time. The time had come for her to march in to reclaim her possible future. Besides, with the exception of Jackson, she'd always gotten what she'd wanted. Brooke couldn't thank her girls enough for convincing her to reach out to Damani, especially after giving him much-needed space.

Brooke reached for the doors and inhaled the smell of the familiar, delicious aroma. Allowing her pride and shyness to shed with each step, she marched to the counter with a confident smile on her face. It took her no time to spot the familiar man bending down behind the cabinet. His hair had grown some, but she could tell it was him by the profile of his nose bridge. She knocked on the counter to grab his attention. When he stood, Brooke poked her tongue in her cheek in slight embarrassment.

"Yes?" The man resembled Damani, but it surely wasn't him. His shoulders were too slender, and though he stood a few inches taller than Damani, he wasn't as handsome.

"I . . . I'm here to see Damani." Flustered, Brooke almost felt embarrassed, as if the guy would chalk it up as a naughty rendezvous. She ran her tongue behind her teeth as he studied her from behind the corner.

His sexy, full lips formed into a smirk. "Damani's not here."

"Oh, so he's off today. I assume he'll be in tomorrow? He's such a workaholic."

He turned his ear to her as if he couldn't hear her. "Excuse me?" The man seemed genuinely confused.

"To-uh-morrow. He will be in tomorrow. Right?" Something about this guy made her feel silly. She hadn't anticipated speaking to another person other than Damani, let alone for this long.

"Sure, if he can pack all his belongings and book a flight by then. He may make it in time for the night shift all the way from Greece." The guy chuckled with pity.

Brooke never felt so stupid. This guy knew something that she didn't, and he rather enjoyed hanging the secret information over her head. "What are you talking about? Is he on vacation?"

"Nope." The guy began wiping the counter with a white cloth. He paused to make eye contact before telling Brooke, "He went back home. It was time."

She could feel her stomach drop to her knees causing her to hold onto the counter. This guy might as well have been speaking Greek, because she didn't understand anything that he told her. "It was time?" Brooke's eyelashes fluttered. "What do you mean it was time?"

"Lady, who are you?" The impatience radiated through his squinted eyes. Obviously, his curiosity had grown as strong as hers.

"I'm Brooke. I was dating him—I'm sure he mentioned me."

He chuckled. "Right."

"We had a misunderstanding, and I came to set him straight." Giving away so many details to this stranger wasn't part of the plan.

The mystery man folded his arms. "I see." Then he positioned his balled hands against the wooden counter to support his weight as he leaned forward. "Look . . ." He twirled a hand as he tried to remember her name. ". . . Brooke. I don't know what scam my brother ran on you, but he was here for a break." He tapped a finger onto his chest. "*I* am the one who went on vacation, and he was the one who took my place while I was gone."

Brooke gasped. "So, he doesn't own this place?" She rested a weak hand over her chest.

Damani's brother froze before he let out a chuckle. He shook his head as he resumed wiping the countertop. "Boy, my big brother got you good, huh?" His eyes glowed with humor. "Owner? *Owner*?"

Brooke squeezed her throat between two fingers as she pointed her nose in the air. "So. What about the townhouse in Arlington?"

"*My* townhouse in Arlington? Were you the one who left behind the pink thong under my bed?"

With her eyes almost out of her head, she squeezed her temples with one hand. She remembered the night Damani took her home after sex without any underwear on. Her silence spoke volumes as she refused to answer that question. It sounded more like an accusation in all honesty.

"Gorgeous, didn't you notice that there weren't any pictures anywhere? I came home a week earlier than expected. Guess what?" Brooke could only raise her eyebrows in horror as she waited to hear the punch line to an unfunny joke. "My pictures were missing, and my home was a mess—well, by my standards. Damani pretty much lied to you on all sides to appeal to you."

"You think?" Brooke snarled. "Tell me. What *is* real about him?"

"His name's Damani Pappas. That is, unless he gave you a different last name." His tongue brushed against the inside of his cheek in amusement.

"No, I got that much. What else?"

"Damani's wife left him because he is self-centered and couldn't leave the ladies alone. He has a weakness for women and will do anything to get one, even if for one night. The good-looking women such as yourself really make him do crazy things."

"He's . . . married?" It felt like someone deposited a lump of coal in her throat.

He nodded with an expression as if it were no big deal. "Yeah."

Brooke felt like a bullet had gone through her chest. Thinking she was moving on and getting over Jackson, she'd gone nowhere. Meanwhile, her handsome, sweet ex, sat across town making another woman happy, according to Summer. If Brooke could crawl, she would've slipped into the nearest hole.

"I feel for you, I really do, but my brother basically took over my life here. I told the staff to treat him like the owner, but Damani really went above and beyond, huh?"

"He did so much for me. He cooked me a meal on our first date, he—"

His brother flipped a hand up. "Whoa. Damani does not cook. He thinks that he is too cute to cook. He brought some food to my house and heated it up."

Confused, Brooke asked, "So, if he's so lousy, why in the world did you set him up in your home and business?"

"I was desperate. I needed a vacation and hadn't seen my mom is a year. He was the only person that I could think of. Running restaurants runs in the family blood—I'm talking aunts, uncles, cousins . . . I mean, he's got that going for him. I knew he was the only one who would jump without worrying about leaving family behind. Plus, Damani sounded like he could use a break from his troubles. He promised me that I would really be helping him out mentally." Damani's brother shrugged. "Won't make that mistake again."

Brooke heard the entrance door swing open. She lost her appetite and her palette for Greek food.

"Look, Brooke. I'm truly sorry about what my brother did to you. And, if I had a chance with you I'd go to strange lengths, too, I suppose. If you'll excuse me, I have a customer." He bit his lower lip. "But, uh, if you ever need a Damani fix, I can play a close second." He tossed the dirty rag back and forth between both hands.

Feeling faint, she frowned. "Don't hold your breath."

There was no way she could ever eat there again. Damani had made a laughing stock out of her. Brooke spun on her heel and came face to face with the next customer, feeling as though she couldn't make a dash fast enough for the front door.

Summer

"That lying jerk! How could I be so stupid? Things like this don't happen to me. I'm officially like those other women who have bad luck with men. I swore I'd never be like them."

The anger and disbelief poured through the phone as Brooke explained how everything she'd shared with Damani turned out to be a joke. I plugged my index finger into my right ear to block out the noisy background.

"And I swore I'd never fall in love and get tied down. Join the club," I quipped.

"Where—where are you?" Brooke sounded annoyed and rightfully so.

I spoke into the phone with my hand cupping my mouth. "I'm at Whole Foods. A live deejay is playing music upstairs. It's this cool thing they do every Thursday, but it's not so good when you're underneath the balcony and on the phone."

"Listen, I have to go. I have an appointment with this client. They are going to drive me nuts. They don't know what they want. And you know what?"

"Yes?" Hunched over with my eyes full of lust, I took inventory of the pastries in the bakery that wouldn't be coming with me.

"I'm not listening to you girls anymore. I haven't spoken to Jackson, and I can imagine how that one would go. Imagine if you woulda never seen him that day and I decided to call him. I would get embarrassed."

I straightened. "Well, Brooke, we were only trying to help. Now you have closure with Damani, and you can date again."

"Closure? Date again? Are you nuts, Summer? He left before I could slap him for lying to me, because I would've slapped him. I'm humiliated. And he's gonna have the last laugh when his brother calls him to tell him that I came looking for him. And, as far as dating again . . . no. Ain't gonna happen. I need a break so I'm going back to having a love affair with my money. I'm done trusting these clowns called men. Such a letdown."

Sighing with a hand on my hip, I struggled with what to say next. "Honey, girl, just calm down. It will all be okay.

Give this time to blow over and focus on work in the meantime, but Brooke Brazile needs to stay open to love. Please don't turn bitter. You're too young for that and that's my job." I knew she would love that and agree. She didn't have to know that I couldn't bear to hear her complain any longer until Mr. Right came.

"Well. I guess bitterness *would* ruin my face. I don't want frown lines before ninety, so thanks, Summer. I'll go for a jog after my clients today. Pray for me. I hate this spoiled bridezilla."

"Focus on the check."

"Oh, honey. I always do." She hung up.

After skating around the store, picking up majority organic products and food, financing the bill off Oliver's dime didn't relieve me of the guilt from shopping here. Even though paying for the four-hundred-dollar bill for ten bags of groceries wouldn't make a dent in the household budget, the same poor girl lived inside of me and cringed. This was my life now—paying for expensive organic food without batting a lash like the rest of these upper-crust residents. If I were still on my own, I'd be shopping at the international market where they didn't sell anything organic. However, Oliver believed that pregnant women and children should eat organic. To me, the organic industry was a scam and warranted an eye roll at that thought every time. Remembering that he just wanted to do the right thing suppressed my irritation.

At my Corvette, I tipped the Whole Foods employee handsomely for loading my car and joked that I could borrow his muscles again once I arrived home.

"I wish I could, miss." He grinned from ear to ear and wished me a happy day. The engine growled once my finger pressed the ignition button and in a half-mile, the drive ended. After unfolding my shopping cart, I carefully loaded the groceries, and pushed it to the elevators. Oliver would kill me if he knew that I did all of this on my own, but depending on a man for simplistic actions didn't quite make it into my DNA.

The walls closed in on me as I tried to delay the inevitable. Ruben needed to know about this baby. After slowly unpacking every item and putting them in their rightful places, I pulled out my iPhone with a shaky hand and scrolled through the contact list to locate Ruben's name and number. Deciding not to overthink it, I inhaled sharply and held my breath while pressing the number that would connect me to my ex-fling.

My hand gripped the kitchen counter for support while counting the rings. One. Two. Three. Oh great! The dreaded question: Do I leave a voicemail or not? I hated that moment of pondering a decision. I cursed at myself for not having that answer before committing to dialing. Four.

I heard a click and waited to discern whether it was a pick-up click or the one before the voicemail.

"Surprise, surprise."

Got my answer. I could hear his grin. The hot Cuban breathed heavily into the receiver as if he'd just rolled off of Fran after having a major orgasm. That moment before lighting the cigarette.

Feeling awkward and mousy, I asked, "Is this a bad time?"

"Summer, Summer. I was surprised to see your name on my screen. Anytime is perfect for you. I'm at the gym. I paused the treadmill just for you, and I don't do that for anybody."

I exhaled the inhale that never really escaped even after greeting him with a question. It was good to know that he wasn't having sex, because that would be a strange moment. I should've known he and Fran weren't raising any ruckus. However, a part of me suspected a new lover by his side.

"Look, can I see you when you have a free spot in your schedule?"

"Are you okay?"

"Just can't get into it over the phone. Can we meet?"

"You mean today?"

"That'd be great," I lied. While it'd be great to get this all over with, nothing would ever fully prepare me for another private moment with Ruben Sotolongo. Nothing. "Well, if possible." I released my grip from the counter in exchange for the back of my neck.

"Sure. I just finished weights, so it won't kill me to forego the treadmill. Lemme grab a quick shower, and then I'll call you back."

"Sounds good."

"I'm happy to hear from you again, Summer. I never stopped thinking about you."

"Um-hm. Bye."

I hung up. Fran told me he was a cheater, and now my name made the list of his dumb bimbo flings. After speaking with him, I couldn't pinpoint my feelings. At least our meeting wasn't secretive. Oliver knew this had to be done and trusted me to go alone. He admitted that he couldn't babysit me and to imply that he needed to would be an insult, despite my many mistakes. While it didn't make him happy, he understood. In deep thought, I folded the reusable shopping bags and waited for Ruben's call.

Emily

Emily unpacked the last box in her new 862-square-foot Southeast condo. After moving from a rowhouse to a condo with no memories, she felt rejuvenated. She felt the difference moving from her five-bedroom rowhouse with all updated appliances to a two bedroom, two-bath condo with somewhat dated appliances, light wooden floors and architectural structure as its selling points. What it did have that the rowhouse didn't was the coziness and a chance for new memories.

Her rowhouse had become crowded with intrusive still-framed images in her head of Eric smiling during their happiest times and of Eric walking away with luggage. Still-framed images flashed of that awful night when she had to put him out again for paying for a night with her best friend. Another image flashed of her arguing with Amber right before Pharr's arrival. Last but not least, the memory of Zach sitting on her couch many times replayed in her head as she chuckled when she thought about trudging home on that windy day after Zach accidentally showed her his lewd video on his phone.

Deciding on a cup of coffee, Emily wiggled her arms into a bumblebee yellow windbreaker over black leggings. She grabbed her keys and debit card from her purse, zipped them into her windbreaker pocket, and headed for the door. Remembering her cell phone at the last minute, she made a beeline to her bedroom, snatched it up from her bed, and headed for the front door once again.

Passing through the glass doors of the lobby, she made her way into the crowd and headed for the closest Starbucks. The sun played peekaboo behind the clouds, indicating a possible storm later. Emily couldn't care less as she became filled with the spirit of gratuity of being in walking distance to stores and coffee shops unlike before. When she lived in her rowhouse, she needed a car to access these kinds of places since her home sat too far into the neighborhood to take a casual stroll for a cup of coffee. Now, instead of always starting the engine to her Jeep, she could just use her two legs, burn extra calories, and enjoy the scenery at the same time.

Emily smiled with pleasure as her ponytail swung behind her head while she headed for the doors of the famous coffee shop. This was the life that she'd waited for. A fresh start with independence was the best feeling next to a vacation. Eric finally made it into her past and didn't know where she lived. Zach lived on his side of town in his own quadrant, so the idea of him making a surprise visit didn't seem so threatening. Even though she liked him a lot, seeing Zach made her think too much of the past. It was all just too close to an era of Eric and a timid Emily, and she didn't like that part.

"What can I get for you?" the young blonde asked through friendly eyes.

Emily loved Starbucks employees; they all seemed genuinely happy to serve customers. She always made it a point to tip them, but she remembered that she didn't have any cash handy.

"A tall, skinny caramel macchiato please."

"Sure." Grabbing the cup with a marker in the other hand, the cashier asked, "Can I get a name?"

"Emily."

"Excellent." She scribbled on the side of the cup and then passed it along to a barista.

Emily smiled back at the cashier before swiping her debit card once she quoted the price. Thanking the cashier and moving to the end counter as she waited for her drink, Emily peeked around the coffee shop as she considered sitting down to enjoy her coffee. The debate ended when she saw a sudden downpour of rain.

Once a male barista called her name, Emily thanked him and snatched it off the counter and found a small table next to the window. She took out her cell phone and explored the internet as she switched her gaze from the phone to the window to watch the rain. Suddenly, Starbucks seemed like the answer for sidewalk peddlers who wanted to escape the rain on this dreary Thursday.

Grateful that she'd made it inside Starbucks before the heavy rainfall, she realized that people sat anywhere they could. Some settled for standing at the window while chatting with someone. Emily prepared herself to be asked to share her table space. It all depended on the company, she decided. She didn't want a creepy or smelly person. She preferred someone without children. Ultimately, she preferred to be alone but knew she couldn't forbid anyone from sitting anywhere.

She shot a text to Brooke to see how she was doing. Brooke wrote back and told Emily that she'd been duped by Damani, ending her text with several exclamation points. When Emily asked what happened, Brooke assured her that she'd call her after she finished her appointments for the day.

Emily shook her head as she realized that maybe they shouldn't have urged Brooke to reach out to Damani. She had also wondered if any of them would have a happy ending. With her eyes on the rain and her mind lost in thought, she twirled her phone through her fingers as the other hand rested under her chin.

A male voice asked, "Would you be mad if I sat here with you?"

It caught Emily off-guard and jarred her from her thoughts. Looking up, she surveyed the tall, lean man towering over her.

Amber

Wriggling under the pleasure of her fingers, Amber cried out in pleasure as Crisanto murmured to her in Spanish. "Oh!" Amber eased into her normal breathing pattern as she composed herself and regained her posture. "*Man.* When you gonna come over here? Lemme suck that tippy tip." She stuck her tongue out as she squealed, "Hehhhh hehhhhhh."

"Baby, I'm on the schedule every single day this week. I asked for more hours. Good news is I'm moving this weekend. So, unless you wanna unpack a box for me . . ."

Amber twisted her mouth in disappointment. "Nah, I'm straight."

"You givin' up on me?"

"Crisanto. You missed my birthday, and I ain't seen you since last week. This over-the-phone action can't be all that I get, you know. I need to feel a warm body."

"I know, I know. But I swear it'll be better when I move to Arlington. I can come scoop you up from the Metro."

Amber moved the phone from her ear and stared at it as if he could see her face. "Uh, the Metro? You can come get me from my house."

"Oh, come on, baby, don't be difficult. You live right next to one, and I can come get you at Ballston Station or something. Relax. You need a car, woman."

Amber shook her head. She couldn't believe this man, or young man, for that matter. "I gotta go, son. I'll call you later."

"Amber? You mad?"

Not known for biting her tongue, she admitted, "Well, I ain't happy."

"Ah, come on, *princesa*. Don't be like that. Don't turn your back on *papi*. You know I'll make it up to you. *Te lo juro*."

If the streets of New York showed her anything, it was that men's promises didn't mean anything. She learned that at the tender age of seventeen. "Bye." She hung up and threw her phone to the other side of the bed. "Pshh." When her eyes caught a glimpse of the time, she jumped up as she remembered that she had a lesson with a student in fifteen minutes.

A loud knock at the door startled her. "Oh, no," she fussed in a whisper as she snapped her white mini skirt together at the waist. "Why is Lynn so early?"

Amber jerked her neck back to check under her shirt to make sure she had on a bra. After seeing her black lace bra, she jerked the door open. Much to her surprise, the tall, handsome man who'd abandoned her at the club stood on the other side of the door.

"Cane?" Her head tilted in disappointment as she studied his stoic face.

"Let me in." Cane pressed a large hand against her door before Amber could object to widen the door for him.

"Um, hello? You cannot just barge in here like this. You ain't payin' no rent here." The door slammed behind him. Cane's decisive expression told her that he had his mind made up to stay and that her words meant nothing. She folded her arms as she squinted. "Not after the way you left me that night at the club."

It felt wrong to admit it, but Cane looked irresistible in his navy blue, fresco wool suit. He closed the distance between them with one giant step. "Shut up," he ordered.

"Say what, asshat?" Angry, Amber pointed a finger at the door with an extended arm. "Scram."

Without saying a word, Cane gripped her ass with both hands and pushed her body against his. She could feel a bulge that'd been missing in her life since Crisanto started picking up more shifts. With forearms pressed against his chest and hands balled into tight fists, Amber growled at him.

"Raise up off me, you asshole." Even Amber hadn't convinced herself that she meant it. But what would he think if she didn't put up a fight?

Cane refused to speak, so he shook his head twice and pressed his lips against hers. His arms gripped her close as if he missed her. They hungrily raced up and down her body and the next thing Amber knew, he picked her up, headed to her couch, and threw her down.

"Cane, get out. I . . . I got a student coming."

Cane got on top of her. Amber became less concerned about the student as his lips sucked on her neck and collarbone. She could feel a big hand under her skirt and between her legs. She decided to make it easy for him by lifting her thigh against his hip. Amber whispered her words with little air or hope. "You really outta go." From unconvincing lips to deaf ears, she struggled with wanting to punch him and letting him have his way. Part of the fun involved putting up the fake fight before throwing in the towel. She could only imagine seventeen-year-old Lynn on the other side with her innocent face hiding behind her too-big red-rimmed eyeglasses.

With quivering breath, Cane reached inside of his jacket pocket, pulled out a foiled packet, and ripped it with his teeth.

"What you doin'? I told you we can't. I got an appointment."

He pointed at himself. "Girl, you sure you don't wanna taste my candy cane?"

When he put it like that, Amber had to get a piece of his sweet stick. She grinned and licked her lips. Pointing a finger at him, she ordered, "You better make up for what you did to me."

"Daaaaaamn, girl." He playfully snarled, "Quit holding grudges and thangs. Sit back and let a man take care of his business."

"All right now, Peppermint Zaddy." Smiling from ear to ear, Amber wiggled her fingers at him. "Give mama some stick."

"You want this big juicy thang, huh?"

"You betta swing that dick over here."

"You gonna like it."

Whoo.

His confidence turned Amber on. She could feel her groin throb. She wanted to feel him. No, she *needed* to know what he had to offer. Each second made her salivate as she waited for the show to get started.

Standing, Cane pushed her skirt to her waist and yanked her black lace panties down so fast she thought he burned her skin. He unbuckled his pants in haste and dropped everything to his ankles to don the condom. Amber saw his dick full of girth aiming between her legs. Before she had time to protest, he fell into her. She doubted she'd ever had one quite that thick.

"Owwwww." The last time someone made her say 'ow,' was the day her virginity was taken.

He grunted, and with his eyes closed, he said, "You can do it, girl. I believe in you."

Cane didn't bring any real rhythm. He simply fell into his own world, disconnected from her. No kisses, no real feels, just jerks.

Amber decided to let herself go since he'd already made it this far. Besides, she didn't kick him out and she allowed him to continue so she decided to make the best of it. She accepted the fact that he wasn't going to get nominated for Best Love of the Year. Therefore, his performance wasn't a real concern. She just wanted to come. Amber could start to feel the rewards of his strokes. It took a minute, but her vagina adjusted, and she began to lose herself in the much-needed action that'd been missing lately.

Okay, okay. This might work.

Her body started to let go to appreciate the sensation. Wouldn't go down as an encounter that she'd have to have again, but it would dust off some of those cobwebs.

Amber settled her arms over his back to caress his head and shoulders. Her legs slid up and down his leg. She raked her toes against his skin with arched feet. "Ohhhhhh, yeeeeeeeah. You can do it, baby. We gettin' there."

With his eyes closed, he turned his nostrils upward. "This some good pussy, girl."

"You gonna beat it up for mama?"

"Talk that trash, girl. Talk it," he demanded with a grunt.

Amber licked her lips. "Mmmmmmmmmm. How this pussy feel, baby?"

"You feel my cane? Can you handle the big stick?"

The pleasure intensified. Amber pinched her eyes shut to focus on the sensation. "I want the stick! Yesss, daddy. Burn me with that stick!" When Amber didn't hear anything back, she decided to focus on the feeling until that, too, changed. Her eyes shot open when his jerking became intermittent. She stared at him with furrowed brows and snarled lips.

With eyes nailed shut, he spoke through gritted teeth. "Mm! Get. That. Candy. Cane. Get. It." His eyes rolled up as his mouth turned into an 'O.' When he finished, his head fell on top of her chest. "Girl."

Amber chastised herself for allowing a man to be intimate with her after dumping her at a club. She shook her upper body to jar him.

"Hey. Nuh-uh, bruh. Get your energy back together. Let's go."

Cane slowly eased himself up. Grinning, he told her, "Oh, my bad, girl." Clearing his throat, he raised off her and stood on his feet. Once he peeled the filled condom off, he dropped it on her floor and pulled up his pants.

As he buckled up, Amber asked, "So what about me? I know you ain't done." She slid her elbows behind her to rest them on the arm of the sofa. "Ain't you gonna finish me off?"

Cane ironed his sleeves with his hands. "You ain't come?"

Heat immediately shot to the top of her head. "Fool, no. You know I didn't."

Avoiding eye contact, he cocked a brow and replied, "Shiiiiiiid. You know what to do."

Realizing that just maybe he played her again, Amber wanted to scream. Jumping up, she pulled up her panties and straightened her skirt.

Amber's hands flew onto her hips. "You lousy jerk. How you gonna leave me hangin'—again?"

Cane shrugged. "Hey. I promised you a taste of the candy cane, and you got it."

Squinting her eyes, Amber realized that he probably held a grudge from their date. "Wait a minute. You still mad about you not gettin' a threesome?"

"Pfft. Sweetie don't flatter yourself. Whatever you don't wanna do, another will. I just came here to bust a convenient nut. Whether or not you got one, that's on you—magician." He flicked his nose with his thumb.

Cussing under her breath, Amber watched as Cane reached for the doorknob then remembered the nasty condom he'd left on her floor. Just as the door had opened, Amber gingerly pinched the messy condom between her thumb and index finger. Racing to the door before it shut, she hurled it at his back and screamed, "Take your nasty seed with you!"

Amber watched as the condom hit his back and then the hallway floor.

With a snicker, he barely turned around when he said, "Come on now. Go 'head with that. You crazy." As he eased himself through his unlocked door, Amber noticed the familiar face of her student standing outside her door in shock.

The appointment with Lynn! The shy girl with brunette hair stared straight at her with unblinking lids before rolling her eyes to the floor then back to Amber.

Shiiiiiiiiiiiit! She couldn't afford to lose a student.

Amber scratched the side of her head with a tilted neck. She pointed briefly at the mess on the floor. "I, uhhh, hate water balloons. Don't you?"

Lynn's eyes slid to the side with parted lips and slightly pinched brows.

Amber didn't know where she stood with the teen, so with a loud clap, she said, "Okay, great. So, missy, did you practice your fingering for playing an ascending scale?"

Summer

The familiar BMW sat in the sunlight in the hotel parking lot. Out of all the cars, my eyes happened to spot his sitting nicely in between two clunky cars. I hadn't a clue as to why Ruben stayed in a hotel, but more than likely, it had to do with losing Fran. After making my way up to the seventh floor, I came face to face with the door that hid the key to my future. Well, somewhat. How this man reacted to my news would determine a lot.

Giving my hair one last comb-through with my hand, I knocked on the door and waited. After what seemed to feel like five seconds, the familiar, sexy Cuban opened the door to reveal a tightly built body regretfully covered in a white button-up shirt. I had to admit, after not seeing him for months and then to come face to face with his good looks, my stomach did a brief flip. Damn!

Kicking out one of his arms, my eyes couldn't help but see the sinew pop from under his short-sleeved shirt. Noticing his well-defined biceps and triceps, I painfully willed myself to look into his eyes. It was for the best given my relationship status. His grown-out, dark brunette hair lay flat against his forehead, slick from a fresh wash and styling product. He looked . . . different. No matter what, he still looked irresistible.

His grin couldn't get any wider. "Summer. Ah. What a pleasure to see you. Please, come in."

His cologne wafted to my nostrils. "Thank you, Ruben." After crossing the threshold of his room, I turned to see his muscles pop again as he closed the door with ease.

Look away, girl.

He approached me but stopped short before coming too close. "I wish I could hug you." Both hands tapped each other at the fingertips.

"I'm with someone now," I told him quickly. Lord knows what happened the last time Ruben and I were in a room together. He almost had his way with my body. That couldn't happen again.

"There's no reason why a lady like you should be alone."

Our eyes locked. The butterfly fluttered in my stomach. I hated it. After all these months of being with Oliver, it didn't make sense to me. It didn't mean I wanted Ruben. Well, sexually, yes. But a relationship with this man didn't exist as an option.

Focus on the reason for your visit, Summer.

"We should get down to why I'm here."

"Of course. First, please, sit." Ruben gestured with his hand. "Sit anywhere, Summer." The spacious room and accommodations indicated a suite and not a basic hotel room. That spelled trouble for him and Fran.

"Thank you, Ruben." My eyes looked around before settling for the edge of his bed, since I already stood at the foot of it. "I can sit here if that's okay with you."

Ruben smiled with a hidden desperation to please me. "Absolutely, Summer. Can I get you something to drink? I know you like champagne. You were always a fan of that stuff."

The sound of his accent brought back a flood of memories. My eyes fell to the carpet with regret of contributing to his marital problems. I tugged at my sweater. It needed to come off. Everything in my mind suffocated my body.

"I can't drink that, Ruben. Water's fine, thanks."

He shrugged and searched the mini fridge as my comment went over his head. Hoping he would ask me why not, it confused me that he didn't say anything about my stomach. Even through my maternity empire dress, he should've still been able to see my weight gain. I stood up, not wanting to waste time. My heartbeat sped with anxiety. It had to be done. The longer I stayed . . .

"Can you tell that I'm not so skinny anymore, Ruben?"

"What?" My question caught him off-guard. With a raised eyebrow, he turned around halfway with a chilled water bottle in his hand.

"Ruben, look at me."

He scratched the back of his head then turned around to fully face me. "You . . . you have . . ." he grunted, "changed some."

"I'm pregnant."

Ruben handed me the water. "Here."

I thanked him and continued with a mumbled, "Well?"

"I was told that a man should keep quiet if he was unsure." His eyes went somewhere, showing me nothing but distance behind his irises despite the grin. Reflection. "I remember being in the supermarket with my mom when I was six. This, uhh, lady came to my mom to ask if she'd ever tried the brand of detergent in her hand. Before my mom could reply, I told the lady, 'Oooh. You're having a baby.'" We shared a quick laugh. "The lady took off before my mom could tell me to apologize. She scolded me and told me that I was wrong, and that the woman was not pregnant. When I got older, she often retold that story with laughter and told me that if I was unsure, then wait for the woman to tell me. Otherwise, pretend like she's skinny."

Sitting back down, he made me laugh with a pointed finger toward him. "Good advice, good advice." At ease, he sat down beside me. It all seemed innocent and not worth making it a big deal.

"Well, congratulations to you and your man, Summer." Ruben's eyes filled with genuine sincerity.

"His name is Oliver."

"Oliver." He digested it with a lowered head. Peering back at me, Ruben said, "Well, be sure to tell Oliver that I said 'congratulations.'"

"Will do, Ruben. Thanks." I bit my lower lip. Technically, Oliver would be a dad.

"I always wanted a baby. But you know, Fran was too scared to try because of her age and all."

A twinge of oddness pricked my body. He would soon find out that his wish would probably come true. "Ahhh. The big F-word."

Ruben laughed. "Yeah. Fran."

Though I didn't care, curiosity got the better of me. "How she doing anyway?"

Ruben's thick eyebrows crinkled. "I'm surprised you care."

"Well, I did you guys wrong. She should be mad at me."

"No, no, no. Fran and I were over long before you stepped in, so please, you can't take all the credit. Summer, how you getting by?"

"Huh? What do you mean?"

"She won't admit it, but I know she tampered with your career. I mean—pfft—she practically owns Northern Virginia and DC."

Not surprised, I didn't want to focus on her. I waved a dismissive hand at him. "Oh, yeah, well she promised me that I could only work in fast food, so it ain't nothing new."

"Man, people don't realize how many CEOs and high-level managers have their positions because her firm placed them there. Corporations love her, because she knows how to find talent. She's so chummy with them and her so-called competitors. It's crazy. I'm lucky to have that friend of mine. He had my back big time."

"I'm fine, I'm fine. Trust me, what she did was nothing compared to what I did."

"What? Sleeping with her husband?"

"Too little time to recount my mistakes, Ruben. Did y'all divorce?"

"Yup. She served me the divorce papers at work."

Hearing Ruben confirm what I'd suspected made me even more thankful for working on my own. "She really wanted to stick it to you, huh?"

He scratched his chin. "Fran likes making points and turning people into examples." He shrugged. "Just gotta stick it out until my condo is ready. Remodeling and what not . . . Just one more week here before I move into my new condo. I've been here for months, Summer, making this establishment rich. It's sickening."

My expression told him that I sympathized. "Where you gonna move?"

"Tysons Corner. She hit me with those beautiful papers the same day my company kicked me out on my ass for excessive tardiness. Fran kept arguing with me in the morning just to make me late, and, boy, did it work. Got a warning and then terminated, all for being late day after day. I knew it was gonna cost me when she made me miss a crucial meeting. Looking back, she was trapping me, but when emotions ran thick, I couldn't crawl out the web. So, I'm good with moving to Tysons Corner. Not a bad place to meet single people, but I always wished that I could have you instead. Summer, I never got over you."

"Ruben . . ." Looking down into my lap, I didn't know what to say. My nerves unraveled as I played with my fingernails.

"I'm not supposed to talk like this, I know. I know you're pregnant and everything. Nothing is the same. I get that." Our eyes met as we read something in each other's expression. "But, Summer, you made me crazy. Unfortunately, I cheated on Fran a few times before you. I was depressed and lonely. I don't think people understand how a lack of connection and arguments can slowly break a relationship. You don't see it coming, but before you know it, you have nothing in common."

"I know." Unsure of my reason for agreeing, I almost regretted admitting that.

"Fran acted like I owed her something after we got married. She wore the pants with me, and that's about as comfortable as me trying to slip into one of her dresses. Can you imagine?"

We must've shared the same image because we laughed simultaneously. When we collected ourselves, our smiles communicated with an equal exchange of fondness in our eyes. What was I doing? Why couldn't I shake Ruben as easily as I could Max? How could I love Oliver but question it every time Ruben's and my eyes met? How could time be of no medicine at all to an ailing affair?

No. Stop it, Summer! Stop it! You will hurt Oliver. Get to the point or get out. Tired of hissing at myself, I said, "Maybe someone should tell you congratulations."

"Huh?" Ruben's eyebrows crinkled again. "Summer, why did you come here? Just to tell me that you and that gu—Oliver are expecting?"

"Congratulations, Ruben. This baby is yours, not Oliver's." It felt like slow motion, when Ruben's eyes widened and mouth dropped.

Emily

Emily beamed at the tall man hovering above her. His hesitant smile told her that he prayed for acceptance and not a rejection. "Sure." Emily sat up and placed her phone on the table in front of her as she studied everything about him.

"Great." He tied his umbrella together with a snap of the string before lowering himself into the chair across from Emily. "Thank you. It's packed in here and evidently, I wasn't the only one to be caught off-guard." Emily nodded with pressed lips as she listened without saying a word. He offered a large, bony hand. "Garrett."

Sliding a hand from between her pinched legs, Emily accepted. "Emily. Nice to meet you, Garrett."

Garrett wasn't the most handsome man she'd met. He owned the suburban-looking style, unlike Eric who appeared more Wall Street, but seemed more polished than Zach. She could do without his tan Dockers and the swooping sandy brown bangs, but other than that, Emily appreciated his height and square-jawbone. That part reminded her of the astute business-man look that she could never quite gravitate away from.

She didn't miss the secret glances her way from his chocolate brown eyes. She giggled. "What?"

"I—" he released a defeated sigh. "I'm sorry. I keep looking at you, because you're beautiful."

Emily bit her lower lip as she giggled again like a teenager. She gandered at the rain falling hard outside, ready to see what adventure a new man could bring. When she was married to Eric, something about the rain usually made her horny, especially when they were home together with nothing to do.

Garrett scratched his head and shrugged. "How's the coffee? Maybe I should get me some."

"Don't bother." Emily didn't understand why she'd been so brash lately. It really must've been because of her last conversation with Eric. "I make a mean cup of coffee at home."

Garrett's eyebrows flattened as he tried to process Emily's insinuation. He leaned forward and whispered, "Wait. Are you inviting me back to your place?"

Emily took one last look at his left hand and saw a naked wedding finger. With a grin, she nodded quickly with a naughty finger hanging at the tip of her tongue.

Garrett shook his head as if to clear his thoughts. "Man, this is the easiest lay of my life. Let's go."

"I live a few blocks down," she reported as she grabbed her coffee and walked under the umbrella with Garrett. Emily didn't know what she called herself doing, but she remembered how well her orgasm fed her in the theatre that night with Zach. It was unexpected, wild, out of character, but safe. And she wanted to do it again.

Summer

"Summer?" With his mouth agape, Ruben blinked slowly, holding both of his palms in the air. "What did you say?"

Without hesitation, I repeated myself. "You are the daddy of this baby. It doesn't belong to Oliver." I threw a hand up. "Well, it shouldn't. The day you had sex with me at your house, you didn't put on a condom nor did you pull out. Oliver and I were *always* careful. The time of conception matches that night." I couldn't take my eyes off his, but Ruben looked everywhere else as he made sense of my words. I couldn't help but feel relieved by my confession.

"And I'm just now finding out, Summer?" Ruben's palms rested against the sides of his head as our gaze met.

Cool as a cucumber, I shrugged. "I had to process everything on my own, too, you know. Besides, I was pregnant for a while before I found out. I didn't have too many tell-tale symptoms."

"I imagine Oliver didn't want me to know." Waiting for my reply, he folded his arms.

"You got that right. But you know what, at the end of the day, this is my baby and this baby deserves to know who his or her father is. You need to be a part of this baby's life."

"Why, Summer? Why you doin' this for me?"

My tone softened as the memory of my mother and dad flooded my brain. "Ruben, my dad died when I was a little girl. Not knowing a parent ain't a fair card to be dealt in life, but you're here and alive." I placed a hand on his shoulder. "I would love for you to be a part of this blessing. Our baby shouldn't have to pay."

In a trance-like state, he repeated, "Our baby . . . huh." Ruben stood with a slow grin taking over his face as he looked heavenward with praying hands. "I'm going to be a daddy and in the kid's life?" His eyes dropped to meet mine. Elated, he pumped a fist in the air and jumped. "I'm going to be a daddy and you the mom?"

Putting up one finger with a firm expression, I told him, "All of this is under one condition though."

His brows dropped slowly back into place. "Wh-what's that?"

"I need to solidify my suspicions by sending you to the draw site, so they can swab you for a sample. I'm going in this week for a non-invasive blood sample. Oliver and I need this proof." I reached into my purse to pull out a piece of paper with all the information he'd need to go from here.

Just a tad deflated, he nodded. "Su-su-sure. Understood. I'd do it, too." Grinning, Ruben's eyes glowed. "Man. You, me, and the baby. I can't believe it. I never thought you'd be in my life again."

Well that makes two of us, buddy.

His words pinched my heart. We sounded like a family. I carried his child. Boom. Like magic, it'd all come together so easily. And just like that, I could have the family that women like Emily and Brooke dreamed of. On the other hand, a man who loved me waited at home. He came fully equipped with no baggage from a previous lifetime. Oliver offered me support in any way, shape, or form. The man even bought me a car and took me into his place when I was down and out on my luck. And still, he wanted to be the father of a baby who didn't share his DNA. As bad as it sounded, I couldn't help but wonder: Did Oliver want to gain a score over Ruben by raising his child, or did he want the baby because he loved me and was prepared to shift into daddy mode? Was I making it too difficult on myself? Should the baby have its family under one roof instead of growing accustomed to visits every other weekend?

Emily

Locked in a kiss, Emily and Garrett eased through the door of her condo with her delicate hands cupping his face, and his long fingers resting on her hips. She blindly kicked the door shut. They both raced to undress him first. To Emily's horror, she realized that her set of living room windows didn't have any curtains, and people in the street could see them from a distance.

Before she had time to change her mind, she decided to be risqué. Eric had accused her of being a bore and was convinced that her future held cats. She would prove him wrong, even if he never found out about it.

Emily led Garrett toward the window and put on a show for any random DC resident or pedestrian to see. Too wrapped up in the moment, Garrett didn't realize or seem to care that they stood on display. Knowing that people could see her nude body wrapped in another man's arms gave her the ultimate sensual rush. Maybe Eric was right. Nothing could be gained by being boring and predictable. If the truth be told, she bored herself, and she felt slightly liberated admitting that. It allowed any last remnants of anger toward Eric to dissipate.

He could never convince her that what he did to her was right, but she could see his point of view regarding her personality. She needed to spice things up.

Garrett scrolled his finger up and down. "Someone's still wearing too many clothes."

Kicking off her shoes, Emily lowered her leggings and panties at the same time. Garrett didn't waste any time pushing her back against the oversized window in one hurried motion.

"I lucked out. My last one." Garrett held up a condom package and ripped into it.

Once he covered himself, Emily leaned in and said, "Well if we need more then I guess you better head to the store."

Garrett pinched her nose. "Naughty woman." He smacked her on her butt.

"Mmmm, naughty is good." Emily tasted his chest with one quick lick, before bringing her mouth to his.

Garrett followed her orders as he lowered her down to her floor. So maybe the show was over, she realized regretfully as they hit the floor, but that didn't mean that no one couldn't see their bodies. The people at a distance would definitely see something, and while Emily was unsure of just how much, even a little show was better than nothing at all.

Summer

I remained seated as I watched Ruben's eyes and thoughts run away with a fantasy.

"Summer. We could be together. Forget that guy. We have names to pick out. I used to get so filled with anger when Fran turned away from the idea of having my baby. Now I thank God that she and I didn't have any meaningful ties. She can have all the money and my job, who cares? I'm better off just because I ain't gotta deal with her."

"Ruben, when I was a little girl, my mom used to sing this song to me every night before I went to bed. My dad used to sing it to me, so when he died, she continued it." Fighting back the tears, I forced a smile. Showing great interest, he watched me speak. "I don't want you to be just a memory to our child. You should be singing those songs to our child—"

"Yes!" Ruben kicked a knee in the air as he pulled an elbow past his waist in celebration. "See, my love, we both want the same thing." He lowered himself beside me. I couldn't talk, because his enthusiasm overrode my need to speak.

His eyes studied mine as a finger wiped a piece of hair from my face. I flinched. Oliver did that to me frequently.

"Summer, you're everything that a man hopes to find. When you walked out my life the night of the party, I was no more good. Fran made it sound like whatever we shared was dirty." Ruben shook his head. "But she was wrong."

Paralyzed by his touch, I listened as he stroked my wavy hair from root to tip. A quick shiver careened down my spine under his touch, but I didn't want him to see that. I wanted to back away from his touch but for some reason, couldn't. Even though the vision of an angry Oliver danced across my mind, it wasn't enough to compel me to fight

Ruben's touch. As usual, the touch was magnetic, and it had a way of pulling me close until the flame flickered under my hand. When I could feel the heat from the danger, then I would know it was time to pull away. Until then, it was like following Dracula upstairs to his lair.

"Summer . . ." Instead of running another stroke of his hand to the tip of my hair, his finger traced my clavicle and the outline of my exposed breast. He was taking it too far and I let him.

Pull back, Summer, pull back.

He had me. Ruben had me. The draw proved to be too strong. It was as if I could see myself falling below the surface of an ocean of magnetic forces pulling me to him. Where was the anchor to keep me afloat? The anchor of loyalty, right and wrong.

He licked his fluffy pink lips as I covered my bottom lip with my teeth. Like an airplane, I could tell that he wanted to land on my lips. Helpless, I couldn't stop him.

He placed a hand behind my neck and eased closer to my face as he whispered, "Summer, I wanna make you all mine." A large hand caressed my nape. Filled with effortless passion, it felt better than any professional massage. The whisper of, "*Te quiero, mi amor*," sucker punched me right into the groin. I didn't know what he said but it sounded great. Somehow, moments with Ruben was the only time I regretted not pursuing Spanish after middle school. The language was all a blur at this point. How did I always find myself in this position with him? Weak and at his mercy. It had to end.

My head and body felt like a separate entity but somehow worked together to get me to the door with my keys in my hand. Trailing closely behind, Ruben turned me around with one hand on my shoulder. My back hit the wall. That large hand eased lower and brushed the top part of my back. It felt so good. He eased closer and whispered, "Do you just want a man, or do you want passion?"

No. Don't. Please, Ruben. Just leave me alone.

I didn't need a mirror to know that a shadow of conflict reflected in my eyes. Or that my eyelids struggled to keep my eyes open. No doubt about it, Ruben and I had passion. What we had was light, fun, but harmful. He was the fire that teachers warned us against. Don't touch it! But what did kids do? They needed to touch, to see—why all the dire warnings? Had my father been alive, this would be the man my daddy would've warned me about. This *would* be the one to get me pregnant.

Ruben stepped closer to me, his hand still on me, his breath closer to my face. Only an inch of space separated us. I wanted to call for help so badly. I wanted to get out of this situation. My soul begged me to save it. I didn't know how to come through for her. He leaned down closer—as if there were any more room to spare—with his face just sitting in front of mine, shaking my groin to the core.

Rubbing my skin tenderly, he asked seductively, "Do you want to live more than you care to exist? Don't you want me to bring you to paradise over and over each morning when you wake up?" His stare dropped to the carpet and slowly rolled up to mine. "*¡Quiero todas las posibilidades contigo! ¿En qué mundo puede existir un hombre sin el roce de una mujer como tú? Quédate conmigo para que puedes ver nuestros sueños se hacen realidad.*"

Something about his accent, something about his Spanish, something about his smoldering eyes, something about our history—it was like a whirlwind of *je ne sais quoi's* that made me forget how my past actions had consequences. Breathing right onto my lips, my knees shook, turning my legs to overcooked noodles. The circuits in my head fizzled like a fried transformer. My tongue licked the inside of my mouth to taste any trace of doubt that I shouldn't be there anymore. The oxygen in my chest became stingy, robbing me of any chance to survive with ease. I squeezed my hand, almost puncturing my palms with the nails that never grew out enough to satisfy an itch, and that reflected my severe state of emergency. He was the professional magician who had the power to steal my last strands of decency. His tricks—though predictable and easily spotted a mile away—still hoodwinked me. Every. Single. Time. And poof! My will to do the right thing escaped me like a thief in a heist.

The magician's finger traced my chin. "I want you. You turn my dick into a hot flame."

Dead. Dead on arrival. *Those lips.* My pussy told me to try them, to see what they tasted like, to see why this magician could snap his fingers to turn me to his side slut again. I also didn't need to pull down my underwear just to know that I was wetter than a tub. And because I'd died, my keys dropped to the floor.

That sound. That sound jarred me. Immediately bending over to retrieve them, I paused upon seeing the Corvette logo on the fob. Still bent, I slowly eased my finger through the key ring, letting it slide down my finger as I straightened. The fob did a lot for me. Woke me up from a no-good trance. Set me back into reality. Holding up the key in front of Ruben, I saw flashes of Oliver's pained face from the night he learned Ruben was the daddy of this baby. Saw a flash of his smile when we hugged on the sofa. His look of accomplishment when he handed me the keys to *my own new car.* It reminded me that we lived in a world of consequences, where a minute of pleasure—however intense or gratifying it might be—could wreak such havoc from which we may never recover.

Talking to myself, I whispered, "Oliver."

This man had saved me, multiple times. What had Ruben ever done for me? Absolutely nothing. Nothing but spit his sperm inside of me. I felt disgusted with myself. My head jerked back as I looked at him as though I'd never seen him before.

My head shook frantically. "N-no. No!"

Ruben squinted his eyes at me, trying to recognize a woman he thought he knew. "Summer, come on."

I threw a hand in his face. "Look. If you wanna see this baby, you better knock this shit off. No more disrespect to Oliver. Keep your greedy hands off my body, quit stepping in my bubble, and keep your Spanish to yourself—unless you're teaching the baby. Am I clear?" My face had never been so stern.

Obviously, he got the picture, because he agreed without hesitation. "No problem here. Today, I will show you that I'm capable of doing whatever's best for our child, and the baby's needs come first."

"Too late for that. I mean it. No more of your shit, Ruben. This is it. It has to be. Last warning." Spinning to face the door, my hand couldn't cover the knob fast enough. The fear that I'd almost backstabbed Oliver kept the pride of my willpower from shining. He *trusted me*. Even if he'd never found out, I was about to burn that bridge, and my own knowledge of that was burden enough. Once I cranked the engine to my Corvette, I checked out of Hotel Ruben, mentally, and emotionally.

Emily

Emily had already come, and with Garrett standing on his knees between her legs, she watched him pull out and remove the condom. Exhausted with a trembling body and unsteady breathing, Emily grinned as she watched him get off. Her hazel eyes focused on his expression, pleased, knowing that she caused the agony of pleasure by the downward turn of his gritted mouth.

"Close your eyes. Gimme some privacy, babe."

With a crooked smile, she agreed reluctantly. "Oookaaaay." Emily honored his wish.

Wondering what the weird request was all about, she got her answer when she felt his unsolicited move of warm splashes against her skin in random places.

Emily jerked when she realized something was going on but didn't know what. She propped herself up by her elbows, and when she saw drops of come all over her legs and lower abdomen, she flipped out, screaming, *"What are you doing*? What did you do?"

Not paying any attention, Garrett didn't seem to hear her as he continued to yank his shaft until nothing else secreted. "Mmmmmfff. Oh, baby, this is so good."

Wide-eyed, Emily crawled backward since he didn't seem to be fazed by her disgust. She couldn't close her mouth. "Oh my! Oh my gosh! You squirted all over me! Y-you squirted all over me!"

Collected with lowered arms and relaxed shoulders, Garrett breathed heavily through an open mouth and lowered eyes. "Baby, I'm sorry. What's the big deal? At least it didn't happen inside of you."

"Quick!" She snapped her fingers. "Go to the kitchen and bring me a towel. Now!"

"All right, all right, relax, cookie. Relax." Standing, he steadied his body with clumsy feet and made his way to the kitchen.

"Don't tell me to relax. You just shot your semen all over me."

Garrett returned with a paper towel. He threw it downward and Emily lurched forward to grab it.

"One?" She dabbled and scraped across her skin. "What am I supposed to do with one? You made a baby factory all over my legs. Go get me another one."

Garrett snapped his head back. "Ugh. Look, I gotta get going." He did as Emily requested and returned with three more paper towels and tossed them at her.

"You shoulda brought me this much in the first place." Irate, Emily snatched the paper towels from her feet and continued to clean herself. "No. You shouldn't have to be bringing me paper towels anyway. What happened to the condom that you had on?"

Sliding one arm into his shirt sleeve, he replied, "I removed it." He pretended to pluck his head. "Duh."

"But *why* would you do that if you weren't done? Have you any manners?"

Looking cocky, Garrett replied, "The idea of cheating on my boring and nagging wife turned me on and it finally happened." He threw his arm toward her. "*With you.*"

What had she done? This was something that she would never do willingly. When Emily realized that she literally didn't know this man, she admitted that that was the risk that she chose to take. At least she knew stuff about Zach and was even his son's teacher. But this guy, she didn't know. She felt sick.

Emily gathered enough strength to stand and walk toward him. "You're *married*?"

Garrett shrugged nonchalantly. "Got kids, too—five in fact."

At the end of her rope, Emily slapped his cheek, leaving a red stain on his skin. It just didn't feel like enough.

With a dropped jaw, Garrett placed a hand there and rubbed it. "Ouch. What the hell you do that for?"

"You. Are. Disgusting! Just repulsive!"

Emily collected his belongings one by one and marched to her balcony.

"No, no, no." Garrett tried to catch up but was too late. "What are—no. D-don't do that. Emily, come on!"

Naked, she didn't care who caught a glimpse as she stood at the sliding door and threw hard enough to send all his garments over the balcony rail with two hands and one good thrust. She slid the door shut in one hurried motion then clicked the lock. Emily headed toward the front door with folded arms and a smile. She turned to the slime ball donned in nothing but an unbuttoned shirt that barely covered his shriveled dick, and calmly said, "Get out."

"No, wait, please," he begged with praying hands. With collapsed brows and glassy eyes, he said, "I am so, so sorry, Emily."

Done with being ruffled, she shrugged with one shoulder and a relentless smile. "No, you're not. You just don't want to be humiliated. I could offer you one of my dresses, but that's too kind. Now," she nodded her head at her door, "you better get out there and collect your snake skin before someone picks it up."

"Emily, *please*, baby. Please." The tears started to brim at his lower eyelids.

"See. You still called me 'baby,' and that's not a term you use for someone other than your wife. Now, if you don't get outta here, I'm calling the cops, because you are officially unwelcomed here."

"But—"

"One!" Emily started with closed eyes.

He placed a hesitant hand on the doorknob. "If you could just—"

Emily stomped her foot and pointed at the door. "*Tú gilipollas*. Get *out*!"

Once Garrett realized that he didn't have a dog in the fight, he went ahead and showed himself out. Slowly. When his last foot hit the other side of her door, Emily took her arm to help the door close faster. Once it slammed, she locked it quickly.

"Arrrrrrh!" Emily couldn't help but cry out in frustration as she realized that the joke fell on her. She couldn't believe that that man made her cross a line that she never knew existed. Being the other woman, even one time, was something at which her parents would shake their fist. Emily couldn't value marriage any more than she already did, especially since she witnessed her mom and dad wrapped in marital bliss since her birth.

Standing naked in the middle of her new living room floor, Emily never felt so nude inside as well as outside and robbed of morality. For the first time that day, she resisted the idea of anyone seeing her vulnerable through her oversized window pane. Totally over the high of public flashing, she crossed her arms over the front of her body to hide both assets. In an effort to put the wrongdoing behind her, Emily raced to the shower to scrub off the scum's residue of sin.

Brooke

After a long day, Brooke snatched her pumps off her feet as she slid the heavy grocery bag onto her kitchen counter. Highly appreciative to be home, she placed a hand on the side of her waist as she struggled to catch her breath after taking the stairs up. She couldn't understand the elevator being out of service in a new building. Realizing that the exercise could've been worse had it not been for her being an avid exerciser, she pushed through the huffing and puffing as she unloaded the grocery items.

The ringing from her cellphone stole her attention. She reached for the phone in her purse. Almost breathing at a steady rhythm, she replied, "Brooke Brazile."

"Oh, uh, yes. You are the person I wanted to speak with. How nice to finally connect with you." The cheerful voice on the other end of the line confused Brooke. On the other hand, she wanted to slap the woman for being so chipper when Brooke hadn't had a chance to rest yet.

"I'm sorry. With whom am I speaking?" Brooke scratched her wind-blown hair as she tried to maintain a professional tone.

"I'm getting married and you came highly recommended—in fact, heard you're the best in the city. Someone was unequivocally convinced that you would be the right woman for this job, even though I heard you charge a pretty penny."

Folding the brown paper bag that carried her groceries, she replied, "Lovely!" Hoping that she didn't overcompensate too much for her lack of genuine enthusiasm while she felt hot and sweaty, she dialed it back with, "So, um, I'm sorry. What's your name again?"

"Justice."

"Justice?"

"Um, hm. Justice Ashby. Listen, I'm getting married this summer and need to start planning now."

"Nice to meet you, Justice. Well, I'm the right wedding planner for the job. What month do you need to be walking down the aisle?" Brooke took a few steps to her window to stare out into the short strip of traffic that led to the main street. A "For Rent" sign caught her eye.

"July. No later than the twentieth. By then my fiancé and I will be doing too much traveling during our vacation break; that's basically our honeymoon. So, can you deliver?"

"Absolutely." Positive that squeezing in another wedding would give her that long overdue ulcer, Brooke located a pen and pencil as she scribbled the number to the space across from her building. "We need to make an appointment."

8: *let's get pissy*

Summer

"I can't wait for this baby to pop out." I spun around wildly in Emily's computer chair in the living room of her condo with my hands gripping the arms for dear life and legs lifted straight out. Her place whipped in blurs of colors with each spin like a merry-go-round, with my friends' frames dragging in the movement as well. "Arrrrrrrrgh."

To pacify me, she said, "You're only a few more weeks away."

Pumping the breaks with a sudden stab of toes into the wooden floor, a concentrated eye roll to the ceiling settled the dizziness and wave of nausea. "Well that was dumb of me."

Amber and Brooke just chuckled at me. They'd been sipping their red wine for a while now in the chairs next to the fireplace.

Holding onto the wine glass with one hand, Brooke flew a flimsy arm straight up into the air. "Thanks for the cozy birthday celebration, guys." She dropped it. "Normally I wouldn't settle for a chill celebration, but man I've been so busy, a lil chill like this is all right."

Straightening my neck, I turned to her. "Honey, thank you for being born today many, many years ago. I'm happy to get out the house a bit. Lately I've been prepping the nursery or watching TV till Oliver gets home."

"Hang on, sis, you almost there." Amber tipped her head at my baby bump.

Emily held up a slice of cake from the kitchen. "Anyone for some more cake?"

Amber waved a hand at her. "Go 'head with that, Ems. It's all you."

"I'm good," I answered.

"Same here," Brooke replied.

"Alllll righty, I tried." She lowered the slice.

Brooke crossed her legs and lifted her glass at us. "Thanks for all the gift cards."

"Of course," we replied.

"It was easy," I told her. "All we had to do was walk into any high-end store and pick up a card with a big value."

"Pshhh," Amber fussed. "Speak for yourself. My wallet couldn't handle that. Right now, my high-end store is Ross. So, she just gon' have to make it work with the Ross gift card I copped for a hundred dollars."

"I ain't mad at cha'." Brooke smirked. "Just know though, that next year this ain't gonna work. I expect a huge blowout, all right?"

Amber rolled her neck to face Brooke. "Sis, what you need is a man to handle your expensive ass. He gon' have to come through for you next time. You'll run a broad ragged."

"A *woman*, Amber, a woman," Emily corrected.

"Can't change a street lady." Amber swept her correction away with a hand.

The alcohol had gotten to Amber a little more than Brooke, because Amber drank more since we'd been here. As a lightweight, Brooke surpassed her limit two glasses ago. She'd already warned us that tonight she'd go all in since it was her birthday. Plus, her job had been wearing her down and she said she needed a day of mental escape. We'd have to see where tonight was going. So far, Amber seemed a bit more bitter with a sharper tongue—which didn't seem possible for a New Yorker, but clearly, I was wrong. More relaxed and not as uppity, Brooke didn't seem to come across as anything but a girl from DC. And Emily seemed to be catering to us while sneaking more sips in than she thought I'd realized. Something told me she'd be the one to crash and burn emotionally before the night was over.

I suppose we all needed it. I couldn't be festive like them, but I needed to be around my girls. It'd been three months since: Ruben found out he was the father of my baby, Brooke leased a building for her business while swearing off all men, Emily and Zach enjoyed sex at random places, and Amber had been sleeping around with Crisanto—well, when she could have him.

Brooke squinted her eyes at Amber. "Oh, yeah, because DC's fiiiiiinest men are just hanging from the historical buildings. I'd do better to steal a broad's man from the alter and make him mine."

I giggled. "Well, don't do *that.*"

"I'm just so pooped from buying and decorating this space and hiring an assistant. Man, but having a building elevated my business to a level I didn't see coming. I'm glad I didn't do this sooner. It's *drai*ning." Brooke shook her head and took a long sip. "Got me drinking and shit. But Mama's gettin' her coins though."

Brooke glimpsed at each of us, one at a time. "You know, I'm finally getting to a point where I've accepted that Jackson ain't coming back, and I ain't chasing. And after finding out that Damani was a dog, I tested for STDs and luckily my tests came back negative. Chile, I was scared."

Laughing, Emily joined us, plopping onto the floor with legs that crossed like a breaded pretzel. "You called me like every night asking, 'Do you think I caught something?'"

We all laughed until Amber informed us of her paranoia. "After messin' with Cane's triflin' dick, I should get a test, too. That's what I shoulda did long time ago."

Brooke gave her the side-eye glance. "Amber." She patted her friend's knee. "You've been givin' Crisanto a lot of neck, too. And, before that, it was the clients. That's a lot of action. I think you're long overdue, boo."

She rolled her eyes. "What? I don't be givin' mouth hugs no more. I should get that test though."

I leaned forward. "Why aren't you and Crisanto an item? I'm not understanding that."

"Bruh scared that a relationship will mess up his concentration while studying the law. He'll be goin' to Georgetown you know. S'pose to be all rigorous and shit."

"You should stick around for that one. You got an ambitious man on your side." Brooke raised the wine glass she could barely see, with lids looking heavier by the second lowering slowly like a sunset over the rim of an endless ocean. "Hang on to that brotha'."

Emily chimed in. "Yeah, that's too bad. Maybe he'll change his mind."

"It's whatever, yo." Amber clapped twice. "All right, y'all, can I blow y'all's minds?" With piqued interests, we waited for her to continue. "You know how I ain't never go to college?" After seeing us agree with nods, Amber planted a hand against her chest. "Your girl ain't do too bad on her SATs."

Surprised, Brooke asked, "You?"

Amber squinted her eyes at Brooke. "Whuh, bitch? A girl from the streets can't be smart?"

Brooke shrugged and took another sip. "I mean . . ."

"Yes, me. May not be that smart in a pacific area, but I am pretty smart, just lazy. Just ain't big on education. Too straight-laced."

Emily raised her finger. "Umm," she grimaced, "I'm sorry. It's 'specific.'"

Out of it, Amber stared past Emily with an empty gaze. "What I say? I said 'spacisic.'"

Emily and I chuckled under our hands.

Brooke shook her head and rolled her eyes. "I'ma need to see some papers." One of her waxed brows arched at Amber.

Amber raised both arms. "I am smart. But I guess no one would never know, because I'm stuck behind a piano all the damn time."

"Have you been getting jobs or gigs?" Brooke asked her.

"Yes. Money has been flowing in more consisily, thanks to your, umm, your ummm, wedding people and all, I got jobs at bougie parties and restaurants." Amber's jewelry-laced hand beat her chest. "But a sis need to know if she gon' eat the next day. Two of my students quit the piano lessons, because the little piss ants think that it's too hard. Really? Who the hell think that they can play a song in two weeks?" She pointed at me because she knew me so well. "Chopsticks don't count, so don't say that."

I grinned and winked at her.

"More sparkling cider," I demanded. Emily circled to the kitchen then topped my portion to the rim. "Thank you, sweetness." She bowed and walked away.

"Summer." Amber pointed a backward palm at me. "You the only one with a man. How's it feel, baby?"

"Damn good." I smiled wider than the Grand Canyon gap.

Emily objected. "Heyyy. That's not fair. I have Zach."

Amber flipped a dismissive hand at her. "Nuh-uh. That don't count. You don't love that man. Set that joker free."

"Or does she?" Brooke asked before sipping.

Emily giggled. "And let go of my penis? No. But how do you make it to that point if you don't take the time to date? We enjoy sex in places when the moment hits, but it's no longer for the high. We just . . . need it when we need it. But other than that, I mean, I call him when I wanna talk to a man. I scroll past Eric's name in my phone and try not to call and cuss his ass out." She blinked multiple times with mock shame. "Sorry for the foul language."

We snickered.

Amber pointed a long, fake nail at her. "You right, you right. Don't nobody need to be throwin' away that guaranteed dick though." She shook her head with closed eyes. "Mm, mm. We don't do that."

"Just hate when I hear him pee. Men's pee sounds too loud and long," Emily complained.

Amber lifted her chin and jerked her head as she said, "*I* love it."

"Ew, why?" I asked chuckling.

"Cuz that means that there's some dick in the house. That's why."

We lowered our heads and shook them with a giggle.

"Wait." Brooke lowered her chin as she studied Emily. "You still have his number in your phone?"

"Whose?" Emily asked. "Oh, Eric?" Her mouthed twisted. "Well, yeah. Don't you still have Jackson's?"

"For what?" Brooke challenged. "Bad enough I remember it by heart."

"I mean . . ." She shrugged as she struggled to supply a reason. ". . . sometimes they come back."

"Pssssh." Brooke swiped the air with a hand. "I don't. If I don't see you, your name and number must go. I hit the delete button the night we broke up. I don't wanna see that name in my phone if I ain't gonna use it. Besides, I know where to find him."

"Well if he calls, he can catch you off-guard," Emily suggested.

"Like I said, I remembered it in the beginning." She shrugged. "But I still got pics of us on my phone. I mean, a lil chocolate, chocolate don't hurt when I'm lonely at night."

Amber hollered with her tongue hanging out as she stretched so Brooke could high-five her. "Right? Don't take it out on the pictures. What those pictures done do to you?"

"Not a damn thang," Brooke replied with a holler. "Shoooot. A girl needs some help sometimes, and it beats pluckin' the bean to some digital dummy that I'll never meet or have never met."

Amber pointed two fingers at her eyes and then at Brooke. "Lemme find out my girl Brooke and I got more in common when she tippin' up the rim."

Brooke patted the back of her head. "I mean, I gotta let my hair down sometimes."

"How long is too long to leave an ex's number in your phone?" I asked. "I mean, I had Ruben's number in my phone when time came to call him about this baby."

Emily pointed at me. "That's right, you did." Her teary eyes widened, subtly suggesting that I'd substantiated her point of view. Emily started to lose the battle to sobriety, and it started to show through her blank stare and slower movements.

"And Oliver don't mind?" Amber asked.

"Guess he never knew. I don't even know why I kept it, you know, after we separated."

"I think subconsciously, you didn't want to let your old life go," Brooke offered. "Or maybe you kept him just in case you and Oliver flatlined. Why else would you want it?"

Maybe Brooke was right. "Maybe I'm bad with closure. I had Max's number and I still do. But we're actually friends. He helped me move out that day, and his wife did, too."

Amber said, "Shiiiiiid. I wish a broad called my man to ask for some help. I'd knock him upside his head if he even thought about it. Betta not ask me either."

I assured her with a chortle, "But we're just honest friends."

"Honest my ass. Your honest vagina still works. And, Summer?" She lowered her chin at me. "We all know a lil wedding band ain't stop you before."

"Ouch." Emily looked away.

Brooke and Amber hollered with laughter and clinked glasses. Amber waved a hand in the air mimicking ocean waves. "Baby girl steam rolled through that marriage. You hea' meh?"

"Shut up!" They drew me into laughter as the two drunk women cackled and smacked hands. It was a good thing that I never told them about Ruben's failed advance toward me. My almost-actions left me too ashamed to tell anyone, and the last thing I wanted was for it to be made light of. Besides, Oliver wouldn't want me to share that with them if I hadn't with him first. No one knew but Ruben and me. It'd have to stay that way.

Amber continued, "As a free bird, you like to keep them options open, baby. Don't you? You know, for a booty call, because I got booty call numbers in my phone. But people who disgust or disappoint me, like a closed-door case like Brooke and Jackson, I delete."

"Well dang, you ain't gotta rub it in that we over."

Amber barely seemed contrite. "Sorry, boo. So, I side with Brooke. When it's over, it's over. Daniel, George, and all them other suckas before them, deleted. Now, it's sadly just Cris, because Cane's dead ass ain't even get me off. Ole girthy-dick self."

"Ew." Emily shuddered. "Why didn't you run when you saw it?"

"Hey, you be quiet over there. At least this fool didn't make it rain on me with his come."

Emily pretended to throw up. "Oh, shut up."

I cleared my throat. "But why'd you bring up the SATs, Amber?"

"I enrolled in community college. I need to see how I feel about school and how I perform before I try a four-year college."

We all shouted with pride at once, "That's awesome, Amber. Good for you."

She flagged a hand at us and looked away sheepishly. "Oh, shut up. Shut up. Y'all makin' a bitch blush."

"Hugs!" Emily struggled to stand but made it to Amber, who pretended to gush as Emily and Brooke smothered her with sloppy hugs.

Amber stood and staggered toward me. "Come here, wobbles." When I struggled to lift my body and baby weight, Amber gently eased me back down. "No. Stay. I'll bend."

"Ohhhh." We embraced as I whispered, "So proud of you." She kissed my cheek before heading back toward her chair.

Emily announced, "And we're gonna have a baby. Cheers!"

The three of us repeated, "Cheers!"

They all staggered in my direction to clink glasses before celebrating with long sips.

Emily said, "We have Brooke's birthday, her new building and moving on strong without a man, I have a new place and a healthy friendship with Zach, Amber is in school and still getting her orgasms." We fell over laughing. "And Summer is about to be a mom in a few weeks with her very honorable man."

Officially July and the last month that I would be pregnant, Oliver and I barely fought, but slight tension drifted between us like an airy pink elephant in the room. With my pregnancy and his awareness of the real daddy, returning to our old fun and carefree selves seemed almost impossible. We spent months tiptoeing as an unspoken attempt to be understanding of each another. I knew I had no right pissing off a man who wanted to step up to another man's baby for the sake of loving me, and he wanted to be considerate of the pregnant woman he loved.

Brooke held up a hand. "Wait." We paused in silence to see what she had to say. "Am I the only one not getting orgasms?"

"Awwwww," we sang in a chorus.

Everyone went back to their prior sitting positions.

Emily suggested, "Well, maybe Summer's not—she's pregnant."

"And in what book supports that theory? Sorry, baby, but don't listen to her. Oliver seems hornier than ever. I farted once when he was in the middle of tasting my ice cream and he still kept licking. Ohhh, how fabulous it is to be pregnant."

Amber stomped her foot. "Dammit, that's what I'm talkin' about. A brotha' who will eat that good ish no matta what. My pussy farted the same night I was with Crisa . . . Cris. We kept it moving."

Delighted, I tilted my head at Amber. "Did you just say 'fawted?'"

"Whuh? I'm from New York."

Giving her the thumbs us, I said, "That accent though, I love it."

Amber sniggered and supped the last portion of her wine.

"Ew." Brooke snarled. "Then maybe I should get a surrogate. Pregnancy just sounds funk*ay*."

"But it's a beautifully funky," I assured her. "And for the right man, you'll embrace all its quirks and funkiness."

"I would have for the 'J' man." She pouted. "Need more wine."

Emily jumped up with a struggle, but once she did, she gave her what she wanted.

Amber shook Brooke's right shoulder. "Now, we not gonna do this on your day. You hear me? Jackson is yesterday's paper and a beauty like you will snag the right guy any day." She turned to Emily. "More wine, please."

"Oh." Emily raced with clumsy feet to fulfill Amber's request.

"Thanks, boo."

Emily took the bottle and stood near the oversized window.

Brooke licked her upper lip in thought. "But you know what? I, too, have a confession."

"What?" we asked with great interest.

"Well, sometimes I think about what his new woman must look like. I wonder if I'm good enough to hold a candle to her. Like maybe he found some super-hot woman to really stick it to me. I think about that a lot, you know. There's always someone better looking than the next. Maybe I'm not as pretty as I think. He never came back, guys. He. Never. Came. Back."

Not knowing what to say to that, we sat in silence, as the three of us exchanged glances. Oblivious to our pupil exchanges, Brooke eyed the floor with the glass of wine in her hands.

Amber rescued us with, "That's just stupid to say." Brooke looked up. "You are gorgeous. But, honey, some women have this bad habit of measuring their immuniny—im-im-hell, you know what I'm sayin'." Brooke nodded, and Emily threw her the right word. "Anyway, we measure that to certain, uhhh, things in life by how beautiful we are. Sadly, you one of them. You think men stick around or treat you differently because you hot? No. Yes, if you in a beauty pageant a face goes a long way. But, honey, over here in real life, men love beauty at first but love to find it in other ways. If you walk around thinkin' these men are as superfisial as you make them to be, then you ain't gon never learn the lessons from your hookups."

"Genius. Just brilliant," I said clapping as Emily nodded with pride.

"That is deep, Ms. Laurent. I wish she just said that as simple as you. Then, what *is* my lesson with Jackson?"

Amber shrugged. "Honey, I dunno. I wasn't in that relationship—you were. But you can have a vagina made of gold trimmings—"

"Hmm," I said. "That sounds good. Where can I find one? I may need it when Oliver wakes up at two in the morning to the cries of another man's baby." They all shook their heads at me. "Sorry," I whispered and spun around in my chair.

"Anyway!" Amber continued. "That still won't make a man stay. Well, okay it could buy some more time, but you know what I mean." Brooke grinned and nodded. "Maybe he thinks he'll always fall short in your eyes and doesn't want to disappoint you because he loves you so much."

Brooke stroked the top of her head. "The irony of it all. I deleted his phone number to show that our book is closed, but a chapter still seems unwritten."

"Sometimes it be's that way," Amber answered. "But what you want the man to do? Look back? You want children and he doesn't. Maybe he'll give up and come back when he can't find a woman who meets that one thingy after passing the rest."

"Thank you for the fantastic advice, Amber, but," Brooke struggled to stand, "this is my party. Forget our woes and men. Let's party." Then she gave up and sat.

"That's all I was tryna' do," Amber said.

I was happy that the black cloud that threatened our night sailed away.

The wine had started to take Emily down. Emily staggered from the window to stand where she was sitting in the living room. "Well, guys, my birthday is in September." She pointed a sloppy finger at us. "Don't forget."

Brooke cheered. "We gonna be wild since my birthday ain't." She raised her glass in the air. "Whew!"

I tittered. "Um, did you guys forget that you have to make it back home?"

"I took a cab," Brooke said before sipping again.

"I ain't got no car so you know I did, so needless to say," Amber took a long swig, "I couldn't give two shits."

"This wine is gooooooooooood." Emily held the bottle up and asked, "Who wants the last drop?"

"Us." Brooke and Amber raised hands simultaneously.

"Here." She poured a quick drop into Brooke's glass and then Amber's. "And here." Then with her head tilted up and lips wrapped around the rim, she finished the rest.

"No waaaaaay," Brooke complained with a pout. "She played us."

Amber started to ease into a laugh. When Brooke joined her, they became hysterical. Watching them cut up made me join them.

Emily spun around and swayed as she struggled to keep balanced. "I didn't tell y'all something else."

"What's that, mama?" Amber looked up.

"I threw that man out naked."

Brooke frowned. "Who?"

"That s-s-s-snake. I don't remember his name. The one who skated all over my legs."

"Skeeted?" I suggested.

She pointed at me. "Right. I forget his name."

Amber's reddish eyes tried to widen. "You threw that man out with no clothes?"

"Bucking naked," Emily confirmed. "Well, almost. I threw him out with a button-up shirt on. That's it."

"Buckin' naked?" Overtaken with humor, Amber lost control. "Girl, I see that when people cross you, you give them the biz."

"Guess so," she said.

Brooke guffawed and then slowly composed herself. "Wait, wait, wait, wait, wait. So, you shoved his clothes into his arms and sent the poor man outside the door?"

Emily held up one finger. "First of all, he cheated on his wife with me and has five children, okay? And no, I threw his crap over the balcony rail butt naked."

I threw my hand up. "Hold up." She raised her brow at me. "You tossed his clothes over the balcony while standing butt naked?"

Emily grinned proudly. "Yup."

"Damn she's a firecracker. I luh this lady!" Amber hooted.

"Now that's called letting someone go with just the shirt on their back," Brooke joked.

"Bet them balls was swingin' under the hem line." Amber slapped her knee as her body jerked with laughter. "Whooo. Whoooo." She fanned her runny eyes. "Errrthing is funny when you drunk."

Brooke set her glass down on the floor. Her voice had become shaky. "So, what? Homeboy walked into the street with no draws on? Just that shirt?" Her hand moved to cover her mouth.

"That's all."

"But what if someone took his clothes by the time he got down there?" I asked.

Emily shrugged and raised the empty bottle. "Not my concern. I did it for all the married women."

"I know that's right," Brooke said as sadness covered her face without warning. "Guys. I hate to say this but, we've *all* slept with married men."

Emily shook her head and snapped her head back. "And I never wanted to be a part of that club." She placed a hand behind her neck, but the other hand didn't relinquish the bottle.

"And I did it on purpose with multiple men." Amber crossed her legs and frowned.

"And you all know my story," I said.

Brooke shook her head. "I feel ya, Emily. I feel your pain. Never wanted to be a part of that club but then Damani forced me into it. Guys, we gotta be more careful. So many men be slippin' those rings off."

Amber said, "The ones I had kept them on."

"Then what does that make us?" Emily asked somberly.

"Some hoes." Amber grinned and then she snickered.

Brooke pointed a finger at Amber. "Speak for yourself, honey. The married men were hoes. We just needed to scratch an itch. Amber—you the only hoe."

"What? I stopped taking money."

One by one, we all succumbed to the humor of it all, though, it really wasn't funny but rather pathetic, however, it sadly led us into splitting our sides. No one in the room had a dry eye.

"You guys better not make me pee on myself. I may have on a dress, but I ain't got no extra pair of draws."

Brooke pointed a shaky finger at Emily through glassy eyes. "Emily may have some that you can wear." She wiped a tear.

Amber pointed out hysterically, "She gon' have to wear Emily's draws, but they ain't gonna fit."

Wide-eyed, Emily asked, "Why not?"

Amber hollered, "Because you too uptight."

Brooke held her heart as she tried to catch her breath. "Her white cotton panties."

Emily's cheeks turned red. With a huge smile she replied, "What? I . . . got nice panties. Really, really nice ones."

I grinned. "Yeah, well, I'm glad I could be the butt of your jokes. And be nice to Emily. If you two continue to misbehave, you'll find yourselves Ubering."

Amber said, "I bet she iron them jokers before wearing them."

Brooke cried out, "The night before, too."

My shoulders rocked in an attempt to conceal my reaction. Amber dropped out of her chair and onto her knees.

Clutching her stomach and falling weak, Brooke fell into the floor with her friend and added, "They probably match her socks."

Emily tilted her head at them. "Oh, well, you two can just suck it, okay? I ain't as rigid as I used to be."

"Yeah, guys," Amber pointed, "she just said, 'ain't.'"

No longer in control, my threshold for tolerating humor had been crossed. I should've used the bathroom sooner, and now my bladder attempted to break free. "Help. I'm gonna pee on Emily's wooden floors." I tried to stand in time from her computer chair. Unfortunately, some pee had already seeped out.

"What?" Brooke looked at Amber in temporary alarm. "She's gonna . . . *her water broke?*"

Amber fell over laughing as she chanted, "You mean her piss broke! My stomach, my stomach, my stomach. Owwww, it hurts."

"Me, tooooo." Brooke bent at the waist as her head gently met the floor. "Owwwwweeeeeeee." She gripped her stomach as the excessive laughter got to her.

Amber tapped her friend's thigh rapidly. "Quick. You're gonna miss her piss. Miss her piss," she chanted harder through her screeching than I thought possible. "Miss her piss on herself."

When she said that, I struggled not to get beside myself and to hold in the urine longer. One look into Emily's hazel eyes revealed matching horror. "Oh, noooooo. Sorry, Ems." The warm liquid raced down my legs and onto my feet. Over my big belly, I soon saw the collection of evidence pool around me. "Nooooo," I whined again. My lips pouted in irritation that I'd have to smell like piss for God knew how long, since I wasn't around the corner from home. Tipsy, Emily couldn't come to my rescue. The other two hyenas were down for the count. As a pregnant woman in another woman's home, I only had myself.

"Guys, it's not funny," I pleaded, but to no avail. Shit just got real.

Emily replied with cupped hands over her mouth as she stared me up and down. "Okay, okay, okay, okay, okay."

She grabbed me by one of my tiny wrists as she slowly led me away. One look back at the hyenas showed me two women with the sniffles and sweaty foreheads with matching glassy eyes. Making their day at least made me happy. We've all been under stress for too long, and this moment proved to be a much-needed relief for all of us. In the distance, I heard the girls cry, "Sorry, Summer." In my opinion, they had nothing to be sorry about; I loved them.

With shaky balance, Emily managed to lead me to her fragrant bathroom. Large sand-colored tiles painted the walls with identical ones covering the floor. She had double sinks, a Jacuzzi tub with a separate shower, and a closed-off toilet. It was a couple's bathroom used by a single woman. What single woman wouldn't love to have a bathroom like this all to herself?

Some women would perhaps feel lonely, but before Oliver, I would've been content. Before Oliver, the bigger meant the better. It didn't make me think of the missing man. Even now, I still had a tough time factoring him into every equation. The free bird still lived inside of me. The trick was not to let Oliver see it.

"Take off your clothes, and I'll wash and dry them for you. Drop your sandals in the sink."

Emily helped me strip down into my bra and soggy underwear. I didn't want to disgust her with too much detail. "Thank you, Emily."

Emily staggered with distant yet present eyes. "Huh?" She swiped a stray hair from her forehead. Before I had a chance to repeat myself, it registered. "Oh. Yeah." She smacked the air. "Don't worry about it." She placed a hand on my back. "Do you need help, sweetie?" Bending down to remove my sandals, she threw them into the sink. I felt better already.

"Emily, you're the best."

One peek in the mirror made me cry. My reflection revealed a big belly hiding blue underwear with a white bra. With my long, wavy hair easing past my shoulders, I felt hideous. The girls poked fun at the wrong woman—

Emily certainly looked better than this. Unable to bear the sight any longer, I threw my palms over my face.

"Oh, nooo." Emily gently removed my hands to show me two concerned eyes traced in runny eyeliner stared back at me. "Don't cry, Summer. What's wrong?" Her wine-laced breath hit my nostrils.

"I don't know, I don't know." My hands flew up then fell against the sides of my thighs. "You're so good to me right now. I'm happy to have you guys in my life. This whole pregnancy thing . . . I'm so scared."

She pointed at herself. "Me, too. I mean, after all that I been through with Eric. Are you serious? Having you ladies here made all the difference. I had Brooke, but you and Amber are a great bonus, too. I love you guys."

"I love you, too, Ems." Her eyes smiled with fondness. "I can't hug you in a bra and wet underwear though."

She giggled as I wiped a tear.

"Get undressed, take a shower," she pointed to a pretty blue robe hanging on the back of the door, "put that robe on. Your clothes . . . be done in thirty." I nodded, and she walked into the door frame on her way out. "Ouch." Turning the corner, she shouted, "More wine, please?"

While in the shower, she came back in to grab my wet clothes and sandals. Pleased, I couldn't believe that she wasn't mad at me. Moments later after the shower and easing back into the living room to join my friends, they spotted me. Emily flagged a pointing finger at the other two and at the area where the pee puddle used to be.

"Look," she said. "They cleaned up the pee while we were gone." She smiled and clapped like a seal. Emily's speech officially slurred.

I bit my lower lip with a grin. For two drunk girls, Brooke and Amber seemed to have composed themselves as they shrugged.

"Ohhh, guys . . ." I wobbled quickly across the room to hug a standing but unsteady Brooke and Amber. I felt

Emily's body smash into ours. We embraced with exhales, giggles, and awws. "Thank you, ladies, for a good cry and laugh."

"You're welcome," they sang.

Amber added, "But, chile, you the one who really gave us the laugh."

"Oh, shut up." I pinched them harder in my hug. We released one another.

Brooke tried to sound sober. "Really, guys. Thank you for this awesome birthday, and it wasn't boring. Emily spillin' the tea 'bout that man, too?" She picked up her glass from the coffee table and pointed it at me. "And her pissy ways?"

We cracked up.

"Oh, you tryna take a cab ride home, huh?" I teased.

"I should call Cane for a good time tonight. A drunk orgasm ain't never hurt nobody."

She started to twerk until Brooke said, "Amber, don't call that man. You ain't gonna get no orgasm from him."

Amber straightened and shrugged in agreement. "Yeah."

Emily pointed at her with a motherly stare. "He respectful to you?"

"Nope. Never. But besides, we screwed once." Amber shot back. "Ever since he barged in before my piano lesson started—"

"Yeah, you shoulda twisted his dick off," barked Brooke before burping. We fanned the air. "Who do he think he is? Don't nobody play with my money."

"Well." Genuinely upset, Amber's face tuned up. "Crisanto wasn't comin' through for me like he shoulda' been. Who says women need to wait for men? Nah, I ain't gonna give Cane no pussy. Still too tight about the last time he did me wrong. Those days are over. And I'm dead-ass right now about that."

"Uh-oh." I eyed her with a cocked brow. "Watch out."

"Besides, I was down for takin' an orgasm for bad treatment. He's a jerk, I know. But I wasn't gonna put up with him when he was out of me."

"Nasty," Emily snarled.

"Oh stop, you fl-flasher," chided Amber. "You do your dirt in public and I do mine at home. You, the teacher, are busy having sex for children to see."

Emily struggled to defend herself. "Weeeeeee are careful and behaving now. Besides, I'm overdue for some careless fun."

"What brought all that on in the first place?" I asked. "Tryna' pick up where Jackson and Brooke left off?"

Brooke looked up with enlarged eyes.

"*No.*" Emily crossed her arms. "What can I say? I was horny one night in the movie, a-a-aaaand Eric thinks I'm boring."

"So, you wanted to prove him wrong?" I asked.

She held up a finger. "*Wanted,* being the operative word, but now I juss like it. It's amazing how much more powerful an orgasm can feel when your brain is having fun. Wild, dirty thoughts."

Amber smirked with closed eyes as she caressed a hand over her chest, clearly drawing joy from a past memory. "Well I don't need no wild thoughts. Just a man who know how to sling it right."

Without a glass in hand, I said, "Here, here. But when I had sex outside with Ruben, it did bring in a different element. That was my first time."

Slurring, Emily confessed, "Doing it in public places becomes addictive."

Brooke looked confounded. "Ion know. Jasson and I did it . . . whereva'." Brooke's eyelids began to close.

Amber suggested, "Maybe your sex life needed a spark cuz in bed it was borin'."

Everyone waited for Emily to respond. She steadied herself with a hand on a barstool. "That could be true." She pointed a finger at her temple. "Nooo, ohh I don't know. I like it and don't plan to quit for now."

"Yeah, until a cop comes knocking on concrete or bricks," I told her.

Brooke and Amber snickered while Emily went to check on my clothes. After she staggered with my hot clothes, she escorted me to her bedroom and closed the doors to give me privacy. When I returned to the living room in my dress and cleaned sandals, Brooke and Amber turned to face me with heavy eyelids.

Brooke barely managed her words. "I gotta go. I gotta meet this Jussice lady tomorrow. Can't even believe I drank too much."

We all agreed with her as Amber struggled to help me stand.

"Oh, well," added Brooke. "The wedding is only three days away and I'ma be free of this chain. I need a vacation."

"We should really plan one," I suggested.

"Sound good," Emily agreed.

"Come on, ladies, let's take the birthday girl home." I reached for Brooke's arm.

"You can drive?" Emily asked.

"From here to Amber's to Penn Quarter to Arlington? It's all good. Let's bounce, y'all."

Emily hugged us goodbye as we thanked her for hosting our best friend's party. The night ended on a beautiful note as I realized that no matter what, I had three amazing sisters and one good time.

9: the wedding planner

Summer

"Great news," Brooke said, breathing heavily into the phone.

I heard the cars honking in the background. "Are you walking?"

"In the street, yes. But do you wanna hear the great news?"

"Sure."

"Justice insists that I bring all three of my friends to the wedding this Saturday. You down?"

"Oh." Oliver's hands gripped my neck as he massaged the tension away between my shoulder blades. "Hang tight. Oliver and I are pressed for private time before the baby comes." I covered the receiver and turned to face him. "Do you mind if I go to the wedding this Saturday?"

"Baby, please go. I want you to have fun before this baby holds you down. Besides, I ain't goin' nowhere, boo. Go have fun." He kissed my lips, melting my heart.

"Thank you, baby. Now get back to work." I winked and turned around as I moved my hand from the receiver and his hand back to my shoulders. "Okay, hon. What time?"

"Three o'clock. It starts at three-thirty, but black people time means bumping it up thirty minutes in hopes that you guys will be on time."

"Maybe you shouldn't have told me the exact time."

"Shat. Look, let's meet at my place. No, wait. I have to be there long before then. Just please, I don't care how you ladies do it. By the way, the others can make it, too. I already asked. Just please be there on time. Okay?"

"Wouldn't miss it for the world. Well, unless the baby comes."

"The baby. Wow. Can't wait. And what about the name and gender?"

"Oliver and I wanna be surprised, but the names—" I shrugged as if she could see. "Who knows, you know. But we got some ideas."

"Gotta go, honey. Call you later with the address." She clicked immediately.

"Baby names and gender?" he asked.

I spun around in the barstool to face him. "Oliver, what are we working with so far? Growing up, I never really thought about having kids."

"Well, didn't you have a favorite doll that you had to name?" He stroked my hair.

I chuckled. "I put no thought behind those names. Got any suggestions?"

"I like the name . . . Ashley. And, uhhh, how about Nicole, Rashida . . ." He squinted as he peered upward in thought.

I poked his hard stomach playfully. "Those ex-girlfriends?"

Oliver wiggled his eyebrows. "Just playin'. I don't think I wanna think of them when we call our daughter's name."

"Good. And if it's a boy?" I twisted from left to right on the stool.

"Oliver, Jr.?" He fell over laughing. "Ollie? Ollie Trollie?"

I couldn't help but crack up. "Get outta' here. How about Omar or Oscar?" I crinkled my nose. "I'm trying to stay in the 'O' family here."

"Ahhhhh. I see. I can't . . ." he shook his head in disapproval with a grin.

Pretending to wipe my forehead, I teased him with a, "Whew. Then what?"

"Please. No last names for first names. I hate that trend."

"What? It makes the man sound stronger."

"Don't try to play me."

"They're just names, Oliver. Okay, then give me some ideas. Well didn't you have some action hero figure as a kid?"

"He-man sounds great." He realized as much as I did that we were two lost souls at this name game. I reached out to hug him close as we laughed.

"The good news is that we have weeks to figure this out. But this is what we get for waiting until the last minute."

"You better hope we have weeks," he pointed out. "I love you Goldie Locks. He plucked my hair.

"I love you, too, Ollie Trollie."

Emily

Zach took a seat on the sofa next to Emily. "Well, baby. How have things been going?"

Emily sighed. "Well, with the summertime and school being out, that means no work for me, so that's great. Just happy that in the past few weeks I've been able to lay low. How have things been going for you? It's been a few weeks since I've seen you, kid."

"I've missed you. But with school out, I took Enzo fishing at Lake Tahoe. Vacation was good. I really wished I coulda taken you, but I didn't need Enzo spreading the word around school next year, you know, his dad chilling with his teacher."

"Good call," Emily assured him with a tap on the knee. "He was a pleasure to have. I'm sure gonna miss him next year."

"Enzo loved you. I just wished I coulda told him that daddy found you amazing, too. So many times, I tried not to laugh when he came home talking about you. I wanted to chime in with him." Zach stroked the back of Emily's head as his hand traveled down the length of her brown tresses.

"Dating anyone right now?" Emily needed to change the subject. She didn't want to talk so serious.

"Nope."

Shucks. He's still holding out. "Why not?"

"Not looking. Besides, one day I hope to be exclusive with you."

"Zach—"

"I know, I know, Emily," he cut her off calmly. "But this is how I feel. I'm not sure what you're waiting for but . . ."

"I have to get rid of all feelings for Eric. He burned me, and I set a fire in his yard, but hey, feelings have a mind of their own that can seem quite arbitrary. What are you gonna do?"

"I can wait. I like you. I'm not in a rush to be with anyone, Emily. I'm a loner, and you're right. I shouldn't have to be with a woman with a divided heart."

Emily settled back against the sofa to fit into the nook of his arm and armpit. He caressed her shoulder. "Are you sleeping with anyone else?"

Thinking before replying, Emily answered. "I have."

In a moment of silence, he replied with an, "I see."

"Does that make you hate me or change your opinion of me?" She pointed her chin upward to catch his gaze.

"No, Emily. I don't like it, but no. We're not a couple—yet. But your honesty is beautiful, because you really didn't have to tell me." Before she could respond, he cupped her face with a hand and turned it, so he could plant a kiss on her mouth.

Zach was a great kisser, she reasoned, but committing to him seemed a bit too much right now. Even though he'd raised the bar by acquiescing to her sexual whims in public, it all failed to suffice. She still couldn't tell if she genuinely liked him or if a part of her entertained him because of her availability. While it sounded awful, acknowledging it as the truth relieved her. When Zach released his mouth from hers, there was nothing left to say so they chose to speak through their beaming eyes.

Amber

"Mmmmmm, Crisanto!" Amber collapsed on top of her lover once her orgasm ended. She rolled over to her side of the bed as she and Crisanto tried to catch their breath.

"Thought I told you to call me Cris." He hopped out of the bed and pulled his jeans over each leg.

"I felt good, so I wasn't worried about your pet peeves or preferences." Amber watched him get dressed, stretching one fit limb into the length of each pant leg. His taut shoulder blades would've been a tease had it not been kissed and caressed already by her lips and acrylic nails.

"Yeah, yeah, yeah." Cris turned to face her with a grin.

"You don't wanna stay for a while?" She rubbed his side of the bed.

"Amber, you know my schedule. I gotta be at work." Cris eased into his shirt and danced each foot into his shoes.

"Cris?" Amber sat up as she narrowed her eyes at him. "Are you seeing someone else? You can tell me." She pulled the sheets over her breasts like a strapless dress.

"I really don't have time for other women, let alone this conversation. I came to get the tip wet." He fastened his belt and stared square into her eyes. Somewhere behind the pupils, Amber read a dare to test him. "And, so what if I am?"

Amber felt a sting to her ego as she shrugged. "I . . . it's not a big deal, Cris. But we did go from some possibilities of something to not much of anything but sex."

"Amber, the first night we met, I had you in my bed. You established our relationship to be like this. What else do you want me to say?"

Looking straight, Amber thought about it for one moment. "Nothing." She rolled her eyes to land on his.

"Nothing at all boo-boo; I feel the same way. I just didn't want to pretend that nothing's changed."

"You're right, Amber. Things have changed. I'm being tested at work so things are intense."

"Or maybe you feel special because you got admitted into *law* school."

He scoffed. "Amber, I don't have time for this, I gotta bounce. But you know what? Maybe it's best to move on from here, you know. Seems like you can't handle not being first. If you decide you can, then hit me up."

Numb with disbelief at his attitude, she replied, "I won't."

"Then there's really nothing left to say." He shook two fingers up and walked away. "*Adiós.*"

Cavalierly, she responded with, "*Adiós.*"

Sometimes, a goodbye really meant goodbye. Sadly, this was one of those times.

Brooke

"Justice has charged everything to the name Celeste Black. Everything." Brooke's assistant turned around to face her. "But the couple is Justice Ashby and Mason Berry."

"So?" Sitting at her desk, Brooke chewed on a bite of salad. Once she swallowed, she asked, "Is that weird, Haysia?" She rubbed her head and fought like hell to work through her hangover. Brooke still didn't know what she was thinking, drinking as much as she did.

Since a professional took a chance on Brooke in college, she decided to pay it forward by taking a chance on a beautiful, Ethiopian college student, Haysia Meseret, who wanted and needed experience as a future wedding planner. Besides, it saved a lot of money since she worked part time with a low hourly rate. It resulted in a win-win situation.

"Brooke. Someone is so nice to pay for all of their things." Haysia's brown eyes glowed.

"Haysia, that's the way it goes. You'll see that a lot in this field. It's her grandma."

Haysia shrugged. "I'm surprised you're not married. You're gorgeous."

Did the little girl think she was having fun being single? Of course she wanted to be married. Before Brooke could become irritated, the compliment changed her reaction. "Thank you, Haysia. Now make sure you call the caterers to remind them of the change in the entrée selection."

"Salmon?"

"And?"

Haysia bit her lower lip as she tried to recall the other item. "I don't know how you remember so much."

"Not only have I been doing it for years, Haysia, but when someone offers you thousands of dollars to get something done, you pull your ass together fast. Lamb."

Summer

I decided to get out of the house since Oliver put in some extra hours at work before the weekend. After sliding my debit card into the parking meter, I opened the door of the corner business that read, "Brazile's Bridal Planning." A petite young lady with gorgeous, copper-colored skin—tenderly kissed by the sun many days—and a head full of tight spiral curls with golden highlights, stood in Brooke's company.

As I came through the door, Brooke jumped up to hug me. "Summer? What are you doing here?" She smelled like lavender and looked pretty in her black sleeveless dress.

"I needed to see the place. I overslept on your opening night and let's be honest—it's time." She made the most of her limited space with beautiful decoration. Just like her home, I could hear the faint sound of lounge/jazz music overhead. The pale-yellow walls kept the place feminine, bright, and professional. Three chic chairs sat in front of two oversized windows with a selection of magazines spread across the coffee table.

Brooke playfully pinched my arm. "Yeah it is."

"This is beautiful. You did good, Brooke."

"Thanks, girlfriend." She did a curtsy. Her hand gestured toward the young lady. "You never met Haysia Meseret—my assistant. Haysia, meet one of my best friends, Summer Stevenson."

Haysia revealed beautiful white teeth as she shook my hand. "So nice to meet you."

I mirrored her expression. "Likewise. I bet you're learning a lot from this wedding guru, huh?"

"She's the best. Her memory and knowledge impress me. I have never met anyone who can do eight things at once. I have a lot to learn."

"Ohhh," Brooke replied with a humble grin. She turned to face me. "Listen, sit tight for a moment, because Justice is coming to touch base with me."

"Who?" I asked.

Brooke chuckled. "Justice. She's the one getting married this Saturday."

"Oh. Right." I rolled my eyes. "The demanding one."

Brooke sliced the air with a rapid hand. "No, no. She's the cool one. Victoria is the brat."

"Ahhhh," I replied.

"Haysia, make her feel at home." Brooke clicked off in her red bottoms to watch the activity on the other side of her glass doors.

Haysia led me to the set of chic chairs and pointed at the magazines perfectly stretched out into a rainbow on the coffee table. "Got your magazines while you sit right here and wait if you like." Her youthful eyes jumped. "Can I get you some coffee, tea, water, or juice? Sorry, Brooke doesn't serve soda, because it's full of sugar and not calming." The regret on Haysia's face said she didn't approve.

Sounded like Brooke, and to that, I had to chuckle. "Thank you, Haysia." I jiggled an Us magazine from the rainbow. "Juice sounds good."

Haysia scurried off while Brooke joined me. Before she could sit down, she spotted a woman outside. "There she is."

"Who?" I turned. As I studied the lady who came through the glass door, Brooke turned to greet her.

"Justice. How are you today?"

Justice hugged Brooke. "Brooke. So good to see you again. Hey, I decided to take your advice and add a vegetarian dish to my menu. Turns out, I do know some of those people." She rolled her eyes and giggled.

"Everyone does these days," Brooke pointed out with a smile. She pinched two fingers together. "Hell, I'm this close to becoming one myself."

"No, I'm just playing. I admire them."

Haysia returned with apple juice, and as I sipped, it was almost impossible not to choke after I recalled the familiar face standing in front of Brooke. Telling Brooke would likely wreck her head as she finished her last stages of planning, or I could let her be blindsided on the wedding day. Maybe Haysia could step in if Brooke didn't find herself in the right headspace. Once I saw Justice step outside with her cell phone, I sprang into action.

Safely hurrying across the floor to meet a happy Brooke, hiding behind a fake smile seemed out of the question. Automatically, I placed both hands on her bare forearms before I spoke. "Brooke." My eyes couldn't hide my horror.

"Summer, what's wrong? Are you going into an early labor?" Her upper eyelids raised and froze.

My finger pointed toward the door. "Is that lady coming back in?"

"Well, yeah."

"Okay, well, I gotta tell you something." I took a quick look outside as the woman chatted away on her cell phone.

"Can it wait?" One look at Brooke's desperate face told me to let her perform in ignorance of what I knew. They say ignorance is bliss and so far, it wasn't a lie.

"Yes." I exhaled with closed eyes. "Yes, yes, don't mind me."

"You sure?"

Looking at her, I knew it was best. "Yeah, yeah. I'm just being silly. Go and take care of her."

Justice stepped back in with her phone to her ear. "Oh, Jay, you're the best. I love you, too." She placed the phone in her purse and with an exhale asked, "So, where were we?"

Jay? Jay? I could let Brooke live in bliss, but the question was how long? It'd be wrong not to offer her a heads up. I needed time with Brooke, but how to go about it all troubled me. The thought of calling Oliver sounded right, until I imagined him scolding me for "getting in the middle." It didn't matter. If I were Brooke, I'd want to know.

Back in the chair with a magazine in front of my face, I pretended to read while watching the women interact. A notification chimed, putting Justice back on her phone again.

After reading her screen, she told Brooke, "I actually have to go meet my fiancé. We got a minor problem with the builder."

Brooke crinkled her nose. "Oh, no. That's no good. Okay, not a problem. Tell him 'hi' for me."

She laughed. "Will do." Justice placed a hand on Brooke's shoulder. "Would you like to come Friday to the rehearsal dinner?"

Brooke replied, "Oh, thank you, Justice, but I rarely attend them. I will need all my sleep to ensure that the big day goes perfectly."

"Well, when you put it that way . . ." They shared a laugh before Justice headed out.

I tossed the smokescreen magazine onto the coffee table and marched back again to my friend. Grabbing her arm, I warned her with, "We need to talk, and we need to do it now." Haysia came over to man the front desk.

Worry washed over Brooke's beautiful face. "Something's been bothering you. Talk to me. What's up?"

"Your client is what's up. Do you know who she is?"

Brooke folded her arms as she expressed disbelief. "Yeah, Justice Ashby. I mean, I'm only planning her wedding, Summer." She stared at me like I was crazy.

"Okay, but what's the name of her fiancé?"

"Mason Berry," she answered with a toss of her hands.

"So, *she* says." Like a lawyer building a compelling case, I folded my arms.

My best friend eyed me like I had a balloon for a head. "Gee, you're full of drama for a little pregnant lady."

"Well. Remember that night I told you about?"

"Uhhh, which one?" she asked, still not taking me seriously.

"The night I saw your ex with that chic." I couldn't wait for her to react or respond. "That was her."

Brooke froze. Her eyes slowly darted between the door and me. With a slow blink she asked, *"That was her?"*

Haysia must have noticed Brooke's awkward footing, because she hurried from around the counter to grip her boss by the elbow. "Oh my, are you okay, Brooke?"

We eased Brooke to the chairs near the windows. She sat down as we hovered above her.

"I mean, she did say that I came highly recommended, and, of course, he would know that." Helplessly, Brooke peered up at me waiting for answers that I didn't have.

"And didn't you just hear her call the person on the other end of the phone 'Jay?'"

Haysia left and came back with water. Brooke took it and sipped it, lost in her daze. "Thanks."

"Oh, my. Now I'm in a professional bind. A-a-and poor Jackson. Poor Mason. Poor Jackson." She held her head.

I was confused. "Poor, Jackson? He's the one screwing another man's woman. He has to be in on it. You did say she said you came highly recommended. See? Who else would know that but him?" Then I bit my lip. That was me last year. Screwing someone else's man.

"The city? I get recommended all the time. And, Summer, unlike you, Jackson wouldn't do that. He's being played."

Taken aback and offended, I said, "Well, gee, thanks. Good to know I'm the only one in this precious world capable of making mistakes."

Her normally-squared shoulders dropped as she sighed. Rubbing her temples, she told me, "I'm—I'm sorry, Summer. These weddings are killing me. I didn't mean to talk to you like that."

Softened, I replied, "So then slow down some, Brooke. Stop taking on so much. You do have Haysia here to help out."

With a desire to please, Haysia nodded anxiously with a smile.

"Jackson can't know about her man. It wouldn't make sense for him to recommend me to her if he wasn't the one marrying her. Jackson wouldn't be no one's second."

I shook my finger. "Ahhh, so true. Then she's cheating on Mason while playing Jackson. She did step outside to take that call."

"Maybe it's his cousin. Sister? Friend?" Haysia suggested with half of a shrug.

"Yes!" I pointed at Brooke. "That devastated sister."

Brooke perked up for a moment but then dropped her shoulders again when she replied, "Her name wasn't Justice. It was umm . . . umm . . . M-Monet."

"Ohhh," Haysia and I moaned.

Brooke clutched her neckline. "My ex is being taken for a fool. That ain't right. How can I stand by this wedding, Summer?"

Cocking a brow, with no hesitation, I answered, "Because you're a professional who was hired to do her job. Now unless you're prepared to forfeit the check, you need to suck it up and stay out of it."

Haysia said, "She's smart, Brooke. Listen to her."

Looking like she just swallowed a bitter pill, Brooke said, "You're right. I have to forget what I know, even if Jackson *has* moved on, even if it is all just a lie. He'll have to figure it all out, I guess. We're not each other's problem."

Wasn't sure how much I believed her.

Brooke stood up and straightened the front of her dress.

"That's right," Haysia replied. "You're such a warrior."

My hands twisted together nervously. Brooke would probably go home and crumble, but I didn't question her. Right now, she needed my support. "G-good."

Brooke didn't move as the will to fight disappeared in her eyes while reality settled in. "But not before I have a good cry." She barged past Haysia and me. "Excuse me." Knowing Brooke, she required space before accepting comfort.

"So, Jackson must've been a big deal?" Haysia looked to me for answers.

I nod once. "Big time."

Her forehead crinkled as she listened. "That's terrible. Do you think she can push through on Saturday?"

"I tell you one thing. You'll probably gain tremendous hands-on experience Saturday. Are you prepared for that?"

Haysia didn't know how to answer. "Yes." She shook her head rapidly with lackadaisical conviction.

"I mean, we're talking taking the place of the woman who works with several idiosyncrasies in order to get things done."

A weak voice behind me said, "I do not. I'm just extremely professional and on top of things." With drooping eyelids, Brooke made her way toward Haysia and me. She threw her arms around my neck. "Thank you. Thank you for not sparing me."

Haysia returned to the desk to take a call.

I squeezed her as a tear fell down my face. "You're welcome, Brooke. I couldn't keep something like this from you."

We stepped back from one another. Brooke said, "All of this could've been avoided if he gave himself a chance to be with me. He was so scared to have kids. Now he's single and probably getting played." She shrugged. "Maybe I should call him after the wedding and tell him what I know."

"No." I grabbed her arms quickly. "Don't even think about it."

"Why? We're both adults."

"Because when you hear that man's voice, it won't go down like you think. All kinds of emotions will flood you. You'll crack, and you will lose. So don't," I implored. My knowledge in that area could be attributed to too many one-on-ones with Ruben.

She placed a finger on her chin. "Hmmm. I don't like the idea of losing, so you win. I've already lost enough and a girl's gotta keep her dignity no matter what. So, thanks again. And happy belated birthday to me from Jackson—the man I can't seem to shake even with a stick in my hand." Brooke chewed on her lip to keep from crying. "Haysia," she called without moving as she located her with her eyes.

"Yes?" Haysia popped up from behind the desk.

Without making eye contact, Brooke told her through gritted teeth, "When you are done with school, focus on your work only. You need to decide between having a man or a fierce career. Got it?"

Scared to disagree and desperate to be the boss's pet, Haysia nodded without hesitation. For me, I couldn't follow suit, so I grabbed Brooke by the arm and turned her back to me.

In a firm whisper, I asked, "What are you doing, Brooke? You cannot say things like that to her."

"What?" she whispered back. "She needs to learn now."

"Learn? Are you her teacher now? You're gonna scare her."

Brooke yanked her arm from my grasp. "Lighten up. Maybe if more women kept it real with the younger generation, they wouldn't grow up with hearts in their eyes and slim pockets."

"Pah-lenty of women have thick pockets with a good man on board."

"Then where is yours? You have the man, but you don't have the pockets. You were chasing Ruben and you even lost your wallet because of him." Unapologetic, Brooke stared at me, waiting for a justification that I couldn't provide.

"Is that what you think of me?" We weren't whispering anymore. It was my turn to wait for her response.

"I'm just stating the facts, sweetheart."

Sweetheart? Did she really?

Her calm demeanor angered me. She didn't seem to care that my toes had been stepped on.

"I don't need my *friend* to call me out on something for which I've already apologized."

"Then if you know what I'm saying to be the truth, then why are you mad?" she challenged haughtily. "Where is the lie?"

"You have been waiting for months to throw shade at me, huh? You've been dying to judge me for losing my job." Did I really have to read my friend in broad daylight in front of her assistant in her own business? Mustering words from shallow breaths and a heaving chest, I shot back, "Are you mad because I wasn't supposed to be the girl to end up with anything? I was a girl making a below-average salary who didn't pin goals on the wall or plan her shit. And God forbid a friend has something to talk about. You always gotta steal the spotlight."

She scoffed with a tilted head and crossed arms. "And how long have you been holding that in, Summer? So whatcha' sayin'? That I'm a bad friend?"

"You see, I think that you have friends because you need a network of sycophants to hear your issues and to indulge you. That's what seems clear to me now. Because you wouldn't trash a friend who just tipped you off about your ex two times now, would you?"

"Summer? I can't condone sexing a married man on purpose. And I certainly can't condone women taking the easy way out by finding men with money. I mean, it could be why you and Amber get along so well."

We both stared at one another unyieldingly with folded arms. Unlocking my tight jaws to speak, I told her, "You're welcome for the heads-up, bitch."

When Brooke's mouth dropped, and dismay repossessed the calm in her eyes, her shoulders slumped as her chest heaved. My blunt friend with many opinions had finally become speechless.

Propelled by anger, I marched to my car, burning rubber to raise up out of Brooke's business, while racing home to wait for Oliver with the realization that it was time to mind my own.

"Shut up, girl," Amber replied, astonished by my news about Brooke and me.

"Nope, we are on the outs and, frankly, right now, I don't even care." I sat on the sofa stroking my hair, explaining my story to Amber.

"I love Brooke, but sometimes she does, you know, like to push. I knew that one day that would come to bite her." She laughed. "Girl, I just thought it would be her and me first, not you and her."

"Me, too, girl. Never saw it coming. I feel bad that this nasty exchange happened, but I do think it's for the best that at least we aired our true feelings. I mean, otherwise, wouldn't what we have been considered fake?"

"We never think one hundred percent great thoughts about people, and sometimes, some things are better left unsaid."

"And other times?"

"They need to be said and heard. But give it all a few days to the point where you two miss each other and then make up."

"Who should reach out first?"

"It's not a game. When the mood hits, you act. Otherwise, you being fake so just keep it one hundred. You don't wanna move into whose-move-is-it-now territory."

"And if the other isn't ready?"

"At least you tried, and you were being true to your feelings. But y'all need to go on and patch this up with the quickness."

"But I called her a bitch."

"Because at the moment it sounded like she was one. She knows it. Just chill."

"I guess."

"You know, Cris and I are over. Not to pull a Brooke—" she chuckled, "—but I have to tell you about me right quick."

"Weren't y'all already over?"

"No. We are done, done. Like you and Brooke. Just kidding! Just kidding!" We shared a laugh. "No, girl, he denies brushing me off more frequently, and I don't like feelin' played. He suggested we go our own ways so I'm like, cool."

"Will you miss him?"

I stood up to the sound of the elevator doors sliding open. Oliver stepped out.

"His penis, sure."

I chuckled. "Hey, listen, sorry to cut this short, but I'll be in touch. Oliver is home."

"Okay. Bye, hon."

"Thanks for helping. Bye, girl."

"All right."

After we hung up, I walked into the living room and met Oliver in the kitchen as he sorted through the mail.

Oliver called to me before I greeted him with a hug. "Baby. What's up?"

"I had better days. You?"

"Same ole, same ole. Why, what happened today?"

"Brooke and I argued." When I told him all about it, he hugged me and looked at me lovingly.

"See, baby, I tried to warn you to butt out. But you know, you were just trying to help. She seemed snobbiest of all of your friends anyway."

"Do you think Emily and Amber are snobby?"

He scratched his chin as he pondered my question. "Snobby . . . hmm. No, not really. No, they cool, they cool, especially Amber. They were just protective of you. But Brooke kind of act like her shit don't stink."

I rubbed my hands on the countertop. "I would still like to consider her as my sister-friend. We just hit a rough patch, but I still love her—snob and all."

"Of course, you do, babe. Yeah, we don't wanna talk smack about her, because that's still your girl. At the end of the day, she's good people, you know. She came over that day with your pack and all of them had guns blazing. That alone makes them cool." Oliver inched toward me with a mischievous grin and smacked me on the butt.

"Ow." I jumped with a grin.

"Get in that room. You've been naughty. Daddy 'O' told you not to mind other people's business but you didn't listen. Go get naked—now." He pointed at our bedroom door.

"Daddy 'O'? Did you just say Daddy 'O'?" I fell over laughing and brushed my hair from my mouth.

"Yes." His eyes widened. "Now go."

"Hmph. And if I refuse?" I folded my arms.

He pointed to his muscles on each arm. "Do you know why I lift weights? To carry a pregnant woman." Before I knew it, Oliver gripped me by the shoulders firmly and gritted his teeth. "I told you to move but you like to be rebellious." He shook me once by the shoulders before lifting me into his arms. I squealed. "That was shrill," he complained as he carried me into the room.

He plopped me gently onto the bed and eased my dress above my thighs and butt. I shifted up and down from right to left to facilitate the process before he snatched it above my head. Unfortunately for me, reluctance moved in the room with us, and my mood plummeted.

"Oliver . . ."

Standing above me, he replied, "Hmm?" as he kissed my neck and shoulder.

"I . . . I feel gross."

He stopped and kneeled in front of me to make eye contact. His fingers lifted my chin. "Why?"

It embarrassed me to open up. After shifting my mouth to one side, I let him in. "My belly is big."

"Because of a baby. Why do pregnant women do this to themselves when everyone else finds them beautiful?"

"I'm used to a flat tummy. And you'd have to be pregnant to understand."

"You're beautiful. And you'll get that stomach in a few weeks. Sweetheart, you have a baby inside of you. What do you expect? I think it's fascinating and cute."

"Even though it's not yours?"

No one could miss his hard swallow when a glisten of hurt flashed in his eyes. But I had to make sure. "Yes."

"I'm sorry for that. For reminding you of that."

"No reminding necessary. I do it every day. But I love you, and what am I gonna do? Hate the kid? One day we will have our own, but for now, let's not focus on whose blood is whose. We have an innocent child with three adults who will love him or her."

My heart melted in the palm of my hands. A smile replaced my frown. "Thank you."

"Now take off that bra and show me those swollen tits."

Giggling, I gripped his neck with my arm and held him close as he fumbled blindly to disband my bra, loving him more today than I did yesterday.

Brooke

Friday night, Brooke walked around her condo in her matching lingerie set sipping wine and listening to ambient music. She wanted to be alone in the privacy of her apartment on the sixth floor of her upscale building. On the ledge of her window in the dining room, she sat watching the cars below on the short strip in front of her building. Everyone had somewhere to be tonight, except for her.

She and Jackson could be at a DC club or at a performance tonight. One of those performances that required ticket purchases online weeks in advance for more than a hundred dollars apiece. It was just one of those nights. How she wished his cherry red Challenger would pull up to that spot in front of her building after a night of fun and romance together. Without him, it was the perfect night to be alone with her feelings. No need to talk to friends or clients. That night, she could reflect on her own thoughts without opinions or judgments.

She almost ignored the ringing cell phone on the dining room table. Deciding against that option, she picked up her Galaxy and answered it. "Hello?"

"Are you sleeping, dear?"

Brooke immediately recognized the familiar voice on the other end.

Through a dull and monotone tone, she replied, "Jacqueline, hi. Long time, no hear. I'm not sleeping."

"I was just thinking about you."

"Why?" Brooke held her head, not feeling too worthy of being on anyone's brain. "I'm sorry, I mean, thank you."

"How have you been, lovely? We haven't chatted lately."

Brook's fingers traced the edge of her dining room table as she listened and talked. "I've—" Her brain raced as she recalled words. *". . . you have friends because you need a network of sycophants to hear your issues and to indulge you."* Deciding not to complain and to work through her issues on her own, Brooke chose to say, "I'm just tired, Jacqueline. I have a wedding to run tomorrow. How are you?" There. Shifting the focus felt much better. She held one bent elbow with the other hand.

"Still blessed, unstressed. I just wanted to see if your heart was mending a little since our last talk."

If anything, Brooke's heart shattered upon hearing Jacqueline's words of concern. Choking on her words, she asked, "Why do you care so much about me and how I'm doing?"

"Why shouldn't I? Brooke, are you okay? You can talk to me."

"He's moved on, and this I know for a fact. His girlfriend is cheating on him, and I have to watch her marry someone else tomorrow."

"My God. Then why did you take this job?"

With the tears rushing down her face, she could feel a watermelon-sized lump grow in her throat. So much for keeping her problems to herself. Hysterical, she answered, "Literally just found out. Backing out now is impossible—not an option." A shaky hand frantically wiped the tears away. She made her way to the sofa and sat there. Supporting her body weight proved impossible now.

"I'm so sorry, Brooke. Losing a love is not easy. Sometimes, people think you cannot love someone so much that you haven't known for long. But I learned it's all about the connection."

Wiping her tears, she agreed. "And you're right, Jacqueline. I felt so connected to him. He was established, handsome, kind, and affable; I can't stop thinking about what I'm missing."

"Don't you believe that someone else can be right for you?"

She had to think about that for a moment. "I've blocked out all possibilities because I want him."

"Brooke? Hear me out. Okay?"

"'Kay." Calmly, she eased into the cushion of her sofa.

"Jackson sounds a lot like you. Are you looking for a male version of Brooke, or do you want him for who he really is?"

"Is my ego out of control you mean? Am I sick or something?"

"Brooke, you're not sick. That's silly. But you need to be open to the fact that your dream man may not be painted with the brush of your choice."

Jacqueline and her puzzles again. She rolled her eyes and threw a hand up. "And what does that *mean*?"

"Dream men don't come from the pages of a fashion magazine or-or-or the frame of a movie. Be open to him making less money, falling short in height, having less hair on his head . . . Some women are single because they can't seem to put their checkboxes away and focus on making a genuine connection."

Her teeth clamped down on her nail. "Great. So be open to dating Homer Simpson. Got it. I'm single because I won't lower my standards."

"Your words, not mine."

"Jackson and I *had* a connection. We just didn't agree in one area."

"A very crucial area. Anyway, look, sleep on it. Get some rest. You have a job to do. Stay out of his business and run your own."

She hung up before Brooke could thank her.

She didn't want to be disturbed, so Brooke turned off her ringer and held the phone close to her chest before standing. Jacqueline told her everything she needed to know, but the last thing she wanted was to let her clients see her with puffy eyes. So, she marched to the refrigerator to pull out her pre-sliced cucumbers and took them to her room and secured them under her eye mask as she turned off her apartment lights before sliding into bed.

"So, are you coming or not?" Brooke demanded to know impatiently as she waited for Amber to reply. Her reflection in a ninety-two-dollar summer outfit pleased her. Brooke wore a black, strapless, lace bodice over a lime green chiffon skirt. It was high in the front, revealing her knees but low in the back. In a tight bun, her sleek hair revealed her beautiful features pronounced with a splash of pink makeup. She took a picture of the moment.

"I—" She sighed. "Brooke, you got Emily and if Summer ain't goin', then someone needs to be with her. Unless you call and re-invite her."

"Amber, I don't have time for this. I'm not quite ready to see her no more than she's ready to see me. Otherwise, we woulda called each other. I'm not in the apologizing mood either. Today, my focus is on looking good and performing like a pro, not pacifying a mean, moody, pregnant lady."

"Exactly. You know she's pregnant and has an excuse. So just call her."

"Not gonna happen today. So, you not coming? It's just Ems?"

"Guess so. But I respect your choice not to push things with Summer."

"All right then. I'll, uh, let you know how it goes."

"Cool. Good luck."

"Yeah."

Grabbing everything that she needed, Brooke headed for the chapel to finish earning every red cent Celeste Black paid to give the cheater, Justice Ashby, that one magical day.

Summer

"Come on, Summer. You guys have to make up sooner or later." Emily pleaded with me over the phone as I popped a few bags of popcorn in the microwave.

"Uhhh, I choose later. What you doin'?" I shook the first hot bag by the corner of the seal.

"Studying myself in the mirror. Hoping my floral-patterned dress is the right choice. *Summer*, get your golden ass to the wedding immediately."

"Nope. She doesn't want to see me. Besides, Amber is coming over to chill with Oliver and me. Well, he gotta make some runs to Home Depot. But afterwards he'll be here." My stomach brushed the top of the countertop as I reached for a big bowl placed on the top shelf of the cabinet.

"That little goat. She's backed down now? I will be sitting in the pew next to whom?"

"Brooke?"

"Oh, please. Wedding coordinators are on the go and this one never sits. She won't have any time for me or until the ceremony starts. Just come."

"You sound violent over there, and I cannot expose my baby to such tempers." My hands carefully guarded the popped kernels from spilling onto the countertop as the tilted bag emptied into the plastic bowl.

"I'ma choke the living shit out of you when I see you. Goodbye, Summer. Have fun with Trader Joe."

I tossed a few pieces of popcorn into my mouth. "Toodles." Luckily, Emily couldn't see the victorious grin on my face.

"Mm."

Brooke

Brooke stepped inside of the chapel and immediately went into hawk-eye mode. Her eyes danced around to confirm that the decorations were in their proper places. She jumped at the quick three taps that popped against her shoulder. Spinning around, she saw her assistant, Haysia.

"Hey, beautiful. You look lovely." Brooke gave her a quick hug.

Wearing a red and black skirt suit with her hair pinned in a French roll, Haysia grinned with excitement at Brooke's acknowledgement. "Thank you." A tiny finger pointed at Brooke. "Wow. You're gonna find a husband tonight."

Brooke looked flattered. "I wouldn't go that far."

"So." She clapped her hands together. "What can I do?"

Brooke snapped back into machine mode. "Seating. We have to make sure that people are sitting where reserved. There was a last-minute issue with time. Call to make sure that the limo driver is on top of time and place. I'll take care of the vendor activity because I have to do all the signing. Oh, and make sure that you keep an extra eye on Justice. She's prone to a sudden emotional outburst because that woman has been frozen through this whole process. She's been numb and she's gonna crack today, so be sensitive and on your toes. Is this too much?"

With parted lips, Haysia didn't blink. "Uh, no."

"Good. Get on it, please. Start with the limo, then the seats, and make sure that our stain remover kit is present and ready for disasters. I'm going to go phone the deejay and meet one of the vendors right quick."

Minutes later, Brooke wrapped up her phone call with the deejay. "Yes, but make sure that you set up in the opposite corner of the buffet table. You are on the wall with three windows. Set up in that corner and please watch your wires so the children won't trip. Thanks." She hung up and called one of the photographers. "Darius, are you on your way? Good. And remember to give my client the fifteen percent discount, please. You almost forgot to do this for my last client remember? I'm bringing you too many jobs to mess up and make me look like a liar. Darius, forget apologies, just stay awake and please be on your way. *Thanks*." She hung up her phone and checked on Haysia.

Set-up moved along nicely, and Haysia's presence helped tremendously. Haysia's need to impress Brooke kept her on top of her duties. She couldn't wait to praise Haysia after the big day, provided that she maintained the momentum.

"Brooooke." The chipper voice behind her came from Justice. "Come here."

Brooke gave her a hug, but she really wanted to take a knife and stab her between the shoulder blades for cheating on her ex.

Once behind closed doors, Justice spun on her heel to face Brooke. "Brooke, please tell me I'm doing the right thing. I have been going strong for so long that I'm tired and wondering if this is all right." Desperate for confirmation, she waited to hear Brooke's input.

The wedding planner wanted to find a bat to beat the bride senseless. Her level of professionalism had never been tested like it'd been in this moment. And that said a lot considering Victoria and her adult temper tantrums. Her temples started to throb, and that was a threat she couldn't afford. Determined to gain clarification she bit. "Justice, do you know why you want to marry Mason?" The judgmental feeling tried to color itself across her face. As a professional, she knew how to erase it, but this time she fought like hell to win that battle.

Justice almost seemed annoyed. "Do I—?" She scoffed. "Of course, I do, Brooke." With a shrug, she asked, "What kind of question is that?"

Brooke crossed her arms and reeled her inner bitch in. "Then go with that. I mean, you said 'yes' for a reason. Right?"

Justice took a moment to consider Brooke's point. Standing, she shook a finger at Brooke. "You—you're right. It's just the jitters."

Brooke took a step to close the gap between them. She placed a hand of mock comfort on Justice's shoulder. Searching her eyes for the truth, Brooke tilted her head. "I mean, no one else matters. Just Mason. He's the only important thing in your life."

Justice nodded and exhaled, obviously too nervous to sense Brooke's underlying suspicion. Brooke knew she played a dangerous game by coming at her client, but in that moment, risking it all meant nothing to her if she could find out the truth.

Justice rubbed her hands anxiously. "Brooke, Mason is my world, and I wouldn't wanna live in it without him. Besides, he is amazing to me. This marriage has to work." She laughed. "I can't wait to drop my last name. I married once, and it was . . ." She shook her head; her eyes grew distant. "My first husband was emotionally abusive. He moved in on me during the most vulnerable time of my life after I'd lost someone so precious to me. I thought his love was gonna fill a void in my heart." Justice shook her head and turned her back to Brooke. Brooke waited for her to continue as she wrestled with her own conflicting feelings toward her client. Justice turned back to face her. "After a year of marriage, he found someone else and thought he could have us both. Thank God my brother pulled me out of that."

Brooke didn't know if she felt satisfied or foolish. Maybe both. Maybe neither. She just didn't get it. None of this made any sense. But one thing remained: Time didn't freeze for that conversation, and the wedding wasn't going to coordinate itself. She jumped back into wedding planner mode and chose to deal with her feelings later.

"Then let's get you married."

When Justice wiped a tear and smiled, Brooke winced. *And there it is. Knew she'd crack and ruin the makeup.*

"Can't wait to get rid of this last name. Should've gone back to Sloan."

Brooke froze. *Sloan? Did she say 'Sloan?'* She shook her head in stupefaction, the horror eclipsed her composure, couldn't mask the reaction in her face. Brooke placed a hand on her stomach. She felt sick. She felt duped. Many thoughts rushed into her head and none of them made sense. They all wanted to take precedence over the other.

Who was this woman to Jackson?

Once Brooke's eyes connected with Justice's, she read the guilt in them before they averted her stare. Justice sighed, her shoulders fell in despair.

"Brooke, I can't do this anymore. Look, I'm sorry. I'm so, so sorry.

Impatient, Brooke asked, "What are you sorry for?"

"Lying to you. It was supposed to work out for everyone."

"What? I don't understand." Brooke almost choked on her own breath. "What was supposed to work?"

"I . . . I wanted the best wedding. Ummm, Jackson— my twin brother—wanted the best wedding for me, considering all that happened to me."

With closed eyes, Brooke shook a hand at Justice. "Whoa, whoa, whoa. You can't be his twin. Her name is, ummm, ummm . . ."

"Monet?"

Her eyes flew open. "Yes!"

"My middle name. Try growing up in Chicago with the name 'Justice,' and see how hard people clown you. I started using my first name in college, but by then, those who know me were too used to 'Monet.'"

"This is all so strange." Brooke placed her hands against her hips. "I feel so duped."

"Nooo, don't. He just knew no one else could do it like you. He knew you would want another event under your belt, and he didn't want to come forth with this information, because he was afraid that it'd be a distraction to you. He thought this would work out if you thought of me as a complete stranger." Justice looked ashamed. On her wedding day, she looked ashamed.

Brooke threw a hand against her hip and exhaled. "What? Did he think I would sabotage you? That's what I'm hearing."

With pleading brows and a hand flagging toward Brooke, she assured her, "Noooo, nooo, it was nothing like that."

She nodded then cleared her throat. "Umm, Justice, I'm sorry you were put in this position. Don't worry about it. It's time to get going. The guests will be here, and we'll be late."

Brooke felt relieved and silly all at the same time. So, at least she knew that he wasn't dating her. Was he single? Brooke didn't know if she should perk up at the thought that he may not have moved on, or still harbor angry feelings at his method of doing things.

"But when was I supposed to find out?"

Justice tapped her fingernails together nervously. "Whenever you ran into him today. But I didn't want you to be blindsided."

Brooke took a step back mentally to preserve her sanity. "It's kind of too late for that." She wanted to tell Justice everything, that her friend had tipped her off to his association with her, but she didn't want the day to flop with her reputation if she lost focus now.

Justice nodded without saying a word. "I'm really sorry, Brooke. This wasn't idea for me—to have things revealed like this. I can see that I've caused you discomfort."

Brooke chuckled to lighten the mood. "Sweetie, discomfort is when you have gas. This is painful. It's like . . . he's been under my nose all this time."

"I understand." Justice seemed to shoulder all the mess between Brooke and Jackson, and Brooke didn't feel right about it.

"Why would you encourage me to bring my friends knowing that Jackson and I would encounter each other?"

"I thought it'd all go down smoother with the support of a friend or two."

"I'm a strong woman. I've made it this far. Please." She smiled as warmly as possible like any professional would do. "This day is about you, not me, and we're losing sight of that. No one paid this much money to make it about me or to watch me sulk." And she didn't need the harsh words from Summer to remind her to remove the focus from her. As a woman of her stature, that came naturally. "Now, forget about it. I'll punch your brother later. Get dressed." Clapping, she told her, "Get moving, Justice. Mason doesn't wanna wait longer than necessary to make you his wife."

Justice fell over laughing. "Well, when you put it that way. I'll get my head on straight and back in the game." She turned and then paused. Turning back around to face Brooke, she said, "And, Brooke?"

"Yeah?"

"Thank you for being a pro about this—personally and professionally."

Warm inside, Brooke's face melted with pride. "My pleasure. Thank you for being a dream client." When

Brooke rolled her wrist to glance at the time, her eyes jumped. "Justice, you gotta move, honey. I'm gonna send Haysia your way."

Giggling, Justice jumped. "Oh. You're right. Thank you so much. This woulda been a disaster without you."

Brooke smiled and turned.

"Brooke." Then she spun around. "I see why you come highly recommended. My brother was right."

After giving her a smile of gratitude, Brooke walked away to prove to Justice and Jackson, that no one else could give them what they knew she could, and that no curve ball could break her stride.

Amber

Amber and I sat on the couch as we chatted about men while the flat screen played *The Devil Wears Prada* in the background. We munched on pizza ordered by Oliver before he left since we demolished the popcorn.

"I think I should take a man break."

"I think you should, too." Grinning at her, I slid the slice of pizza into my mouth and took a bite. "Give that pussy a break."

"Oh, you real funny now. Huh, Wobbles?"

I swallowed and then added, "Just sayin'. I mean, dealing with men can be complicated. I got a baby in my tummy because of my hormones. Stupid men."

Amber swallowed as she rested her eyes on me. "Maybe I need to quit sleeping with men so fast, especially on the first night. I was gonna have sex with Cane the first night had we not pissed each other off."

"Oliver and I did it on the first night. Ruben and I had sex on the first night, but I always had the feeling that we could have blossomed into something if it originally weren't for Fran."

"Do you wish you coulda explored that?" Amber asked before taking a bite.

I couldn't answer right away but lying didn't do any good. "Well, I think I had a hard time leaving him alone not just because we were forbidden, but if you take Fran out of the equation, there was something mysterious about him that I wanted to explore. He was magnetic, and looking back, I had to leave him alone because that man could make a woman do bad things. When I met Oliver, he made me feel safe and good again. I felt like a bad skank with Ruben." I shook my head vehemently. "It was intoxicating at first, but after Fran came into the picture, it became poisonous."

"Wow." That was all Amber could say, so she continued to eat. "Could you resist him now? Like do you ever wonder what coulda been? Say like, there was no Oliver now, would you pursue Ruben, baby or no baby?"

I fingered my hair with one hand and held the crust of my pizza in the other. Sighing, I replied, "Resisting him ain't easy. He's suave, hot, and exotic. He's speaks Spanish. That's hot man! I, uhhh, think I would see how Ruben and I could be without Oliver, Fran, or the baby in the picture." I shook a finger at her. "But you know, Oliver is really in my heart. Like, if you want to have smoking sex, you go to the Cuban. But if you wanna come home every day to something real, stable, and attentive, that's my Black Hawaiian." I giggled. "And we do have great sex."

"But Ruben is the better lover?"

With a gaping mouth and a laugh caught in my throat, wagging a finger at her, I let it out and replied, "Girl, no. I'm not even gonna let you start with me."

Amber smiled. "Girl, you an international mess. Mmmm, you don't even have to say it, sis." Empty handed, she rubbed her thighs and shins. "Ruben got that drug dick, huh? That magic stick!" Splitting at the sides, she collapsed facedown into the cushion beside her. Sitting up to collect herself, she fanned her face as I shook my head with a grin.

"You're a mess."

"What do you think about Emily and her public indiscretions?"

"I think she should be really careful, or just stop."

"But it's hot, right?"

"Hot, yes. But she is a teacher. If someone caught her, it could mess up her career."

Amber shook her head. "Teachers can't do nothing, man. As long as they teach, people shouldn't care. Teachers need to have a life and orgasms, too. I think it's cool for her, but my sex is so hot, I don't need spectators to lead me up."

"Why'd she start anyway . . . I still don't get that part."

"Dunno. She mentioned proving Eric wrong when he insulted her."

"Yeah, she did, but I mean, he can't see it. So, how's it count?"

Amber shrugged and stretched her arms on the top of the couch as she yawned. "I guess because she knows. You know when people call you fat in school, and, as an adult, you lose the weight, and even if they can't see it, you wanna prove them wrong?"

"Got it. Guys can really mess us up, huh?"

"And girls, too. We as women, are at a point where sometimes we try to impress girls just as much if not more, than the men. And we ain't even tryna date them!"

"Competition." I waggled my head. "Competition."

Amber's attention seemed to drift into another atmosphere, but before I could call her out on it, she looked at me with deep concern. "Summer, I'm glad I met you. I've met so many women over the years, but as you can tell, I can't keep many female friends."

"Awww." I smiled. "You're one of those chicks. Every woman knows a chick like you."

Her somber expression told me she needed to express her sentiments. "Seriously. I can barely hold onto Brooke, but thanks to you and Emily being mad chill, I can handle her. Without you guys, I couldn't of remained friends with her long enough to see what she really about. I'm glad I did though, cuz it ain't good to hang with people all the time because it's easy. I learn from her."

Pleased to hear that, I concurred even though we were on the outs. "Like what?"

"I don't know. Brooke tries to make people do more than what they do. She doesn't settle for average. She takes pride in standing out and going above and beyond without apologizing for it." Amber pointed a finger in the air. "But what I like most about her is that she does it clean. She doesn't step on people's backs just to best them."

I found it humble of Amber and admirable that she could speak so highly of someone she felt strained with at times, but I couldn't help but wonder why. "And what makes you bring her up? You jumped from me to her." I tilted my head in confusion.

Without another thought, and as if she anticipated that specific inquiry, Amber answered, "I don't want you and Brooke to go on another day on the outs. You guys gotta face each other and work it out."

"Believe me, I'm not gonna parry the situation forever, Amber. I just need my own time, that's all. I have a baby in my stomach, she has the wedding, and I think we're both stressed."

"Okay, that's fine, but that's neither here or there. That was the problem. Where's the solution?"

I narrowed my eyes at her with mock suspicion. "Did you come visit so you can work on me?"

Amber winked.

In all sincerity, I told her, "Just another reason why I love you."

Brooke

"Here Comes the Bride" started. Brooke allowed herself a moment to collect herself in the back of the church. Haysia had a seat in the last row reserved just for her boss. Raptly watching the bride, everyone turned around to see Justice walk to the altar. The groom waited in the front wearing a nervous but happy expression as he watched Justice commence her down the aisle. Before Brooke could slide into her designated row, she waited to the left like a statue behind the bride to keep from dimming any part of Justice's shine. She decided to wait for the bride to make a few steps first. Justice turned back around once and acknowledged Brooke with one nod and a smile, and from there, Brooke knew her client was officially good to go. Proud papa fought his tears as he linked arms with his daughter. A harsh reminder that she'd never have that. That moment never hurt any less each time Brooke saw it.

She'd met the parents earlier when they were dying to meet her upon their arrival to the church. As they thanked Brooke for a job well done, the wheels in her head spun to figure out how much they knew. They both appeared to be in their fifties, healthy eaters—but not too plump—festooned in fine clothes with a sprinkle of gold and costume jewelry. Brooke could actually see the resemblance Jackson and Justice bore to their parents. Justice had daddy's wide eyes and longer nose. Jackson resembled mommy, stealing her full lips and eyes. Jackson. What would he look like? Would he try to spot her out?

Brooke watched the bride inch down the aisle at the pace of a worm before her eyes darted about to see the faces that went with the back of the heads she'd seen moments ago. Brooke always found it delightful to witness the faces of the people who appeared happy for the bride and groom, but especially for the brides since weddings seemed to be more about them.

The people in the back always seemed less emotional, as the most invested people obviously sat in the front. Coworkers, neighbors, and people who came just to be nice, watched from the back. Brooke studied the bridesmaids. Dramatic with plastered smiles from ear-to-ear while sparring with the mean thoughts echoing in their heads about still being single. Then there stood the one or two genuinely happy friends. The calmest of faces without appearing aloof. One look into at least one best friend of the bride, and you could see the relief that the struggle to find love had ended. With her heart pumping in her gut, Brooke decided to scan for the brother. No more stalling. Looking for him reminded Brooke of the chocolate cake that'd soon come after eating the vegetables during dinner. No one salivated over vegetables, but they had to be consumed. In fairness, she loved her vegetables. But when did they hold a candle to chocolate cake? In fact, she'd eaten her veggies for weeks already. Now the time had come to make room for dessert. Where was her chocolate cake, dammit?

Brooke craned her neck to find the tall piece of decadence. Three tall men stood in the first pew. The first one—very dark, clean to the hills, young and bald—played with his linked fingers. It wasn't him. The second man searched the place with darting eyes, looking for the girl to holler at during the reception—not him either. Brooke struggled to make out the last tall man because the tall woman with a lot of girth wore a hat which blocked the man. When the bride made it closer to the groom, the officiate instructed everyone to sit. The lady with a lot of girth gave up quickly and took her seat, but the tall men lowered slowly. Smiling, the last tall man refused to turn around to face forward until his eyes found what they must've been looking for. Arching an eyebrow, he grinned at Brooke. Her heart dropped from her gut to the floor. An invisible sucker punch to her lungs stole a breath or two. She couldn't return the same expression, just a hard stare into her ex-lover's eyes had to do. Her lips parted just enough to help her breathe better. Even in a daze, she noted his appearance. He changed a little. Instead of a goatee, he wore a beard now. Certainly, he had to see what he did to her. She gripped the backing of the pew in front of her with weak fingers stressed by nerves. In Brooke's world, she'd experienced a mini earthquake. It was rattled, shaken out of place.

Haysia whispered, "Brooke, you can sit." But she couldn't, and neither could the man. Everything became a blur in slow motion.

Paying no attention to what she may've looked like to other people and oblivious that everyone in the pews were sitting, Brooke couldn't take her eyes off the now sitting man who nodded at her with a grin before turning around. Snapping back into reality, Brooke slowly took her seat.

Haysia leaned over. "Are you okay?"

When Brooke finally managed to look at her assistant through a blank stare, she saw furrowed eyebrows. "That was him."

Confused, she asked, "Who?"

"The man who won't return my heart."

"I can't believe I missed her walk down the aisle." Emily stomped her foot and pouted.

"Well, where did you go?" Brooke whispered as the bride and groom headed down the aisle.

She rubbed her stomach. "To the bathroom. I had too much fiber last night if you know what I mean." Emily sucked her teeth at herself in irritation as she grimaced.

"I found him." The butterflies in her stomach flapped wildly about. Her stomach began to ache. Eventually she'd have to see him face to face. For now, the memory of seeing him with distance between them haunted her. He looked exactly the same: very handsome but sexier. And that shouldn't be possible.

"Who?"

Brooke turned to face her friend with a solid expression. Emily got the silent memo because she cupped her hands over her mouth.

"Oh, my gosh. Seriously? No joke?"

"No joke. He's Justice's brother. Stop now. Calm down before he sees you and thinks I'm pressed."

"But you are. He's gonna come."

"If he doesn't have a woman, then yes, I would love to see him. I've been waiting for this moment for an eternity."

Emily couldn't fight back the tear that raced down her cheek. "I'm so happy for you."

Brooke smacked her friend's arm lightly. "Girl, I'm the one who's supposed to be crying, not you." She smiled. "But I gotta go. Pictures are about to be taken outside, and I have to control the crowd. Excuse me. Stick close to me when you can." With that, Brooke left a fussy and emotional Emily to fend for herself as she went back to work.

Brooke couldn't discern her heart from her stomach. Shaking from her fingers to her legs, she still had a job to do that required a composed image to dress her vulnerability from the families and friends gathered outside as her nerves battled her happiness. She knew that man, and it would be a matter of time before he would meet her outside for some alone time, or at least to catch up. She wanted to call Summer to tell her the latest and how things weren't as they appeared, but she couldn't. It hurt her that she couldn't just pick up her cell and phone her friend. She just wasn't ready. Plus, she didn't have the time. She didn't even have the time to tell Emily about her conversation with Justice before the wedding started.

Fortunately, the entire process of picture-taking went along smoothly. Brooke helped Darius by maintaining the crowd and rounding up the people needed per click. After a few successful shots, Justice looked at her and said, "Brooke, don't worry. My mom wanted to do the rest of this part, you know, direct and supervise with the photographer since she'll be hanging many photos in her house."

"Congratulations, sweetie." Brooke took Justice's free hand in both of hers and shook it.

"Thank you. I mean you gave me the Brooke experience and then some. I feel sorry for your competitors."

Brooke laughed and gushed on the inside. She didn't want to hold Justice up, so she told her she would see her at the reception.

"Please, Brooke, whatever you do, don't work too hard. You coordinated everything so well that this ship is running smoothly. You've done enough. Chill a little bit. Bye." The photographer had her and Mason's attention as everyone who wanted to see stepped to the side to watch the flicks catch this important moment. Turning around to look for Emily and Haysia, Brooke bumped into someone else.

"Ooh!" When she recognized the tan suit before her gaze reached his face, she saw the answer to her prayers. "Jackson."

Standing with his hands in his pockets with squinted eyes, he said, "Brooke."

Her knees were as solid as a jellyfish, her stomach tossed like a salad, and her heart raced like a Nascar driver upon hearing his voice. How she longed to hear that voice and the familiar way he said her name just one more time. Maybe it hadn't been a year, but *it'd been so long*. Brooke placed a hand over her heart.

"I can't believe—how—how are you?"

He chuckled. "You did your thing, girl. You did your thing. I couldn't let no one else create this special moment for my sister, but you."

"You guys barely look alike . . . well, kind of. I can kind of see the subtle resemblance." Brooke felt like a fool as she grasped for the right thing to say while he took in the moment as calm as a cucumber. "I see you grew in the rest of your facial hair. I like it." She loved it.

Jackson replied with his trademark sexy grin. His eyes rolled to the bride and groom. Something told Brooke that he was over her or just guarded. On the other hand, a part of him appeared nervous because he came across slightly fidgety with his hidden hands and averted eyes. It killed her not to just throw out a question regarding his relationship status.

When he didn't reply, Brooke said in a semi-defeated tone, "Well, thank you for the recommendation." *Where is the passion?* She had to wonder if that really mattered since she wanted kids and he didn't.

"I didn't answer your question." He tilted his head and flicked his tongue to moisten his lips.

That tickled her vagina.

"Which was what?"

"I've been doing great. Just been drowning in work and hanging with my boys."

Translation: pussy hunting. Brooke knew better and bit her lip to fight the sting.

"Working and working out. Gotta stay cut and lean, ya know?"

Again, for the ladies.

She giggled. "I do. Same here, but you know, without the cut."

"Still got those abs I like?"

Brooke's stomach dropped. "What do you think? I can show you."

Did I just say that?

She bit her lower lip again as a pressure point for the embarrassment.

He released a short, manly chuckle. It always sounded sexy. "We may be able to catch up."

"Will someone be jealous?" Brooke didn't want to spend another minute with doubts. She had to be sure this man didn't have a ball and chain of no kind.

Calm and collected, Jackson replied, "Don't worry about it," he scoffed.

Wow. Did he just . . .

Curious, he asked, "Guess you know Justice is Monet?"

Playing it cool, Brooke's eyes crinkled. "Yeah, no thanks to you."

He smiled handsomely. "I didn't want to complicate this for her . . . given our history." He pointed back and forth between the two of them.

"I heard. She told me everything already."

"Well, we can catch up later. I gotta get going to the reception." Jackson never removed his hands from his pockets as he twisted slightly from left to right.

"You're right, you're right. I have to get back to work."

Her eyes darted beyond Jackson and onto Emily who stood there with crossed arms and a smile. It made Jackson turn around. She waved.

"Oh, it's Emily." He waved at her with a sincere smile and turned back to face Brooke. "Wow. Your crew. Where they at?"

"The other two couldn't come."

"How they doing?"

She didn't want to complicate things, so she replied with a simple, "They're great, thanks. They mention you from time to time." Brooke had to put the blame on them.

"Really. Why?"

Brooke hated when men asked why at certain comments. "Umm, well, they miss you I guess."

"Oh. Just them." He smirked.

Brooke didn't know what to say. "Y-yeah." Nervously, she twisted her fingers.

From friendly eyes to a cold stare, he said, "See you at the reception. Brooke."

"Okay." She waved a hand up. "It was nice to see you."

"Yup." He walked away leaving Brooke heartbroken all over again.

Emily

Ready to explode with a wide grin, Emily asked, "Girl, he looks delicious. What did he say?"

"I . . ." Brooke seemed confused and shut down. "I don't know. It was like he'd lost interest, like seeing me wasn't a big deal. I don't think I ever considered that he would be over me without having someone else in his life. That's difficult, more than I thought. At least with someone else in the picture, the wiped-out feelings make sense. But when the feelings seem bleak and no one has taken your place, it feels sickening."

Emily wished that Amber could be there to offer her a line of wisdom, which seemed weird coming from a woman who didn't do relationships. Then there was Summer as another option, but she wasn't talking to Brooke. Emily sighed as her eyes moved above Brooke's head and to Jackson's back. He stood there talking to the bride and groom. He seemed slightly more animated.

Emily wanted things to go right for Jackson and her friend, but all she could say was, "Well, at least you finally have that encounter that you've been dying to have."

Brooke replied with, "But now I feel more lost than ever."

"Well, is he coming to the reception?" The possibility lifted Emily's dragging expression.

Brooke nodded. "Yeah."

"Okay then." Emily nudged her friend's shoulder. "There's still more time. Make something happen. Don't let his mood discourage you. You don't know why he feels like that. It could be you, or it could be something else. Just use this time you have with him in a way that you won't regret."

It was at that moment that Emily felt like she had decent advice to offer. Brooke hugged her and escaped with Haysia. Emily took the quick moment alone to call Amber to inform her of the day's major event.

Summer

I couldn't believe my ears. "Brooke got to see Jackson? And he's the brother of the bride? That makes so much sense now. Guess I was wrong but somewhat right. You know, I said he was the side piece, but this is even better. Well, I'm happy for Brooke." That was the truth. Being mad didn't spell the end of our friendship. I still wanted the best for Brooke.

Amber nodded, her expression plain. "Yes. Finally, man. Cuz I was about to go snatch that fool up and bring him to her doorstep."

"*Right*." Speaking of doorsteps, Oliver came through ours via the elevator, so I spilled the news to him after he greeted us.

With two grocery bags in his arms, he froze. "Are you kiddin'? So, the Jackson mystery is solved?"

"Yup," we replied.

"Case closed," Amber added.

"It's about damn time. Well I'm happy for all of you guys." He headed to the kitchen to place the bags on the counter. "I'm also happy that Brooke can get some answers—and maybe some dick."

"*Oliver*." The grin across my face was unwelcomed.

Finding his comment all too funny, Amber cackled. "That's what I'm talking about, Oliver. We do have some new material to work with though." Amber stood. "And on that note, I think I should be heading home."

"Already?" Amber held out her hand to help me stand. "Thanks."

"Hard to remember you're not skinny Minnie right now, huh?"

I squinted my eyes at her. "Jokes."

Oliver walked over to kiss Amber on the cheek and to send her off with a hug. "Thank you, beauty, for staying with my princess. I'm glad she wasn't alone on this day."

Amber replied, "Awww, it's no problem. I hate weddings."

"Well, if we have one, you better come to it," Oliver warned playfully pointing a finger at her.

I hope my face didn't reflect the feeling of my sinking heart. *Marriage*? I've gone from moving in with a man, to being in a relationship, to carrying a baby, and now possibly considering marriage in less than a year of moving out on my own? No, no, no, no, no. This sounded like Emily or Brooke's dream, not mine. Suddenly, I felt lightheaded and had to sit. They both noticed.

"Are you okay, sweetie?"

"Yup, yup. Sorry. Just light-headed."

Amber pointed her thumb behind her. "Let me go." She hugged me goodbye with a kiss on my forehead. "Take it easy, chile."

I cracked a tense smile. "I will. Thank you for being here with me."

"No problem. It was fun."

"Let me walk you out real quick." Oliver walked her to the front door, and we said our final goodbyes before she left. He marched back to me in a hurry. "Come here, baby. Let's get you to the bed." He guided me with a hand against my lower back and the other against my stomach.

"Sounds good." All the resting in the world couldn't suppress my anxiety about the possibility of marriage.

Brooke

Brooke stepped inside of the country club for the reception. Everybody from the chapel came to the extravagant reception in Bethesda, Maryland. Jackson stood nowhere in sight, but she knew he had to be there.

"Brooke!" Justice flagged her down with a quick wave of the hand. Brooke approached her.

"Hey, bride, how's married life?" Brooke joked.

"Hmmmm, the whole hour of bliss has been fantastic. Why do people divorce? Who says married people can't get along? I don't know what they're talking about," she teased.

Brooke laughed. "Well, now that it's official, you seem so happy."

"Look, I just wanted to tell you that I know we paid you to handle the reception as well, but honestly, we don't care. You can still dip if you want. I mean, don't think we're kicking you out or anything, but you gotta be exhausted." She could tell that Brooke was about to put up a fight. "No. You've worked so hard on this and it came out flawless under your control. I cannot wait to put my experience on social media."

Brooke couldn't hide her emotions. "Thank you," she managed as Justice reeled her in with a hug. "Thank you."

Justice smacked her on the back of the shoulder. "Go mingle, you hottie. Maybe we'll be planning your wedding soon."

"Oh, whoa." Brooke laughed. "I wouldn't go that far. Good luck."

"Best to you, Brooke." Brooke watched the bride turn and leave as she joined the crowd of people. Across the room, she spotted the face that made the experience more worth it than the recommendations and money combined: Jackson. There he was, standing against the wall on the other side of the room, eyeing her. Brooke grinned at him before heading out the door.

"Brooke?" A very deep voice that she didn't recognize called her name. Upon spinning around on her heel, she saw the groom.

"Oh, hey, Mason. I hope this day was everything you wanted."

He shook her hand. "I wish her grandma woulda let me pay for this. You were worth every penny." He also had a slight lisp. "Thank you." He took his handkerchief and wiped his sweaty forehead. His hand swallowed hers with a wedding ring pressed into her tiny fingers. Brooke couldn't get her hand back fast enough from the tight grip.

The achy hand whipped over her heart. "You're so kind. Your wife was a very easy client. Wish they were all like her."

"My wife . . ." He bugged his eyes upon saying the word, "Wow."

"Nice, huh?"

"Well, I have a circle of friends who can afford you when their time comes, so keep a look-out. Thanks, Brooke. Take care."

"Good luck and thanks," she called as he headed toward the party.

Brooke turned to catch some fresh air and to be alone with the hopes of seeing Jackson again. Until then, she reveled in the calm breeze and green hills. It appeared that everyone was inside but her. Some people still pulled up in their cars with gifts, and some people came out for a quick smoke, so Brooke moved to the side of the club.

"Hey, you."

Inside, Brooke smiled when she heard the familiar voice. She turned to see him standing with his hands in his tanned trouser pockets wearing a crisp, light blue button-up. Her knight in shining armor. Brooke gave him a cautious smile.

"Hey. You lost the jacket, huh?"

"Excuse me?"

Awkwardly mapping her hand over her chest, she repeated, "The jacket . . . you ditched it."

He smirked upon her clarification. "Right. I had to get more comfortable."

"You look . . . very handsome."

"You look beautiful, but, when don't you?" He smiled and walked closer to close the distance. They were finally alone. *Yesssss.*

"You were always smooth with words." Though he stood close, Brooke wanted him to get personal. In fact, inside of her, to be exact.

He grinned. "Is that what you think? That I ain't sincere?" A large hand sprawled across his chest.

"No. I think you're always truthful."

"Good." His eyes shot down at the pavement before hitting hers again.

She reached out to gently tug his beard. "Looks good on you. What made you grow this?"

Even past his smile, Brooke could read his reluctance to speak on it. "Nothing. I just stopped shaving for a few days and decided to keep it going." He shrugged. "That's all. Whatcha been up to?"

"The same. Work and friends. But I . . . I did wonder how you were doing?"

"You didn't have to wonder," he said softly.

Brooke's stomach flipped, and her knees weren't as dependable as usual. He made her want to abscond into the green pasture until he sexed her until her vagina shut down. She licked her lips as she tried to ignore the growing sensation growing between her legs.

He lifted a brow. "You coulda' called."

"I couldn't call, that would've been odd."

"I don't think so. We didn't have to be like strangers."

"Well, then, why didn't you call?"

He shrugged. "What was left to say? You seemed so determined to leave and find what you needed out of life. I didn't wanna block your happiness. I loved you too much to do you like that."

Brooke wanted to faint. He reminded her that he loved her, but she wanted to hear that he still did. "And now?"

"Now what?"

"I don't know. How do you feel about everything now? Did you move on?"

"Are you asking me what I want from this moment?" He rubbed his chin before lowering it as he cleared his throat, studying her through narrow eyes, awaiting the truth.

Brooke tugged at her index fingers. *Come on, bitch. Go all in, go all in.* "Uhhh, well?" She tilted her head. "You might as well tell me since we're here."

"I went on dates, of course. I know you did."

"I saw one guy. He turned out to be a lying loser. But he's in Greece now and forever."

"So, just one guy, huh?" Jackson chuckled.

"Why's that funny?" Brooke asked, slightly offended.

"Because that sounds like you. Systematic. Careful."

"Well, it's not my fault you decided to chase skirts."

He laughed quickly. "I didn't have to chase, they came to me."

"Whatever, Jackson." She folded her arms and looked away.

"You wanted me to sit at home and wait for your call or something? I'm sorry." He turned an ear to her and cupped a hand behind it. "Are you saying that you're jealous even though you walked away?"

The magnetic pull between them was killing Brooke. She felt like he wanted to see her break first and that he enjoyed their game of exchanges. Maybe she should indulge him.

"I'm not jealous. But you had no problem moving on, I see."

He turned his face to her again. "Oh, don't be stupid."

"Excuse me?"

"You're waiting to hear details but too full of pride to ask. If you're suffering now, it's because of you."

Brooke raised a brow at him with a pinched forehead. "Oh, please. Don't flatter yourself."

He stepped back with a raised eyebrow as well. "I don't have to, baby. You're doing it now."

Brooke didn't like where this was going so she decided to throw in the towel for now. She didn't know if she wanted to cry or throw up. "I don't . . . I can't . . ." Brooke walked past him, but a sudden tight grip on her arm pulled her back.

"Where you going? I didn't say I was done with you." Jackson backed her up against the siding of the country club. Thankfully, no one could see the wedding planner backed against the wall. How could they have so much privacy at such a big event?

Brooke's hard stare lost steam as she peered up into his eyes. They brimmed with frustration. He slightly lowered his face to hers. His breath rained on her skin, so she crossed her legs at the knees. She barely had room to kick he was standing so close.

"Careful," she warned with mustered irritation. "You're lucky I like you."

Jackson pinned her against the wall with both hands gripping her arms. "What do you wanna hear? Stop playing games."

Frustration gripped his face like a stroke, but she dared think that passion flickered behind the former emotion as well. Brooke bit the inside of her cheeks. Fighting back tears, in a shaky and louder voice, she replied, "I don't care, Jackson, I don't care who you put your penis in all night long."

"*Yes, you do,*" he insisted as she tried to wiggle out of his firm grip. "You want to know if I made another woman scream, if I tasted her, ate her, rolled the tip of my tongue to her clitoris . . . gave it to her all-night long. Don't you?"

She wanted to cry. He wanted to torture her, pay her back for leaving him that night. "Let me go, let me go," she insisted.

Jackson ignored her demands as he spoke faster. "You wanna know if they were more beautiful than you, if I compared them to you, if I fell in love, if I forgot about you, if I enjoyed sex with them more than you—"

Brooke smacked his face. Heaving, she watched him rub his cheek. He turned to look at her with eyes as cold as ice. They didn't say a word. Brooke wondered if she went too far. Maybe they both went too far.

Jackson placed his hands on the sides of her neck, moving one down her throat and then up to her chin. She didn't know what he was going to do next. Frozen in fear, Brooke waited to see her fate as she wished that she could talk. His eyes pierced into hers one last time before he placed his lips over hers.

Starving, Jackson's lips and tongue explored her mouth. He groaned as his hands madly caressed her back and nape. He pulled back long enough to say, "You wanna know if this dick been somewhere else, don't you?" Jackson sucked her lips and then her neck. He whispered, "You just wanna hear how I use my dick, huh? If I ran my dick all up in another woman, the way I did with you. Don't you?" He nibbled her neck and then her ear. "You want me to beat that pussy up, don't you?" His hands slipped between her legs and pinched the insides of her thighs. Brooke moved her head from left to right as she felt herself losing control through expressive moans. Jackson took her hands and pinned them above her head.

"Please, Jackson. Please don't . . ." she whispered. "I want you all over again."

"How badly?" he demanded as he gnawed on her neck. "Huh? How badly do you want this dick?"

"I want it. I want it so badly. Do it like you did before."

"Girl, before ain't gonna have nothing on us. I'ma run this cock so far up in you, you gonna feel it in your dreams."

Better? Wow. There were no complaints before, so she couldn't imagine that he had more tricks up his sleeve.

"Are you seeing anyone else?" she asked while her horniness out-weighed her pride.

"No." Brooke's neck and chest muffled his mouth. "Shut the hell up, woman. I wanna be inside of you *now*."

Even though her area of paradise felt like an inferno, she had to take control of the situation before someone caught them. "We can't, Jackson. Not here." She tapped his shoulders.

Brooke did a number on him. With unsteady breathing and dopey eyelids, Jackson tried to collect himself with a cleared throat and attempt to straighten his shirt. "Let's go." He grabbed her hands and ran as she struggled to keep up in her heels.

"Ouch, wait," Brooke pleaded.

Impatient, he ordered, "Come on." Before Brooke knew it, he swooped her up in his arms as he carried her across the pavement and into the parking lot.

Brooke's arms flung over his shoulders. "They can't see the wedding planner like this."

"I don't need no one's permission." With determination in his step, Jackson eased her onto her feet when they stopped in front of his red Challenger.

"I've missed this car," she told him earnestly.

He opened her door. "Well, get in."

"Wait. I parked in this row, too." She searched a few cars down and saw her BMW. "See." She pointed with her finger. "Tell me where we're going so I can follow you."

"I guess that makes sense. A hotel down the street. Don't worry, it's a five-star."

She eyed him suspiciously, "Did you plan this?"

"I won't tell you everything and you know that." He grabbed her before she could walk off and planted a long kiss on her lips. When they pulled away, he told her, "Drive safely and stay close." Brooke nodded and headed to her car.

Brooke couldn't believe that she and Jackson were about to happen, so she called Emily.

"Brooke? Are you smoking a cigarette in bed with Jackson now because you guys climaxed?"

Brooke giggled. "You stupid, you know that?"

"I'm sorry I couldn't stay behind. My stomach was killing me."

"Yeah, yeah. But hey, I'm following him in my car to the hotel. We're about to have hot sex. He almost got it on the side of the country club wall outside. Your cup of tea, huh?"

Emily fell over laughing. "Ohhhh. I'm jealous. I should call Zach tonight. Let him stroke me out."

"Look, I gotta call you later—like tomorrow. We're here." She sang in a loud opera voice, "I'm about to get laid."

"Girl, let him knock it out. Enjoy."

"Oh, sweetie, I hope he murders this pussy."

"Um. Wow. Listen to you. That's my cue. Bye."

Brooke threw her phone into her purse as she parked her car. Hopping out, she made her way toward him. Jackson stood at the bumper of his car and took her by the hand to lead her to the receptionist. She loved how much he wanted her. She missed him and really wanted to know if he belonged to her again. Brooke sat in a chair as she waited for him to handle the transaction and when he snatched the key card from the man behind the desk, Brooke stood to join her ex-flame.

Grinning, he laced his hand into hers and led Brooke to the elevators. An older couple came in the same elevator. Brooke and Jackson shook their heads since they wanted privacy. Their room waited on the eighth floor, but the couple departed when the doors opened on the fifth. As soon as they stepped off, Jackson snatched Brooke and pressed her against the elevator wall.

"Did you ever think of me?"

"Every day." Her eyelashes batted involuntarily as she fought the wave of anxiety in her midsection. "Did *you* think of me?"

When the elevator stopped on the eighth floor, Jackson grinned and tried to pull her out when the doors opened. She froze inside of it.

"Well?" she insisted. Brooke felt certain that Jackson could tell that she needed some reciprocation of admission.

The doors were about to close with him on the opposite side. He threw up an arm to block it, long enough to say, "I did," he assured her tenderly.

"Then why did you avoid my question?" Brooke folded her arms.

As he took a while to ponder her question, he threw his arm up again to block the sliding doors. "Because I don't care to admit how much your leaving got to me. That's why. A man wants the woman to know that she already knows without saying a word. Now can we go?"

"We can go," Brooke agreed with an accomplished expression. He turned away. "Oh, wait, wait, wait, Jackson."

He stopped in his tracks. "Yes, Brooke?" He spun back around to face her with limited patience.

"Did the other women compare?"

The doors tried to slide, so he stepped forward to catch it for the third time.

With a smirk, reluctantly he replied, "No." He eased toward her, blocking the doors with his body. "Not a day passed by that I didn't think of you. I dreamed of running into you, but you met your match, Brooke Brazile. I wasn't going to beg you or chase a woman who wrote me off."

It sounded harsh coming from his lips. "Jackson," she started lovingly, "I didn't want you to think that I wrote you off."

"Can we do this in the room, please?"

"Wait. I have to speak while I have the nerve." He sighed with a closed mouth and hands hidden in pockets. Brooke continued. "Jackson, I just felt that we couldn't get past what the other wanted."

"And what if we still can't? Should we just let the doors to the elevator close on us now while standing on opposite sides? I'm not prepared to discuss the future with you right now. It's too soon. I'm not sure if we're the same people who met all those months back."

Feeling slightly injured in her heart, Brooke bit her lip and stared at the carpet. "I want you soooo badly."

He touched her chin. "Let's forget about the rules tonight. All I know is that I want you. Now."

"I'm scared that it's just lust tonight."

"It's familiar lust," he joked. "I remember how everything about you felt. I want you, Brooke, tonight. No talking, no explaining, no games."

"And then what?"

He shrugged. "And then we talk. We talk about whatever eases your soul and mind."

After the quick intestinal somersaults, Brooke felt uneasy—pissed actually. She felt like the only thing between them had been nothing but labyrinthine dialogue. Brooke saluted and grabbed his hand. He led her to room 805. Spacious, clean, and nicely decorated.

The things on her mind weighed her down and blocked her from wanting his touch. She wanted it, and in fact, her vagina ached at the thought. However, knowing who she was, she couldn't rest until he heard what she had to say.

"Jackson. We need to talk. We're alone now."

Jackson ran his tongue across his lower lip and tapped his foot with crossed arms. "All right. Go for it."

"This isn't easy for me . . . just lying down with the man who crushed my heart like nothing has ever happened. I want you. You *know* I do."

"Then what's stopping you?" Unfolding his arms, his hands slid into his pockets.

"It's not fair to pretend like you don't know. The truth is . . ." The lump in her throat developed and pushed its way into her vocal chords. She didn't care to will the tears away that steamed her eyes. Her heart stomped so emphatically that she swore it'd fall to the floor. "The truth is, Jackson, I love you so much but all I want to do is hate you, and I can't stop and now I hate myself for that!"

With a fisted mouth and furrowed brows, Jackson talked over her. "Oh, yeah, well you think it's easy for me, Brooke? Like I don't wish that I could go back to that day in the coffee house and pretend like I never saw you? You're not the only one feeling like shit."

Angry hands flew to the sides of her head. Hysterical, she couldn't help but shout at him. "Then stop this madness. It's all on you, Jackson. Make us stop bleeding. Because the cut hurts, and I can't stand to lose any more blood."

With wild gesturing hands, his level of frustration matched hers. "What am I supposed to do? You always have all the answers. What are we supposed to do, Brooke Brazile? As it is, we're like two dumb deer not knowing which car to avoid."

"You tell me that we're gonna have children, that's what."

Jackson's head shook. "Baby, I can't do that. Don't throw things in my mouth like that. How about you tell me that I'll be enough—that we can have a fulfilling life, just you and me?"

Through gritted teeth she replied, "Because I can't promise you that. It's not fair."

"Then you can't budge, and I can't budge."

Brooke folded her arms and looked away; Jackson didn't take his eyes off her. They stood in silence, thinking.

"You see. I didn't wanna ruin this moment, baby. I just wanted one moment to be with you without all the worries."

Brooke stole a quick glance at him before giving him her back. "Does it always have to be about you? This time, *I* wanted something. I wanted to deal."

Brooke could feel Jackson standing at a distance. Stiff. She listened for words, for a shuffle—anything. Finally, after what felt like eons, he came to her. A bolt zipped through her spine and all the way to the back of her knees when he placed his hands on both arms.

"Baby, listen."

She could feel his breath against the back of her neck when he spoke. No way in hell would she turn around. "Listening."

"Brooke, I—let's not ruin this moment. We need this moment, but it can't be about anything else, because we need to reconnect first. Right?"

"I'm scared."

"Who wouldn't be? But I need something from you. One favor. But you have the power."

That piqued her willingness to participate. "Tell me and I'll consider."

In a lower and caressing tone, he suggested, "Give in to me, give in to us."

His lips massaged her skin with traces around her neck and shoulders, sending lightning bolts through her groin. Already, Brooke's temperature rose, just from his body against hers.

Unconvincingly, she softly replied, "Maybe we shouldn't." She tried it. Even she couldn't convince a dummy.

"Come on, sweetie. Let me do something to you." Those irresistible fingers trickled up and down her arms, waking the senses under her skin. "Let me remind you why I had you screaming many nights."

Jackson slid one arm over her chest and buckled it with his fist against his opposite shoulder. His pointy elbow sat between her heaping breasts. He possessively placed his hand flat against the top of her chest, owning her, sweeping her into another world where nothing else mattered. Worries flew out the door, questions evaporated as Brooke decided to just go along with it, no matter what. When he slid his other arm around her stomach, her muscles contracted, subtracting her inner strength. She wanted to crumble into his being, if that were at all possible. She didn't want to exist in a world without him. His world made her feel safe, wanted . . . sexy!

The finger on his traveling hand swerved over her midsection, and down under the hem of her skirt and then under her panties. He popped into it with a greedy but easy hand, controlling his desire. Jackson brought his lips down to Brooke's ear and whispered, "Yeah, I'm gonna touch you."

Her stomach stumbled over itself. He had so much power over her. Brooke closed her eyes and clenched her jaws together, swallowing hard, preparing herself to be at the mercy of this man. This was the part where she couldn't be the wedding planner in control. This was the part where she would let this man demolish her will, eat her soul for breakfast, and send her into a sexual hole of submission. He had a hold on her, a possession, and she was the lady held happily at hostage.

She'd waited for so long to have this moment, and now that it'd arrived, it just had to last forever. How could she want to be anywhere else? Jackson was her everything. Last year, the nights after the breakup, and right now. A secret tear fell from her eye—of goodness and overwhelming emotion. The heat from his body always soothed her, broke down her barriers, placed her on a pedestal, made her feel like she was worth it all. Even though Brooke knew her worth before him, something about the right man loving her felt indescribable, like she was a warrior's princess. Someone besides herself for the first time in her life believed in her. Saw value in her. And she didn't want to lose that.

She rolled her neck back to rest her head against his shoulder. Brooke prepared herself to accept the easy agony. His finger warmed up her clitoris with a few slow strokes. She moaned. Bit her lower lip. Jackson's finger caused a fire from the friction of his skin and her delicate lining, drawing a heatwave under her panties.

He spoke in nothing but whispers. "You like that, baby, huh?" When Brooke nodded, he placed a kiss on her earlobe.

Jackson ran his finger up and down between her lips, making sure to always hit that sweet spot. She could feel his eyes watching her every reaction, even without opening them. Investigating her. Ensuring her level of sexual satisfaction.

Using his thumb and middle finger to separate her lips, his index finger ran slow, delicious circles around the inside of them. His finger always graced the clitoris with each lap. But when he wanted more, he dove deeper into her ebony, surfing his finger around the inside of her walls with a thumb constantly massaging that crucial pinnacle of power. A multitasker he was, because his hand lowered from his shoulder to cup one of her breasts under the bodice. His thumb and middle finger pinched her hard nipple, while the index finger rubbed across the tip, electrifying her senses and causing chaos throughout her body.

Brooke's brows pinched as her mouth went parched. He stripped her ability to make it against his advances, stripped away all her methods of survival with pleasure this great in combination with love. It was a deadly combo. Love and deep passion never went over easy on someone's soul. It ripped them to nothing and reduced bodies to empty bags of nerves that received mere punishment at the mercy of someone else's exploration. What could she say? This man wanted it all and she'd let him suck her out of her own existence. This was him. This was Jackson. The man who made her helpless under his hands without making her feel foolish.

She wrapped her arms behind his head with her head rolled to the side, arching her back, barely containing all the goodness that hit her simultaneously. At this point, his finger bathed in her reaction. It'd become a slippery mess, one that moved Jackson to taste.

When Brooke felt his finger pop out of her pie, she turned to see him taste her filling. Sticking his tongue out to meet two fingers, he wiped her over his tongue, locking his eyes into hers as he sampled. Watching his tongue roll around inside a closed mouth, Brooke inhaled sharply when he eased toward her. He gripped both sides of her face, inched his face toward hers as his fingers gently knocked on her lips.

"Open your mouth for daddy. Taste."

Brooke felt slightly hesitant but figured that with Jackson, they should have no boundaries. The amount of trust installed in him would never fail her, despite the night he broke her heart. There was no limit as to how many times she'd play his fool. Not when she felt this spellbound. What was she going to do with herself? He owned a piece of real estate under her skin, and she had no clue how to make him sell it back to her.

Besides, Brooke was one to stand by her product, so she opened her mouth and did just that as he slid those coated fingers into her mouth. To her, it tasted like Jackson since he really didn't leave much behind. He grabbed her face again and moved in for a rapacious kiss.

His hands eased up to her hair, as he gingerly figured out how to release her tresses from on top. It swept her shoulders on cue. Moving behind her again, Jackson lowered himself behind her. His fingers trickled under her skirt to lift it up as he hid underneath it. Holding her steady at the hips with two strong hands, Jackson placed slow and sensual kisses over her ass before biting into a cheek. With a finger inserted inside her mouth, she bit her nail, enjoying his dirty intimacy. One stroke of his tongue against her butt made her vagina dance. She felt the bridge of his nose slip into the insides of her ass at the very bottom. After a placed kiss, he stood to grab her by the base of her neck and shoulders. His fingers walked down to locate the zipper on the back of her bodice, causing it to fall from her frame. She heard the slow ripping sound of the zipper before his hands gripped the sides of her skirt. Taking control, Jackson turned her around and stepped back to say, "Undress yourself for me."

Studying her moves with unwavering eye contact, Jackson watched as Brooke hypnotized him with her eyes as she did what he instructed. With pursed lips, she looped her fingers inside her skirt, slowly and gently rocking her hips side to side to accommodate the material as it slid down her hips and thighs. Finally, the skirt dropped to the carpet, pooling at her ankles.

Jackson inhaled through his nostrils with a raised eyebrow as the sight of her semi-nude body piqued his desire. Brooke noticed his dick came to. It awoke from its coma, very alive and well. She clamped her lower lip to catch any salivation.

Standing in her black lace bra and thong, now she could enjoy the strip show. He undid his shirt, one button at a time without looking away. He couldn't peel the button-up shirt off his muscular arms fast enough to get to her. Finally, he stood in nothing but slacks. Brooke raced to Jackson like a cheetah in the wild to work his Philipp Plein belt.

Before Brooke could finish, Jackson gripped the back of her head with a fistful of hair to cover her lips with his.

Relentlessly, Brooke fingered his buckle while she indulged in the kiss. Like a tornado, Jackson's tongue twisted around hers while gripping a huge chunk of ass in one hand. He decided to help her move the process along by taking over the removal of his buckle and pants. With black boxer briefs and her lingerie serving as the only material between them, Jackson yanked her against his body.

Staring into her eyes, he told her, "I miss pounding the shit out of you."

Brooke's heart sped up as his words tickled her pussy.

Whatever you want, Jackson. Whatever you want.

With weary eyes, she could barely get the words out. "I want that meat. I've missed that stick, Jackson."

Jackson dropped to his knees in an instant to nibble on her lips through the lace material. Brooke cried out in pleasure with her neck snapped back. The thong glided down her legs as he undressed her. Never in her life had she been so grateful to be on time with her Brazilian waxes. In her head, she always boasted that Brooke Brazile did her Brazilians.

"Always on top of her game," he mumbled.

Smirking with silent pleasure as her head faced the ceiling, Brooke cried out when she felt Jackson taking licks from her Brazilian-flavored cream. Hastily, he raised one of her legs onto his shoulder to dive his tongue in deeper. Standing, he picked her up without changing her position and eased her onto the edge of the bed. Bending at the knees, Jackson placed one arm under her thigh as he inserted his tongue between her opening, coloring her canvass until she came. Brooke sucked in a sharp breath under his spell with a quivering midsection and curled toes. A million tears on her pillow at night made this moment worth it as she cried out his name in satisfaction with flailing arms.

Wanting more, Brooke leaned forward and pulled his dick from his underwear. "I want you to take everything and leave nothing behind."

A pleased grin slid over his face when he chuckled. Brooke crawled backwards until she reached the top of the bed. Jackson walked on his knees to her chest. Straddling her stomach without resting his weight on top of her tiny midsection, he parked his length between her breasts and then took her hands and placed them on the outer parts of her breasts. Jackson pushed her boobs together before removing his hands and drove his cock back and forth. Every time he went forward, Brooke let the tip into her mouth. In and out it came. His glaze hit her chin and chest as he suffocated his manhood with her mountains.

Brooke lifted her head to take more of him in with each stroke. Greedy and impatient, she grabbed his length and shoved it into her mouth. For all the lost nights between them, she sucked. For every weep that sang through her bedroom after a day's worth of work ending in no one to come home to, she sucked. For every photo she refused to erase and had to face, she sucked. And finally, for every skipped heartbeat at the thought of him moving on without her, she devoured.

Dropping his head backward, Jackson responded to her successful blowjob with clenched fists and a mighty grunt. No doubt existed within her whether to swallow his goodness. She wanted to. She wanted *all* of him. Besides, didn't he have all of her?

Brooke's stressed neck collapsed back onto the pillow. Jackson's head lowered and after a few seconds of deep breathing, he told her, "You weren't supposed to go in for the kill. I wanted to stab you first with my dagger, girl."

Brooke broke into laughter as she slid her hands through her hair. "What can I say? You're hard to resist."

Jackson rolled onto his back to settle beside her. Brooke questioned if she should face him. She didn't know what he wanted. Where did they stand?

"Don't be a stranger. Let me see that gorgeous face." He rolled to his side.

Grinning, Brooke did the same to face him. "What?"

"What? What do you mean 'what?' You use me for my goodies and then you don't know me?" he joked, stroking her butt and thigh mindlessly.

She rubbed his shoulder. "You're crazy."

He offered her a warm smile. "It's crazy being here with you right now."

"I *know*. I need someone to pinch me. I really don't believe it."

"I still remember what it was like to hold you in my arms."

"How about you refresh my memory?"

He reached for her as she turned and slid her bottom into his groin. "Glad to do it. I missed you, baby." One of his arms hung around her chest like a necklace.

"You did?"

"What do you think, just because I'm a man I don't have feelings?"

Brooke didn't know what to say. She didn't even know how long she had with him before they went their separate ways again. Her heart stung at that realization. "I just thou—thiiiiink, that you managed well without me. You know? I never heard from you again."

Grateful that he couldn't see her misty eyes, she pushed her lips inward to help keep it together.

"Neither did I. I broke your heart, but I really pissed you off. I let you down so badly, Brooke Brazile, I just didn't know how to lift you back up again."

Brooke didn't want to talk anymore about the past. It hurt too much.

"Just . . . hold me right now. We don't have to say a word." She rubbed her hand over his shielding arm. The feeling compared to the comfort of returning home after being on vacation for way too long. And he simply felt like home. Warm . . . cozy . . . familiar.

After they fell asleep for a brief nap, they woke up. Brooke flipped over to face him. She caught the look of awe across his face.

"Can't believe I'm with Brazile again."

She pinched his cheek and let her hand fall to his neck. "Shhhh. Less talking, more touching."

His face glowed. "Oh, yeah?" He moved over her body and used his muscular triceps to hold himself up. "I never quite gave you the big dick yet, huh?"

She shook her head. "No. Mm-mmm. You didn't."

Jackson lowered his lips over her nipple, tracing her areola with the tip of his tongue, clamping down on her nipple with his teeth. Taking it all in, he sucked and tickled the tip of it. One of his hands gripped her breast to double her sensation. She moaned under his touch. Raced her hands up and down his beautiful back. His hand moved from her breast to between her legs to stir the pot a little. His fingers punished her, made her legs switch up and down in a fight against too much synchronized sweetness. Releasing her from his mouth, he moved over hers and tasted her lips. One hand went under her back and the other in her hair. Brooke felt he couldn't get enough of her. Before she knew it, Jackson had thrown himself into her, and with one raw thrust he sent her head back with eyes pinched shut.

She opened her eyes to make sure the man that she'd long for shared a real moment with her. She saw a man with a hand gripping the top of the headboard with an intense expression as he pounded into her fervidly. Brooke realized this man and all his passion could be the death of her. She wanted him on a level no other man would ever be sure to reach. He was the perfect man with clothes on, while holding her hand, while having a conversation with her, or while filling up the space beside her doing nothing at all. Jackson had her in the cup of his big hand, and she felt powerless to do anything about it. What scared her was the idea that she almost didn't care. She didn't mind being captive to his spell in the bed or out. She just knew she had to have him all day, every day. What was a girl to do?

I cannot. This dick though . . .

Rendered speechless, Brooke felt Jackson's tongue over hers. His tongue never felt so ravenous. Time apart had affected him as well. Jackson rolled off her, turning her over as well. He kissed her back, taking licks at it with his tongue, then moved in behind her to work her from the back. Brooke threw a hand backward to feel his toned butt flex with each push and to make sure no inches were without a home. She needed every bit he had to give.

Jackson slid a hand around her side to reach her nipple and pinched her hard while he swung a hand over her hip and down to her paradise to find her clitoris. Brooke cried out so loud, she feared the hotel manager would come to kick them out.

This sensation though . . .

She didn't care—she couldn't care. Jackson was throwing it down harder than ever, and hearing his labored breathing turned her on more. He pinched her harder on the very tip of her nipple, sending that delectable pain straight to her vagina, making it even more impossible to fight that burn that increased between her legs.

"Daddy!" Brooke called out when she experienced the beating of the orgasmic drum that removed her soul from her body. Her ears rang, her toes shot upward. She knew Jackson came when he squeezed her breast like a water balloon followed by a hungry grunt.

Tired, Brooke collapsed forward into a fetal position.

Jackson chuckled. "You alive over there?"

Throwing a halting hand behind her, Brooke warned playfully, "Stay back, you."

Jackson caressed her butt. "I went easy on you."

"Tuh. Whateva. My coochie is in recovery right now." She winced as she rolled over to face him.

Jackson closed in on her to nibble her neck. He came up long enough to look her in the eyes to ask enticingly, "What do you want, Brooke?" in a hot whisper.

Thrown off, she replied, "Excuse me?"

"We last talked in 2016. We don't know each other like we did—or thought. I wanna put it all on the table now. What . . . do you want?"

Brooke hesitated, knowing that she might lose it all as she engaged in a deadlock stare with her lover. It came down to all or nothing; she could win or lose. With parted lips and hazy eyes, Jackson waited patiently, almost silently daring her to say the words.

"I want to be yours. Forever." Brooke closed her eyes and opened them to find him staring at her with a grin. She caressed his face. "What happens now? I go home and you go to yours?"

"It should be clear now where I stand."

"Do I want this more than you?" She examined the tips of her hair between her fingers.

"I want you the same. I think you know that." Appearing reluctant, he proceeded. "The last time we were together, I threw myself into you like I did with no other woman. This time, I'm not sure what's gonna make you walk out that door."

"Is that what I'm sensing? Is there a ray of reluctance?"

"Of course." He blinked. "Brooke, you wanting a child and me not wanting one broke us up. That's serious."

"And now? Do you want one?" Brooke's heart stopped, because his answer would affect her future in a way that she knew he was aware of. She stared at the ends of her hair to shield herself from his stare.

"I could be selfish or greedy and tell you what I think you still wanna hear, but all I can tell you is that I don't know."

"Are you totally against it like you were before?" Her thighs tightened as she waited to hear that there would be no foreseeable obstacles in their relationship.

"No." He folded his arms behind his head. "I don't know. I don't wanna fail you. I wanna make you happy. I do. But you're a woman who doesn't bend easily." Jackson's face turned solemn. "And you shouldn't."

Releasing her hair, she reached over to place a hand on his knee to tell him, "I'm not ready to throw in the towel."

Jackson smirked. "Brooke, I didn't like how things went down in Georgetown the night we broke up, or I should say, the night you broke it off with me. You walked away like I was a car salesman trying to sell you an overpriced lemon. Obviously, you didn't look back, you just forgot that you met me. I was crazy about you. What did I tell you the night you walked away?"

"That you would always love me."

"Right. I meant it, because I mean what I say. You need to trust me."

"I will." Brooke didn't hesitate; he had her at his mercy. Living without him again was no longer an option.

"Get up. I wanna take you somewhere very special."

Delighted with promising words and thrilled by his investment in her, she leapt to her feet and located her clothes with a limp. Pieces were everywhere, but together, they dressed and headed to their cars.

At Jackson's suggestion, Brooke dropped her car off at her home. They drove to Georgetown in his Challenger. "Tell me, what made you get a car? My suggestion?"

"Something like that," she replied with a smile. "I love coming here on this short strip. There's so much life with crowds of young and quirky people standing around, eating, and just chatting with friends."

Jackson placed a hand on her knee and rubbed it. "My car missed you."

"I missed it. We have many good memories in here." Her dimples flashed with excitement.

Jackson winked. "Not the right ones though."

"I don't think this car is made to handle sex in the back."

"We can try to test that theory then. One day."

"I'm down. But for now, you punished this vagina of mine when you were on top. Let it rest."

He laughed. "What can I say? Girl, you got the good stuff." They laughed together.

After finding an available parallel spot, Jackson opened the door for his girlfriend and then they eased into the crowd. Holding hands, Brooke felt protected and proud with a tall, delicious man like Jackson by her side. They walked down the street, and as the crowd thinned out, Brooke turned to him to ask, "Where you taking us, Jackson? There are no more stores here. We're about to hit the gas station and a neighborhood. You know someone here?"

"Nope. Well, yes. Someone used to live here?"

Puzzled, Brooke asked, "Huh? Then if they moved, why should we come?"

Jackson stopped them at the base of a very long, narrow staircase. He pointed a finger upward to direct her attention to the top. "You see these concrete stairs?"

"Yeah." Brooke didn't see the relevancy. She did notice that the stairs were steep and very long.

"Well, Regan used to live here."

Brooke chuckled. "The President didn't live here, silly. They all stay at the White House."

"No, not him, you silly girl. Regan, the little girl possessed by the demon from *The Exorcist*." He said it so casually that Brooke felt the need to slap his shoulder.

Brooke squealed with wide eyes. "Get me outta here!"

"You look so cute when you do that with your eyes when you get all scared and shit." Humored, he laughed at her and ignored her plea to flee.

"Jackson! Are you *insane*? This is some freaky shit, and I wanna leave—*now*."

Unfazed by her serious demeanor, Jackson replied, "You call yourself a true Washingtonian, but you were unaware that a movie that made history like that was shot here?" He pointed to the house adjacent to the staircase. "But ain't this cool?"

"I'm leaving." Brooke walked away. Without breaking stride, she turned back to tell him, "I'm not trying to have that mess come get me."

He pointed a thumb behind him. "But, Brooke, do you think the owners ever have a possession up in there?" She shot him one last look of annoyance before leaving his sight. He called, "Look! No one else is scared!"

Back in the car and with folded arms, Brooke lectured, "Jackson, I cannot believe you did that to me. You call that a date?"

"Yes, one that you will never forget."

The fact that he didn't seem to find any problem with it appalled her. "But, you're serious, huh? You have absolutely no problem with the fact that you spooked me?"

"No. You need to relax. I had to shake your world up a bit. It's too controlled."

"What? It wasn't controlled when you broke my heart and couldn't see things my way." Brooke studied his profile as she waited for him to answer. He threw a hand up. *Low blow, Brooke, low blow.*

"I'm sorry."

"It's all right."

"Still don't like what you just did."

"How could anyone manage weddings like you do? I saw the fruit of your work and not only was I impressed, but it turned me on. I thought to myself, this girl really knows what it means to take control."

Brooke still hadn't softened. "Your sister's tight deadline was the biggest challenge. She was easy. She didn't ask for too much. Besides, I had help, you know—my assistant."

"Please. You managed that and more before she came into your life. What did she do, set up flowers?" He sneered.

"No. Excuse you, but she worked hard, and she impressed me."

"She wasn't there in the beginning. You came this far on your own. So, I wanted to throw a monkey wrench in your perfect existence. You know, give you some fun."

Irritated, Brooke folded her arms. "Yes, let's talk monkey wrenches and how you recommended me while staying in the cut."

Jackson smirked. "I already explained myself."

"Well finding out from your sister that you set this all up shook me up. And did you know that Summer told me that she saw you touching a woman's face in National Harbor, who happened to be your sister?"

"Wh—" Jackson stopped at a red light and turned to face her. He snickered. "That day she came to visit me to tell me how worried she was about me. Yeah, I always squeeze her face. She's adorable when she gets all protective of me. Poor, Summer. She ran back to tell her little girlfriend that I had one myself." He cocked his head back and laughed. "Women are funny. Always gossiping."

Brooke felt silly and rolled her eyes. "Just shut up and drive."

"Back to funnier things. This is a reconnection date that you and I will remember. You shoulda seen your face." Jackson tried to suppress his chuckle with a loose hand over his mouth.

Brooke couldn't help but release a subtle snicker of her own. "Were you trying to give me nightmares? I do live alone you know. Scare me too much and you'll find me in your bed each night."

"I won't complain. You can stay in my bed as much as you like."

Brooke's tense face eased into a pleased smirk. Staring out the window, she couldn't believe that he'd returned to her life once again. It felt right to tell him, "I'm glad that we're together again. I'm not sure how long it will last, but I'll enjoy each morning waking up knowing that I'm yours again, no matter whose bed I'm in."

Jackson stole glances at her as he drove. "In the hotel, you said forever . . . that's how long you want us to last."

"Yes." The rhythm of her heart increased to a quick skip.

"Well, then."

Summer

Not bothering to sit up, I blindly picked up my ringing cell phone on the nightstand with a groggy voice. "Hello?" I forgot to screen my call in my sleepy state. Oliver grunted.

"Good morning, Summer." The tone sounded guarded.

It was too early to play guessing games. "Who is this?" I tried to shield the sun from my eyes.

"It's Brooke."

Surprised and happy to hear from her, my heart skipped a beat. "Really? Brooke? So early?"

"Yeah. Well, it's not that early. It's ten forty-three."

"Right." I sat up without checking my clock.

"I couldn't let another day pass with us on the outs. Can you meet me and the girls for breakfast?"

"Love to. Where?" I peeled the comforter off my body.

"In your neck of the woods. Rail One."

"Umm, sure. I'll be there in half-an-hour."

"Sure. We'll wait. Emily's gonna bring Amber."

"Cool. See you soon. Bye."

"Bye, Summer."

Dressed in blue shorts and a floral top, I entered the diner and sat at the table where Brooke waited alone. Glad we could speak alone first, I did wish the other two were there to cushion the awkwardness.

"Hey, there," I said, squeezing into the booth.

"Summer." Her grin was bigger than I expected. "So nice to see you. I—" She shifted uncomfortably. "I wanted to talk to you and clear the air before the girls got here."

I smiled. "Here's your chance."

"I'm sorry. I took my emotions out on a helpful friend who really saved me from being blindsided. I was the bitch."

Brooke's gesture touched my heart as the sincerity peeked from behind her brown eyes.

"I'm sorry that I called you that. I take no pride in using that word and especially on a friend. Do you accept my apology?"

Choked up with one tear streaming down her cheek, she agreed. "Sure. I was dying to call you last night, and it felt strange not doing it."

I felt shy about asking but proceeded anyway. "So, do you think badly of me because of my lifestyle choices over the past months?"

Brooke flicked her hand at me. "Oh, that." She opened her napkin to unwrap the spoon. "We should just forget about those nasty comments and words." When she saw me staring at her expectantly, her answered changed to, "No, Summer. I—I mean, yes, you were careless with Ruben but we all have careless moments, but I don't judge you. I'm embarrassed by my behavior, that's all."

"Thank you for being honest. That's the Brooke I respect. And sorry for essentially calling you an attention whore."

Brooke giggled and waved a hand. "Girl, who are we trying to kid? I like my sycophants."

We gave into a bout of laughter with hands over our chests with beaming eyes.

"Girl, please. I have no shame with that." Brooke flipped her hair back with a sassy hand. "Please."

I banged the table lightly. "So, what happened? I know you saw Jackson." I sat on the edge of my seat, waiting to hear possible good news."

She rolled her eyes with happiness. "Oh, I *saw* him all right."

"Yeah?"

"Well, we made love, confessed our feelings, and I went for the gusto and told him I wanted forever." Brooke grinned so wide I thought her mouth would rip her face.

"Girl, you are beaming. Now, what'd he say?" I leaned in forward as if she were disclosing the secret to perky breasts after pregnancy.

"Well, he didn't disagree, but he didn't propose or anything either." She saw the ladies and patted the edge of the table. "Shhhh, they're here."

Before I could turn around to see for myself, Emily and Amber came sashaying to our table. Brooke moved over for Amber, and I for Emily.

"Well, well, well," Amber pointed out. "So glad to see two of my favorite three ladies together again."

"Oh, we are over that blow-up. Yesterday's paper," Brooke replied.

"Just tell us about Jackson," Emily demanded with raised eyebrows and a big smile.

Brooke shared everything again, but in more detail. Emily and Amber shared a high-five with Brooke and Emily asked, "Is there going to be a wedding?"

Brooke shook her head. "Not even sure, but I hope so. I really do." She placed a hand over her heart and gasped with a smile before proclaiming, "I love him. I really love him."

Emily nodded and placed a hand over Brooke's hand. "I understand, Brooke. You can't shake some loves. You just can't. You know I'm glad I'm finally over Eric, because it was so crippling to want something that you cannot have. You know, I think I had to be daring with these guys just to sleep with them, because my heart wasn't in it. Yeah, a piece of me wanted to prove to myself that he wasn't right, that I wasn't a boring teacher with a sad love life. But the more I thought about it, the more I realized that I needed that extra stimulation to make it to a point of arousal because my heart was tied to him."

I glanced at her suspiciously. "You are ca-razy. I could get moving just fine with another man if Oliver and I fell apart. I don't see any reason in not coming just because my heart is broken."

Amber's laugh spurted out. "Riiiight?"

Brooke chuckled. "Yeah," she said. "You must be different in that department than me, because I thought about Jackson on the way to my first date with Damani. But when time came to perform, my vagina was ready." We fell over laughing, even Emily.

"Sad, isn't it? Eric has broken my heart and trust but, yet, it took a long time to get over him. Y'all." She balled up a fist. "When I love a man, *I love.*"

"Well, to love half-heartedly is a waste of time, don't you think?" Brooke asked.

I couldn't help but feel the sting in my heart upon hearing Brooke's words. I just didn't know what it meant and the purpose of the reaction. Mentally, I shrugged it off and re-engaged with the conversation among my girlfriends.

Amber said, "Well, I know I'm sick and tired of these bills," she spilled with a toss of her napkin. "I can't seem to catch up. You guys know the last time I could afford to shop?" Our unblinking stare told her to continue. "Since my birthday when Brooke gave me the gift cards." She pouted. "For real y'all, how pathetic is that?"

Emily smirked. "First-world problems, huh?"

Amber patted her chest. "Okay, I'm sorry, not to sound spoiled, but this just shows how I can't afford to do anything but try to pay bills. Going legit is tough yo."

"I'm sorry," Brooke told her. That was a rare moment. Brooke rarely expressed herself so softly.

"Thanks, Brooke. Last year you tried to warn ole girl. I shoulda been savin'. But I gotta believe that something will work out. Think about it. You guys all had a come-up since knowing me. Emily moved outta her five-bedroom home and into a cute condo, Brooke is renting a space for her business, and Summer went from her basic apartment into Chez Oliver. And me? I'm still the chick in Southwest in a raggedy ass apartment. You know them upgrades started in the units people are moving out of. My building is changing. And with the area being all upscale now, it's so hard to make it here. Had to sign a new lease the other day, decided on a six-month lease, and the rent has already gone up. With the gentrification of Southwest, y'all, I'm tellin' you, I don't know what I'ma do."

Rubbing my belly, I told them, "Sounds like I got out in time. It looks like a new world over there."

"But it's just sad. I see people moving out all the time. Spoke with someone at the CVS one day. Told me that the low-income families feel out of place in neighborhoods they've been in for years. Even a cup of coffee ain't a roll of quarters for them no more." Amber rubbed her temples.

Emily shook her head, looking occupied in her lost stare. "Very sad. I can't imagine." She wagged her finger at Amber. "You should have made it a two-year lease if possible or one more year at the least."

"Why?" Amber tilted her head. "Don't think I can stay too much longer anyway."

"Well, you just made that possibility even higher. It may be tighter for you, but if you can manage the increase now for six months, then you're looking at another possible increase sooner—in six months. With a longer lease, that's more time away from another increase."

Amber buried her face in her hands. When she revealed her frowning face, she asked, "Bihhhh, now you tell me?"

Unfazed, Emily shrugged. "Now you know."

Brooke squeezed her lips together in thought and told Amber, "Well, you used to want the uppity life and now you have it. Southwest ain't quite the little dog no more. So, stop your complaining, Amber. For real. You'd be facing the same thing in New York."

"You right."

I tried to make her feel better by reminding her of the truth. "Amber, did you forget you used to live on a friend's couch before getting your own spot? And I would still be right across the street from you had I not met a man who wanted to take me in. Stop being so hard on yourself."

Amber asked, "Do you think of it as a man saved you? Besides, you recruit, and that brings in a nice penny."

"Actually, I've stopped. I've been too tired with setting up the nursery, and Oliver wants me to sit back and do— uh, not much of anything."

Amber's eyes bulged at my words. "My goodness, girl. This man just loves you. Do you think he saved you? Yes or no?"

It sickened me to think of anyone 'saving' me, let alone a man. "To be fair and honest, yes. My savings was a joke. It wasn't enough to do much of anything in the long run. And if it weren't for Fran or at least that first week, or Oliver, I think I would've had to move back to Delaware with my mom."

"Don't be foolish, you coulda moved in with me," Amber said. "It woulda been fun." She playfully rolled her eyes. "You cop the couch and pay half of the rent while I handle the other."

"Yeah," I pointed a finger at her. "So much fun."

"I was lonely," Emily added. "So, I probably would have snatched you up first."

Brooke said, "Hallelujah." She fanned herself. "I love you, Summer, but I can't say I wanna live with someone. Well, maybe my boo, of course, but I wouldn't want to see a friend homeless." She flashed a lasting and warm smile.

"That's good enough." I rubbed her balled-up hand that rested on the table.

Brooke sighed. "Guys, I'm not sure how long Jackson and I will last, but I do wanna tell you guys the moment I knew y'all were special. And I don't know if you guys went home and talked about me behind my back."

We laughed.

"But one day it hit me that you guys put up with my constant whining about Jackson. Thank you."

"Same here," Emily said. "I knew you guys were cool, too, for putting up with my crazy moods regarding Eric. I think I would have avoided me, if I were you." Her glassy eyes lowered. She nodded her head. "Yeah. So, thanks. I needed that support." When her voice broke, I rubbed her back.

Amber cleared her throat. "Me, too." She chuckled. "You guys didn't really judge me for my lifestyle choices, and I knew then you guys were worth my time." She made us laugh for a moment, even though she had furrowed eyebrows and tensed lips to fight back any emotion.

"My turn," I said. "I knew you guys were special when you helped me through the Ruben thing, and, like Amber, there wasn't a lot of judgment just *my* obsessive whining. Plus, I knew we were all onto something each time we met up like this—together. I never had this before."

Brooke stuck a finger up. "Look, I've been judgmental, and you guys knew that. I'm working on that, okay?"

"You? Judgmental?" we teased simultaneously. "Nah, no, get out of here." We laughed, ate, and for the first time, we were all somewhat merry.

10: a new season

Summer

It'd been a great past week and a half. The girls surprised me with a baby shower on Saturday that Oliver managed to hide from me as well. He'd given the girls a key to the apartment while he took me out for an afternoon movie. It was a stupid, short comedy, but it was a quick diversion to keep me trapped from returning home. When we returned, Jackson, Zach, and my mom were there with the girls, waiting for our return.

I'd entered with a priceless expression full of shock upon seeing the nicely decorated living room. At that moment, I realized just how blessed my life turned out to be. The men ran away upstairs to give us our privacy. It was Brooke's great idea to bring the men together. Amber thought the idea seemed fantastic and didn't seem to mind that she was the only one without a plus one. Her only focus these days was money, and she blamed the diversion of men as the reason for her perpetual state of being broke.

My mom even stayed for two days in hopes that I'd go into labor. She promised to return once she found out my water broke. The whole event was a success. Besides, why wouldn't it have been? Brooke had arranged it.

Brooke

Brooke answered her cell phone. "Hello?"

"I need to see you tonight."

"*Hey*, baby. On a Wednesday night?" She grinned from ear-to-ear at her desk.

"I need to see you tonight. I won't take no for an answer." Wow, he sounded so serious.

"Does it sound like I was going to turn you down?"

"I'm gonna pick you up."

"It's only been three days," she teased.

"That's unacceptable. We need to have a talk. What time do you get off?" His serious tone persisted. Brooke really didn't know how to take it.

"Ummm, okay. You win, though there really wasn't much of a fight. Pick me up at five-thirty."

"Goodbye." When he hung up suddenly, the chill sent down her spine told her that she didn't know how to read what just happened.

Amber

Amber sat up on her couch when she heard the knock at her door. She knew it had to be—well, she wasn't sure. Her girlfriends would never show up without a call. She wasn't expecting anyone else. Normally, she would peek through her peephole, but she didn't feel like it was necessary. Her jaw fell open when she saw the man standing on the other side of the door.

"*What are you doing here*? Just because you know where I live doesn't mean you have to use my address."

He invited himself in; she didn't miss his demanding personality.

"Amber, I'm going to get straight to the point." Amber slammed the door behind her and spun around.

"Ummm, sir! You cannot just barge through my door. I didn't invite you in." She folded her arms at his nerve.

"You opened the door, so you weren't really against seeing me," he justified with outstretched arms.

"I failed to use my peephole. Don't flatter yourself. Now, why you here?"

Holding up both palms, he replied, "I know I did you . . . wrong."

"That's an understatement. You really did me greasy. We ended this mess. After all this time, why now?"

"Because I miss you. I had fun with you. I was wrong."

Through gritted teeth, Amber replied with anger, "You. Think. You. Are. All. That."

"But I had fun with you. My life is nothing but work. I'm sorry, Amber."

"Don't you have another hoe bunny you can find to replace me?"

He shoved his hands into his pocket with a low-hanging head. "I was a jerk. But Amber, we had something, whether you can admit it or not. I wasn't expecting nothing to come of us, but something blossomed. Sometimes, men need space to see it. Well, the dumb ones anyway."

Exhausted by the verbal sparring, Amber said, "Just get to the point already."

"Look at you. You are one hot mama. The sex between us was nothing that I've ever experienced. I'm bored without you." He chuckled. "Straight-out bored. I'm tired of living alone. It gets old quick. Let's say you move out of this dump—"

"Heeey," Amber objected. "I . . ." She nodded as she searched for the right response. "I like this place. It's my home."

"And that's the only reason why you should. But I can give you more, something better. You'll love the closet. It's all yours. I have something for you if you need more convincing."

Confused, Amber watched and waited as he fumbled in what appeared to be his oversized pocket. When his hand fished out a little black box, Amber cupped her mouth and tried to keep her balance with spaghetti legs.

"Oh."

"Move in with me."

Feeling catatonic, Amber stood there for a full minute. "Well, what's in it?" she squealed. Her heart raced anxiously.

"Amber, tell me yes, and I will open it. But if you decline, then you'll never know. What's it gonna be?"

Amber thought about how she would be at an advantage for once in her life. She wouldn't have to do life alone anymore. She could actually get out of her financial bind. She knew what she had to do.

"All right, then. All right."

She jumped up and down and wrapped her legs around his sides. She knew in her heart that they did have fun together. And perhaps, she was going to be in a relationship.

Brooke

Brooke stood on the corner as she watched the red Challenger roll up beside the curb. She knew better than to approach the car. Jackson stepped out and without saying a word, he greeted her with a firm kiss on her lips. He placed a hand on her lower back and helped her into his car before hopping in on his side and placing a hand on her bare leg.

"I'm sure you're hungry, baby. Right?"

"Of course, babe."

"All right then." Jackson pushed on the clutch and shifted into first gear, made a U-turn, and roared into the traffic on Seventh Street.

After sitting in twenty minutes of traffic while listening to dance music, they arrived at Ici Urban Bistro, an upscale Northwest restaurant. "I've never been here before," Brooke said. "I'm loving the ambience." He pulled her chair out before taking his.

"You know how we do." He grinned and cracked open the menu. "You know I'm paying, right?" He winked.

She playfully snaked her neck at him. "If you ever want some of this good stuff again you will." In no time, their server showed up with an introduction, and Jackson requested the wine menu.

"Let's check out the wine menu first," he told Brooke. "French or American?"

Brooke's eyes scrolled over the menu, before responding with, "French and you choose the color."

"Let's have a bottle of Chateau Ducru-Beaucaillou, Grand Cru Classe, 2003."

With wide eyes, Brooke looked up immediately. "Boy, that's some good French there."

Jackson winked with a smirk.

"Very good." The server collected the wine menus with a smile and walked away.

"Jackson, that bottle is just five dollars under four hundred dollars. Maybe you should—"

"You sayin' women like cheap men now?" he questioned with eyes above the top of the menu.

Choosing her response wisely, Brooke replied softly with a smile, "Oh, come on. You know that's not what I meant. I'm just saying that you don't have to do so much. I'm not too big on alcoholic beverages."

"I'm not either, but I'm in a celebratory mood. We're together." They smiled at each other.

His gestures and words melted her heart. "You right, you right." Brooke studied the menu. "So, what made you choose this restaurant? It looks promising."

"Ohhh, I had to see what the rave was all about among my co-workers. I've heard nothing but good remarks, so I had to come check it out." When the server returned to pour the wine, Jackson ordered a rib-eye steak and Brooke ordered an ahi tuna.

"The wine tastes great," Brooke said with delight. Jackson agreed. "So, you made tonight sound so mandatory. What did we need to talk about?"

Setting his glass down, he answered, "Oh yeah, about that." He cleared his throat. "Let's talk about us and why you love me."

"Oh. A little random, but okay." She smiled and traced the rim of her glass with an index finger. "You are freaking sexy and behind all of that allure is a secure gentleman with a great work ethic. You're kind, loving, attentive, and highly affectionate. You're magnetic. And most importantly, you know how to treat me."

"I like that answer."

When he didn't smile, Brooke felt like she was on a job interview, like there was a right or wrong answer.

"Good." She bit her lower lip in slight disappointment. Not knowing where he was going with this information rubbed her the wrong way. "Is this why we met?"

"Yes. It's all about me, baby, all the time."

Brooke couldn't hide her frown or the hurt in her eyes. Instantly, Jackson leaned forward and rubbed her hand. "Hey, relax, Brooke. Baby, I'm just playin', come on now. I wanted to tell you that I hope you never change. I love you. I love the way you handle your business fearlessly. I love your work ethic, your drive, your passion for life, and, most of all, I love how you put yourself first." The words touched her heart. He held her hand. "Listen, when you left me, I admired how you put yourself first by honoring your needs. You didn't let a man change you. I wasn't gonna challenge that."

"But now . . . we're back. What does this mean?"

"It means that I'm open with time, if you can accept that. Right now, Brooke, honestly, I just wanna enjoy you. You know, when my sister said she was getting married I knew it was the only chance I had to catch up with you."

"I love you, and I trust you with my life. Never in my life have I trusted anyone like this before. It feels strange but good." A tear fell down her face. "I've also cried more times this month than my whole life I believe. I feel like you've changed me."

"I want to make you happy every day, Brooke." His voice tightened in his throat. "And, umm, if I could devour you in this place, I would."

"Can we go? I don't even need this right now. Just you."

"Yeah, we can do that." Jackson flagged down the server and explained that nothing was wrong but that they changed their minds about staying. The server understood and hurried off to accommodate the changes. Paying for the wine, Jackson left a very handsome tip in the amount suitable for a dine-in as they vamoosed.

Grabbing her panties, he complained, "What is this shit still doing on? Take this off."

Standing partially naked in front of him in her bedroom, Jackson didn't wait for her to act. Brooke wasn't even quick enough. Reacting off the hunger of lust, Jackson yanked her panties off so fast, Brooke didn't even see them disappear.

Wow. He wants me so badly.

The agony in his face reflected his need. He lowered her to the bed, and when he crawled over her, Jackson lowered his face. With his cheek pressed against hers and his lips breathing over her ear, he told, "I want you seven days a week, anywhere. I want to make you beg and rip the sheets. I want your stomach to tremble, your legs to grip me into possession, and your pussy to cry for mercy."

See, this is the suave shit that I miss.

Brooke felt his dick pierce her and in a matter of seconds, he'd established a rhythm made from a push of a set of muscular butt cheeks with his head resting beside her shoulder as he lay it into her. He brought some form of wonderful pain onto her, unleashing the fiery of a man who'd walked too many miles without aid in sight. A tear developed as she figured that she was home. *He* was home. Her heart had never felt so whole. Though she didn't mean to think and preferred to just shut up and enjoy the ride, she couldn't help it. This man meant everything to her. He had the power to destroy her again, from the inside out, but she didn't care, and didn't believe that he would do that. Now she knew what people meant when they pleaded for one more night with a former flame. No one knew what to do with the aftermath of one more night, just that they had to have it with the faith that they could sort it all out later.

Brooke took each thrust until it broke down her walls. Slowly, they crumbled away. Before she knew it, Jackson had gripped her as he rolled over, putting her on top of him. Straddling him, she arched her back until her hardened nipples saluted him. Brooke lined herself up and took him again, committing to a riding motion as her hands danced over her hair. With a cocked neck, she closed her eyes and let her hips do all the work. Enjoying the touch of his fingers squeezing her nipples, she lost herself in a world full of daisies and fields of green. His raw shaft inflicted that burn that flicked into a fire, and when she felt that orgasm quaking from the pit of her womanhood, her mouth opened and sang a tune of liberation. Letting her noise out with her fingers in her mouth, Brooke's head and back curled so far back, she thought she'd never straighten again. She felt Jackson's big hands against her thighs to help her cope. She knew that he'd wait on her, and that it must've been punishment for him. She gripped his hands, and as their fingers intertwined, he succumbed as well. Jackson grunted and said, "*Shit.*"

She'd blown his mind. Released, Brooke eased her head and back upright and peered downward to meet his gaze. Trying to capture a workable breathing pattern, Brooke collapsed forward and rested on his shoulder to recover. He always felt good. So good, that she wished that she could lose all her excess calories by making love to Jackson instead of heading to the gym. But identifying that thought as unrealistic, Brooke smiled when the idea occurred that he'd always make one hell of a dessert.

Emily

The next morning, Emily rushed to answer the loud knock at her door. When she yanked it open, she figured she had to be hallucinating. "*Eric?*" Her tiny hands couldn't move. They locked into two balled fists at her sides. "How in the world did you find me here? *What* are you doing here?"

Eric's demeanor surprised her. His approach was even more shocking. "I would like to talk to you. Please, Emily."

Tension hit her in the neck, and she thought she would go blind with anger. "No. Go away." She didn't trust him, and she certainly didn't want to be drawn back into his web of hurt.

He held up his palms. "Emily. Would you hear me out?"

She couldn't say anything as her mind drew a quick analysis of their past to determine what she should do. "You talk on that side of my door, not inside." Emily was proud for being authentically firm with him. Her tone reflected it as well.

"Fair enough."

Emily studied his face. Still handsome with a square jawbone and salt and pepper hair, it appeared as though a little bit more salt had been sprinkled since the last time. Could be because of her actions to exact revenge. She allowed herself to lower her stare, only if for a moment. Of course, his lean body wore an expensive three-piece business suit. Still fit, still sexy. If she acted carelessly, she'd find herself vulnerable again to his pleas and promises.

Eric clenched his jawbone. "Emily, things went too far between us, and for what? I understand I hurt you when you found out I slept with that friend of yours, and we made things worse from there. You left highly inappropriate photos at my job, and I said some pretty disgusting things to you."

He still didn't manage to erase her irritation. "So, why are you here? The way I see it, we can conclude that you hate me, and I hate you. We're even."

"But, that's just it, Emily. I should hate you, but I don't. I can't. Where did we go wrong?"

"I don't know. Let's see." Emily held up one finger. "Your dad manipulated the hell out of you, so you left me."

She held up another finger. "You treated me like gum on the bottom of your shoe." Then the second finger. "You slept with my friend and tried to hide it. So, that's three and four." She held up one last finger. "You insulted me badly. One little act of revenge is not that bad. You pushed me too far." She didn't know how she made it through the list with a trembling voice and rapid breathing.

He nodded. "Fair enough." He cleared his throat. "That's exactly where we went wrong. But I met another woman."

Struggling not to rip her own hair out with hands placed on the sides of her head, with bugged eyes and gritted teeth, Emily asked angrily, "Why are you telling me? My God, have you any shame, Eric? I mean, you just don't quit, do you?"

Talking over her angry ramblings, Eric spoke calmly but loudly, "She even asked me to move in with her, she wanted to discuss our future, marriage, and kids." Over Emily's voice he pushed through until he finally said, "But I wanna be with you."

Once the words floated into her ears, Emily stopped talking. Without blinking, his eyes smiled into hers. "Gorgeous, I know who you are. I don't need to learn who you are again. Yeah, I was severely pissed at you, and then I laughed. It was all my fault and you stood up for you, for love. I wanna be with you."

Brooke

"Hello?" Haysia answered the front desk phone.

Brooke sat off to the side at her desk scribbling notes onto her calendar before heading to the two new potential clients sitting in her waiting area.

"Wait. That doesn't make sense. You would like us to plan your wedding?" Haysia asked. Brooke couldn't help but notice the look of confusion on Haysia's face.

"Is there a problem, Haysia? That *is* what we do." Brooke whispered loud enough for her assistant to hear.

Haysia ignored her and Brooke rose to her feet, ready to approach Haysia if she needed help.

"I . . . I don't understand, sir. You said you would like us to coordinate your wedding to whom? I'm sorry, sir." Haysia held up an index finger to Brooke.

Brooke's hand rested on her hip as she tapped her desk with a finger. Brooke folded her arms, wondering if Haysia could pull off dealing with an adverse customer.

"Okay, so I just want to make sure I get this straight. You would like to have us coordinate your wedding. You are the groom, correct?" Haysia waited for his response. "Okay, and you said you will be marrying Brooke Brazile?"

Brooke's eyes widened. "Is this a sick joke?"

Haysia grimaced. "Well, okay, sir, what is your name?" Haysia managed to avert Brooke's gaze throughout the whole conversation. However, when Haysia learned of his name, her eyes widened as she looked at Brooke. "Jackson Sloan?"

Brooke's jaw dropped. The floor felt yanked from underneath her feet. Everything started to move in slow motion as her knees went soft. Haysia lowered the phone receiver to her chest with a look of confusion and horror, while Brooke tried to keep her head from spinning. They heard the bell ring at the front door. Brooke and Haysia's eyes noticed the man walking through the door on his cell phone.

With a grin and cell phone against his ear, Jackson continued their phone conversation in the middle of Brooke's entrance. "Yes, I said that I am Jackson Sloan, and I would like to have you coordinate my wedding to Brooke Brazile."

Brooke couldn't move. She couldn't breathe. She couldn't think. The two potential clients and Haysia just stood in awe, watching Jackson stare at Brooke. When she finally eased around the corner of her desk and to Jackson, he kneeled before her with a fourteen-karat, black gold band, three-stoned princess-cut ring.

"Will you marry me?" Jackson peered up at her for the first time, as she'd become used to looking upward.

Brooke couldn't believe the beauty of the black gold-banded ring. When she stared at it for so long, he said, "You are like no other woman I have ever met, so the ring should reflect that. But if you don't like it—"

"Shut up, shut up," she told him in the shakiest voice. "I will marry you with a ring made of cat hair. Yes! Yes, Jackson, I will marry you! Get up!" Standing, Brooke flung herself into his arms as he spun her around.

"Ohhhh," the women and Haysia said. They clapped louder than the sound of Brooke's heart against her chest. Jackson grabbed her face and planted a kiss full of love and passion on her lips.

Summer

I called the girls one-by-one since this would likely be our last night out before my parenthood materialized. We needed to have that one night that I could remember where we laughed and shared the events of our week before my freedom would become limited.

"Oh, absolutely I'm down," Emily said.

After hanging up with Emily and calling Amber, she replied with, "Girl. Yes. When and where?" Informing her of the details, we promised to see each other later and hung up. Brooke was last on the list, so I shot her a text with a message to call me back as soon as possible since she didn't pick up her phone.

Sitting on the couch—which seemed to be the norm these days—I jumped when my phone rang with Brooke's name across the screen. Swiping across the screen to answer the call, I said, "Brooke Brazile, finally. We are going out tonight. Me and the girls, that is. Care to join?"

"Yes! Count me in. When and where?" Noticing her abnormal amount of enthusiasm, we hung up after she received the information. Since my pace had become slower in every task lately, it seemed more sensible to prepare for tonight right away.

Hours later, I stepped outside and waited for the girls to spot me. One of the upsides to being pregnant was watching everyone around me accommodate "the pregnant woman." My friends agreed that I shouldn't have to travel far, especially since going into labor seemed probable any day now. I chose Tysons Corner, the Shay Lounge. We could all use a break from DC. Brooke and Emily approached me first, and then Amber crossed the street. Obviously, she'd taken the Metro.

"Well, well, well," Brooke started. "I'm surprised we're not in G-town tonight."

Emily hugged me and then I reached for Brooke. Amber came in and swooped one big hug over all of us. I waved my hand at Brooke. "Nah, I'm sick of that place. We need to hang out around my neck of the woods now."

"We've been doing that with Rail One. Duh. Besides. no one told you to move to Virginia," Emily sassed with a hand on her hip.

I laughed. "Well, my man is here."

"Summer, your car is a bucket, and since I scooped Emily up, that leaves the Beamer." Brooke clapped and twirled a finger. "Let's go."

Amber pulled out a set of keys from her purse and dangled them on her finger in the air and teasingly said, "Or does it?"

Everyone's mouth dropped with Brooke noticing the emblem on the key fob. She grabbed it in her hand and asked, "Is that a Mercedes? No wonder you rejected my offer to pick you up."

"Yup." Her smile could no longer fit on her face.

Through a smiling, dropped jaw, I asked, "Girl, what kind of trick did you turn last night?"

"Apparently the right ones." Emily answered. "Wait. You're from New York. You stole it, didn't you?"

"I resent that." Amber pretended to be offended. "Just follow me to my whip and we can get to Tysons Corner by way of the Mercedes."

"I must have done something wrong in my life," Brooke determined.

"Wow. Now, who's moved up?" I chuckled and lightly jabbed my elbow into Brooke's side. She could barely find any humor in the situation, because she was still trying to process it.

Amber led us to the opposite street and pressed the button on her alarm to disarm the car. "Parking was horrible. I had to park all the way over here."

"You have the G-Class SUV?" Emily gawked. "No way. Eric had one but sold it. He couldn't stand the size after a while. But it is fully loaded inside."

I told her, "We don't care about Eric anymore, remember?"

Emily tightened her lips at me with raised eyebrows before she hopped into the back.

"Pregnant lady gets the front," I called.

Emily replied, "Noooo, you get the front because you know where we're going."

"Well, not really," I admitted. "I just pinpointed it on Google maps. Now, I do know you have to hop on I-66 west." When I didn't say anything else, Amber looked at me with an expression that read, *does it look like I know where to go?*

"Right," I said. "You wouldn't have a clue, Metro girl."

"Uh duh, ya' think?" Amber replied with a slap on her forehead. "Or could it be because I'm not from here?"

Nodding, I told Amber the address as she tapped the address into the navigation system.

Once we hopped on the highway, Emily tapped Amber on the shoulder. Amber glanced up into the rearview mirror to look at her. "Yeah?"

"So really, Amber. Whose car is this?"

Amber smirked. "Fine." She reached into her shirt and pulled a chain out from underneath. "He gave me this. It's a diamond pendant from Tiffany."

"Whoaaaaa," Emily and I gushed.

Brooke's hand flung out. Impatient, she asked, "*Who*? Who gave you all of this? And show me at the restaurant, because we can't see it from back here."

After seconds of silence and the three of us hanging on a cliff of curiosity, Amber finally spoke up. "It's Daniel."

We gasp and inhaled.

"Daniel stopped by and he-he wanted me back. That joker said life ain't right without me."

Leaning forward, Brooke knocked Amber in the arm. "After that jerk denied you. Oh, no, sis, you got the wrong one. Mm-mm." She waved a disapproving hand as she sat back into her seat.

Emily cleared her throat. "Ohhhh, come on, Brooke. That can be romantic. He's lost without her and wants her back." She nodded her head with certainty. "I . . . think it's a good thing."

Brooke snapped. "Are you on crack?"

Emily smacked the side of my seat. "Summer, what do you think?"

Amber grinned my way. "Yeah, Summer, what do you think?"

I rolled my lips between my teeth with uncertainty of how to respond. "Pfft, I mean, it's her call. She's a grown woman, Brooke. I think we need to trust her judgement. Amber has . . . shown us that she is on a much more mature path."

"I agree," Emily cheered.

Looking pleased, Amber said, "Thank you, Summer. See Brooke. You're out."

Brooke replied, "Well, if she's more mature, that's all the reason why you should steer clear before he drags you back down. Once again Amber, you let material things snag you."

"Oh, please, Brooke. Do you know if Jackson wants kids yet?"

Low blow, alert.

I clapped my hands. "Ladies, *please.*"

Leaning forward, Brooke palmed a hand at me. "No, it's okay, Summer. Amber, you don't know what you're talking about."

"I know that Jackson throws that dick down and you go down for the count."

With a finger pointed up, Brooke opened her mouth to reply, then froze. "You—you know what. You right. You are absolutely right, Amber. Jackson's got that good dick and it's so, so good that I just gotta have it. My nah-nah so good, he put a ring on it."

We all covered our mouths. "What?" we asked.

I said, "Shut the front do'."

Immediately, Amber pulled over onto the shoulder and then struggled to locate the map lights. When she did, Brooke placed a hand forward.

"See? Look."

"Woooooooooow," Emily gushed. "This night really is full of surprises."

Grinning, my fingers traced the stone. "That's different, Brooke."

"You like it?"

"I do, Brooke, I do. Wow. Miracles do happen."

Brooke pointed a finger at me. "No. A miracle would be you and Oliver doing this."

In an instant, I tried to disguise my panic with a display of amusement. So, I laughed. "Miracles are so few and far between."

Amber dropped Brooke's hand and said, "Well, bitch. You got me. You win." She put the car into drive and joined the flow of traffic on the highway.

Emily fanned her face. "Ohhh. I wanna cry. This is such a beautiful and enlightening night. We've spent so much time vacillating between decisions and it just feels so good to be in a good place. Look at us."

Nodding in harmony, Amber suggested we celebrate in the car with music. She blared music the rest of the distance until we reached our destination. About twenty minutes later, we arrived at Shay Lounge. Valet took over the parking, so we hopped right out and headed indoors. Since it was Thursday night, we entered free of charge. We planned to make the best of the night.

Between the dancing, eating, and drinking, especially on Amber and Emily's end, we really had the time of our lives. We had to fight off several attempts from men offering us drinks, rides home, or just invites to the dance floor. Amber ignored the men and even the ones who measured up as her type. Whatever she and Daniel established this time around must've been legit. Even Emily stuck tight to the group. I supposed they just wanted to make it a true girls' night out.

Sitting at the bar, I noticed that Amber was on her fourth drink, so I decided to remind her that she wasn't a Metro girl tonight. "Hey there, you may wanna take it easy, honey. You drove us here."

Amber pointed her hot pink press-on nails at her chest. "Hey. I know how to handle my liquor."

"Yeah, well you make sure you know how to handle that wheel," Brooke warned.

"Or you'll have to stay in Ballston with me tonight," I told her.

Amber shook her head. "No, no. Daniel is gonna miss me tonight. I mean, I moved in already."

Emily looked taken aback. "Man. That was fast."

Brooke shook her head in disapproval.

I told Amber, "Well, sweetie, I think he wants you alive for the long run."

Brooke clutched her temples. "Amber." She looked up. "He dissed you in the worst possible way. Do you really wanna be with a man who would do that to you?"

"Honey. Welcome to adulthood of doin' what you gotta do to survive." She opened her arms. "I don't have any help. I'm goin' to school now, lessons are a bit slow, and-and I got a sister who needs me. It's pussy for help. What's the problem? He wins, I win." She gulped the last of her Sex on the Beach.

I noticed Emily's finger in her mouth. She appeared nervous, almost guilty. Suspicious, I squinted at her. "You have been so quiet tonight. What's up with you?"

Emily peeked around with her eyes and clenched her teeth together. "I'm getting married."

I told her, "I didn't know Zach and you were this strong."

Brooke gently pushed her shoulder. "Yeah. I thought you weren't feeling him like that.

"Aaaaaaaaaaaah!" We all screamed in excitement.

"How crazy is this?" Amber shouted. "Bartender. We need a Hypnotic shot!"

"No, no, we don't." I canceled the order with the cute bartender. He smiled and nodded. "Amber." I slammed my hand on the countertop. "Stop drinking so much. Daniel won't like it. Do you want him to send you back to your top-tiered hood?"

Almost drunk off her ass by now, Amber fell over laughing. "No. No, I don't." Her eyes darted around. "I'm rich! *I am* rich now! I don't have to work so hard, I don't have to worry about bills. I can just shop now. I can hit the mall with leisure."

Brooke winced. "Calm down, girl. Calm down. You're hurting my ears. And besides, don't get too comfortable with a man taking care of you. Keep working and save your money this time."

"Bitch, please," Amber replied with a hand at the side of Brooke's face. "I'm gonna parrrrtaaaaaay!"

Brooke shook her head as she eyed Emily and me. We shrugged and took a sip of our drinks. I knew better than to lecture someone about life choices and a drunk person at that. Life taught me to judge no one. People needed to find their own light. I did notice that Emily remained quiet, and I couldn't shake the feeling that she looked guilty about something.

"Emily." I waved a hand in front of her face. "You, ummm, have a fiancé now. Do you regret the engagement to Zach?"

"Yeah, we forgave him for whipping out his penis," Brooke said as we laughed.

"Ohhh, the dick man!" Amber hooted. "Make sure he doesn't do it as you guys exchange vows. I'll bite that tip off!" She chortled in her stool like a pig.

Brooke's shoulders wiggled up and down as she tried to suppress her laughter.

"I can bite it off if he whips that pink thing out!" Amber threatened. "Grrrrrr."

The ridiculousness of it all made me laugh. I leaned forward and rested my head in my folded arms on the bar. This was crazy. Sitting up again, I just saw Amber growling at herself at the mirror behind the bartender.

"Grrrrrrrr." She snapped her teeth together like a pit bull. "Gimme that little ping-a-ling, boy." She snapped her hand out at her reflection as she growled.

Embarrassed and trembling with laughter, I ducked my head down in my folded arms again.

Emily had tears in her eyes from cracking up so hard. "Stop it, guys. Stop it. It's not Zach."

In a wavy voice and glassy eyes, Amber sobered up enough to ask, "It isn't?"

"No?" Bewildered, Brooke's face twisted.

I raised my head and tilted it at Emily. "You know, this night just keeps on getting weirder. Who's the man then?"

Emily bit her lower lip in shame. "I . . . uhh. I . . . I . . . I should go ho—uhh, yeah."

Amber blurted, "Girl I'ma smack the hell outta you. Tell us in Spanish or tell us in English! Just please, spill the freakin' tea." She smacked her hand on the wooden bar between each word. "Who is the man?"

I grabbed Emily's shoulders. She had a blank glassy stare with parted lips. "Sweetheart, the truth. Who is he?"

Emily looked at Brooke and Amber and pointed at each of them as she spoke. "Well, if you can have a man from your past and if you can have a man from yours, then I can, too."

Brooke pointed a finger in the air. "Hold up. The flavor of your tea is Eric Grey?"

"Eric?" we screeched. Emily shook her head reluctantly.

I cheesed at Brooke. "I like what you did there, Brooke."

With a proud grin, she replied, "Thank you."

"Well, this is your choice," I told her. "Own it. Be proud."

"No," Brooke interjected. "No, no, no. He hurt you *too* many times."

"Brooke," Emily replied, "Save it, honey. Not everyone can be perfect like Jackson. Besides, couples can grow and become stronger from distress."

"Yeah?" Brooke challenged. "Like who? The ones I know just break up."

"Look at you and Jackson. He wanted a baby and you didn't," Emily reminded her.

"Yes. Exactly. We broke up because of that. Now we'll just play it by ear." Through gritted teeth and wide eyes, Brooke discreetly reminded her, "But he slept with your *friend*." Her eyes flicked to Amber, who was hidden behind Brooke's head. "How can you be with a man who knows the flavor of your friend's Kool-Aid?"

Amber heard her. "Man, why you gotta bring up old shit?"

Emily slammed a hand on the countertop. "Brooke! I know exactly what he and I have been through and what we have to overcome. I don't need you to remind me. Goodness. Why can't you just say congratulations to someone without doing a trend analysis in your head first? No one asked for your opinion. It is what it is. If we fail, then we fail. If we don't, then it was truly meant to be."

Amber tapped Brooke on the shoulder. When Brooke turned around, with her drink in her hand, Amber told her with a matter-of-fact expression, "She told you," and sipped her drink through the straw.

Turning back to Emily, Brooke snarled at her. "Well, fine. Congratulations, Emily." She spun in her seat to face Amber. "Congratulations, Amber." Amber nodded with a smile.

Emily replied. "Thank you. But it doesn't matter if you mean it or not, Brooke. It's gonna happen."

"Well where's the ring?" asked Brooke.

"I'm smaller than when he first met me. He had to get it resized."

Looking at me, Amber asked, "Where's yours? You and Oliver better get movin'. Baby gonna be here."

That knot resurfaced in my throat. I held up a hand and before taking a sip of my iced tea, I assured her, "Nah. We good. I'm good. He's, umm, yeah, good."

"Nervous much?" Brooke teased.

I flashed a strained smile at her. "Noooo. I just need to get this baby out. She, he, or whatever this baby is, needs to be out of my stomach. Tired of being fat."

Emily reminded me, "You're pregnant, not fat."

Brooke said, "Yeah, don't worry. We'd tell you the truth."

I shrugged. "Well, let's just say that I've never weighed over five pounds my normal body weight."

"Lucky you," Brooke and Emily replied simultaneously. Brooke added, "Like the rest of these Washingtonian exercise-holics, we have to work for our bodies."

I decided to lighten the mood, and it seemed to work. "Okay, ladies. Let's start with Amber and go down the line to Brooke and Emily. Tell us how it all happened."

Amber seemed to have sobered up enough to tell us about Daniel's sudden and shocking appearance.

Brooke waited until Amber froze with a glow. "Ugh, I still can't believe you."

Without turning her head toward Brooke, Amber gave her the side eye and looked at her with an insincere grin full of sarcasm. Throwing a hand out, she said, "The shade is real. Whatcha tryna say?"

Face palming myself, I shook my head before removing my hand to watch the explosion occur.

Brooke inhaled before exhaling her opinion. "You went easy on him, huh? It'd be remiss of me as your friend to say nothing. Maybe that's how Summer and Emily do things, but not me."

Irritated, Amber slammed a hand on the countertop of the bar. "Whadiya talkin' about?"

"I'm talking about this man degrading you with a denial and then once *he* determined that you were worthy," Brooke posed like a bunny with both hands bent downward, "the chocolate bunny goes hopping back."

"Heffa, ain't cha kettle black, too? Tuh. Your man didn't even want children and still don't, but you gonna marry him? Now who sold out on her dreams?"

Emily briefly enlarged her eyes. She arched a brow with lips folded inward, clearly pleading the fifth with no interest in adjudicating or taking sides. I couldn't do that. These ladies meant too much to me, and the purpose of tonight didn't intend to serve unnecessary drama. I already knew Amber; she was a headstrong woman who didn't appreciate being told what to do. As a woman of many opinions, Brooke stood up for her beliefs and sometimes with reckless abandon.

"Hey? Hey, ladies? C-could we just stop? We don't—"

My words fell on deaf ears. Words from two different women competed to be heard over clacking glasses, shaking ice, and music. This was what happened when alcohol became another friend among us.

Amber slid her neck from left to right and twirled her finger toward Brooke. "Honey, just because you went to college and got your little condo don't mean your boo-boo hole don't stank, too."

"Damn right I got that condo. But guess what? But guess what? Brooke did it on her own. She did it on her own. And I actually don't need a college degree for my job. But I still got the job done. No excuses. I never took a penny from no man. In fact, *no*body. So, it can be done."

"Guess what, Brooke? I like having sex. I like dick. But I loooove money even more. And if I can get it from only one man just for gettin' him and me off, then I will do that."

"Why can't you work at a coffee shop? Or, a donut shop? The mall?" Brooke rolled her eyes to the ceiling and flipped out her hand. "A restaurant. You have charisma. Get tips. You can leave with cash in hand just like you're used to, except your jaws won't have to do any work and your knees won't have to bend."

"Ouch." Emily buttoned her lips with her fingers.

"*Ladies*. Stop," I implored.

"Don't worry about her, Summer." Amber took another sip of liquid courage. "She just wants to be the mother to us that she never had. Don't pay old girl no mind." She cavalierly brushed the air and sipped again staring straight.

All three of our jaws dropped. She took one droopy-eyed look at us and shrugged.

"That's how we play that game," she bitterly told herself.

Brooke stretched both arms before her with a gaped mouth and unblinking wide eyes. "Okay, okay. Guess that's one less mouth to feed at my wedding."

"I don't need that crusty invite. Hoes don't believe in forever anyway, right?"

Using my shattered heart to propel my creativity, I covertly poured my water on the floor below my stool and between my legs and cried, "My water!"

"Huh?" Brooke's head snapped back in my direction.

"My water broke! Yeah, I think it broke."

Amber's straw slid from between her lips. "Say whuh now?"

Brooke told her, "Bitch get up. Her water broke for the baby. I got the tab."

Emily clapped like a happy seal with cheekbones as high as her forehead. "This is excellent. Our baby is here." She spun and rolled off the stool to stand by my side.

Brooke slapped two generous bills down and came to my other side. "Let's go."

Amber took one last long sip until her cheeks caved inward."

Emily asked, "What are you *doing*, Amber? The girl is gonna pop. Come *on*."

"Oh, all right, all right. You know I'll do anything for my girl, Summer. That's the only reason why I'm cutting this short."

Brooke told her, "Um, you're cutting this short because there's a baby inside of her who needs medical care, regardless of the person."

"Chill, I got this. I got this."

Emily panicked. "Oh, no. Who can drive? We've all been drinking."

"Let's just get her to the car first," Brooke suggested.

Calm, I peered at their expression while they figured this all out. Then I remembered that I needed to feel pain when Emily looked at me with crinkled brows.

"Uh—owwwwww, oh, ow. Please," I begged through gritted teeth, "we need to hurry."

Actually, I'd grown tired of the place and the pettiness of my friends and couldn't take another moment of this claustrophobic nightmare. *Black people. Always acting up.* I shook my head.

The three ladies escorted me out with drunk feet shuffling as they warned people in our path, "Watch out, pregnant lady coming through."

Finally through the double doors to freedom, the stiff air—humid and neutral—felt as good as a gulp of water to a deprived tongue on a desert. A little relief went a long way.

Once valet pulled out Amber's man's Mercedes, they tried to ease me into the backseat. Instead, I straightened up and gently pushed Amber to the side and said, "Move, girl. Get in."

"You can't—you're in labor," Emily squealed.

"Or is she?" Brooke challenged with folded arms.

"What?" Emily tilted her head.

Amber squinted but probably because she just couldn't see straight.

"Are you serious?" Emily threw up her hands with all the joy robbed from her face. "You scammed us."

"I'm so sorry, Emily. You didn't deserve this." I waved my finger between Amber and Brooke. "You two were driving me nuts and have completely screwed up this night.

They both pointed at each other. "It was her fault," Brooke and Amber said.

"I don't wanna hear it. You both ruined it for Emily and me." I nodded at the car. "Now get in the car."

Emily started to head toward the passenger side. "Thanks a lot guys."

"Emily." Brooke waited until Emily turned her way, and then pointed at the back door. "Why don't you come sit back here with me?"

Emily sighed and fulfilled her request. I rolled my eyes and hopped in.

Amber marched to the other side. "No one cares, Brooke."

Once we all buckled up, I started the engine and headed toward the highway.

"Well, now that we all know Summer was playing us, I would like my money back from someone." I peeked up at Brooke through the rearview mirror and frowned. "Emily? Please tell Amber that I need to be reimbursed."

They just didn't learn. I shook my head.

Emily inhaled. "Amber?"

"Yes, sweet one?"

"Brooke would like to be reimbursed for the . . . drinks." She shrugged, obviously uncomfortable with being the mediator.

"Emily? Please tell Brooke to blow me, especially since I let her ride in this whip free of gas charge."

Emily sighed. She cleared her throat and turned to Brooke. Dryly, she said, "Oh, hell, you heard her. What do you want me to say?"

I watched the women in the back just about as much as I did the road. Brooke pursed her lips and then leaned over to whisper in Emily's ear.

Emily cupped her mouth with both hands and with wide eyes she whispered, "No, I can't say that."

"Do it," Brooke demanded in a high whisper.

Sighing, Emily said, "Amber. Brooke said that since blowing people seems to be your specialty and you're strapped for cash, then why don't you blow her instead?"

Starved of patience, I chewed my lips.

The whole car went silent for a moment. The first sign of noise came from Amber. What sounded like a scoff actually turned into laughter. As the rest of us observed dubiously, she became more hysterical. Convinced that she was genuinely amused by Brooke's opprobrium, we all eased into songs of laughter.

Wiping a tear from my eye, I told them, "I can't with you guys," with a hand on my stomach.

Brooke said, "I'm not thinking about Amber, and she never thinks about any of us." She chuckled. "That's why we always work out in the end."

Amber grinned Brooke's way. "Yeah. Brooke's a tough broad."

The wedding planner turned to the teacher. "Hey, you."

"What's up?"

"If I confronted one friend, I gotta confront the other."

Emily sounded guarded. "Okay. Go ahead."

"Sweetie, are you sure? Just—are you sure?"

"I said 'yes,' didn't I?"

"But you don't have to."

I saw Brooke's hand stroke the back of Emily's head. "He hurt you so many times."

Emily brushed Brooke's hand from her as she pulled her head away from her touch. "I'm not a child, Brooke. I don't need to be questioned just because Jackson seems so perfect next to Eric and Daniel. And Amber's right. You have your own problem with Jackson to worry about that a marriage can't fix. So . . ." She shook her head and looked out the window.

Brooke took a moment before she said anything. She nodded her head faintly with a blank stare. I shifted my gaze back to the taillights in front of me.

"Okay. I get it. You and Amber have all the answers, even if these men have shown you guys their true colors. And to be clear, Jackson and I aren't standing in front of the same crossroads from last year. Our distance proved that we can't live without one another. And . . . I trust him. I trust in our love this time to get us to the place I want us to be in."

Clearing my throat, I decided to speak up. "Brooke?" Our eyes met in the rearview mirror. "Baby, Eric is proving his love with a ring. Daniel wants to make it up to Amber by taking her in for what he wants. It's a win-win."

"But she didn't hold Daniel accountable for what he did. She made it easy for him."

Amber turned her neck. "Honey, I ain't in love. I don't want anything from him aside from his bucks and shelter, and he just want me to play in his meat district. I know he ain't husband material. And I don't want him to be. Sis, no foul. I love you for your mama-bear protection. You are like the mother I need sometimes. But, baby, I'm from New York. I've seen worse, and I've earned my stripes. This lioness is gonna be aight."

I looked at her with a toothless smile of admiration and saw her wink at Brooke.

Brooke reached forward to rub Amber's shoulder.

I arched a brow and looked at Emily. "Emily?"

She turned to look at Brooke. "I mean, if I can forgive Amber and Eric . . ."

"*Shut up.*" Brooke laughed and ruffled Emily's head. She laughed and bumped Brooke with her shoulder.

"I heard that," Amber said.

All the girls nodded off as I drove with just my thoughts to keep me company. Soon, I would meet my baby. Soon, *Oliver and I* would meet *our* baby. My life would have another life-changing event, and then after this, I didn't want change to knock on my door for a while.

Twenty minutes later, I pulled up to the curb in front of my building to let the girls out before parking Amber's truck in the garage with my car. Brooke swore she could drive Emily home safely and promised to call me when she arrived home. I called an understanding and grateful Daniel for Amber to explain her late whereabouts since I refused to let her endanger herself or others. Amber slept on my couch until eight in the morning. It appeared that she really did have a man who genuinely appreciated his New York piano player for the polished street girl that she was, and for that, I felt relieved.

It'd been days since hanging out with my girls. One of those days included a trip to the doctor, and most recently, labor pains. This morning, I sprawled across the couch flicking through random channels before settling on a chick flick. The little runt couldn't come soon enough. I missed seeing an actual figure in the mirror and sleeping in various positions. Besides, waddling only contributed to my insecurities and moving at a glacial pace consequently heightened my guilt for not enjoying long walks pre-pregnancy. Most of all, I just wanted to meet my baby.

"Baby! Help me find my jeans!" another baby cried from another room.

Struggling to stand, I'd just about doddered to our bedroom to find jeans all over the floor. "Well, which ones?"

Standing over the pool of denim with a look of defeat, Oliver folded his arms. "I . . . I don't know."

He'd been a mess lately and had gotten used to me teasing him. However, now my casual outlook on his behavior had turned into genuine concern. Something seemed off about him.

"Baby, are you okay?"

Looking at me, he replied with a shoulder shrug. I crossed his heap of clothes to place my hands on his muscular shoulders as I pouted mockingly. "Yes, you do know. So, tell me. I can take it."

"I can't find my jeans." Oliver's expression insisted that nothing else bothered him, but his eyes said otherwise.

"If you don't know which jeans you need, then why are you making a fuss about a specific pair that seems to be misplaced?" I insisted.

After he exhaled, Oliver sat on the bed. "Summer, this baby is coming, and I feel unprepared."

I sat beside him and caressed his back. "The nursery is done. We have clothes and items, and the baby shower was a success. Baby, I think we are all prepared here."

"Everywhere but mentally." He appeared anxious with constant exhales and repeated swipes of his palms up and down his thighs. He jumped back up. "I've never been a dad before."

"Oliver." I held up a palm to stop him. "Calm down. Neither one of us knows what we're doing, but we just have to man and woman-up to the challenge." I stood up and caressed his shoulders. "We'll be fine."

Oliver laughed and sat back down and then I did, too. "You have no choice but to say that, he's coming from your belly."

I punched him on the shoulder. "She."

"He."

I pointed my finger at him. "Well you better not leave us hanging if it's a girl."

"I won't," he assured me in a tender tone.

Rubbing my baby bump, I said, "Good."

"What do you wanna do today? I can't go to work until that baby comes."

"Oh, please, I will be— Ow! Owwwww! Oliver." A very intense contraction hit me.

Oliver gripped my elbow. "What should we do? Go to the hospital?"

"Help me up, baby." Oliver eased me to my feet.

"No. Uh, I don't know. I should, uhhh, do the breathing exercises that we learned."

Panic struck his face. "Which one?"

"Umm, I don't know. The one that, ummm, you know," I winded a finger, "the one breath per second one. Or is it minute?"

He looked confused. "Summer, a breath per minute? You'd be blue or dead."

I nodded frantically. "Right."

He placed praying hands in front of his face. "Okay, let's chill. Chill. It's the slow breathing, baby." Confident, he waved a finger at me. "Yeah."

"Yes!" A sharp pain hit as I rubbed my belly.

"How do you breathe slowly?"

"Right. Y-y-you, umm, breath through the nostrils and let it out with the mouth. Right?"

He nodded quickly again. "Yeah, yeah, yeah."

Implementing the correct breathing pattern, the realization that my wish had been granted to physically commence motherhood stole any sense of bravery.

Looking into his strained eyes, I winced and grimaced while executing my breathing exercises. Oliver did it with me. "Please stop. You look like a mirror of me, but more nervous." When an unusual pressure hit my pelvis, I felt a popping sensation. Before I had a chance to comb through my own suspicions or questions, a gush of fluid raced down my leggings and puddled on the carpet. "Oliver," I yelled, even though he stood right in front of me with eyes wide of terror. "Hand me my phone. It's in the living room. My water just broke."

With his palms in the air, he looked down at his carpet horrified. "Oh, shi—"

"Get it! Go!" I yelled.

Oliver ran off and came back in record time. "Here."

I snatched the phone and scrolled until I found my mom's number. When she picked up, I said, "Mom, when can you get here? The water broke."

Alarmed, she replied, "Oh, sweet, Lord. My shift ends in thirty. Is that fine?"

"Yeah, yeah, Mom, that's cool. Just, please, *drive safely.*"

"Oh, well, of course. I will see you tonight, pumpkin. Ooooh!" My mom could barely contain her excitement. "See you tonight. Yay!"

"Bye, Mom. I love you."

"I love you, too."

Hanging up, I said, "Sorry about your carpet, man. Too bad I didn't do this on the wooden floor.

"I don't care about that." With visibly shot nerves, Oliver started to pace.

I dialed Amber and she picked up. "Hey! Virginia Hospital Center. Tell everyone. My water broke."

"Oh. My. God. This is wonderful. Oh. Oh. Oh."

"Amber. Focus, honey. Call friends."

"Okay, okay, okay. Bye."

After hanging up, I cried out when another contraction hit. "Oh, boy. This is happening. I'm gonna be a mom. I don't want to deliver this baby! I'm scared!"

Oliver stopped pacing to stare at me. With one hand flipped outward, he asked, "Well what do you want me to do about it? It's too late for a middle wife to have it."

"Midwife. And, no, you mean surrogate."

"Oh, yeah, that gate thingy."

I rolled my eyes with a sigh.

Flustered, Oliver dropped to his knees beside the bed and began to pray.

"*What are you doing?* Babe. We have to go."

Oliver peeked at me through one eye. "Baby. I need God to help us."

"Yes. But, please, can we pray in the car, while you drive? This is becoming a hot mess."

Popping back up, Oliver looked at me for answers.

With the phone in my hands again, I blurted, "We need to call Ruben."

"He can wait, Summer," Oliver barked with pinched brows.

"No, he cannot. You need to respect that, as the father, he should be included in the labor as well."

"Oh, my gosh. Whatever." He turned away.

"You think I'm happy about this? You knew we had to do this. Is this going to work for you, Oliver? And get my overnight bag. I gotta go."

Oliver walked to the closet and snatched up the duffel bag. "We'll call everyone from the car."

He assisted me to the elevator with an arm behind me. This moment was the most intimate one between us yet, despite the tension seconds ago.

Oliver bent down to kiss me behind the closing doors. "You scared, baby? I know I am."

Fighting through the pain, I nodded with a tear. "Yes. I'm scared of the birthing part. But I wanna know who this kid is . . . what the baby will look like. I'm so excited to meet our baby."

Oliver's eyes glistened. His voice went partial. "Me, too, Summer. I love you."

"Ohhhh. I love you, baby."

He helped me out of the elevator and toward our designated spaces. When I saw a grey truck instead of a Corvette, anger took over. Pointing, I told him, "Look. Some asshole stole our space, baby. And where's my Corvette if yours is in the other space? Someone stole my car!" I realized.

"Wait, baby, wait." Oliver stretched an arm out to disarm the truck. "This Suburban is yours, ours, whatever. Sweetie, a baby's not fit for our cars. I can't ride in pink if you need your truck, so, it had to go. Plus, that Corvette belonged to a single, carefree woman. Not a mother. It was time to upgrade, boo."

I was touched, I really was. However, the little one inside me demanded all my emotions and attention, so I just nodded with a faint smile. He helped me to the passenger side. Once he opened the door to reveal black leather seats, the smell of the familiar new car scent hit me. Oliver strapped me in before closing my door to head to the driver side. Once in, he started the car and drove off after buckling up.

With a different breathing pattern, through gritted teeth, I told him, "We. Need. To. Call. People."

"I don't know how to work this hands-free thing in this car." He wiggled his fingers at me. "Gimme your phone."

"Shoot." I tossed it to him. "Ruben."

"Fine, I'll call the damn man." He was hostile, too.

He dialed Ruben's number on speakerphone. He picked up after the second ring. Of course. "Ruben, man, what's up? It's Oliver."

Another sharp pain hit. "Owwww!"

Ruben cleared his throat. "Oh, of course. Hey, Oliver, how it's going? Everything okay?"

"Summer's going into labor. Meet us at Virginia Hospital Center."

"What?"

I felt bad for Oliver as Ruben expressed his excitement. Wow. I'd really gotten myself into something.

"This—this is amazing!" Ruben rejoiced.

Dryly, Oliver replied, "Ain't it tho?"

I looked up at an irritated Oliver. He shook his head and hung up.

Wiggling in my seat, I ordered, "Punch it."

"We're almost there, baby. Almost there." He placed a comforting hand on my leg.

Once there with Oliver by my side and the girls in the waiting room, five hours later, my baby entered the world. As the baby slid out with the aid of the doctors, they announced, "It's a girl!"

My whole outlook on the baby changed, like life made sense and that my purpose had become clear and strong. Her precious vocal chords sang like music on a clear summer day. She cried with two shaky fists, almost hinting that she felt pissed to leave her cubby of comfort. Her chunky legs kicked aimlessly like her best defense again the touches of any human contact. But when they placed her in my arms, the world around us felt right. She sensed that shift, too. Though fussy, she calmed down as my Amazonian hair sheltered her from the stares, lights, and commotion.

"I know, baby," I whispered. "I know."

Smiling at her, nothing else seemed to matter. She was the world I didn't know I wanted to exist. And it was more than important to me to be a part of it. What could she teach me? I wanted to know. Looking up, it became clear that she wasn't the only being crying. Oliver cried with two quiet tears and a balled fist to his mouth. The wait was over. I was a mom. A proud and happy mom who knew I would do anything to protect her. I couldn't wait to pass the baby to my mom, so she could meet her first grandchild.

"We're a legit family now," Oliver said as he stroked the top of my head.

I looked up at him with a grin. "Hold her."

Oliver inhaled with a quiver and spread arms. Once he had her, the love showed in his eyes. "What a cutie pie. She's gonna have your color."

I chuckled. "Too soon to tell, I believe."

"Have you thought of a name?"

Replying with a nod, her name came to me without a doubt. It was like God chose the name for my daughter and with tears, my mouth said, "Autumn. Autumn Stevenson."

Laughing, Oliver hugged Autumn and me. "That's adorable, babe."

For the first time, I felt protected. Felt like a family of my own. Nothing could harm me, nothing could hurt me. On cloud nine, I felt untouchable. "Go get the girls, baby?"

Oliver nodded and straightened. He passed Autumn to me.

"Baby, thank you."

He kissed me one more time before leaving. Then he spun around. "I'm gonna call Ruben. He's beyond late. At this rate, your mom will beat him. Traffic must've gotten her. Man. Who shows up late for their own baby's birth?"

"Wow. You're right. Okay. Sounds good."

His suggestion surprised me. Perhaps Oliver felt more secure in Ruben's presence. After the doctors cleaned me up, the girls rushed through the door in awe carrying balloons.

"Ohhhhhhhh," they cried. "She's beautiful."

I glowed at their presence. My heart felt whole. My friends' love was as close as possible to a mother's love. Speaking of mothers, I wanted mine. Holding my daughter out to see who would get first grabs, I told them, "Meet, Autumn."

Emily covered her mouth in surprise. "Autumn? Summer and Autumn? Really?"

I nodded proudly. "Really."

As Emily took the baby, Brooke shoved her body into me. "Oh, sweetie. This is surreal. Congratulations, honey." She squeezed me with tears running down her face.

I rubbed her back. "Thank you, Brooke. Thank you."

Amber sat close to me and squeezed my hand. "You did good, Summer. You did good."

"Someone has it all," Emily teased with a grin.

"All right now," Brooke said. "Don't hog the second season. Give her to me, too."

We laughed.

"These are the days, huh?" Amber commented.

"It's a new season. One that I will never forget," I replied.

Emily stood to take pictures of everyone with the baby. Then Brooke took Emily's picture with Autumn.

"Our first social media baby," Emily said.

I shrugged. "Yeah, you know I don't have a profile. Well—only my recruiting profile."

Amber handed my daughter back to me. I observed her precious little face, her heart-shaped lips, her perfect tiny ten fingers and toes, and button nose. I told them, "My eight pounds of joy." As if on cue, Autumn looked up at me with her honey-colored eyes. Tears bombarded mine. My finger flew under my nose to catch the sniffles.

"Awwww," they gushed.

Our attention turned to the sound of motion at the door. Lurking at the door and making no attempt to join us, Oliver barely passed the threshold as he wore a face of a zombie. He didn't approach us.

Emily pointed and giggled. "Look, he's so stunned to be a father that he can't move or talk."

We chuckled. They congratulated him one at a time.

"Yeah," he gripped his cell phone nervously, "thanks."

I noticed his hard swallow and found his shift in demeanor perplexing. "Honey. When is Ruben coming? He's so late."

"Oh, no," Amber said. "A late father. Not dependable already. Can him," she joked.

Oliver rubbed the top of his head as it hung low. He didn't want to look at me. I felt strange.

"*Hey, you,* what's wrong?" I cradled and patted Autumn in my arms. "When's he coming, honey? Wh-what's wrong?"

Walking toward me with slow feet, Oliver asked, "Can we have the room for a moment, please?"

Brooke nodded and patted a hand against Emily's shoulder to urge her forward. The three ladies headed toward the door without saying a word.

What was his problem? Why couldn't he just tell me where Ruben was? Why did Oliver feel the need to be alone with me, knowing that my girls needed to be a part of this crucial moment? They were practically my sisters at this point.

I didn't know how worked up he'd gotten me until I spoke. "Huh? No, they don't have to go leave. This is crazy, Oliver. Just go on and speak."

My friends froze in their tracks, staring at me, waiting for the final decision.

With his back to my friends, Oliver lifted a brow at me with a slight tilt of his head, and then I got the message. He needed to come first.

There I was again, not trusting Oliver with a situation. I really had to remove the invisible second-place medal dangling around his neck. After all, he did agree to father Autumn.

Nodding, I told them, "Yeah, I'll catch you guys up in a minute."

"Of course," Brooke replied with a nod and half smile.

I watched the girls head out and waited for the door to close behind them before asking, "Now, could you please tell me what this demeanor of yours is all about?"

Oliver held his arms out. "Can I have her?" He didn't smile as he sat beside me on the bed.

"Are you sure you want her? I mean, you don't look too happy, kid."

"Summer, this beautiful tot has already got me wrapped around her tiny finger. Let me have her."

"Of course." Transferring my baby into his arms, defining his mood eluded me. What was it that he didn't want to tell me?"

With closed eyes, Oliver pressed Autumn close to his chest, kissing her forehead. "Aww, there you go." I could sense him tuning me out as he brought our child closer into his world. He needed this moment, and I guess he had to do it before Ruben got here. And here I was, trying to deny him this necessary and tender moment between him and Autumn when all he needed was a moment before reality would step in with Ruben marching through that door, proud and boisterous. See, I had a lot to learn.

"Did you know that I'm your daddy?"

I agreed. He was the daddy, but I felt like she needed to hear it from Ruben first. Wasn't that how it should go? I was already confused. How would I know when he was out of line?

His brought one of her miniature hands to his mouth to kiss her fingers. "I have lots of money. I have lots of love. And you can have both, as much as you want. Whatever your tiny heart needs, you shall have. Do you hear me? I pledge this to you on day one."

My eyes darted quickly between his face and Autumns. Her reply was a yawn. His was . . . glassy eyes. Autumn made him cry. A quick knock of his shoulder against his face erased the tear going down his cheek.

What is going on, Oliver?

He sniffled once and then turned to me with somber eyes.

I tipped my head to one side and smiled. "I didn't know you would be so emotional, baby." He almost convinced me that maybe he needed to fall into my bosom for comfort.

"Summer, she's going to need me."

"Of course. Of course, baby." I chuckled and pinched her toe gently while using the baby tone I detested used by adults when I said, "This little girl is gonna have tons of love from all three of us."

"Summer?" Oliver moved one of his hands to my legs and caressed it.

"Did you ever get in touch with Ruben?" I extended my neck to peek over his head and toward the door.

"Yes and no." His mouth pursed, his eyes briefly averted mine until he noticed mine chasing his stare.

I snapped at him with my fingers to grab his attention. "Hey, you."

"Summer, Fran picked up his phone."

My arms flew out as my neck rolled with my eyes. "Oh, of course she did. And so, it begins." I straightened my head to look at Oliver. "You see, this was exactly what I was dread—"

"There was an accident, Summer."

I squinted my eyes at him as my arms lowered slowly onto the bed. "Wh-what what do you mean he was in an accident? Is he all right? Or wait, I bet this was his way of escaping fatherhood and somehow, he cut a deal with Fran so—"

"He's dead."

"Impossible," I whispered.

"Apparently, he was rushing a bit too fast to get here. Fran was upset, noise was in the background . . . it was all too real, baby."

I had to let it register. Oliver just said that Ruben died in a car crash. Every time our eyes locked it confirmed that I heard him correctly. Ruben was dead. My little girl no longer had a chance to meet her biological father. I only had four great years with my dad, and those memories were a blur. For all intents and purposes, I might as well have never met him. However, Autumn didn't even have one day. Just like me, she would be deprived of knowing her daddy.

Heat ripped through my throat as the shocking news registered. For my daughter's sake, I wanted to scream. The idea of us having that one tragedy in common before anything else broke my heart. With a racing heartbeat, my head felt light. Nothing came out of my mouth. Shaking my head, I looked away. I didn't have time to blame anyone, though no one stood at fault. He squeezed my trembling hands to offer silent comfort.

Finally, I told him, "This year has really tested me, but only because of my own faults and actions." My fingers played with the thread of the blanket. "I just wanted to make it to the top on my own. My dream was to be like Fran and own my own recruiting agency one day. Because of my actions, screwing her husband meant screwing myself. Then I met you and dragged you into my madness." My words were interrupted by sniffles and jerks of breath as I struggled to regain control of my breathing while stifling tears.

Oliver had a look of pity on his face. "Summer, there's nothing I would take back if it meant not having you in my life."

"I just don't understand why you want me so much," I whined. "I am so irresponsible."

"His death is not a ticket for you to recount your mistakes. I am proud of you for pushing through in life."

"That's all? Like, what else was I supposed to do? Slit my wrists or something? I don't get a gold star for hanging in there," I replied bitterly. "What have I done so far that will make Autumn proud of me one day?"

Oliver didn't say anything. After a moment of silence between us, he replied, "There's still time you know. You can make your mark by the time Autumn is old enough to talk. Today is not the last day for improvement, baby."

Once again, the black cloud moved back above my head. My emotions boiled over, and I had to release them like vomit. I cried uncontrollably at his choice of words. "But, Ruben . . . it was his last day."

Oliver nodded. "Yes, Summer. But he was happy, and he tried to get here."

"Why did that idiot rush anyway? I'm in a bed. It's not like I was going anywhere," I cried.

"Summer," Oliver said, caressing me anywhere he could place his hands. "Autumn needs you to be strong. She still has me. It may not be my blood, it may not be my DNA, but she can be mine. I can be the daddy she was meant to have. I will be the rock you two can lean on."

This was the uneven terrain that my mom warned me about. The rocky part where he would have to pick me up. A quick sob escaped my lips before I grabbed him close. Over his shoulder, my mom stood in the distance looking lost, as if she didn't know if she should make contact with Autumn first or just comfort me. And it was then I realized, that even moms didn't always have all the answers.

One look at Autumn told me that when she became old enough to hear the truth about her daddy's identity, I'd be wearing the same lost expression as my mother. But as a daughter, my mom's presence reminded me that nothing could ever come between a child and a mother's bond. Sighing, I straightened my shoulders and realigned my energy, because I was a mother now. And no matter how many years a woman had on this planet, sometimes a daughter just needed her mother. Therefore, Autumn would always need me, even in her most disappointed hour. Finding comfort in that, I affirmed that Autumn and I were going to be all right, because even though her father had passed on, her presence brought me nothing but tranquility.

Please remember to leave a review on Amazon. I appreciate your feedback!

Follow me @ . . .
Facebook: www.facebook.com/dawn.wright.54738
Instagram: dawnwright_author
Twitter: Dawn Wright@_dawn_wright
Email me at: authordawnwright@gmail.com
Sign up for my newsletters to find out what's new at
www.dawnwrightbooks.com/newsletter/
To learn more about Dawn Wright visit
www.dawnwrightbooks.com

acknowledgements

Proofreader: Dianne McCann
Editor: Richard "Tony" Held
Cover design by Les
Cover Model Photography by Evan
Christopher Photography
Cover Model: Starleigh Caldwell

The Capital Trilogy
Capital Encounters (book one)
Capital Consequences (book two)
Capital Resolutions (book three)

Next Release: Capital Resolutions, summer 2018

About the Author

Before committing to writing novels, Dawn Wright, spent a decent amount of time teaching and studying business, while having a fascination for the corporate environment.

Determined to someday make the workforce a place where employees would want to work without dread, she made it her mission to obtain her master's in human resource management. However, in her last semester, two classes away from graduation in fact, she pulled out her laptop for other than studying or Internet surfing and decided to give life to Capital Encounters. Unaware that this book would lead to a trilogy, she set it to the side to keep from compromising her GPA. After years of countless and persistent prayers, she realized that her book didn't have to be second to a traditional career, but that by stepping out on faith, it was just time to say goodbye to what was expected and hello to passion.

Dawn Wright currently lives in Alexandria, VA as a full-time writer. She frequents DC when she and her boyfriend feel like crossing the bridge. Ever since writing her first book, there's never been a time that she doesn't visit DC without feeling like her characters are right down the street.

www.ingramcontent.com/pod-product-compliance
Lightning Source LLC
Chambersburg PA
CBHW071545030726
47593CB00001BA/41

9 780998 078724